HALF OF THE HUMAN RACE

Anthony Quinn was born in Liverpool in 1964.
Since 1998 he has been the film critic of the
Independent. His first novel, *The Rescue Man*
(2009), won the Authors' Club Best First Novel
Award.

ALSO BY ANTHONY QUINN

The Rescue Man

ANTHONY QUINN

Half of the
Human Race

VINTAGE BOOKS
London

Published by Vintage 2012

2 4 6 8 10 9 7 5 3 1

Copyright © Anthony Quinn 2011

Anthony Quinn has asserted his right under the Copyright, Designs
and Patents Act 1988 to be identified as the author of this work

First published in Great Britain in 2011 by
Jonathan Cape

Vintage
Random House, 20 Vauxhall Bridge Road,
London SW1V 2SA

www.vintage-books.co.uk

Addresses for companies within The Random House Group
Limited can be found at: www.randomhouse.co.uk/offices.htm

The Random House Group Limited Reg. No. 954009

A CIP catalogue record for this book
is available from the British Library

ISBN 9780099531944

The Random House Group Limited supports The Forest
Stewardship Council (FSC®), the leading international forest
certification organisation. Our books carrying the FSC label are
printed on FSC® certified paper. FSC is the only forest certification
scheme endorsed by the leading environmental organisations,
including Greenpeace. Our paper procurement policy can be found at
www.randomhouse.co.uk/environment

Typeset in Palatino by Palimpsest Book Production Limited,
Falkirk, Stirlingshire

Printed and bound by CPI Group (UK) Ltd, Croydon CR0 4YY

for Rachel, MLC

We know what we are, but know not what we may be.

Ophelia, Hamlet, 4.4

It is little I repair to the matches of the Southron
  folk,
Though my own red roses there may blow;
It is little I repair to the matches of the Southron
  folk,
Though the red roses crest the caps, I know.
For the field is full of shades as I near the shadowy
  coast,
And a ghostly batsman plays to the bowling of a
  ghost,
And I look through my tears on a soundless-
  clapping host
As the run-stealers flicker to and fro,
          To and fro:–
O my Hornby and my Barlow long ago!

'At Lord's', Francis Thompson

Half of the
Human Race

PROLOGUE

So it had come to this, she thought, as the last light of the afternoon shrank away. She had first heard the distant collection of footsteps and muffled voices descending from the gallery above, and now, like a shambling beast, it was stopping at each door on her own ward; the metal shiver of keys on a chain, the clank of the lock, a brief scuffle; shouts. Then the slam of the door followed by a long silence, which was the most unnerving sound of all. She checked the makeshift blockade of table and chair and bed she had raised against the door. How long would it hold? Her heart was beating hard, and a plume of nausea writhed in her stomach. She had not eaten for four days.

With no company to relieve her solitude – without even a book to read – she had taken to distracting herself with thoughts of other crises she had outfaced. The most trying had come at the age of nine when she had succumbed to acute rheumatic fever; she remembered how it made her joints ache and disfigured her skin with rashes, but at the time it was the snailing tedium of the weeks in hospital that had most excruciated her. It was some days after being brought home that she caught her father unawares, sobbing in a way she had not seen before. (Only her mother ever cried like that.) Disturbed, she had backed away, and gone in search of her sister to ask, 'What is the matter with Pa?'

Her sister, with no gift for tactfulness, had replied, 'He was crying because of you. You were going to die.' Though she was winded by this revelation, she did not bring the matter up with her father until years later, by which time he was able to admit that certain doctors had despaired of her condition. 'But I never thought so,' he added proudly, as if his own gambling instincts were a sounder judge of mortality than the reasonings of medical science.

It puzzled her sometimes that such a momentous experience had not left a greater impression on her. But it is a sadness of childhood, and perhaps a mercy, too, that so much of it does go by without notice. The weeks and years silt up elsewhere, and only afterwards do we sift the residue for meaning. More vivid to her, now as then, was an incident two years prior to her illness, on a day that had already been set aside for memorialising. It was the Queen's Diamond Jubilee, June of 1897, and in the evening her family and various cousins had gone to the West End for the fireworks display in Green Park. The crowds were more overwhelming than anyone had anticipated, and somehow in the jostling dark she and her brother, Fred, had become detached from the family party. She knew her parents would be frantic, but an hour and more of wandering brought no sight of them. As the sky above them fizzed and crumped with showers of light, she realised that they were lost, but decided that Fred, two years her junior at five, must not be allowed to know. So she explained to him in a grown-up voice she found from somewhere that an adventure lay ahead: tonight they were going to find their own way back home. Holding his hand tight, she began tramping along the main road by which they had arrived, eventually spotting the omnibus she hoped would take them in the right direction. She almost hauled him up the narrow winding steps. They sat on the knifeboard seat behind the driver, whose frequent 'woahs' and clucks to his horse delighted

Fred even more than the novelty of being 'on top', with the masses of pedestrians streaming below. Either through negligence or a spirit of holiday goodwill, the conductor didn't trouble them for a fare, and when he called out 'Any for the Angel?' she hurried them both downstairs and onto Upper Street. By the time they arrived home their mother was at the gate, watching the street; their father had already gone to the police station.

The story of Jubilee Night became a family favourite, and her precocious navigation of the journey from Green Park to Islington established her, in her father's eyes at least, as a clever and capable girl. She loved to hear him boast of her thus, and, peering down the shadowy hallway of her future, she conceived a hope that she might make something of herself. Once outside the protective cordon of his regard, however, the difficulty of such an ambition became apparent. Even among men who were her father's friends she met a solid wall of indifference. Society did not want women to be clever and capable; it wanted them to be pliant, pretty, incurious, domestic, accommodating and, generally, silent. They were designed for no purpose other than filling and feathering the nest considerately provided for them, and to seek beyond that pinched horizon was to risk disapproval. One day she overheard a lady friend asking her mother why on earth she had let her daughter apply to medical college. 'Don't you want her ever to get *married*?'

It puzzled at her at first, this assumption of subservience, for it seemed to be founded on nothing more than the tendency of women's voices to be hushed and small, and men's voices to be hard and loud. As she grew into her teens, she wondered if some mysterious unspoken principle lay behind the imbalance. Was there an intrinsic flaw in womankind that determined they should exist as a separate class, ignored and unrepresented? The idea was laughable, and yet almost everyone seemed to abide by it. She could

3

recall the moment – she was lying on her bed in moody contemplation one evening, before the dinner gong went – when she realised how it had come to be that men should have the upper hand, give the orders, make the laws, arrange the world. And the reason was simple – *because they said so*. She wasn't sure if she was more appalled at the banality of this formulation or the iniquity that had inspired it. But the shock of it made her half rise from the bed. No wonder they sounded so loud and confident. They were the important ones, just because they said so.

The voices were outside her cell. She heard someone recite her name and number. The small partition in the door was drawn back, and she saw a face at the spyhole. More muttering, and then a key turned in the lock. But the door held fast, with her chair wedged beneath the handle. This was fortified by the planks of her bed set lengthwise between the door and the window. She felt quite proud of this construction. It was difficult to tell how many of them were heaving and cursing beyond the threshold. First an arm poked through, blindly scrabbling for purchase in the gloom. When a head appeared, she picked up the chamber pot ready to throw, distantly aware of her own panicked shouts and her heart hammering furiously to be let out of its cage. The tortured wood began to screech and splinter. Not long now.

PART ONE

A Little Learning

1

They had stopped on the sward where it flattened towards the edge of the promontory, with the shadow of the castle behind them and a panorama of the coast in front. Picnic blankets had been laid down, and a hamper was being unpacked by the younger and more enthusiastic Beaumont cousins. Down below they could see striped bathing huts ranked along the shore, and dozens, tens of dozens, of holidaymakers staking their place in the crush, paddling in the surf or reclining on the shingle. The sea swayed and glistened, hurriedly folding itself into thin white undulations as it lapped the shoreline. The noonday sun, growing fierce, had prompted matrons to take cover beneath the black blooms of their parasols. Further in the distance the pier was aflutter with Union Jack pennants, a harbinger of the Coronation less than two weeks away.

One of the picnicking family stood slightly apart, her gaze absorbed by a spectacle way down to the right. Opinion divided as to whether Connie Callaway was a beauty. Somewhat gawky, and taller than she would have liked, she carried herself with a certain hesitancy, as if reluctant to be noticed. From her father she had inherited a strong jawline that looked at a certain angle almost masculine; yet this severity was counterpointed by an expressive mouth, delicately fluted nose, and eyes of liquid brown that glittered when she laughed, bewitching even those – not a few – who considered her 'odd-looking'. Those eyes were focused upon a cricket match, and even at this distance she could hear the tiny click as ball touched bat. The ground, once a water meadow, was unusual in being situated right in the centre of town, and thus vulnerable to a council notoriously eager to sell it off. The sight of chalky figures shimmering at the wicket had an instantly soothing effect upon Connie's nerves. She detested picnics: essentially, one took a pile of sandwiches for a walk, settled oneself on a scratchy tartan rug, then waited for the wasps to show up. But in spite of a naturally forthright temperament she had taught herself, in the course of her twenty-one years, the virtue of graciousness: she would not impose an irritable mood on her companions.

There followed a burst of activity on the pitch. A batsman had slashed a ball through the covers, beating the ring of fielders and panicking a party of seagulls that had settled near the boundary rope; the birds scattered and exploded in an upward flurry. A drowsy ripple of applause rose with them, and Connie instinctively clapped too. Her cousin Louis had sidled up next to her and was also scrutinising the game, one hand in his pocket, the other shielding his eyes against the sun. He was two years older, a short, dapper man whose expression always seemed to be savouring some private amusement.

'There's a sight to gladden the heart,' he said, gazing past Connie, who murmured her agreement. 'I wonder if Maitland's there today . . .'

'Who's that?' she asked.

'Oh, pal of mine from Oxford – a Blue. I know he's been playing for M—shire.'

'Shall we go and see?'

Louis gave her a sidelong look. 'We could put the idea to this lot.' He nodded over his shoulder at their kinfolk, who were now busily distributing sandwiches and beakers of home-made lemonade among themselves. Connie pursed her mouth as she silently gauged 'this lot'. The custom on family holidays was to do things together, and the preponderance of females among them militated against the likelihood of an afternoon's cricket. Her older sister, Olivia, would have none of it, she knew, even if Lionel, her fiancé, was willing. Their mother might just be persuaded; she had developed a neutral tolerance of the game from her late husband's enthusiasm. As for Louis's mother, Jemima, and his three sisters – her devoted affection for them did not incline her to confidence in their docility. Her mother was calling them over. As she settled herself on the rug, she said, to nobody in particular, 'There's cricket in town today. I thought we might wander down there.'

Mrs Callaway, who would formerly have looked to her husband for an answer to this, merely tilted her head in a way that offered no clue to her desires.

'Cricket is a bore,' said Alice flatly. At sixteen she was the oldest of the Beaumont girls.

'I disagree,' said Connie, keeping her tone bright. 'It is slow, and complicated. But not a bore.'

'Well,' said Lionel, with a meditative sniff, 'if we can get a seat in the members' stand . . . We don't want to be with the plebs.'

Connie wondered, not for the first time, how prepared she was to have Lionel for a brother-in-law. He was at Barings, and even today wore a waistcoat, stiff collar and bow tie, as if fearful of dispensing with his banker's uniform. His concession to the holiday spirit was the temporary retirement of his dark worsted suit for a pair of grey flannels, with deck shoes instead of brogues. The matter of the cricket was put aside while they involved themselves in the picnic. The sun, hoisted high, seemed to have tweaked up its glare another notch. Connie felt a bead of perspiration trickle down the small of her back, and wished they had found a more shaded spot for their lunch. The glass of lemonade was sweating in her hand. Looking to distract herself, she turned to her aunt and said, 'That's a lovely hat, Mima. Is it new?'

Jemima, younger and more at ease than Connie's mother, though widowed like her, smiled from under the hat's wide brim at her niece.

'It is. I actually meant to keep it for the big day, but I couldn't resist putting it on when I saw the weather this morning.'

Connie nodded, and sensed an opportunity for mischief. 'By the "big day" I assume you mean the procession in London next Saturday.'

Jemima blinked her soft grey eyes uncomprehendingly. 'Ahm . . . next Saturday?'

'Yes! The procession of all the suffrage societies to the Albert Hall. They say there's going to be quite the most enormous turnout.'

'She's being provocative, Mima,' Olivia cut in humourlessly. 'She knows you meant the Coronation.' Connie's elder by four years, Olivia had her sister's high forehead, a forbidding stare and a tongue that was quick to judgement. Connie was perhaps unique among the family in not being frightened of her.

'What's "suffrage"?' asked Flora, Jemima's youngest.

'It means the right to vote in an election,' replied Connie crisply. 'The procession will be a way of asking the government to give that right to women.'

Flora frowned as she digested this information. 'But – do women want to vote?'

'Good question,' said Olivia. 'Most women *don't* want to – just a crowd of harpies who are making trouble because they think they're the same as men.'

'And if you want to know what a harpy is, Flora,' said Connie, placing her hand with mock primness on her breast, 'behold.'

'But really, Constance, what do you hope to achieve?' her sister pursued. 'By insisting on the vote you inflict a burden on women – one that most will thoroughly resent.'

Connie laughed, and shook her head. At moments like this it seemed remarkable to her that she and Olivia were blood relatives. 'In time they'll find it not such a burden after all. Don't you think so, Ma?'

Mrs Callaway sighed in such a way as to suggest she had heard this argument before. 'I have no view on the matter at all, as you know – but I'd rather you didn't turn our luncheon into a debating society.' She was directing a vaguely beseeching look at both of her daughters.

Lionel, ignoring this last plea, adopted a tone of resonant authority. 'I read in *The Times* recently that they canvassed women in seventy-odd districts and less than fifteen per cent replied that they were in favour of the vote. *Thirty-eight per cent*,' he said, with a pause that infuriated Connie, 'declared that they were opposed to female suffrage. Which tells you enough.'

Jecca, Louis's fourteen-year-old middle sister, was assiduously calculating a sum with her fingers. 'So – fifteen, thirty-eight . . . what about the other, um, forty-seven per cent?'

'Oh,' said Connie, with an exaggerated shrug, 'they're probably just harpies.'

By the time they had finished the sandwiches and the remainder of Jemima's walnut cake, the treacly heat was making them quite uncomfortable. Flora and Jecca were positively fractious. Connie thought that this might be the moment to refloat the idea of the cricket, and looked over at Louis, who read the entreaty in her eyes. He stood up and briskly cleared his throat.

'Right then, this is what we'll do. Clear up here, then stroll down to the cricket. If my pal's at the ground we'll be able to get seats in the pavilion – some welcome shade for the ladies. Girls,' he added, turning to his sisters, 'if you really don't like it you can go to the beach instead.'

They began gathering up the detritus of lunch. Connie, inwardly, was astonished. Her lobbying for the cricket had met with blank indifference. Yet Louis had carried it off without a peep from any of them. He hadn't even couched it as a suggestion – he had said, 'This is what we'll do,' and they had simply complied with it. Without needing to enquire too deeply she knew why, and it was not because Louis had bullied or wheedled. He had no need to. He was a man, he had spoken, and that was enough.

Louis's surmise that his friend might be playing had proven correct, and soon he was ushering the family through the members' gate and into a row of seats. The high scent of baking grass and sun-blistered wood permeated the air. The pavilion, built in the mid-1880s, was ambitiously modelled on the one at Lord's in its mixture of mauve brick, wrought-iron balconies and large plate-glass windows. It had been funded for the Priory by a local businessman who hoped to raise the town's profile as a cricketing venue. M—shire, the county cricket club, had shared a home with Sussex in nearby Brighton, though the addition of this huge pavilion and the enduring charm of the ground itself had persuaded the county to transfer its patronage to the Priory. The town, overshadowed for so long by its more glamorous neighbour down the coast, had rejoiced.

The family had arrived at an opportune moment. Surrey, the visitors, had been bowled out by the middle of the afternoon, and M—shire's opening pair of batsmen were now clattering down the shadowed steps and through the gate. A loud volley of applause echoed over the ground.

Connie had turned on hearing their footfall and caught a glimpse of the older of the pair as he passed, a tall, broad-shouldered figure with a heavy moustache and a striped club tie raffishly belted around his waist. The bat looked almost puny in his hands. She thought she recognised him, though he looked somewhat older. Louis had briefly disappeared, and she knew that none of her family would have a clue – apart from Lionel, whose conversation she was reluctant to engage. Spotting a boy selling scorecards on the boundary's edge, she called him over and paid him his tuppence. Her eye scanned the card, and there was his name at the top of the order: A. E. Tamburlain.

Some minutes later Louis returned, and beamingly introduced his cricketer friend to the family. The latter, tall and loose-limbed, was named Will Maitland. He shook hands with Mrs Callaway and Jemima, then with Olivia and Lionel, and directed a short grave nod to the girls, who blushed at the handsome stranger in his flannels. Connie, seated slightly apart, was the last to be introduced, and unlike the others stood up to take his hand. Louis, dwarfed like a referee between two prizefighters, smiled at his cousin.

'Mr Maitland,' she said, 'thank you for accommodating us. I thought it was members only'.

'It is,' Will admitted. 'But I couldn't disappoint Beau here – I mean, Louis – particularly when he's brought along such agreeable company.'

Connie allowed herself a slow smile at this gallantry. She sensed him frankly appraising her from beneath his club cap, and to deflect this attention she gestured towards the square.

'I see Mr Tamburlain is playing today.'

Will followed her gaze. 'Yes – hence the crowd.'

'Well, they've come to see one of the greats,' Louis broke in. At that, a sound like a rifle crack suddenly pierced the air. Tamburlain had just hit his first boundary of the afternoon, and Louis, pleased to have his words so ring-ingly affirmed, shouted, 'Shot, sir!'

As the applause subsided, Connie turned back to Will. 'I wonder if it's difficult for someone of his stature – I mean, after playing for England, and Sussex –'

'– to come and play for a little club like ours?' said Will, with a wry half-smile. 'I think Tam enjoys it. He could hardly be more appreciated here. And there are worse teams to play for.'

'I didn't mean –' Connie was blushing at her unintended slight, but it was lost to notice by a commotion out on the square. The county's first wicket had fallen. Will said, 'I'd better get padded up. I go in at four these days.'

'Good for you, Will,' cried Louis, surprised. 'With any luck you'll get to bat with Tam.'

Will winked, and turned to Connie. 'Very nice to meet you, Miss Callaway. I do hope you enjoy the game.' He nodded abruptly to both of them and walked off to the dressing room.

The shadows had begun to lengthen over the field as the afternoon wore on. Alice, Jecca and Flora had departed for the beach with Olivia, leaving Lionel to entertain Jemima and his future mother-in-law. This allowed Connie both the leisure to watch the game unfold and to interrogate Louis in some detail about his friend Maitland.

'Mm?' said Louis, his gaze focused on the middle. 'His people live down here, or at least, his mother and sister do – Oh, *shot!*'

Connie clapped along with her cousin. 'And his father?'

'Um . . . died a few years ago. Made a fortune as a wine and spirits importer.'

'Oh. So he didn't join the family business?' Connie was failing to suppress a rising inquisitive note in her voice, which Louis, absorbed in the cricket, had not yet registered.

'No . . . Will studied Law at Magdalen. At one time he was destined for the Bar. But it didn't appeal to him half as much as wielding the willow. So when he came into his inheritance he dropped out and joined M—shire. I suppose this must be his second or third season here.'

Once the second wicket fell, the subject of their discussion emerged from the pavilion and stalked out to the blazing middle. Will nodded to Tam at the other end before taking his guard, then looked around for gaps in the field. He felt in determined, if not quite confident, mood, and the forward-defensive push at his first ball was severely correct. At the end of the over he looked down the wicket at his senior partner: Tam sometimes liked to have a quick chat between overs, but today his frown of concentration was pronounced, and Will decided not to disturb him. The first ball of the next over bounced high and reared past Tam's chin, prompting 'ooohs' from the crowd. He stared back down at the bowler, who, perhaps carried away by the idea of rattling the celebrity, overpitched his next ball. Tam drove it fast and straight, so straight that it almost took Will's head off at the non-striker's end. He managed to duck just in time, and watched the ball as it went, one bounce, over the rope at long on. With a faint smile Tam lifted his hand to Will in apology.

Hearing the vicious *whirr* of that ball as it scorched past his ear reminded him of the first time he had encountered Andrew Endall Tamburlain – as an opponent. Like so many boys of his generation he had idolised 'The Great Tam', the batsman who had rivalled W. G. Grace in popularity and ought to have captained England; but it was not until the summer of 1906 when Will was making his debut for the Varsity against Sussex at the Parks that he came face to face with him. Tam, in his last season for the county, was flogging the Oxford bowling to all corners of the ground. Will had never seen anyone hit the ball so hard. On his fourteenth birthday he had received the gift of a 'Tamburlain Repeater' bat, so called for the rifle-like sound of its celebrant's shots, but he had not yet experienced their force at close quarters. Fielding at point, Will mistimed his dive at one of Tam's fizzing square cuts; he heard the ball rather than saw it, and next thing it had ricocheted off the turf and gut-punched him. He lay there, winded and gasping for breath, until a couple of his teammates came over to check on him. As he rose unsteadily to his feet he caught sight of Tam standing at his crease and shaking his head in annoyance: that ungainly block had deprived him of four runs.

It would be the last time that Will or anyone else managed to stop one that afternoon. His abiding memory was of Tam's swing, which was clean and swift and true, like the old gardener he had once watched cutting down a tree in his parents' orchard. Tam's tightly bulked musculature aided his stroke-playing but wasn't the source of its majesty. His secret lay in his timing, which could create the illusion that he had barely touched the ball. Sometimes it was a conventional pull or hook; at others it was an outrageous scoop at a good-length delivery that was heading for middle-and-leg. Up it would soar, climbing on a diagonal into the soft volume of air, so high you had to squint, less an object in flight than the point of a vertiginous construction, like a church steeple or a weathervane. But the shot he best recalled that day was one of Tam's least characteristic, a drive square off the front foot past gully for four. It seemed to flow straight from his bat over the rope in one silky flourish.

'Aye. That was the one,' Tam said later, meeting his young admirer with an approving nod. 'It went like butter.'

Will never forgot the phrase. From that moment on he wanted to know how it would feel to play that shot: to make it go like butter.

* * *

That was five years ago. Lulled by this current of memory, Will abruptly resurfaced in the present. He had got himself into difficulties, his timing all out of sorts. Tam meanwhile had gained an ominous fluency, and was entertaining the crowd with his repertoire of favourite shots. The Surrey bowling was hardly menacing, but it was competent, and Will knew that he really needed to play himself in rather than try to emulate his senior partner's big hitting. What he knew he ought to do and what he felt driven to do, however, were at war in his mind. Now he was facing a medium pacer whose nagging accuracy had pinned him down. For some reason he found himself going for cavalier strokes and misjudging them, which only heightened the impression of his overeagerness to grandstand. Tam had sensed that something was amiss, and had come down the wicket to have a word.

'All right, Bluey?' he said. This had been his nickname for Will ever since he heard that the club had signed up an Oxford Blue.

Will shook his head. 'Can't seem to time it today.'

'Well, there's no hurry. Just hold steady and wait for the bad'un – we can make a pile of runs here.' There was a kindliness in Tam's flat Lancastrian accent, and Will felt emboldened by his companionable use of 'we' rather than 'you'. It implied that they were equals, run-getters-in-arms. A few balls later the bowler at the pavilion end sent down a long hop and Will gratefully heaved it over the midwicket boundary. At last! The applause crackled pleasantly in his ears. He glanced down at Tam, whose cheerful wink seemed to him like a benediction. Strange, he thought, how a single moment's lapse could change everything. He'd been scratching around for twenty minutes, playing and missing, hopelessly out of touch. Now the opposition had gifted him a loose one and the shackles were off; he was free to fill his boots. Such were his thoughts as he faced his next ball,

17

which struck a divot and climbed suddenly. Will was into his stroke before he could adjust to the ball's altered trajectory. It hit his bat on the splice and arced high, high into the air, you could almost hear the collective intake of breath. His heart froze as he looked up – the ball had height but no distance – and as it steepled and fell towards the man fielding at square leg, Will knew his time at the crease was over and done with. It was like a foreglimpse of dying. He had already started trudging back to the pavilion when he heard the roars of the Surrey players behind him celebrating the catch.

The sun was just disappearing over the cliffs when play finished for the day. The others had left for the hotel about an hour before. As the fielding side converged on the pavilion and their spiked boots clinked on the steps, Louis called out to Tam, trailing a little way behind, 'Well played, Tam!' The latter looked up to the stalls on hearing this tribute and lifted the brim of his cap in acknowledgement. Louis turned his face in delight to Connie, as if to say, *Did you see that?*

'I suppose we should go and say cheer-o to Will,' he added, and Connie followed him as he edged past the departing spectators and through the pavilion's tall glass doors. A bouquet of linseed oil, tobacco smoke and sweat hung about the murky entrance hall as Louis stood on tiptoe trying to spot his friend amid the jostle of weary cricketers and ground staff. Connie, glancing off towards a changing room, saw a man sitting alone, bare to his waist, with a towel draped over his head. She recognised him in spite of his shrouded face, and called over to Louis.

'Isn't that him?'

He nodded and entered the room, while Connie modestly held back, watching. She couldn't hear what was said above the clamour of voices around her, but she did see him pulling back the towel from his head as he talked to Louis. During this short colloquy Will glanced through the door at her, and though she felt the impropriety of staring at a half-naked stranger, she did not avert her eyes. His torso, she noticed, was lean and rangy. He held her gaze for a moment, then turned back to Louis. The hall was bustling now, and the two men disappeared from view as more white-clad figures filed past into the dressing room. Connie walked back outside and took a seat in the emptying stalls, where she opened a packet of cigarettes and lit one.

A few moments later, Louis emerged through the doors and did a small double take as he noticed the cigarette in her hand. Connie expelled a plume of smoke and said, 'Please, do *not* mention this to my mother.'

'Mum's the word,' said Louis, then chuckled at his accidental witticism.

They strolled back along the esplanade to their hotel, serenaded by the screeching of plump herring gulls overhead. From below they could hear the rattle of bathing huts being hauled up the beach for the day. Louis was enthusing over a mighty six that Tam had struck earlier in the afternoon. The ball, which had flown over the wall into South Terrace, had ended up in someone's drawing room. They had all heard the faintly comical explosion of tinkling glass.

'That's the benefit of such a compact ground,' he explained, mimicking the shot for Connie's instruction. 'You see a lot of big sixes.'

'And a lot of broken windows, by the sound,' Connie added, before continuing. 'Your friend, Mr Maitland, looked glum.'

'Hmm, poor old Will missed out today.'

'It's a shame we won't see him play tomorrow.' They were due to return to London the next day.

'Yes . . . though Will did mention a party that's being held tonight. It's the club's fiftieth anniversary, or something.'

'Oh. He invited you?'

'Mm. As a matter of fact, he invited you too. But I wasn't sure you'd be interested.'

'Why ever not?' she asked, surprised.

'Well . . . the company is mostly male, and the atmosphere may be – a little rowdy . . .'

Connie smiled. 'Nice of you to be so protective, Lou, but I'm sure that my delicate sensibility can cope.'

'Capital!' said Louis, who continued boyishly practising his forward-defensive strokes, left elbow thrust outwards, oblivious to the passers-by on their early-evening promenade.

Dinner was prolonged by Lionel, who peevishly voiced dissatisfaction with the temperature of his Dover sole, and then made a fuss about the wine that proved, on inspection, not to be corked after all. Even Olivia looked rather put out by his pedantic line of argument with the head waiter. It was a little embarrassing, because everyone could tell that the waiter (who behaved impeccably) knew more than Lionel – everyone, that is, but Lionel himself. The dining room fronted onto the sea, and the windows of the Royal Victoria had been opened to accommodate the warmth of the evening. A pleasant sea-salty tang wafted through the air, with only the faintest scent of horse manure trailing behind. Alice, Jecca and Flora had attached themselves to another family at the hotel who were taking them to the evening performance at the Pier. The adults would perhaps play bridge, as long as Mrs Callaway's slight neurasthenia allowed; she had not come down this evening, and Connie, once dinner was over, had gone immediately to her room.

'I'm quite all right, darling,' said Mrs Callaway, supine on her bed with the curtains drawn. 'You go out with Louis. Don't worry about me.'

Connie sometimes wondered if her mother's martyred

tone was born of calculation, or if it came, in fact, quite naturally to her. Its quiet plaintiveness had the same result, in any event, prompting in Connie a mixture of guilt and exasperation. Tactfully, she refrained from voicing it. In the three years since her husband's death, Mrs Callaway, passive by nature, had sunk into a kind of elegant lassitude from which her younger daughter, out of love and duty, would try very gently to rouse her.

'Ma,' said Connie, plumping the pillows behind her mother's head, 'if you feel well enough, they need a fourth for bridge downstairs.'

Mrs Callaway nodded, and waved her hand in dismissal. Connie waited for a few moments. Then, as she opened the door to leave, she heard a feeble little cough behind her. The voice quavered again.

'Darling, perhaps you *could* fetch me a bowl of the soup before you leave.'

The Wellington was one in a long terrace of creamy stucco hotels on the Queens Parade, and as Connie and Louis approached they could hear the jaunty strains of a piano from somewhere inside. A horse-drawn cab had just pulled up at the entrance, and out of it stepped two young men they had seen that afternoon in the Priory pavilion. Both now sported boaters and blazers, and, once Connie saw them close up, matching moustaches. She briefly reflected on how difficult it would be to kiss a man with facial hair. Now Louis was leading her through the vestibule and down a corridor, following the sound of the piano and the gathering hum of conversation. As soon as she entered the room Connie sensed many eyes turning to her. There were other women present, but most of them were hotel staff carrying pints of ale and champagne buckets draped in napkins. The acrid stench of cigar smoke seemed to Connie at that moment the essence of hearty masculine camaraderie, even more so than the desultory caws of laughter and the sing-song that had just started up. 'Daisy Bell' was plainly a Priory favourite, and as Connie stood at the bar waiting for Louis to be served, a young man boomed out behind her ear: '. . . *I'm half crazy / All for the love of youuu!*' and favoured her with a wink when she turned. Not wishing to be thought prim, she offered him a half-smile in return. Louis, edging through the crush, glanced around nervously and seemed at once to realise that Connie had become the cynosure of the room. As he handed over a glass he leaned towards her, raising his voice above the braying chorus: 'Are you, er, all right with this place?'

She was touched by Louis's expression of solicitude, realising at that moment how typical it was of him. Rather than shout back, she simply patted his arm and smiled. She still found it disconcerting to be ogled, though she had to admit it was oddly gratifying, too. When the song finished, the man who had winked at her leaned over and said, with a chuckle in his voice, 'So . . . what brings a nice girl like you to a place like this?'

'Oh, probably just the same thing as you,' Connie replied, raising her glass cheerily. The man, blazered and brilliantined, hoisted his eyebrows at this.

'I'm not sure we're thinking about *quite* the same thing,' he drawled, at which remark Louis stepped in, his face darkening.

'That's enough of that,' he said, glaring at him. 'You're talking to a lady.'

The man looked down at Louis, stifled a guffaw, and turned to Connie. 'I'm sorry – is this your little brother?'

Louis lurched towards him, but was prevented from further obligation by the arrival of Will, who said in a good-humoured tone, 'Now, Beau, take no notice of this chap. Revill here is our resident joker, and I'm sure he'll apologise to Miss Callaway for any . . . unseemly remark.'

Revill, holding forth his palms in a gesture of innocence, glanced at Connie. 'Miss – my sincere apologies.'

Connie heard no sincerity in them, but wanted the scene over with, so she nodded briefly then looked away. Will dismissed Revill with a jerk of his head, then conducted his guests into a billiard room on the other side of the corridor. He introduced Louis to a small cluster of his Priory colleagues before inviting Connie to sit with him at a table in the corner.

'That was a timely intervention,' she said, looking over her glass at him.

'Your cousin is quite the bantam, isn't he?' said Will, who proceeded to talk of his friendship with Louis at Oxford; as he did so, Connie took the chance to study him more closely. Will's face in repose was brooding, though there seemed little of moodiness about him. He had an abstracted gaze at times, and she couldn't help noticing his long eyelashes, almost like a girl's. She thought there might be something rather spoilt about the set of his mouth. He was asking her whether she liked the south coast.

'Very much. This is our first time down here – we used to go to the Continent.'

'Oh, whereabouts?'

'Mostly to the Riviera, sometimes to Lake Como. But then my father died and we – well, we couldn't any longer because –' She stopped, and coloured at having blundered towards an intimacy. Will, sensing her embarrassment, filled the space. 'I lost my father when I was twelve. A heart attack.'

'I'm sorry,' said Connie, with a sympathetic lowering of her gaze.

'We were pretty close,' he continued, with a rueful smile. 'He taught me a lot about cricket.'

'So did mine!' said Connie, her eyes bright with enthusiasm. 'Pa used to take me and my brother to watch the MCC.'

Will merely nodded, and Connie realised then what she ought to have said. 'I'm sure that your father would be . . . very proud of you.'

'Hmm. Not if he'd seen that shot I played today.'

Connie smiled. 'Well, that was unfortunate. But . . .' She sensed an interesting topic ahead, and wanted to see if he would take the bait. Will was alert to the significant pause she had left.

'"But" what?'

Connie didn't require a further prompt. 'I was going to say – *but* you don't quite help yourself as a batsman. You seemed too keen to compete with Mr Tamburlain's quick scoring, when it would have been more sensible to support him. And the ball you got out to was exactly a consequence of that eagerness – you went too early into the stroke and were caught on the crease. But that may be to do with technique . . .' She was talking earnestly, hurriedly, in the hope that Will might sooner appreciate her understanding. But his gaze had dropped as she spoke, and she wondered why. Now he looked at her again, and said, distantly, 'My – technique?'

Not sensing any danger, she continued. 'Yes. It seems to me – I hope you don't mind my saying – you hardly move your feet at all. You're rooted to the crease, and seem unsure whether to go forward or back . . .'

Will was listening, though hardly able to believe his ears. It was a shock to him, for he came of a class and generation of men who were disposed to regard a lady's opinion as merely decorative. He might have found her impertinence amusing were it not also for her apparent conviction that she was *doing him a favour*. The temerity of the girl! Connie's stream of talk had begun to dry as she perceived a certain tension in his silence. Will shook his head for a moment, as if he were surfacing from a daze, and spoke with cold deliberation.

'Actually, I do – that is, I *do* mind your saying. May I ask, Miss Callaway – have you ever played cricket yourself?'

Connie, startled by his unfriendly tone, shook her head.

'I thought not,' said Will. 'So you've no experience of facing a cricket ball that's coming at you like a rocket from twenty-two yards. You've no experience of making quick decisions, or of compiling an innings, or indeed of anything that pertains to the discipline of batsmanship. And yet –' he allowed himself an abrupt chuckle '– you presume to tell me about the niceties of "technique"?'

Connie was quiet for a moment, and fixed a measuring look on him. It was not resentment she felt so much as disappointment. His charm had proven as brittle as a teatime wafer; beneath it was only petulance and condescension.

'I'm sorry that you take offence at something I meant quite innocently. It's true that I've never played cricket – I have never had the opportunity – but surely that does not disqualify me from having an *opinion*. I dare say you have never made an armchair, but you'd not hesitate to say whether the one you're sitting upon is comfortable or not. No, I haven't learned "the discipline of batsmanship", as you call it, but I have watched enough cricket in my life to know whether a player has acquired a sufficiency. And you, Mr Maitland, have not.'

Will could not tell if it was anger or incredulity that had hold of his tongue. He looked at her as one might at a lunatic or a child who had just stumbled upon the gift of eloquence. He even experienced a small shiver of alarm. Hitherto he had enjoyed the company of women without ever feeling an obligation to take them quite seriously. He excepted his mother from this. He took her very seriously indeed. Connie, meanwhile, was pulling on her gloves. She saw the expression of stunned bemusement clenching Will's face.

'I'm sure you would rather be talking to your friends,' she said, standing up and feeling glad of her height, for once. She would keep a civil tongue. Will, surprised at her suddenness, also rose to his feet. Despite his annoyance, he was not blind to his obligations as a gentleman.

'Miss Callaway,' he said, swallowing hard, 'I am at a loss as to – I fear we have misunderstood one another – your forwardness –'

'Don't concern yourself, Mr Maitland,' she replied calmly. 'I think the misunderstanding was mine. I believed you to be . . . other than you are. And now I'll bid you good evening.'

She stepped past him before he had time to remonstrate with her further. She would leave a message at reception to let Louis know that she had gone. On her way through the vestibule she had to pass through a thick knot of revellers, one or two of whom stared at her with candid interest. The tallest of them, who had been talking, now broke off to clear a path for her as she advanced. Tamburlain. He looked much older close to, his skin darkly blotched and his huge black moustache flecked with grey. As she caught his eye he bowed, gravely, and said, 'Miss.' She nodded her thanks and walked out into the night.

As the sea bucked and heaved beneath the esplanade, Connie leaned on her elbows against the railing and stared into the dark. An imperceptibly fine spume had dampened the night air, and when she licked her upper lip it tasted of salt. She felt a light-headed exhilaration. Among her family she was known to be combative – in spite of their closeness, she and her father had had the most tremendous rows – but it was not her inclination to be so with near-strangers. She thought back to the look of surprise that seized Will's countenance, and felt triumphant. It occurred to her now that he had never been addressed so frankly by a woman before. Well, he should accustom himself to it. A batsqueak of conscience told her that she might have exercised a little more tact. But this was swiftly drowned out by the flood of indignant scorn on recalling his sullen self-importance. 'The discipline of batsmanship' – what pomposity! She knew she was right, and that he had made a fool of himself. It was a pity, really. She had rather liked his face.

2

On the morning of the following Saturday Connie was in her father's study, drawing her finger along a neatly serried shelf of *Wisden* Almanacks. The collection abruptly ended with the edition of 1908, the year that Donald Callaway had departed this life. Those numerals inscribed on its spine had rendered the volume a kind of memorial in her eyes. The year was a turning point for her, for all of the family, marking the age when he was alive – and everything after, when he was not. It was a divide as absolute to her as BC and AD. When she plucked a *Wisden* from the shelf and opened its brittle pages her nose took in the scent of dust and time, with the faintest melancholy traces of her father's pipe smoke. A jovial, gregarious man, he was well known among his City peers for daring speculations that would nearly always yield dividends, and he had kept his wife and children – two daughters and a younger son – in the comfortable security of a large house in Islington. His fabled luck in the markets had not, alas, insured him against cardiac failure. One autumn morning a colleague had found him slumped over the desk in his Cheapside office. Connie had happened to be looking out of the morning-room window at Thornhill Crescent when the policeman opened the front gate and walked up the path, his heavy step the harbinger of ill tidings.

As the shock of his death reverberated through the family,

another followed swiftly in its wake. Without precisely understanding his occupation, Connie knew that a broker undertook certain risks as a matter of course, and she only had to
read a newspaper to appreciate how suddenly financial ruin
could engulf an apparently safe institution. Yet when the
family's solicitor, Mr Napier, had presented himself at the
house some weeks after the funeral to read the will, no one
was at all prepared for the news that their late paterfamilias
had been, to all intents and purposes, bankrupt. In the months
leading up to his death, Donald Callaway had borrowed
heavily on a diamond-mining venture in South Africa, only
to see it collapse without warning, leaving himself and other
leading brokers in the City recklessly overcommitted. Mr
Napier's quiet, measured tones as he related this were in
notable contrast to the exclamations of dismay from Connie's
mother and sister, who at one point resorted to the disbeliever's
rhetorical fallback, namely that 'there must be some mistake'.
There was no mistake. Once certain creditors had been satisfied, the will would leave nothing to the family but the house
they lived in. Unable to bear the broken expression on her
mother's face, Connie looked at Fred, her brother, who grimaced and said, in an undertone, 'Crikey.' He was due to go
up to Cambridge the following year, and, in the stunned
minutes that followed the solicitor's disabling revelation,
Connie knew that Fred would now be calculating the greatly
increased odds against his being able to do so.

In the forlorn discussions that ensued over the next few
days the widow and her children took stock – ironic phrase
– and made some hard decisions about the future. Julia
Callaway had brought to her marriage a modest fortune
of her own, which was mostly intact at the time of her
husband's death. This would allow her to maintain
the running of the household, though at a reduced level;
the cook would be retained, along with a maid. The other
servants would have to be dismissed. All extravagances

– the carriage and pair, visits to the theatre, the accounts at Jones Brothers and at Nicoll's on Regent Street – would be henceforth curtailed. Holidays on the Continent were now unthinkable. As to their individual futures, there was enough money, just, to see Fred through his final year at Uppingham and thence to Cambridge, but Olivia and Constance would be obliged to seek gainful employment in order to make ends meet. Olivia, who had no ambition other than to marry well, greeted this new imposition with a look of candid horror. Connie, more independent-minded than her sister, had been about to start her second year at the London School of Medicine for Women.

If Connie had felt more encouraged she might have enquired into the possible connections between her father's business failure and his sudden death. Was the heart attack consequent on the shock of his undoing, or was he predisposed to the condition? When she broached the subject with her mother, however, she had met with a pursed rebuff that seemed to warn against further enquiry, and Olivia's response was even more brusque. In spite of this, Connie had an intuition that her mother and her sister had talked privately between themselves on that same subject. She might have felt hurt at this perceived exclusion but instead she tried to bury her curiosity, if not her sense of grief, in the conscientious pursuit of her first job. She secured this, ironically, through an enthusiasm of her late father's. A passionate reader, Donald Callaway had for years patronised a small but well-regarded bookshop in Camden Town, and in so doing had become friendly with the owner, Mr Hignett, a man of his own age, outlook and clubbable habits. Connie, who had inherited her father's bookishness, was herself on good terms with him, both through his attendance at the Callaway dinner table and at the shop, where she was often dispatched to collect her father's latest parcel of books.

Having noticed Mr Hignett at the funeral, she decided to write to him at the shop, and was rewarded with a letter in which he initially expressed puzzlement at her interest but went on to indicate that, if she were quite serious, he would gladly find her a position. A month later Connie started there as an assistant. The work was of an unchallenging nature; she found the cataloguing and stacking quite dull, but she enjoyed corresponding with out-of-town customers and minding the shop during the quieter hours when she could have a little reading time to herself at the counter. She got on well with the two young women who worked there, and Hignett's manager, zealous only in his talent for delegation, left them to run the place more or less by themselves. She would set off from home each morning just before eight to open the shop, and at just after six in the evening be ready to lock up. Others might have been downcast by this sudden change in routine and perhaps even humiliated by the obligation to work in 'trade'. Connie, fighting the impulse to self-pity, mourned the abrupt cessation of her medical studies, but she knew it was only through her father's liberal-minded view of the world that she had been allowed to pursue higher education in the first place.

She was skimming a *Wisden* profile of A. E. Tamburlain –

> debut for Sussex, 1889; featured as one of the Five Cricketers of the Year in 1893; 16 Test appearances for England; *annus mirabilis* in 1899, when he hit four centuries in successive matches and scored the quickest hundred (44 minutes) in county history; moved to M—shire, 1906

– when the door of the study creaked open and Olivia entered. Connie, seated on the top of her father's old library steps, looked down and bade her good morning.

'What are you doing here?' Olivia asked. In reply Connie

held up the little volume; her sister regarded it with indifference, and then began to wander about the room, pausing now and then. It was a sign that meant she had something to say. 'Aren't you working this morning?'

Connie shook her head. 'I've taken the day off. You surely haven't forgotten?'

Olivia looked blank, and then, remembering, clicked her tongue in exasperation. 'You're not really going, are you?'

'Of course I'm going! We gather at the Embankment for half past four, and the procession starts an hour later. Just think – all those women marching together –'

'Yes. Just *think*,' said Olivia sarcastically. 'It's really rather common, marching.'

'Common' was Olivia's most damning epithet, and covered a multitude of apparently innocent activities. Funny stories were common, so too was holding hands, kissing on the lips, whistling in the street and riding a bicycle – all of which Connie happened to enjoy. Anything from Germany and France was common, unless it was wine and, possibly, opera. Organ-grinders, flower sellers, paperboys were *unutterably* common. Connie suspected that bookshop assistants would be similarly tarred, though Olivia had refrained from saying so.

'I might also call in to see Mr Brigstock on my way.'

'Oh . . . him.' Her sister seemed less certain in her response to this. 'Are you sure he's quite – a gentleman?'

Connie laughed. 'I do hope so. He's asked me to sit for him.'

'*What?!*' Olivia looked horrified. 'Of all the – you've surely refused?'

Connie shrugged, enjoying her sister's outrage. 'I haven't given him an answer yet. Though I suppose it's rather an honour.'

Olivia merely scowled at this and resumed pacing the room. On another day she would have expatiated on

32

the character of Mr Brigstock, whose reputation as a painter did not, in her view, excuse the distasteful sight of his dirty fingernails. But Connie could tell that she had something else on her mind. She had turned back to her *Wisden* when she heard Olivia halt again, and sigh.

'Lionel,' she began, 'has suggested to me that I – stop working. He wants me to help prepare the house.' Connie heard this without surprise. Olivia had not adapted to their reduced circumstances with anything like the good grace of her sister. She had been teaching, unhappily, at a junior school in Holloway for nearly two years. The pupils she liked well enough – her cast of mind was naturally pedagogic – but her staff colleagues she regarded as petty-minded, cliquish and, no doubt, common. Nor would she have been slow in communicating her disdain: she did not suffer many kinds of people gladly.

After considering this news for some moments, Connie said, 'And what is your own inclination?'

'Well, of course I'd prefer not to work.'

'There is no "of course" about it. You studied for a year to qualify. It has furnished you with an income. Does that not count for something?'

Olivia shrugged, and Connie realised at that moment the decision had already been made. It was merely her approval that was being sought. Olivia would marry Lionel the following summer; she would then bear his children and run his home. Even if Connie could accept the surrender of one's life to a man, she could not quite face the idea of that man being Lionel. She sometimes wondered if her aversion to him was simply physical: perhaps once she had grown accustomed to his mean slot of a mouth, his carefully oiled hair and his nasal voice all would be well. But even in that unlikely event, she could not deceive herself as to his oafish manners, his deafness to pomposity and – so common to his sex – the immovable sense of his own importance. And yet Olivia could abide all of this just because he was rich and would keep her in a grand style. There was only one question arising in the matter that intrigued Connie, and thus far she had managed to resist asking it. Now would be the moment. She closed the *Wisden*, and looked straight ahead as she spoke.

'Do you – love him that much?'

Olivia looked over at her and frowned. 'What a question. Why do you suppose I agreed to marry him?'

Connie knew that, were she to answer truthfully at this point, the ensuing *froideur* would touch the Arctic. Her conviction was that Olivia would never have accepted Lionel while their father was alive and the family's fortune still intact. Her sister's self-esteem and discernment would have inclined her to choose a husband on the basis of something other than a career at Barings and the promise of a large house in west London. Even if Lionel's innate conservatism and snobbishness accorded with her own, Olivia would not have been blind to the kind of man she was marrying. But Connie loved her, in spite of their differences, and kept her own counsel.

'I suppose, then . . . you must do as you see fit,' she said to Olivia, in a tone as neutral as she could manage.

The heat of the day had taken away her appetite. Connie excused herself from lunch and set off from the house wearing stout lace-up boots, though they hardly matched her wrap coat and summer bonnet. There was a good deal of walking ahead. Thornhill Crescent, where the family had lived for nearly twenty years, was close to the teeming slovenliness of Caledonian Road, whose fish shops, pawn-brokers and second-hand furniture sellers seemed quite alien to the genteel respectability of their home. Connie recalled as a girl asking her father, 'Are we middle class or upper class?' With an amused look he had replied, 'The in-between class, I think.' Only Olivia of them all had openly expressed her distaste for living cheek by jowl with shopkeepers and costermongers.

Connie's journey took her past unlovely sights – gasworks, coal depots, towering warehouses – before she gained the outskirts of Camden Town. Yet what she felt amid the thickening clatter of the streets, of wheels clicking on cobbles, of trotting horses and the jingling of tramcar bells, was not disgust, but excitement, a sudden blood-tingling sense of her own potential. Connie wanted to be worth something in the world, and she was not of an age or temperament to be discouraged: there was a future before her to grasp. The roar of traffic on Camden High Street grew louder, and on calling in at a tobacconist's shop she had to close the door behind her simply to make herself heard. She was about to buy her usual Player's, but spotting the name of another brand familiar to her, she bought them instead. More expensive, but she imagined the choice might impress him.

The consciousness of this small extravagance also delighted her as she continued down the High Street, stopping at junctions every so often to let a cavalcade of cyclists, motor cars and trams pour across the thoroughfare. This pulse of headlong movement never failed to amaze, the criss-crossing of so much human and mechanical motivation, and all apparently oblivious to everything but its own need to press on. The sense of the city as some monstrous, million-footed organism would have been disturbing to some – her mother, for one – yet to Connie it seemed a thing of enchantment, of infinite possibility.

She had reached Mornington Crescent, and only now did it occur to her that Brigstock might not be at home. Who would want to be stuck indoors on a day as warm as this? She followed the curve of the road until she came to his door, a dull, weather-beaten burgundy colour with a dusty crescent fanlight overhanging it. She tapped the knocker, and was answered some moments later by an ancient-looking landlady who thought Mr Brigstock might be in, 'though I 'aven't seen 'ide nor 'air of 'im'. Connie, invited to enter, took in the smell of mice and mildew as she walked down the hall and up the uncarpeted stairs. The house, which had doubtless been a smart address back in Regency times, had a tumbledown atmosphere a century later, though she sensed its air of dingy neglect would be to Brigstock's liking. She came to the second-floor landing where a cat, black with white paws, like spats, was curled on the bottom step. At Connie's arrival the creature rose languidly and began to pad up the staircase, like a spoilt child conducting a guest through the house. Connie called out a greeting but met with no response, so she followed the cat past the kitchen and living room, and up the next flight of stairs. Before she had reached the top the smell of turpentine and oils wafted down, mixed with tobacco smoke. She put her head round the door as the cat minced in ahead of her.

'Hullo, Maud,' said the painter, without taking his eyes off the canvas he was working on.

'Hullo to you too,' replied Connie. He had not heard her soft step, and looked round in mild surprise.

'Why, if it isn't Miss Callaway,' he said, smiling genially, though without bothering to stand up and greet her. 'Please, come in – have a seat.'

'Your landlady seemed not to know whether you were at home,' said Connie, wandering in and looking about her. She had not been to his studio before, though an invitation had been extended some time ago. Taking off her gloves and bonnet, she folded herself onto an old horsehair sofa whose blanket was coated in cat hairs. Canvases and frames were propped higgledy-piggledy against the walls. Lemony daylight flooded through an open skylight, and a casual arrangement of mirrors lent the room a deceptive sense of space. Brigstock had laid down his brush and was wiping his hands with a rag.

'I keep, um, irregular hours,' he said by way of explanation. 'I don't believe I've seen Mrs Geraghty all week. Did she seem to be missing me?'

Connie laughed. 'Not that one would notice.'

Brigstock sighed, then focused his gaze upon her. 'I've been wondering when you'd drop by.'

'I happened to be walking this way,' Connie said. 'I've not made a special trip.'

He acknowledged the slight rebuff by a tolerant inclination of his head. Connie was telling the truth, but she did feel glad to see him again. She also felt as if they were resuming an interrupted conversation. Brigstock had a drawling ironic voice which fell agreeably on her ear, though she was never sure how much of his talk was meant to be taken seriously. He was a man in his late forties, with a relaxed slouch that seemed of a piece with his rather unconventional style. His face and neck were tribally smudged and flecked with paint, and his clothes, while reasonably clean, carried the air of the pawn shop. He wore no collar, and his shirt was unbuttoned to his chest; his dark, curly hair hung to his neck, and seemed never to have known a brush or comb. Connie supposed it the calculated look of the 'starving artist', though she had gathered that Brigstock was far from being poor.

He was now looking at her very steadily. 'It's quite alarming –' he said, and stopped.

'What is?' asked Connie with an uncertain smile.

'How pleased I am to see you.' He spoke as if he couldn't quite believe the words himself. 'I've always been with Wilde – you know, "youth is a gift wasted on the young". But you make an honourable exception.'

'Do you rehearse this sort of flattery, Mr Brigstock?'

'Oh, please, call me Dab. "Mr Brigstock" makes me sound like a bank manager.'

37

Connie rose from the sofa and made her way around the easel where he sat. Brigstock had made a reputation from nudes, but he was also known for his scenes of London lowlife. The canvas before him today was of a music hall, as seen from the vertiginous angle of the audience in the gallery. It was gaily coloured, yet Connie discerned in the watching figures an inexpressible melancholy.

'I was at the Bedford the other night. Couldn't get this picture out of my head. I do love a music hall . . . they give one so many ideas.'

Connie nodded at it approvingly. 'It's very good,' she said.

'Do you swear it?' asked Brigstock with sudden intensity, and they both laughed. He reached over for his cigarettes and offered her one, but Connie declined, and dipped into her coat pocket.

'Have one of mine,' she said, breaking the seal on the packet. Brigstock arched his eyebrows as he took one.

'Sullivans? There's fancy . . .'

They smoked for a while in silence. It was odd, Connie thought, how they had become companionable on such a brief acquaintance. They had met some months before when an establishment selling artists' supplies opened next door to Hignett's bookshop. When Connie first saw him she had mistaken his dishevelled appearance for destitution; only when he appeared up close had she realised his dowdy attire was a kind of raffishness. She watched him out of the corner of her eye, and rather liked his air of abstraction as he pored over a book. Then she had become conscious that, more often, *he* was watching *her*, until one day during a lull he had sidled up to the counter as she sat reading and asked about the book in which she was absorbed. Connie had held forth its spine for the man's inspection – it was a Rhoda Broughton novel – confident that he would never have heard of the lady. Brigstock had taken in the title, and nodded.

'Not one of her best,' he had said, astonishing her.

After that, they had talked to one another whenever he had visited the shop. He would sometimes make a show of asking her about a new novel or book of poetry, although it soon became clear that his interest centred upon her rather than literary chit-chat. Their acquaintance entered a new phase one Sunday afternoon when, out walking on Hampstead Heath with Olivia and her mother, she happened to see Brigstock ambling towards them. He had caught her eye, but with an unexpected delicacy of manner he refrained from greeting her until she hailed him. Connie proceeded with introductions, and was briefly mortified to notice Olivia affording the stranger her frankest head-to-toe appraisal, like a beady dowager inspecting a suitor for her niece. Brigstock, dressed for the occasion and too suave to mind such scrutiny, was already making himself agreeable to Mrs Callaway, who by the end of this little encounter seemed utterly beguiled by him. As they walked off she quietly confessed her admiration of his 'beautiful manners' and thought that for an artist he was – no higher praise – 'quite respectable'. Olivia was also favourably impressed, though when her mother suggested inviting him to dinner, she demurred. 'Did you see the dirt under his fingernails?'

Connie had also entertained the idea of inviting him to dinner and rejected it, though not for any unease about his personal grooming. She suspected that Brigstock was a little spoony about her, and while the thought of his infatuation was pleasing, she did not want to be seen to encourage any advances. Now, as they sat there smoking together, she wondered if she should test him.

'Awfully warm, isn't it?' she said absently.

'I should say so. Too warm to be wearing . . .' Brigstock had a mischievous glitter in his eyes.

'Yes?' she prompted.

'. . . anything but a smile.' Connie looked away, so as to

hide what was, indeed, a smile. 'Have you thought any more about my offer?' he continued.

'Oh, is it an *offer*, then? I imagined you to be making a request.'

Brigstock shrugged, and pulled a droll face. 'I can make it a request, of course.'

Connie was silent for a moment, then said, 'I expect you would prefer . . . without clothes?'

Brigstock allowed himself a slow smirk. 'Why would you expect that? I rather like you in your clothes.'

Connie blushed furiously, perceiving that she had been tricked into forwardness. Brigstock, seeing her flustered, came to the rescue.

'Forgive me, Miss Callaway, I already have a number of models who pose for me – professionally – and there would be a *frightful* fuss if they got wind that another young lady was taking work from them.'

'I feel rather – foolish –'

'Truly, they're as touchy as sopranos,' he added, talking over her. 'But you'd do me a great service if you agreed to sit – for an hour or two?'

Connie, still embarrassed, only nodded. Brigstock rose and walked over to his work desk, returning with a little camp-stool and a wooden drawing board with ivory-coloured sheets of paper clipped against it. He took out a stubby pencil from his waistcoat pocket and examined its point.

'You mean to – begin?' she asked, startled.

'If you have a moment.'

She glanced at her watch. 'I'm meeting a friend at half past four . . .'

'I'll be sure to let you go in good time. No, don't get up – I'd like you just where you're sitting.' He had seated himself on the stool, and was now making a few preliminary marks. The cat, which had been skulking around the room since Connie arrived, now joined her on the sofa.

'Maud,' he said, 'get off there, please.' The cat ignored him, and curled up next to Connie. For the next half-hour Brigstock worked silently, his eyes shifting from his drawing board to Connie and back again. It had grown so warm that she briefly daydreamed of throwing off her clothes and disporting herself in the nude, but then his remark about liking her in clothes re-echoed within and made her cringe. She studied his lean, unshaven jaw and furrowed brow, then his long, bony hands; she wondered how they would feel on her skin. It occurred to her that Brigstock was the sort of man to whom women devoted themselves; he carried an air of sexual experience, but also of sexual competence – something quite different. He would perhaps pride himself on his ability to make a woman feel . . . whatever it was she was meant to feel. It frustrated her that she hadn't even the language to describe it. She, who had spent her whole life reading romantic novels. Would he be surprised by her innocence? Probably not: he was not the surprisable type.

Brigstock seemed to emerge from a trance. 'So . . .' he began, still focused on his board, 'this friend you're meeting. A young man?'

Connie shook her head. 'A young woman – we've been friends since school.'

'How sweet.'

'We're joining the procession this afternoon.'

'Procession – for what?'

'An international procession of women suffragists. We start at the Embankment, and then march through town to the Albert Hall. You haven't read about it?' Brigstock shook his head, and Connie sighed with slight irritation. 'I suppose you regard women's suffrage as rather absurd.'

'You assume a great deal about me, Miss Callaway, most of it erroneous. Suffrage does not seem to me at all absurd. I think that any measure intended to raise women from their present state of ignorance is to be encouraged.'

'So you think women ignorant, then?'

'The vast majority, yes. And men are to blame. They have kept women at a childish stage of development, and then make complaint that they are childish. We cannot hope for any kind of social progress until women are intellectually trained as men are. Why do you smile?'

'Because I have never heard a man speak such common sense before. Indeed, I feel I should insist you march with us this afternoon. We have a common cause, after all.'

Brigstock shook his head. 'No, no. I don't join movements, and I certainly don't go marching. Besides, giving the vote to women is not necessarily to emancipate them. There will be many still sunk in drudgery, and just as many idling away their time until marriage offers.'

'Marriage is sometimes the only means of escape a woman has.'

'True – but what a disastrous basis on which to wed! If I made the laws no girl should be allowed to grow up without a profession, however rich her family. Then there would be no reason for them to mope and maunder in useless waiting. In the long term men would benefit from it, too – they would have wives with whom they could share a proper conversation and intellectual respect. And everything that a marriage of equals has to offer.'

Such as a sexual relationship, Connie wanted to say, but did not dare. 'My sister works in teaching, which she loathes. Her fiancé has advised her to give it up in anticipation of their marriage, and I assure you, she is delighted to comply.'

'Teaching is a puzzler. Men become schoolteachers after solid preparation. Women enter the profession mainly because there is nothing else for them to do. I dare say your sister might have prospered in another line of work, but her choice was limited. Could not the same be said of yourself? Is it really your heart's desire to work in a bookshop?'

42

'I like it there,' said Connie mildly. 'But there are things I would much rather do.'

'Such as?'

A sad smile crept over her features. 'You'll laugh to hear it.'

'Unlikely – given what you know of my views.'

'Well, I had rather a serious illness when I was younger. I was in hospital for weeks – it felt like years at the time – but there was a surgeon there who was friendly to me. Much friendlier than the nurses. I remember being in his consulting room and always staring at a full-length diagram of the human anatomy, all the bones, the arteries and what have you. I became rather fascinated with it, and during the days and weeks of being confined I learned every single part. The surgeon, Mr Swain, was quite charmed by this, I recall, and joked that I'd soon be joining the Royal College of Surgeons, or some such. For years after I wondered if I *could* be a surgeon – it seemed to me so noble. Heroic, almost. But the commonest line of advice was that *nursing* would be the profession best suited to a girl . . .'

Her voice tailed off. Brigstock, who had been listening intently, said, 'Could you not have applied to a medical college?'

'I did. And studied for a year at the London School of Medicine for Women. But in the autumn my father died, and we discovered that he had left his finances in some disorder. A living had to be earned, and so –' She spread out her palms in a gesture of philosophical resignation.

'That's unfortunate,' said Brigstock musingly. 'I rather like the idea of you wielding a scalpel. You don't fear the sight of blood, then?'

'No. Do you?'

'Only my own,' he chuckled, and took out his watch. 'I suppose you ought to be getting along. There's a tram that runs from here down to Trafalgar Square – mustn't be late for your march.'

Connie put out the cigarette she'd been smoking. 'So I can't persuade you to accompany us?' she said archly.

'I think not.'

'Even for a worthy cause?'

'As the poet wrote, "They also serve who only stand and wait."'

'That's a rather lyrical way of evading responsibility.'

'*Touché*,' said Brigstock, laughing. He rose to help her into her coat. 'Before you go, perhaps you'd care to look at this.' He unclipped the sheet of paper on which he had been sketching and handed it to Connie. He had caught her well, she thought: the relaxed posture on the couch, head propped against hand, and seated alongside her, the lazily curled feline. Beneath it he had written, in a tiny cursive, 'Constance and Maud. 17 June 1911', and initialled it DAB.

'What does DAB actually stand for?' she said.

'Denton Adolphus. Heaven knows what my parents were thinking of. But "Dab" is rather appropriate, for my line of work. It was a nickname at school.'

She moved towards the door.

'Thank you for sitting for me,' he said. She smiled by way of reply, and offered her hand. He clasped it warmly, and they bid one another goodbye.

As soon as Connie stepped off the tram she saw Lily waiting at their designated spot on Northumberland Avenue. The marchers were by now milling around in vast numbers, and it took Connie a minute to push a way through them to reach her.

'There you are!' cried Lily, relief in her voice. She puffed out her cheeks as she leaned in to kiss her. 'I thought we'd missed each other.'

'Sorry I'm late, Lil. The tram took such ages – I ought to have gone on the Tube.'

'Not likely! You'd melt on a day like this.' Lily was wearing a huge straw bonnet with daisies festooned around the brim. The two friends were of an age – they had both just turned twenty-one – though Lily's round, innocent-looking face and small stature belied her years. She worked as secretary to the headmistress of a Camden girls' school and was regularly mistaken, to her chagrin, for one of the pupils. She was now adjusting her bonnet in the reflection of a shop window.

'You don't think it's too much?' she said, pointing at her headgear.

Connie shook her head. 'You look lovely – like the Queen of the May.'

The crowds of women marchers had suddenly thickened around them, and the air seemed to crackle with excitement. Everywhere the eye looked was a medley of white, purple and green, on banners, flags and sashes. Mounted policemen were patrolling the edges of the swelling scene. From behind they heard the rousing boom of a bass drum, and in the hush which followed a speaker had mounted a temporary platform at the top of the street. She now delivered a short address through a megaphone.

'Women – the multitudes I see gathered here today give proof, if any were needed, that the cause of suffrage goes from strength to strength. Let me remind you of what our chosen colours signify: white for purity, green for hope, purple for loyalty. This is a Coronation procession, and out of respect and loyalty to our new King we have laid down our weapons and called a truce to the war. Yes, a war! – for that is what we have been waging. If woman is to be kept no longer in subjection, but a human being with her own powers and responsibilities, she must become a soldier. Today we demonstrate our commitment to the cause by

45

marching. On another day, we may be obliged to fight, to suffer violence and imprisonment. But we will do so because we know that right is on our side, and this government shall everywhere hear our voice – *Votes for Women!'*

The crowds cheered wildly and echoed her cry, though when Connie had looked about her during this address she had noted that the mood was far from unanimous. At the mention of 'war' she had seen some women shaking their heads. She suspected that most of the marchers assembled today had not involved themselves in militancy – the riotous demonstrations, the altercations with police, the unruly behaviour in the courts – and she had not herself known anyone who had. She remembered the first time she had read newspaper reports of 'suffragettes' being forcibly fed in prison, and felt cold horror. It sounded like a fiendish torture from a Gothic novel. She could not even contemplate the idea without feeling sick.

The bands had started up, and the massing lines of marchers were on the move. Around Trafalgar Square and the roads leading off it, wheel traffic was now suspended; no vehicle could have made it through the huge current of women walking seven or eight abreast, banners raised high. Some had come in historical costume, a living pageant of famous women down the ages – Joan of Arc, Queen Elizabeth, Grace Darling, Florence Nightingale, Charlotte Brontë. There were representatives from mills, match factories, clothworkers' guilds. So many hundreds of different unions, from all corners of the kingdom! Connie glanced at the banner just behind, blazoned in large white letters – GOD BEFRIEND US, AS OUR CAUSE IS JUST. As they turned into Pall Mall the stolid, compla-cent facades of the gentlemen's clubs stared down. A procession of this kind might march past every week, she thought, and meet only indifference. Through the raised window of one majestic soot-blackened edifice she glimpsed shadows moving about. Here they all were, pouring through the heart of male clubland, and yet none of its denizens seemed in the least disturbed by their intrusion. If, as that lady alleged, they were engaged in a war, then this afternoon's skirmish would have to be considered a disappointment. The enemy had not even bothered to stir from its trenches.

As if sensing her despondency, a little knot of marchers ahead of them had started up a rallying song.

> Shout, shout, up with your song!
> Cry with the wind for the dawn is breaking.
> March, march, swing you along,
> Wide blows our banner and hope is waking.

After a few more lines of this, Lily looked round and cupped her hand over Connie's ear in order to make herself heard.

'What an awful song!'

She smiled her agreement, and gave Lily's arm a squeeze.

> Song with its story, dreams with their glory,
> Lo! they call, and glad is their word!

It sounded so earnest and jolly – and yet so galumphing. Connie imagined Brigstock hearing the lyric and curling his lip in sardonic disdain. No wonder he took such a pitying view of women . . . She would prove her mettle one day and show him that a woman need not be a meek drudge or a domestic pet. But for the moment she would have to put up with the fatuous words of this marching song.

They had just turned the corner into St James's Street when they heard a strident wolf whistle. A party of five or six swells, in tails and toppers, had been sauntering along the pavement and come to a halt. One of them, with a monocle fixed over his eye, had spotted Lily and called to his pals in a tone of braying insolence, 'I say, shouldn't that child be at home tucked up in bed?'

Lily flushed angrily, and made to reply, but Connie steered her away. 'Ignore them, Lil. They're buffoons, and drunk, by the sound of it.'

The monocled man was now alongside them, and addressed Connie directly. 'Ah, miss, you there – don't you wish you were a man?'

'No,' Connie fired back. 'Don't you?' The man's companions guffawed at this, and one of them clapped him heartily on the back, dislodging his monocle.

'Ouch! A hit, Reggie, a palpable hit.' As the cracks and sniggering continued, another of them was heard to say, incredulously, 'Votes for women? Good Lord – whatever next?' Connie had started to walk away, but now turned back. She looked the man in the eye, keeping her voice perfectly even.

'Whatever next? After the vote, I dare say women shall take the jobs, too. We have the will. We only need to find the way. And the likes of you – *gentlemen* – will be left wondering whatever happened to the good old days.'

The men were briefly stunned into silence; if she had ranted they would have laughed, but she had spoken with calm command. She took in their glazed eyes and blotched, well-fed faces, but she had already turned on her heel and taken Lily's arm by the time their satirical cries of 'Oooh' and 'Hark at her' were piercing the air. The two friends were halfway up the street when they heard the cry of 'Bloody toms!'

Lily looked at Connie, and the surprise mirrored on each other's face sent them into convulsions of laughter. Not even another chorus of 'The March of the Women' could quash their high spirits as they walked on.

3

Will had mistimed his journey across town, and now the hansom he had taken outside his flat in Devonshire Place was hopelessly adrift of his destination. It was Thursday morning, the day of the Coronation, and he had failed to take into account how many streets would be closed or blocked off to wheel traffic in anticipation of the royal event. He had arranged to meet his mother and sister off the train at Charing Cross and thence conduct them to the party in time to watch the King and Queen's procession from Westminster Abbey. It was not a duty of unmitigated delight to him – he would rather have been at Lord's watching the MCC play Cambridge University – but he knew how excited they were, and he wouldn't dare let them down. His cab had been obliged to take a circuitous journey to the station and was now snailing through the backstreets at the south end of Bloomsbury.

Had passers-by spotted him on the street earlier, attired in matutinal grey with a silk tie (purple, in honour of the day) fastened by an emerald pin, they would have assumed him to be a fellow at ease in the world, probably well off and blessed with a certain physical charm. His clean-shaven face was unusual among his peers, though he would have worn a beard if the bristles had not sprouted so patchily on his chin. That proved to his advantage, for shaving lent his features an open friendliness they would not otherwise have enjoyed. From his sporty, wide-stepping gait one might have expected him to talk in boisterous tones, but his voice was soft and pleasant, and he used it sparingly, almost shyly. It had already failed to attract the attention of the cabbie, seated above with the clatter of wheels and hooves harsh in his ear; Will realised, too late, he ought to have waited for a motor cab.

After weeks of blazing sunshine the day had begun disobligingly muggy and overcast. A cortège of smudged grey clouds was just now passing overhead. Since leaving the south coast for London by train the night before, Will had been brooding on his current abysmal form with the bat. He had not scored a fifty all season, and, as he secretly admitted to himself, he had not seemed likely to. Loss of form was painful for any batsman, but for Will it chafed the more so after such an auspicious start to his M—shire career. He had announced himself there two years ago with a century on his debut; the rest of the summer yielded three more, and an aggregate just short of 1,400 runs – a club record for a player in his first season. His second season had shown the first one to be no fluke: he registered three hundreds in May alone, hit a double century in July (the first at the Priory for seven years) and ended second to Tamburlain as the club's top scorer. Yet it was the manner in which he compiled his runs that had caught the eye. His buccaneering style had thrilled the crowds, and he had begun to score almost as quickly as Tam, from whom he had copied a favourite ploy of swivelling on his front foot and swatting across the line at balls down the legside; it had kept fielders at midwicket busy all summer. Newspaper reports were soon comparing the two men, one citing Will as the young pretender to Tam's crown, for which he was ragged in the club's changing room. Yet he was secretly gratified. To be mentioned in the same breath as Tam was an accolade in itself.

The early weeks of the 1911 season, however, had brought him crashing down to earth. He had collected a pair in his first game – ominous beginning – and for the rest of May he failed to make a score higher than thirty. His timing of the ball, immaculate the previous summer, had gone to pieces, and his vulnerability to swing-bowling had been horribly exposed. It was baffling as well as disturbing: he hadn't consciously changed anything about his batting, and yet where once reigned fluency and grace there was now only a desperate struggle for survival at the crease. His bat might as well have had holes in it for all the good it was doing him at present. At first he blamed his luck; then, when his poor run continued into June, he realised his problems might have a deeper root. It was a blow to his self-esteem, but he had eventually made up his mind to seek out wise counsel, and his spirits lifted at the prospect of a likely supplier being present this afternoon.

The cab had at last pulled up at Charing Cross, where the bank holiday crowds were streaming forth from the concourse, flags in hand. A riot of Union Jack bunting had foamed over the Strand; it coursed between railings, along parapets, across windows. Having paid his cabman he waded against the flow of the oncoming masses until he spotted his mother and Eleanor in matching straw hats and cream-coloured dresses. They were standing next to an alarming assortment of bags and cases. Good Lord, thought Will, how many days are they planning to stay? Arranging his features into an expression of mild penitence, he hurried over.

'Hullo, Mother,' he called brightly. 'Sorry I'm late. My cab's just been halfway around town trying to get here.'

'Hullo, darling,' said Mrs Maitland, fiddling with her gloves and proffering her cheek to be kissed. She looked up at the lowering, mouse-grey sky, which was now beginning to grumble. 'Proper summer weather,' she remarked archly. 'Three fine days and a thunderstorm.'

'You seem to have a lot of luggage,' said Will, looking about them.

'A porter helped us,' she replied, missing the point.

'Packed train. I had some old woman almost sitting on my knee,' said Eleanor, a pert seventeen-year-old whose fair skin almost shone against the ambient gloom. As she offered her cheek to be kissed, Will took in competing scents of perfume and perspiration. The air around them felt as thick as pudding.

'What on earth is in the crate?'

'Champagne, of course. It won't do to arrive empty-handed.'

'I'm afraid we'll have to. We can't carry this lot all the way to St James's Street.'

'Surely we can take a cab?'

He shook his head. 'The roads are all closed off. It's on foot from here.'

'*Well*,' Mrs Maitland protested at this inconvenience. There was a steely gleam in her eye which Will knew of old. 'I suppose we'd better get started then.'

'I'll go and store these at left luggage,' he said.

Once he had done so, he began to lead his mother and sister through the heaving press of bodies in Trafalgar Square and Pall Mall. At junctions, pickets of police milled about in anticipation. As they passed through the jostling crowds, Will occasionally glanced at the faces of strangers and discerned the same expression in them. What was it, exactly? A vague, deferential, somewhat bovine curiosity. So many thousands of people tramping the streets, so much discomfort and fuss and waiting endured merely for the chance to pay homage to someone who was, after all, a mortal like themselves. One had to wonder at the point of it. He recalled a similar summer's day in 1897 when the family had assembled in his father's office, high up in a building on Cheapside, to watch the Queen's Diamond Jubilee procession through

London. Will was nine at the time, and he and his young cousins had been solemnly advised to remember this day so that they could tell *their* children about it in years to come. All Will could now bring to mind was the sight of a little black bundle holding a parasol as protection against the blazing sunshine. 'That's Queen Victoria!' his mother had said, pointing excitedly from the window, but he felt disappointed that such a famous personage could look so dumpy and insignificant. Someone else had pointed out to him the two horsemen in white uniform flanking the royal carriage: on one side her son, the Prince of Wales, and on the other her grandson, the Kaiser. Later that day Will had been sick from an excess of ice cream. He supposed that, were he ever to have children, they would be less than enthralled by his reminiscences.

'*William!*' It was his mother, and judging by her peeved tone he had not been paying attention.

'Sorry?' he said.

'I said, how much further is it?' They were struggling between the stands and the multitudinous humanity thronging the west end of Pall Mall, where pavement space had been squeezed into a narrow two-way channel. Above the street every available peephole seemed to have five or six spectators, on roofs, windowsills, ledges. Nimble youngsters were hanging like monkeys off the lamp posts.

'Just round the next corner,' he reassured them. Nearby he heard a blackguard bawling out some popular song, and soon other voices were joining in. From behind Will felt someone barge violently against him, though no apology was offered. He glanced at his watch. They would have had an hour's play at Lord's by now. He would like to have been there. In fact, he would like to have been anywhere other than among these revelling hordes. A stray line of Latin poetry, one of few to fasten on his unpoetic consciousness, came to him:

Odi profanum vulgus et arceo.

'I hate and shun the common rabble,' he muttered to himself. If only he could.

'I beg your pardon?' said his mother.

'Nothing. Here we are.' They had turned into St James's Street, where a few doors along from a bootmaker's stood a tall mansion block; Will rang the bell and they were admitted by a doorman. An electric lift took them to one of the upper floors, and then they were entering a grand drawing room, with wide bow windows and a balcony overlooking the street. Fresh-cut flowers festooned every surface. A party of mostly young men were already heaping plates with food – Westphalia ham, ruby-red slices of beef, rolled ox tongue, chicken livers – from a buffet table. In the far corner someone was playing a waltz at the piano. Their host, a young man of rakish demeanour, boomingly addressed them.

'William, greetings! Mrs Maitland, I presume,' he said, bowing deeply, '. . . and the *delightful* young Miss Maitland. Welcome, all!' Reggie's conviviality began at such an inflated pitch that there seemed a danger he might float away on a cloud of gaseous goodwill. Mrs Maitland, used to deference, inclined her head regally. Eleanor merely giggled.

'This is Reggie Culver,' said Will, half smiling at the affectation of his friend's monocle.

'I'm sorry to say that our champagne is presently boiling away in the luggage room at Charing Cross. There wasn't a cab to be had.'

'Ah, don't fret, dear lady,' cried Reggie. 'We've *gallons* of the stuff here. Now do start helping yourself to luncheon – you must be famished after all that *walking*.'

Will left his mother and Eleanor in Reggie's company and strolled out onto the balcony. A wooden pole had been secured against its wrought-iron rail and a huge Union Jack hung out. The red in the flag was the colour of old blood.

He looked down onto the street, from this vantage a shifting, murmurous sea of hats – caps, bowlers, boaters, bonnets – that stretched all the way up towards Piccadilly. Across the way he could see figures leaning out of the windows, and even lurking high up between the chimney pots, where the pigeons made their strutting patrol. A bird's-eye view – to land on a rooftop whenever the fancy took you. What larks . . . His ornithological reverie was interrupted by two men who had joined him on the balcony. Archie Holbrook and Algy Tregear, friends from college days, had since thickened prosperously around the middle and were now looking uncomfortably warm in tails and waistcoats.

'Hullo, Will,' said Archie, holding a flute of champagne in one fist and a pheasant's egg in the other.

Will smiled. 'I've never seen you two look so smart.'

'All in honour of – the King!'

'The King!' repeated Algy, and both of them snapped to attention and chortlingly raised their glasses. Will turned back to survey the street.

'What news of our special guest?' asked Archie.

'Oh, he said he'd be coming. But I wouldn't be surprised if he'd stopped for refreshment somewhere on the way.'

Will knew better than to make a cast-iron guarantee where A. E. Tamburlain was concerned. The man's habit was to arrive late at parties, or else not at all. His social appetites were in some circles as legendary as his batting feats. When Will had first arrived at the Priory, he had been nervous of Tam, and not merely because he had revered him for so long. He had got wind of Tam's 'blooding' of new recruits. The night before his debut Will had been introduced to 'Mr Tamburlain' at the Priory clubhouse.

'Ah, the Blue,' said Tam, a twinkle beneath his saturnine brow. He turned to the little coterie of clubmen and camp-followers who usually congregated around him. 'I've heard these Varsity men have no head for ale – they fall down at the sniff of a barmaid's apron. Hope we won't have to carry you home.'

Then he and two of his familiars took Will out on the town, starting with oysters and pints of champagne at the Wellington. They proceeded to a dance, where they drank well past midnight and Tam sang 'If It Wasn't For the Houses In Between' to a banjo accompaniment. Between two and five thirty they played poker and whist in another hotel lounge, and having pocketed his winnings, Tam insisted they all went out for a dawn paddle by the Pier. A breakfast of porridge and kippers followed, after which Will was allowed to go home and catch up on some sleep before the match began at eleven that morning. He didn't have to be carried, although, given his condition, he would have appreciated it.

Mrs Maitland, in search of diversion, had now stepped onto the balcony. Will, already faintly exhausted by her company, introduced his friends.

'This is my mother – Archie Holbrook, Algy Tregear.'

Mrs Maitland peered at them. 'Reggie – Archie – Algy – quite the gathering of diminutives. I dare say you know William from Oxford.' She spoke, as ever, with a brusque patrician confidence that stopped just short of rudeness. Archie, untypically meek, admitted that they did.

'Did you have a pleasant journey here, Mrs Maitland?' asked Algy.

'Three hours on the train,' she replied tersely, as if it had somehow been Algy's fault, 'then a footslog down Pall Mall I'd rather have been spared.'

'Closed to traffic,' Will said.

'I do sympathise,' Algy pursued. 'Only last Saturday we were tootling down here from Marylebone when we found all the streets blocked off by the police. Had to abandon the motor and walk it.'

'A ladies' march – for suffrage,' Archie explained.

Mrs Maitland emitted a sound somewhere between a bark and a shriek. 'Oh, will those creatures give us no peace! If they *had* the vote they wouldn't know what to do with it.'

Archie chuckled at this. 'I wish you could have seen this couple we ran into, just outside the flat here. The impudence of them! Shouting and carrying on . . . Poor old Reggie innocently asked one of them, "Madam, do you wish you were a man?" To which this hoyden screamed in reply, "No – do you?"'

Will burst out laughing at this. His mother looked sharply at him.

'You may laugh, William, but these women are a menace. There's not a scrap of modesty or decency about them.'

'I dare say,' Will said, smiling, 'though you can't deny that one a certain wit.'

Mrs Maitland harrumphed at even this concession. Will, who had not properly considered the idea of suffrage for longer than half a minute, was nevertheless surprised by his mother's antipathy. He had supposed her to be one who might find such a cause congenial. Privileged by birth and imperious by temperament, Sylvia Maitland had a formidable talent for getting her own way. Her force of character had been tested when her husband died unexpectedly in 1899. With no obvious successor to the directorship of Maitland's Wine and Spirits, she had stepped into the breach and enlisted her brother as partner in the day-to-day running of the business. Her fierce energy had done the rest. She was someone Will would not readily have crossed. Only once had he been obliged to, when, three years ago, he had abandoned the law and signed professional terms as a cricketer. He was still not certain she had forgiven him for it. The repeated twitch in her cheek now was enough to warn him off engaging with her in an argument as to the pros and cons of 'the vote'.

A waiter had just refilled their glasses when a noise was collected out of the muggy afternoon. Because the flat was high above the street, the approach of the Coronation party from Westminster Abbey was heard almost as if it were a distant mumble of thunder. Will guessed that the procession was still a long way off. At that moment he found Eleanor at his side.

'Will, you-know-who's arrived and he's looking for you.'

He excused himself and followed her inside. A little knot of men had already gathered about Tam like eager courtiers. Will held back for a moment, watching the guest of honour at work, shaking hands, modestly fielding compliments. It still seemed remarkable to him that he and Tam had become close. He had known senior professionals who quietly but indisputably resented new recruits, and Tam, now into his forties, might have allowed himself such animus, particularly towards one who reminded him of his own youthful verve. Yet far from cold-shouldering Will, the senior man had adopted him; perhaps the truly self-assured have no need of rivals. The early amity forged as batting partners – Tam was at the other end when 'Bluey' reached that debut hundred – gradually extended beyond the raucous confines of the changing room and entered a new phase on their discovering a mutual love of fishing. In the contented hours spent on boats and riverbanks, where only a skylark's yearning trills might be heard, Will discovered another side to the glamorous, buccaneering cricketer of public renown.

One afternoon the previous summer, as they finished off a lunch of potted herring, and a bottle of Pol Roger lolled at the end of a string in the shallows of the cooling river, Tam had talked for the first time about his family. Though born in Lancashire, he had lived 'all over', on account of his father's job as a travelling salesman. The family had eventually settled on the M—shire coast, where Tamburlain Senior's commercial fortunes had, after a period of debt, tipped into a steep decline. Drink had hastened the crisis. Tam returned home from school one day to find his father hanged by the neck in his garden shed. Will had been disturbed, not only by the content of this history but by Tam's assumption that he, Will, was an appropriate confidant. Hitherto their talk had been limited to the safe familiarities of cricket and beer and fishing. This tragedy had cast Tam in a new light – the son of a suicide – and in the telling it seemed to breach the boundaries set by their relationship. He would really have preferred not to know, rather than have to wonder what else might be wrong with his friend.

Now, as Will edged towards the group, he could see a man animatedly recalling a shot of Tam's he had once witnessed, while the hero of his anecdote maintained a polite, slightly glazed expression, as if he had heard this somewhere before. And, as Will knew, he *had* heard it before, many times, because Tam's naturally gregarious instincts brought him into contact with men who would always want to reminisce about the days of his batting prime – those tumultuous innings of the 1890s that had suddenly turned matches. As his interlocutor prattled on, Will caught Tam's eye, and the latter saluted him with an almost imperceptible lift of his chin. A few minutes later, once another scrum of well-wishers had been dodged, the two men found themselves seated together on a gleaming chesterfield. Tam, cigar in hand, shook his head and sighed.

'Terrible thing, Blue,' he said, 'but after a while you weary even of *praise*.'

'What story was that fellow delighting you with?'

'Oh . . . a six I hit at the Priory – landed on top of a passing tram in South Terrace.'

'I never saw that one,' Will admitted.

'You wouldn't have done, it was years ago.' He stared at his glowing cigar, and added, 'They were all years ago.'

'It's natural that people want to talk to you. You're still the best.'

Tam gave a rueful chuckle. 'Don't you start.'

Will paused. 'Actually, I wanted to ask you something . . .'

'Oh aye?' said Tam, squinting through his smoke.

'Have you ever had a truly wretched run with the bat – I mean, so bad that you could never see it ending?'

'Of course. Every cricketer does – you know that.'

Will gave a mournful nod. 'I suppose so.'

Tam paused, and puffed meditatively on his cigar. 'This game . . . it preys on doubts. Why is it that some days you can middle every ball, then others you can't lay the bat on anything? Never easy to understand why you're having a bad trot. But it wouldn't be cricket without them doubts.'

'Yes, but how do you conquer them? Is it talent, or luck?'

Tam's expression was Delphic. 'Talent *is* luck, half of the time. That magnificent square cut that goes for four runs might have been caught at point, if only the fielder hadn't moved a couple of feet sideways the previous ball.'

Will sensed that Tam wouldn't offer advice unless he was directly asked for it. He took a deep breath. 'Look, Tam, you've seen how badly I've been playing this season. Is there anything – I mean *anything* – I can do?'

Tam tapped the side of his head. 'The problem might be up here, as I said. Do you have . . . worries?'

'Yes, I have worries,' Will groaned, despairing of these generalities. 'I'm worried I'll never make any runs again.'

'Well,' said the senior man, 'have you changed something, p'raps – something that's affected your confidence?'

'Nothing that I can think of.'

'Then it might be something you *need* to change. Don't forget, bowlers are always looking for a weakness, a flaw they can work on to get you out. P'raps they've spotted a chink in your armour, so to speak . . .' Tam's eyes, watchful beneath his brow, were fixed on Will, who now felt uneasy as well as despondent.

'Have you, er, spotted one?'

'You tell me, Bluey.'

Will shrugged, considering, and remembered a recent conversation on this very subject. It might be worth a try. 'Could it be my feet not moving properly? I seem to be getting caught on the crease of late. I'm not sure if I'm meant to go forward or back.'

Tam nodded sagely, as if this were the answer he'd been waiting for. 'You've just been a bit stiff-legged lately, that's all. If you don't move your feet you're not in a position to play the right shot –'

'It can't be just that,' Will interrupted.

'No. But it's a start. Your great advantage is having a quick eye – like me.' Tam was not a braggart, but he had no truck with false modesty. 'Speed of eye's a gift, there's no learning it. Keeping your head still, moving your feet – that's just technique.'

'Technique,' repeated Will. He suppressed an abrupt shiver of mortification.

'Next time we're at the nets, I'll give you some pointers,' said Tam. 'In the meantime, stop worrying about it. You'll be back in the runs, I promise.'

While they had been talking more guests had arrived and were now congregating around the balcony. As they rose and followed the drift to the doors, Will noticed two or three of the men stepping aside to let Tam through, and the reflected dazzle from his friend's celebrity fell on him like a balm. The distant alarums heard twenty minutes before were gathering to a climax; it seemed edged almost

61

with panic. The royal procession was yet to turn into St James's Street, but the noise waxing from Pall Mall had created a thrum of anticipation across the teeming masses below, pushing little waves of hysteria in front of it. Louder, louder, the roar climbed, cacophonous and exhilarated, until a tidal wave of cheering, whistling, clapping seemed to engulf the very rooftops. And then, from Reggie's balcony, they could see the vanguard of caparisoned horses make the turn, prancing up the street in a torrid blaze of colours, somewhat unreal, like a child's tin soldiers. The noise now entered a feverish new dimension as the royal carriage, like a giant silver gravy boat, wheeled into view, and Will's gaze was held by the stunned majestic glitter of the newly crowned monarch and his queen, waving her gloved hand somewhat nervously, first this side, then that. It felt to him as if the crowds were trying to outdo their own pleading displays of deference, as if a collective will in the celebrations were as vital to the success of the day as the tiny royal pair whose progress was being so exuberantly saluted. On the street, hats had been torn off and whirled in the air like so many spinning tops. For one lady on their balcony the excitement was too acute; the colour had fled from her face, and she was tottering backwards in a swoon. Two men had taken charge and were leading the victim away in an odd stumbling dance, while other ladies murmured sympathetic 'oohs' in their wake. Will caught Eleanor's expression – a comical widening of the eyes – and smiled.

The carriage was now directly below them, and the King and Queen so close that, had the crowd's tumult been less deafening, someone might have called from the balcony to draw their attention. Whether prompted by a heightening of patriotic fervour, or a consciousness that the royal pair would soon be passing by and out of their sight forever, someone sitting at Reggie's grand piano had seized the moment and was now plonking out the notes of the only song it could have been permissible to play.

> *God save our gracious King*
> *Long live our noble King*
> *God save the King!*

Will had joined in, and now their raised voices could be heard through the din. All of the men around him had spontaneously removed their hats. The tune caught on, delirious and unstoppable; down on the street they were roaring out the words, too. Later, people would swear that they had seen the King turn and incline the royal head in acknowledgement of the anthem.

> *Send him victo-o-orius*
> *Happy and glo-o-o-orius*
> *Long to reign over us*
> *God save the King!*

As the familiar cadences fell into place, Will looked around him and felt something extraordinary take hold. The prayer contained in the words had lit up the faces around him in a jubilant glow. Without quite understanding why, his eyes began to moisten. Order had been drawn out of chaos. That misanthropic spasm he'd experienced towards the 'common rabble' a few hours before – a deplorable impulse of snobbery, entirely unworthy of him. Here they stood at the beginning of a new era, a sovereign people with a new king; they lived in the greatest country on earth, at the greatest possible time. Hot tears were rolling down his cheeks, blurring his sight, and though he considered such a reaction unmanly he was quite beyond helping himself. Tam's deep Lancastrian voice – a basso profundo that started somewhere in his chest – sounded behind him, and Will felt a giddy sort of elation oxygenating his lungs; it felt as though he had been reprieved. 'You'll be back in the runs, I promise,' Tam had said. He had promised! Will choked down a happy sob, and reassured himself that all would be well. There was nothing he couldn't do.

4

Russell Square was a trench of raw fog as Connie peered through the window of the motor cab. It was an evening in November, and not the sort that would have drawn anybody onto the streets unless it were vitally necessary. The cab was nosing into a lane from which it had emerged some minutes previously.

'I think our driver is lost,' said Connie, wiping the condensation from the glass.

'No wonder,' said Lily. 'I can't make out a thing from this side.'

They were passing by gas lamps that floated and glimmered against the enshrouding gloom. The address they had given the cabbie was a hall in an obscure back lane of Holborn, an area which neither she nor Lily had had much cause to investigate before. The hall was that evening's venue for an emergency meeting of their local suffragist group, prompted by rumours that the Conciliation Bill, on which so many hopes were riding, had been effectively scuppered by the prime minister and Lloyd George.

Connie rapped on the glass and asked the cabman to stop. 'I think we might find our own way from here,' she called. They stepped out into the blurred night, and having taken their bearings started up a narrow side street where the Georgian terraces stared down, black and glassy.

'Ugh!' cried Lily, spluttering. 'I've just got a mouthful of that fog. Are you sure this is the right direction, Con?'

'Pretty sure,' said Connie, feeling less so as they blundered on through the clinging veils of white mist. 'Let's just keep going.'

Her pretended certainty paid off when, a minute or so later, they came in sight of the appointed hall, a thin slice of gaslight just visible through the oaken double doors at its front. Inside, the meeting was already under way, and the lighting disclosed a much larger gathering than Connie had anticipated. Edging their way along one of the back rows they eventually found a vacant spot, somewhat distant from the stage but useful as a vantage to survey the two hundred or so congregants. From their demeanour and dress Connie speculated that they were 'women of assured circumstances' – she had read the phrase in *The Times* – and some, to judge from the diamond flashing like a bayonet on the hand of the woman next to her, rather more than assured. Perhaps it was only such women who had the time to devote to a cause; the rest either didn't care or else were too busy trying to make a living. She shifted in her seat and focused on the woman who had just stepped up to the podium. Her name was Louisa Gray, a leading light of the National Union of Women's Suffrage Societies, and a speaker Connie had admired at the Albert Hall meeting in June.

Miss Gray's voice was marked by a pleasingly melodic lilt. '. . . and present circumstances seem even less hopeful. We have been grievously wronged by the intransigence of this government. In protesting against their treatment, and in asking for what is rightfully ours, we have endured contempt, physical degradation, even imprisonment. Now, after two years of forbearance while they wavered on this Conciliation Bill, we gather that the prime minister's new purpose is to reform suffrage – for *men*! Could anything be better calculated to add insult to injury? Yet I would urge you, all of you here present, not to be discouraged. In the long perspective this will seem but a brief setback on the road to freedom. We will endure, and we will oblige this government to listen to us. How? By continuing to make an intolerable nuisance of ourselves! We have already done so by confounding them on census night, by refusing to pay taxes, by applying to our MPs, by writing to the newspapers, by openly proclaiming our cause in public places. We will not let them rest. We will be gadflies on their rump, pricking them, provoking them, until they concede that the best way of dealing with an intolerable nuisance is to remove the cause which drives it. After the fuss we have created they will regard negotiation not merely as a duty, but as a relief. So I say to you: onwards!'

Her words were being applauded when a commotion arose near the front. A lady had stood up, although it was plain from the noise she was making that her neighbours in the audience were reluctant to give her the floor. Miss Gray, apparently recognising the protester, signalled to them to let the woman speak. Once she had turned her face to the assembled, Connie also recognised her. It was Marianne Garnett, a woman whose energetic militancy had bounced her from Speakers' Corner to Holloway Prison and back. Becomingly attired in purple and black – a veil had concealed her identity up to this point – Mrs Garnett spoke in tones that had less melody but greater resonance than did Miss Gray's.

'I thank Miss Gray for the opportunity to speak,' she said, with a gracious bow, 'and I approve entirely her determination to make an intolerable nuisance of herself. In an ideal world she would persuade the government to repent of its ignorance. But we live in a world that is as far from ideal as can be conceived. Let us be clear about what has happened. The Conciliation Bill has been – to use Lloyd George's boastful word – *torpedoed*. The truce we offered them has now been exposed as a futile delay. We have kept the peace, we have refrained from outrages – we have, once again, been overlooked. This government does not intend to honour our goodwill with a concession of its own. It is my belief that they never did. Constitutional means of persuasion have failed, utterly. So what is left to us? I say that Asquith and his cronies *will* listen to the argument of stones breaking glass –' At this, a chorus of boos and groans sprang up, and women on both sides of the hall rose in protest. But Mrs Garnett merely raised her voice over them. 'We are already treated as outlaws. Why then should the government be surprised if we behave as outlaws? I am a wife and mother of two young children, yet I am ready to leave a happy home for a prison cell. *Will any of you here do the same?'*

At this, the meeting degenerated into an unseemly shoving match; Mrs Garnett's harangue had inflamed the mood, and a scuffle broke out between the handful of militants who had come to her aid and certain National Union members, whose professed aversion to violence evidently did not preclude manhandling their unruly opponents. Connie and Lily were too astonished to do anything but stare as a couple of bruisers, hired in case of a police raid, stomped into the fray, seized Mrs Garnett and frogmarched her down the side of the hall towards the exit. Cries of 'Shame!' echoed across the room. While a semblance of order was being fitfully restored, Connie leaned over and whispered in Lily's ear, 'Let's go.' Lily seemed surprised, but she promptly followed as her friend made a retreat from the hall.

They came out into the fog-bound evening in time to see the woman at the centre of the fracas upbraiding the men who had ejected her. A third man in a cap, who had come to her defence, now seemed to be occupying the role of referee between the parties, as Mrs Garnett, with remarkable calmness, explained to the bruisers the immemorial British prerogative of free speech, and their own shameful part in denying it to her. After some minutes of not being able to get a word in edgeways, her two antagonists shrugged and withdrew, tossing oaths behind them. Connie took Lily's arm and, with a faltering step, approached the indomitable lady.

'Mrs Garnett?'

The woman looked round, and Connie saw an imperious glitter in her eyes. 'Yes?'

'We've just been listening to you speak –'

'Then I thank you,' she cut in crisply. 'Few others were, it seems.'

The man in the cap was now whispering deferentially to her, and with a brisk nod he trotted off. She began smoothing down her ruffled skirts, seemingly oblivious to the two young women off to her side. Connie glanced at Lily, who had pulled a quizzical face; then she said, 'You don't remember us, do you?'

Mrs Garnett's magnificent head turned again to face them. Frowning, she said, 'I don't believe I do.'

'We used to know you as Marianne Brooke. At St Joan's?'

Her eyes gave a sudden, startled blink. 'St Joan's . . .' she said, her breath pluming in the night air. She looked searchingly from one to the other. 'I seem to – are you . . . Constance?'

Connie smiled. 'I am – and this is Lily.'

'Lily – *yes!*' she said with a little sigh, the light of recognition now kindling in her dark eyes. 'Well, fancy that! It must be all of – eight years for me, I suppose. St Joan's. I haven't thought of the place in ages.'

'*Audere est facere*,' said Lily with a giggle. Mrs Garnett gave an amused nod on hearing their old school motto.

'"To dare is to do" . . . I can think of some who might profit from that lesson,' she added archly, glancing back at the hall from which they had emerged. 'I wonder what Miss Dolan would say if she could see us now.' The name of their severely religious headmistress reduced them abruptly to silence – and Connie's droll vocal mimickry ('Bow your heads for the blessing, gels') roused them to laughter. They heard the engine before they saw the twin headlamps of a motor car swim through the fog. It pulled to a halt by the kerb where they were standing.

'My husband's driver, Stansfield,' explained Mrs Garnett, of the man behind the wheel, the same one she had lately dispatched in their presence. He was now stepping round to open the passenger door. 'I'm sure I can take you somewhere,' she said, by way of invitation.

Connie thanked her, but declined the offer as unnecessary – at which Mrs Garnett snorted. 'On a night like this? In with you.'

A quick glance between the friends signalled an agreement not to argue. Once they were settled on the dimpled leather seats, the driver turned to his employer.

'Where to, ma'am?'

Mrs Garnett told him an address in Mayfair, and they were off. 'I'm having supper at my club,' she explained. 'That sounds rather like a man, doesn't it? But Stanny will take you wherever you need to go.'

As Mrs Garnett's cedarwood scent permeated the car's interior and the fog pressed damply against the windows, Connie enjoyed a nervous shiver of excitement: it was the first time she had been in a private car. Even the throb of the vehicle's engine suddenly sounded glamorous. She felt madly curious about the woman bundled up next to her. In recent years Marianne Garnett's name had become familiar in the papers; their own connection to her at school – mutely adoring at the time, as juniors will be to the head girl – had been eclipsed by her continuing celebrity as a spearhead of the militants. This was a woman who had been photographed talking to Lloyd George and Asquith, and later in conversation with two Whitehall policemen (who happened to be arresting her). She had attained the spotlight very quickly. Yet it was an unambiguous personal reference made at the end of her speech that came back to Connie now.

'So – you have children, Mrs Garnett?'

'It's *Marianne*, please. Only the press and the politicians refer to me as "Mrs Garnett" – and often something worse. Yes, I have two girls. A three-year-old, and an infant of six months.'

'Good grief,' said Lily. 'How do you find the time to – um . . .'

'Well, I've been indisposed most of this year, but really it's all fallen together quite nicely. I had my baby during a truce, and now I can return to the fray – like a giant refreshed!'

At the foot of Shaftesbury Avenue a horse had slipped in the fog and brought down chaos, but Marianne's driver simply veered up a side street and bypassed the delay. To her enquiry about their lives since St Joan's, Lily shyly mentioned her secretarial work.

'Ah, I know that school. Jane Clowes, the headmistress? I've met her at charitable dinners. And yourself, Constance – I now recall you being quite the bookworm.'

Connie gave a half-smile, flattered that Marianne should remember this. 'Well, perhaps that decided me – I work at Hignett's bookshop, in Camden.'

Marianne looked at her curiously. 'And that satisfies you?'

'I'm not sure,' replied Connie, honestly. 'But it's a living.'

The car had pulled to a halt on the forecourt of a tall red-brick mansion in South Audley Street. From the upper windows lights blazed through the fog. Marianne rubbed a little hole through the clouded window and said, 'Here we are. It only now occurs to me – I do apologise – perhaps you'd like to join me for supper?'

Connie and Lily looked momentarily taken aback, prompting a delighted ripple of laughter from Marianne. 'You two! You look as though I'd asked you to take Stanny's place at the wheel. Don't be alarmed. It's known as the Cavendish Club – "for ladies". All quite respectable, I assure you.'

'If you're quite certain . . .' said Connie, wondering if they were properly dressed, and what indeed 'proper dress' in such an establishment might entail. They stepped out of the car, and Marianne, tapping at the driver's window, had a few quick words with Stanny. He tipped his cap and drove off.

'Where does he go?' asked Connie, staring after him.

Marianne shrugged. 'Oh, I think he just drives around. Shall we?'

She led them to the club's door, where a peremptory knock admitted them. They trailed a servant up a balustraded staircase, its oak-panelled walls hung with oils of solemnly profiled grandees. As they passed along a corridor to the dining room, two ladies, stately as galleons and wrapped up in furs, nodded at Marianne, who offered a casual salutation. Under the dazzle of the room's electric chandeliers, their hostess cut an almost frighteningly imperial figure. Her head looked sculpted, like the carved prow of a ship, and around it her thick brown hair had been coiled in a glossy chignon; pale-skinned and dark-eyed, she had a slightly uptilted chin that seemed, like a pugilist's, ready for combat – which was just as well, thought Connie, who was about the same height yet had not mastered that frank self-confidence, the swagger and brightness which distinguished Marianne's bearing. She ought to have been painted by Sargent. A waiter had sidled up to their table, and was reeling off the evening's menu.

'No loin of beef, then?' said Marianne, disappointed. 'Very well – I'll have the mulligatawny, then the poussin.'

Connie and Lily, not daring to catch one another's eye, both chose the duck breast in port-wine sauce and aspic. 'Oh, and we'll have the Latite – in a jug, please,' called Marianne to the departing waiter.

Lily was staring around the room. 'I've never seen the like,' she said, in a wondering tone. 'A supper room where the women are at leisure and the men wait on them, hand and foot.'

'The world turned upside down,' said Connie wryly.

'One day soon it won't look at all unusual,' said Marianne. 'Men can sense it coming. That's why they're clinging so desperately to what they've got.'

'What you said about the Conciliation Bill – is there really no chance of it being passed?'

Marianne shook her head. 'None whatever. Asquith will make sure of it. He simply doesn't like the idea of women being enfranchised – for one thing, it may create more Conservatives than Liberals. For another, I gather his wife's taste for parliamentary gossip has got her into trouble. From this he seems to have assumed that any woman involved in politics is a liability.'

'But this government has shown that it will negotiate,' argued Connie. 'Look at how they eventually made peace with the unions in the summer. The dockworkers, the railwaymen – they went on strike –'

'Exactly! They did something that obliged the government to listen. The strikes meant that food was rotting in warehouses, that travelling was well-nigh impossible. The country was being brought to its knees. But women – we have no such economic leverage. No bargaining tool. Without that, *pace* Miss Gray's optimistic forecast, I see no likelihood of a constitutional about-face.' Marianne paused, and then continued in a more musing tone. 'We live in a time of war, and we have to equip ourselves to fight it. Nobody else will supply us with weapons. Miss Gray and her kind insist that militancy is favoured only by a minority. But those who are ready to suffer in person and reputation for a cause they love are always in a minority. And given what we *have* suffered, the wonder is not that there are so few, but that there are so many.'

Lily, pensively toying with her glass, said in a quiet voice, 'I admire the courage . . . but, speaking truthfully, I couldn't bear to go to prison.'

Connie had been thinking precisely the same thing. Her earliest impression of incarceration was gleaned from visiting the huge suffragette bazaar at the Prince's Skating Rink in the spring of 1909. She had inspected there a replica prison cell, designed to show the public the mean, cramped conditions that women were being forced to occupy: the thought of it terrified her. That day had also been the one occasion she had seen Mrs Pankhurst up close, seated at a bric-a-brac stall; she would call out in a profoundly bored and distant voice, 'Pretty little vase – just a shilling.' Connie had been too shy to talk to her.

'Believe me,' said Marianne, 'when I first started, just the thought of going out to lecture the public filled me with dread. But I steeled myself to it, and by the time we began our campaigns I was used to rough treatment – I had been kicked, punched, pelted, spat upon . . . and that was before the police got hold of us! By that stage, being arrested didn't seem such a grievous fate.'

'Yes, but – prison?'

'It was grim, I have to say. And if you were on the strike, well –' Marianne broke off as a waiter arrived at their table, and she leaned back. 'Perhaps I should save that delightful reminiscence for another time. Let's not ruin our supper.' Connie felt at once relieved and frustrated at the interruption. She dreaded to know what Marianne had experienced, and yet she could not suppress a horrible curiosity goading her on, wanting to hear the worst. While they ate, Connie studied her more closely. To think of the advantages this woman had enjoyed – a wealthy, artistic family in Chelsea, education at Girton, two children, a husband who could afford a driver – and yet she had set them at naught in pursuit of a cause. *The* cause. Strange, too, that she in no way conformed to the 'suffragette' of stereotype – a winged fury, if one were to believe the *Daily Mail*. For all the fanaticism that swirled about her, for all the execration heaped on her, Marianne seemed absolutely sane and self-possessed. There was no ostentatious martyrdom about her, though there had been something irresistible, almost majestic, in the way she had stood up to address that meeting in the hall. Even Olivia, sullen foe of suffrage, would have been awed into silence by this woman's cool command.

Marianne had summoned the waiter to refill their glasses, and now raised her own to Connie and Lily. 'A toast, I think. To the school, of course, and to friends reunited – if I may have the honour of calling you friends.'

Connie had felt certain that the toast was going to be 'Votes for Women', yet Marianne had instead invoked the spirit of personal amity. The woman's charisma was boundless, oceanic – you could drown in it, if you weren't careful. As their plates were being cleared, she suggested they take their coffee in the adjacent room, and gestured them through. Here, with the lamps turned low, conspiratorial clusters of women were reclining on sofas and armchairs, and waiters swanned discreetly around the tables. Marianne proffered a fanned pack of cigarettes; Connie took one, and returned the favour with a light.

'Ah,' sighed Marianne, exhaling a thin column of smoke. 'I confess – if it came to a choice between the right to vote and the right to smoke, I would prove a disgrace to our sex.'

They were still savouring this irreverence when Connie noticed the entrance into the room of a certain lady, whom Marianne plainly recognised, for she pursed her lips in amused disfavour. 'And talking of a disgrace . . .'

Lily, half turning, asked in an undertone as to her meaning.

'I'm sure you've heard of Greville Foulkes.' She had named a Liberal backbencher who had gained notoriety as one of Parliament's most vociferous anti-suffragists.

'He's a scoundrel,' said Lily, with feeling.

'True enough,' agreed Marianne. 'I gather he is preparing a motion that any homeowner who catches a woman damaging his property should be entitled to horsewhip her.'

'No!'

'I'm afraid so. *That* lady is his wife, Meredith – and hardly less poisonous in her views than he is.'

'You know her?'

'We've exchanged . . . unpleasantries. My husband works at the Foreign Office, so we move in similar circles. She introduced herself one evening, and thereafter became inescapable.'

Connie peered across the room to where Mrs Foulkes was engaged with a company of superior-looking ladies. From her frequent tirades on behalf of the National Anti-Suffrage League, as reported in *The Times*, one might have imagined her to be kin of Wilde's Lady Bracknell – 'a monster without being a myth'. But the lady in question was not much older than thirty, elegantly attired and altogether more human-looking than Connie had envisaged. She turned to Marianne.

'It's rather confounding – she really doesn't look . . . the type.'

'The whole idea of an Anti-Suffrage League is confounding,' replied Marianne, 'not to say ridiculous. What's to be done about women who start a political campaign that aims to exclude their sisters from politics?'

'Perhaps she can answer that question herself,' murmured Connie, directing her eyes at the woman approaching their table, and then back to Marianne. This ought to be interesting, she thought.

'Mrs Garnett,' said Meredith Foulkes, canting her head very slightly. Marianne responded with a smile that did not reach to her eyes. Two prizefighters waiting for the bell to ring might have put more warmth into a greeting.

'I see your Conciliation Bill has run into trouble,' said Mrs Foulkes with a distant smirk. 'Should we be prepared for a return to your former tactics?'

'I couldn't possibly say,' Marianne replied coolly. 'But I'll be sure to send you notice if we do.'

Mrs Foulkes glanced at Connie and Lily. 'I trust you've not been filling these young ladies' heads with subversive ideas.'

'They're perfectly capable of forming their own ideas. We were educated at the same school.' Connie felt a surge of pride at this declaration of solidarity, though she kept silent. 'Be kind enough to tell Mr Foulkes, by the way, that if he takes to carrying a horsewhip in the streets he had better know how to use it.'

'Oh, I think my husband has more important things to do than flogging miscreants.'

'Of course. It would be typical of him to hire others to do his dirty work.'

'Well,' said Mrs Foulkes, slightly narrowing her gaze, 'I think if he encountered *you* he might make a personal exception.'

Marianne's eyes flashed wickedly. 'I'll be waiting for him – if he dares.'

Mrs Foulkes offered a slow, ironic nod, and was about to turn away when she looked again at Connie and Lily. 'Ladies, before I bid you good evening, allow me to advise you – have a care for the society you keep.' She tilted her chin once more at Marianne, and turned on her heel.

Lily drew in her breath suddenly. 'Of all the *nerve*! "The society you keep" . . . as if we want her advice!'

Marianne's expression was ambiguous as she said, 'She paid you a sort of compliment, all the same. She sees that you have the right fire.'

Connie glanced uncertainly at Lily. 'Fire?'

'Yes,' said Marianne, looking from one to the other. 'Now that we have started this war, we have to finish it. We face Mrs Foulkes and her "antis" on one side, Miss Gray and her law-abiding sisters on the other, and the government right in the middle. We need you – with all your courage, all your fire – to go forth and rout them.'

Her voice had dropped low as she spoke, but the gleam in her eye indicated that a challenge was being thrown down, and for the first time that evening Connie wondered if Marianne's charm and generosity had been merely the smokescreen for a recruiting drive. Disappointment touched its limp hand to her heart. It now seemed that the sentimental ties of their alma mater had been useful rather than important to Marianne, a means of binding them to the cause. She had called them both friends, but would she still if they refused to join up?

'What would you have us do?' asked Lily.

'You'll know what you have to do,' said Marianne simply.

'And go to prison for it?'

'If necessary. But we would go in the satisfaction that our cause is great – the greatest the world has ever known. It is to free half of the human race.' She let her words hang in the air before adding, 'May we count on you?'

They finished talking as the clock on the mantelpiece struck half past midnight. They bid Marianne and her driver goodnight, and watched the car disappear into the fog. For a while Connie and Lily walked in silence, both deep in contemplation, their boots ringing on the Mayfair flagstones.

As they approached Oxford Street, they heard the jingle of a tram's bell, and then saw its length rumble crossways. Connie was trying to order her thoughts, uncertain as to what had been the most revelatory aspect of their evening – it already felt like a memorable one. At length she turned to Lily, muffled up against the cold, and mused, 'Do you remember how we were all rather in love with her at school?'

Lily nodded. 'And d'you know? – I think I still am.'

Some days later Connie was busy in the stockroom when the youngest assistant, Clara, poked her head round the corner to say that there was 'a gentleman' upstairs asking for her. It was likely to be someone from the vast army of publishers' representatives eager to promote their spring catalogues. Connie had recently taken over as manager of the bookshop after Hignett got wind that the previous incumbent had crossed the line from delegation into downright negligence: Connie, indeed, had been de facto the controlling influence there for several months before her appointment was made official. Now she spent more time inhaling dust from the stacked shelves in the basement, where old stock seemed to have bred in the dark like mushrooms. In all, it felt rather less satisfying than a promotion ought to have done.

She ascended the winding iron staircase to the shop floor, where the feeble grey light of a November morning was leaking through the mullioned windows. She saw the outline of his back, and when he turned she was surprised by the sight of Brigstock, who had not visited the shop in several months. She had begun to think he had left the country.

'I *did* leave the country,' he said. 'Returned last week. I've been in Paris for the last four months, getting through a tremendous amount of work. Sorry, I ought to have written you a card.'

Connie half smiled at his presumption, touching in its

way, that he had been missed. He looked little changed, aside from the flamboyant fur-collared coat and the shading of a feathery beard. A gleam danced in his eyes, though she couldn't be sure if he favoured every young woman he met in this way. He was now slouching against the sales counter and looking about the shop like a man with time on his hands. Connie coughed lightly, and said, 'Is there anything in particular you're looking for?'

He swung round to face her. 'Oh, no. I only stopped by to ask if you'd care to hear a little music this evening.'

'The opera?'

Brigstock laughed. 'I'm afraid not. They've just reopened the music hall round the corner from my digs, and I have a yearning to visit the old place again. What do you say?'

Connie hardly knew. She had never been to a music hall before, and the idea of it appealed to her. But what message would accepting such an invitation convey to its proposer? She *had* thought of Brigstock occasionally, but more in wonder at his absence than in some romantic reverie.

'All right,' she said. 'I close up here at about half past six.'

'Splendid! I shall return for you then. We'll dine before the show begins.' He doffed his homburg in genteel fashion, and with a sidelong glance at young Clara, who had been gawping, he strolled out. When he had disappeared from view, Clara sidled up to Connie and said, in a conspiratorial undertone, 'He's got a lot smarter since he was last here.'

At the appointed hour Brigstock tapped at the shop's glass-fronted door. Connie, who had just finished cashing up for the day, clapped shut her accounts ledger, locked her desk and, with a brief nod through the window, signalled to him that she would be one minute. She had retrieved her coat and hat from the office downstairs when she glimpsed herself in the spotted looking glass at the staircase turn. She quickly fixed her hair before going up to join him.

The lamplighters had just visited the narrow lane where the bookshop stood, illumining the night with a dingy glare. Brigstock led her a little way up Camden High Street before halting outside an eating house. It was a place patronised in the main by office clerks, nightwatchmen, lowly journalists and the like. The hot breath of boiled meats wafted through an open window. Brigstock directed an enquiring look at Connie.

'It's not the Café Royal, I grant you, but they serve a decent chop here.'

'If you don't mind it, I see no reason why I should.'

They entered a long room divided at intervals by wooden benches and patrolled by waiters in aprons. Voices echoed off the tiled walls, and gas jets flared on their brackets. They took a booth and sat facing one another. Brigstock cast a cursory eye over the menu before discarding it, then looked at Connie.

'I thought of you the other week. I had a letter from an old friend of mine, inviting me to watch him perform an operation.'

'Er . . . and you thought of me?'

'I should explain. Cluett is a surgeon at the London, and I've been at him for a while to let me watch a . . . procedure. Well, he's at last agreed to smuggle me into his theatre.'

'Why ever would you wish to see such a thing?'

'Natural morbidity,' he shrugged. 'And I have an odd notion that it might make a painting.'

'Oh . . .'

'But that's not my point. I seem to recall a conversation we had some months ago about your own ambitions in that line. I thought that you might care to accompany me.'

'Yes – but medicine is not a career I can afford to think about any longer.'

Brigstock nodded. 'Maybe so. But surely it would interest you for its own sake? The opportunity to watch a sawbones – sorry, a surgeon – intimately at work doesn't happen along too often.'

Connie paused, considering. 'It *is* something that interests me –'

'Well, then! Once I have the lie of the land, I'll ask Cluett if he'll allow me to bring a guest.'

'Even if she's a woman?'

'Oh, he's a modern sort of fellow.'

'Like yourself,' she said with a faint smile.

'You know my views on the sexes. Though I must say, these suffragettes are making it a devil of a business to get about town. I'd only just arrived at Victoria the other afternoon, called in at my tailor's and next thing a stone comes flying through the window. Missed me by inches!'

'Do you deplore such tactics?'

'I did at that moment,' Brigstock said with a laugh, and then looked thoughtful. 'The sound of breaking glass is a good way to create a stir in the newspapers. But I'm not sure that sort of thing won't turn public sympathy against them – or should I say, *you*?'

'I've not been throwing stones, I assure you,' said Connie. 'But I did happen to meet Marianne Garnett the other night . . .'

'Ah. One of the Pankhurst mob. How did you manage that?'

'I'd met her before. We were at school together.'

'Rather a spitfire, isn't she? I saw a photograph of her in *The Times* braining some policeman outside Parliament.'

'She's not the crazed harridan they claim. Only very . . . determined.'

'I should say!' cried Brigstock. '*Hostibus eveniat lenta puella meis.*' Connie looked blank. 'It's Propertius – "Let a placid girl be my enemy's lot." I do admire a woman with spirit.'

'Marianne Garnett is certainly that.'

'I wasn't thinking of Mrs Garnett,' he replied, his gaze across the table so candid that Connie had to look away.

They dined on some acceptable chops – Brigstock had got that right – and Connie also forced down half a pint of porter. The bitter, yeasty taste of it was still in her mouth as they headed off to the music hall, its lighted facade gaudily refulgent against the gloom, like an ocean-going liner floating through a black night. The last time Connie had noticed the place it had been masked in scaffolding.

'That's a sight to gladden the eye,' said Brigstock. 'There's really nothing like an English music hall.'

In the foyer there rose an expectant clamour that bordered on rowdiness. The evening's programme had already begun, but from the sound of the laughter and the clink of glasses at the bar it seemed that some had found entertainment enough outside the auditorium. Brigstock led Connie through the crush and up the stairs, the reek of cheap cigars, orange peel and stale beer thick in their nostrils. At the top he handed a ticket to the attendant, who conducted them along a corridor; their destination turned out to be a private box. Connie hoisted her eyebrows in surprise.

'I'd usually go to the gallery,' he said, raising his voice above the hoots and cat calls that were already raining down from the cheap seats, 'but I thought it mightn't be the most agreeable introduction.'

'. . . Very nice of you,' she said, almost shouting in his ear. They settled into seats of a slightly grubby crimson plush. Raucous cries and whistles cut the air, and Connie peered over the balcony to discover the cause. A troupe of acrobats were fumbling their way through an act whose want of finesse had provoked the onlookers to loud derision. A minute later they were hurrying off the stage, to everyone's satisfaction. At her side, Brigstock had pulled loose the ribbon on his portfolio and was fixing a loose leaf onto its boards. As the din from the audience continued, Connie became distracted between what was happening onstage and the spectacle of the gallery opposite, where a sea of faces loomed in and out of the semi-darkness. Some leaned on their elbows, others had propped their feet against the safety rails. Framed beneath by the gilded mouldings of the balcony, and above by plaster cupids, these spectators became a kind of theatre in themselves, pointing, cackling or merely staring for minutes at a time.

Onstage the acts came and went – a trick cyclist, an illusionist, a pair of mashers, a sword-swallower, another troupe of tumblers – while the crowd responded with desultory applause; nothing really enchanted them, or Brigstock, who barely looked at the entertainment. His eyes roamed over the stalls, the circle, the gallery of shadowed faces overhead, and then dipped back to his sketch. He was quite absorbed. It was flattering, she conceded, that he had sought her company this evening, though she didn't altogether trust him to behave. She had been flirted with before, when Fred invited 'chaps' from college to dinner at Thornhill Crescent. She had even been wooed, briefly, by the son of one of her father's colleagues in the City, handsome and clever enough, but much too eager to impress. Like other men, Spencer Nairn knew how to talk *at* her, but not to her. His courtship had proceeded with such confidence that the way in which his face seemed to collapse through stages of mortified confusion as she politely but unequivocally turned down his proposal was interesting to behold. His retreat from the room felt so piteous that she was half minded to call him back. Wisely, she had not. But she felt much less self-assured when faced with a man to whom she was attracted.

She looked sidelong at Brigstock, bent over his drawing. His confiding manner – suddenly leaning over to whisper some droll remark in her ear – was born of someone at ease in the company of women. She liked the feeling of his breath on her neck, and now suspected that his choice of venue this evening was precisely calculated to allow him this liberty. The more closely she pondered it, the more certain became her conviction that he, to some degree, desired her. It was a thrill to realise it, to feel the power of one's physical allure upon a man. The insult currently hurled at women who campaigned for the vote was 'unsexed', a word symptomatic of a vague alarm that masculine authority, in and out of the bedroom, was under threat. Unsexed. She could not imagine Brigstock bandying the word about: had he not declared his partiality to 'a woman with spirit'? For all his charm, however, she had to concede that he was *old*, perhaps nearly fifty, and that it would be wrong to encourage his fancies. He was looking at her now, and in his expression she no longer saw mere regard, but hopefulness. She knew that she would have to tread with care – the male ego was a frail thing. The audience had at last risen to enthusiasm at the appearance of a fellow in loud checks. The orchestra accompanied him.

> Now it really is a wery pretty garden
> And Chingford on the eastward can be seen.
> Wiv a ladder and some glasses
> You can see to 'ackney Marshes,
> If it wasn't for the 'ouses in between.

Connie looked across at the gallery, at the rows of faces roaring out the words, and as she joined in herself she recognised the song as a favourite of her father's – she could almost hear him singing it now in his mellifluous tenor. If only she could return home and tell him, 'Pa, you remember that old song you used to do . . .' – she could picture his face beaming at the thought. And there it was again, that needling sensation, whenever his face rose in her memory,

85

of something unresolved, mysterious, in the suddenness of his death. Or was it simply that death was always mysterious?

> *Now it really is a wery pretty garden*
> *And right outside the poplar can be seen.*
> *If I 'ad a rope and pulley,*
> *I could feel the breeze more fully.*
> *If it wasn't for the 'ouses in between.*

Unwillingly, her eyes began to moisten as the desperate jauntiness of the tune took hold. She had sat stony-faced through love duets at Covent Garden, through requiems at the Bechstein Hall, but now here she was, reduced to tears by a tuppenny-ha'penny canting song. Brigstock had glanced in her direction, and his expression changed in an instant to alarm.

'My dear girl . . .' she heard him say.

Connie shook her head, unable to speak. She would be all right in a minute, she felt sure, so long as he didn't touch her. But then, right on cue, he took her hand in his, and patted it gently. At that, her shoulders began to quiver, and the tears began to spot her lap. She couldn't help herself, and at Brigstock's whispered entreaty she took his handkerchief and let him steer her outside past the waiters and stragglers. The bar downstairs was still in a roar as they emerged into the night.

'At least allow me to pour you a brandy in my rooms,' said the painter, his hand resting solicitously on her elbow as they walked towards Mornington Crescent.

'I'm quite well, thank you, Mr Brigstock. I'm only sorry that I interrupted your evening.'

'Constance, please.' It was the first time he had addressed her thus, and it created a little frisson in the air between them. It seemed that more than mere familiarity was being risked. 'May I presume to ask what has distressed you? Is it something I've said?'

She shook her head, though she heard in his tone an assumption that it *was* something to do with him. Could it be that he had mistaken her tears as evidence of romantic distraction? Her impulse was to correct him immediately, but she feared that attempting to explain something that touched so tenderly upon her father's memory would set her off again. She bit it back, and kept silent. Camden High Street was still lively at this hour, and they had to navigate a pavement crowded with men and women pouring out of its public houses. Outside one, a penny-whistle player tootled merrily, while a ruffian associate holding forth a cap importuned the passers-by. Connie, feeling more in command of herself, stopped and turned to Brigstock.

'I'll wait here, if you don't mind. A tram will be along soon.'

Brigstock returned a look of concern. 'I'll flag down a cab for you.'

'No, don't.' She was thinking of the needless expense, but regretted her brusque reply. 'But if you'd be kind enough to wait with me . . .'

He made a gesture of impatience. 'For heaven's sake! You don't imagine I would just *leave* you here – at the mercy of the drinking classes?'

Connie half smiled at that, and felt relieved as she spotted a tram in the distance. She had the impression that there was a matter unspoken between them, but now was not the time to broach it. As the tramcar shuddered to a halt, Brigstock took up her hand for the second time that evening, and pressed it to his lips. He fixed her with an earnest, enquiring look.

'Would you – at a more convenient time – explain . . . ?'

Connie nodded. 'Yes. I will,' she said, and boarding the

tram she found a seat. Through the window she watched his figure recede into the distance, his arm raised in farewell. Her hand still trembled as she held a match to her Sullivan. Yes, explain. She would have to tell him that, much as he might wish it otherwise, her tears had nothing to do with him; that she acknowledged the depth of his feeling for her but, alas, could not reciprocate it.

These thoughts preoccupied her as she stepped off the tram and walked back to Thornhill Crescent. They persisted after she had doused her bedside lamp and rested her head on the pillow. She sensed an urgency about disabusing Brigstock, who might even now be planning his declaration scene. It would be a mercy to nip his hopes in the bud. Her dreams were troubled by confused reverberations from the music hall – somehow, she had ended up onstage apologising for the hopeless acrobats, while the audience almost as one bayed abuse at her – and she woke in a state of bewildered relief.

With the resolve of last night still uppermost in her mind, Connie hid herself away in the bookshop's office all morning, rehearsing her lines to him until she had them by heart. As midday came around she left the shop on the pretext of going to luncheon, and bent her steps towards the painter's rooms in Mornington Crescent. She had made up her face carefully, and the expensive loden coat she had borrowed from her mother provoked a tiny appraising double take from the landlady. Pursuing her heartbeat up the stairs she pictured Brigstock's surprise on seeing her, so soon after their last meeting. At her knock she heard footsteps ambling along the corridor, and the door swung open.

'Miss Callaway,' he said pleasantly, not surprised in the way she had anticipated. 'Please, come in.'

Without catching his eye, she entered, and he led her into a small parlour overlooking the back of Mornington

Crescent station. As she stood gazing out, a train rumbling down below made the window vibrate in its frame. He asked her to sit down, but she refused, aware that the tentative intimacy of the night before had subtly changed. Daylight seemed to have put a different complexion on the matter.

'Are you recovered from . . . ?' He had a slightly puzzled air.

'Thank you, yes. Mr Brigstock, I wanted to say –'

At that moment, a door off the corridor was heard to creak open, followed by the light slapping patter of bare feet on floorboards. Connie, frozen to the spot, looked at Brigstock, whose expression hadn't altered. Presently a young dark-haired woman, sleep-dazed and wrapped in a thin dressing gown, peered into the room. Her gaze unconcernedly took in Connie.

'Uh, 'scuse me,' she muttered, and dozily withdrew.

Brigstock didn't appear to have noticed the interruption. His eyes held the same enquiring gleam, and must have taken in the furious blush now suffusing Connie's face. She turned again to the window in a belated effort to hide it.

'You were going to tell me something,' he said coaxingly.

She paused, trying to collect herself, wondering at her naivety – the pity she had felt for him and his old man's infatuation. Little did she know! Summoning her will, she faced him. 'I wished only –' she began, a catch in her voice. 'I wished only to apologise for my selfish behaviour, and to thank you for – your understanding. Good day to you.'

She didn't wait to hear his reply, brushing past him and hurrying down the stairs. She felt the awkwardness of her exit keenly, but her only object was to be out of that house. The roar and bustle of the street barely impinged on her as she quickened her step, mortified each time she replayed the scene in her head – his quizzical look, the peacock flash of the girl's dressing gown – but grateful nevertheless that her mission of 'mercy' had been so abruptly torpedoed.

5

'I wish I had hands like yours,' said Connie, holding Lily's hands across the table and examining them as if she were a fairground palmist. 'They're so neat and womanly. Look at mine,' she continued, wrinkling her nose. 'The size of them . . . they look more like feet!'

Lily giggled, quickly checking them herself to see if the comparison was just. They were having tea at the Corner House in Coventry Street. Connie had taken to staring at hands a good deal of late. It had started when a friend of her brother Fred's, a medical student, had come to dinner just before Christmas and she had idly recounted to him her girlish ambitions of becoming a surgeon. The young man, with no more than a glance, remarked that it was a pity she hadn't pursued them, for her hands (if she didn't mind him saying) looked strong and bony, 'like a man's'. The initial effect of this observation was to make her grateful that she so often wore gloves. Then she began to wonder if there wasn't something in it – if her future really did lie, as it were, in her hands. In the new year she had dug out some of her old medical textbooks, and spent most of her free evenings studying at the new public library at the corner of Thornhill Square and Lofting Road.

It was now the 1st of March, a day off, and she had spent the afternoon wandering around the West End in search of a new lawn coat. As a rule she preferred to shop for clothes on her own: the opinions of friends, however well meaning, were apt to confuse her dependable instincts. And Lily, in any case, seemed in too difficult a mood to be of much help. Connie caught her checking her watch again, but when she had mentioned this half an hour before Lily became rather snappish. She was well versed in her friend's moods, but today's seemed quite different, an indecipherable compound of reticence and skittishness. Might there be a man in the background? Just then a waitress was passing their table.

'Shall we have another pot, Lil?'

Lily shook her head emphatically. 'No, I must be getting along.'

'Oh.' Connie put just enough enquiry into the syllable to invite an explanation.

'I have to meet someone – in the Strand,' she said, then called to the waitress for the bill.

Her curiosity piqued, Connie said airily, 'I'm going that way, too. D'you mind the company?'

'Fine,' replied Lily, with a terseness that suggested it was anything but. Well, thought Connie, this did sound like a man, and if Lily was going to be mysterious about it then she would feel no compunction in tagging along. Outside, a pale late-afternoon sunlight glistened on the rain-rinsed pavements. They skirted the stuttering traffic that was coming from Piccadilly and walked on through Leicester Square; a newsvendor was barking out the headlines of the *Standard*'s late edition. Connie sensed an urgency in Lily's gait, and felt suddenly aggrieved that she had not been taken into her confidence.

'You know, you can tell me, Lil,' she said with a sidelong look.

'Tell you what?'

'If there's a new sweetheart in the offing.'

Lily clicked her tongue and sighed irritably. 'It's really nothing like that.'

'Then why so secretive? And why has it put you in such a mood?'

Lily stopped and glared at Connie, who flinched. What had she done to merit that look? They were standing on St Martin's Lane, with shoppers streaming by on either side of them. Lily was now looking about the street, apparently in search of something.

'All right, then – you asked,' she muttered, and almost dragged Connie by the arm across the road. She led her into a narrow passageway of blackened bricks and reeking drain-pipes, stepping inside the murky embrasure of a tradesman's doorway that screened them completely from the street.

'What on earth – ?'

'Shh,' hissed Lily, who had now unclasped her handbag. From it she produced something wrapped in a canary-coloured duster. With a furtive check against passers-by, Lily unrolled the cloth, and there, incongruous but unarguable, lay a hammer. Its varnished handle and metal head gleamed brand new. For a few stunned moments Connie simply gazed at it. Only when her eyes caught the expression of dread and defiance on Lily's face did she finally understand.

'Oh, Lil . . .'

Lily swallowed hard, and seemed about to speak. Instead, she rolled up the hammer in the cloth and replaced it in her handbag. Then, with another glance at her watch, she stepped out of the shadowed doorway and back into the street. Connie, left staring at nothing, hurried after her.

'Lily, wait.'

'I haven't got time,' she said without breaking stride. 'I'm supposed to be there at quarter to six.'

'I'm just – Who's put you up to this? Was it Marianne?'

'Not directly. She introduced me to one of her . . . lieutenants.'

'At a meeting? Why didn't you tell me?'

'You were busy. With your books, remember?' There was an accusing note in her voice that made Connie shrink. She had been preoccupied, it was true, but it seemed inconceivable that the militants should have got their claws into Lily without her even noticing. When Marianne had asked them that night in November if they could be counted upon, they had both been doubtful. The prospect of prison seemed too grotesque to bear thinking about. But something – someone – had changed Lily's mind, and any minute now she was going to take an irreversible step. Ahead of them, the Strand was a honking fury of motor cabs and buses. She clutched at Lily's arm.

'Please, think about this. You don't have to do it.'

Lily paused, reluctantly. Her face was deathly pale, but it was her voice, the quiet decision in it, that frightened Connie. 'No, you're wrong. I do have to do it.' She held her gaze a moment longer, then, with a little skip, darted across the road. She was briefly lost amid the traffic, reappearing at the corner of Villiers Street, where she stood surveying the crowds, left and right. An agony of suspense finally drove Connie to cross the road herself, and as she walked towards her friend she wondered, in a flash of desperation, if she might snatch Lily's bag out of her hand and make off with it.

On seeing her approach, Lily half turned away, as if from a troublesome acquaintance one hopes to avoid. 'I can't let you do this,' Connie said.

'For God's sake, keep your voice down,' Lily replied in a sharp undertone. 'There are policemen everywhere.'

'Lil, I implore you –'

But Lily was looking beyond Connie's shoulder. 'That's her,' she said, and as she moved away she began to open her handbag. Connie saw a woman twenty yards up the street nodding at Lily's approach, and then caught a glint of metal in her gloved hand. Lily had stopped in front of a silversmith's, its huge plate-glass windows holding a mirror to the Strand's ceaseless toing and froing. From the direction of St Martin-in-the-Fields bells rang out, announcing the hour. Connie sensed her own reflection gravitating across the shopfront when, as in a dream where perverse and unlikely events occur within a familiar setting, she watched Lily swing the hammer against the glass. It sounded a thin metallic clunk and bounced off, leaving the pane intact. Office workers on their way home looked round in curiosity. She swung again, harder, and this time the glass broke with an affronted squeal. A neat hole opened up, with spiderweb cracks vectoring in every direction; her third and fourth blows sent the whole thing crashing in. From along the street came answering sounds of shattered glass. A man, his lips twisted in rage, came hurrying out of the shop door and bellowed, 'Oi, you bloody hellcat!'

Lily, ignoring him, had moved on to the next window, and was about to deal it the same treatment when the man, a good foot taller than the assailant, dragged her back by the hair. She cried out in pain. Connie, who had been immobilised with horror up to this point, instinctively moved to her friend's defence.

'Stop that,' she shouted, and clutched hold of the man's tailcoat. She heard the material rip in her hands as he jerked away. Turning, he hissed, 'Fucking cow!'

The violent shove he gave Connie sent her flying head first towards the window, the one Lily had been about to break. She heard an onlooker's startled 'Oh!' as her face smacked against the glass. The shock of impact dazed her – it had caught her flush on the nose – and she staggered against a lamp post in an effort to stay upright. She straightened her hat.

'Are you all right, miss?' she heard someone ask, and then mixed in with the echoes of tinkling glass came the quick high shrills of a whistle. Lily, grappling still with the silversmith's man, called out, 'Connie! It's the police – run for it!'

It took Connie a few seconds to realise that she was now in danger – was it aiding and abetting? – and, her nose still smarting, she looked round to see two, no, three policemen dodging through the crowds towards them. Mechanically she turned and broke into a hustling kind of run, her boots crunching over glass where the other woman was still bashing out her own splintery chaos from the shop windows. She appeared to be enjoying herself. Panic lent lightness to Connie's feet as she brushed past sandwich-board men and startled shoppers, who scattered out of the way of this careering madwoman. She slowed for a moment as her nose began to drip – she touched it and found blood on her glove – then turned to see one of the policemen wrestle the hammer-wielding woman to the ground. His colleague was looking up the street, and having spotted her was now in pursuit. How absurd, she thought, to be chased up the Strand by a bobby! It sounded like something from a music-hall song. But her wildly beating heart urged her to run as fast as she could: which, given her hobble skirt, was not fast enough. Another glance behind told her the policeman was gaining.

A motor cab some yards ahead was turning into a side street, and without thinking she followed it. Ahead of her she saw the glittering facade of the Savoy, its forecourt thronged with porters, cabmen and bejewelled guests. Slowing to a more decorous trot, she removed a glove and held it to her nose. She had just nodded at the liveried doorman when, behind her, she heard a shout. 'Stop that woman!'

Without turning, Connie darted through the revolving doors and into the hotel foyer. Where now? Strangers idled about, heedless of her plight. She trotted across the chequered floor and almost collided with a bellboy.

'The ladies' cloakroom?' she said, her mouth still muffled by the glove.

'That way, miss. Just follow the signs.'

She ducked into a corridor, not seeing any signs. Around

the next corner, a group of men in evening dress were ambling towards her. She turned her face away from them, fearful of their scrutiny. The dazzle of the white walls and the electric lights oppressed her senses. Further down the corridor another man in tails was hurrying to catch up with the others. She didn't look at him, either – but he looked at her, and stopped very suddenly.

'Miss Callaway?'

She glanced up, and took a few seconds to recognise – the cricketer.

'Mr . . . Maitland –' His face was frowning in alarm. 'Good heavens. You're bleeding –'

'Yes, the ladies?' she interrupted.

'Of course,' he said, with a little bow. He escorted her along the corridor, and stopped at a door marked WC. Connie pushed it open and was about to enter when she turned back to Will.

'Would you be kind enough to assist me?'

He looked momentarily disconcerted. 'In there?'

'If you wouldn't mind.'

The hushed, unpeopled chamber, mingling a floral perfume with detergent, held for Will an air of trespass. A continuous line of mirrors tracked their approach to the sink, where he plucked a cotton flannel from the stack and hovered around Connie.

'Please, allow me,' he said, removing her hat, tipping her head back and gently pinching the bridge of her nose with the cloth. 'This should staunch the flow.' Connie's eyes watered with the pain, but she submitted to it as quietly as she could. After a minute or two Will removed the flannel, ran it under the tap and wiped the crusted blood from around her nose and lips.

'Thank you,' she said, squinting at him. He gazed back at her.

'What on earth happened to you?'

Haltingly, she recounted the incident on the Strand, the windows, her misidentification and pursuit by the police.

'Should you not simply explain the mistake to them?'

Connie shook her head. 'They'll arrest me first. I wonder, would it be possible for me to slip out the back?'

'You wait here. I'll go and reconnoitre,' he said. Connie felt reassured by the military seriousness of his tone. Once he had left the room, she turned to the mirror to take stock. Her nose was pinkish, swollen, throbbing. Her eyes were smudged as if from weeping. The front of her blouse was polka-dotted with blood. Her whole body felt damp with sweat. What a fright! Will returned a few minutes later, his brow knitted with concern.

'Well, the place is overrun with policemen – back and front.'

'Oh, no,' she said, a tremble in her voice. 'What shall I do?'

Will put his hands on his hips, hoping that the posture lent him an air of command. 'What we'll do is . . . find a way out.' He went over to a lavatory stall and held open the door for her. 'Wait in here a moment.' Seeing her uncertain look, he added, 'I'll be back, don't worry.'

She heard his footsteps retreating across the tiled floor, and then out. Locked in the dark, she thought now about Lily. It was her absolute unflinching determination that had taken Connie by surprise. A window-smashing suffragette: her own best friend. It didn't matter how close you were to someone, people would always be a mystery to one another. She suddenly tensed at the approach of voices, echoing off the lavatory tiles. They were muffled and male, two or possibly three of them.

'. . . said he saw her come in here . . .'

'. . . must've done – look at this.' The glove. Connie knew at once – she had left it there by the sink without noticing. The voices had dropped to a mutter. She held her breath as she pictured the scene outside. A bloodstained glove, only one stall in the row occupied . . . She was cornered. A light knock sounded on the door.

'Um, 'scuse me, miss?' came a man's voice. Connie, now seated, swallowed hard – hesitation would damn her – and called out in a tone of high, matronly outrage, 'Do you mind?' She had recalled to life the voice of Miss Dolan, her headmistress – but did it sound like a sixty-year-old lady to them?

'Beg your pardon, ma'am.' The voice was all deference; the footsteps backed away, then receded from earshot. Connie, her heart pounding still, laid her head against the cool marble wall. It occurred to her just then that her school-days hadn't been entirely wasted.

Will, meanwhile, had just turned the corner when he saw two policemen emerge from the Ladies and come down the corridor. He busied himself with a boot button as they passed. So they had gone in and found – no one? Mystified, he sidled back into the room, and found the stall door closed, exactly as before. He knocked and called her name. The lock snapped back, and there she was, pale-faced and trembling.

'I thought you'd bolted! How did you . . . ?' he said.

Connie heaved a sigh. 'A small talent for mimicry. Since I was a girl.'

Will shook his head in wonder. 'Impressive . . .'

'Thank God you told me to hide in there,' she said, edging out past him. She looked around for the nearly incriminating glove, but of course they had taken it. In the mirror she saw Will holding what looked like a lady's hat and coat.

'What have you got there?'

'Your disguise. I'm afraid you'll have to leave that one behind,' he said, pointing to the felt navy cloche that Connie was wearing. It was a new one, though she had to concede that its flame-coloured silk band might draw attention. Will hung it on a hook inside the door, and handed its replacement to her. It was black silk, with a long veil. He held up the arms of a coat for her to try.

'Did you – take these things?'

Will gave her a dubious look. 'Well I didn't have time to go and buy them. There was nobody minding the cloakroom . . .' She looked appalled, so he said, 'Fine, I'll send them back once we're done with them. But for now . . .'

Connie collected herself, and tried on the hat and coat. They were quite a good fit. He straightened the veil over her face, and gave her an appraising look.

'Hmm. Not bad. You could pass for a young duchess just returned from a spa in Baden-Baden.' For the first time that afternoon, Connie laughed.

Will returned a smile. 'Right. Button up that coat – best not to show those bloodstains.' Connie did as he requested, and checked herself in the mirror. He was now crooking his arm in invitation.

'You're coming with me?' she asked.

'Of course. We're two guests at the hotel on our way out for the evening.' His cleverness would save her yet, she thought. The police had pursued a single woman into the hotel; they would not suspect a couple coming out.

'Thank you,' she said, patting his forearm. They stepped out of the Ladies and down the corridor, arms linked, and paused just before they entered the foyer. Policemen were still posted there, watching people as they exited. Will dipped his head towards her ear.

'Slow march,' he whispered. 'Nice and steady.'

Connie felt horribly self-conscious in her borrowed – stolen – finery, but she feigned nonchalance as best she could. They were halfway across the foyer when Will, in a moment of insane boldness, addressed a passing policeman.

'What's going on, Constable?'

'We're looking for a young woman, in connection to some damage of commercial property.' He leaned in chummy conspiracy towards Will. 'More window-smashing, I'm afraid.'

Will shook his head sorrowfully. 'D'you hear that, my dear?'

Connie, her powers of improvisation exhausted for the moment, merely nodded. The policeman seemed about to move on when another came alongside them. With a creeping horror Connie recognised him as the one who had first given chase. He was staring at her interestedly.

'Miss . . . if you'd be good enough to show your face.'

Will gave an incredulous laugh and said, 'What on earth is this about?'

The man was not to be cowed. 'Just doing our job, sir. Miss – please?'

Connie tried to compose her features as she slowly lifted the veil. The policeman's expression had changed. He had recognised her, she knew it.

'Could you tell me your whereabouts this afternoon?'

Connie's voice felt dry in her throat. 'I've – I've been here. At the hotel.'

The man looked disappointed in her. 'I think we both know –'

Will interrupted him. 'Constable, your colleague mentioned something about windows being smashed. I can assure you –' he paused to gesture at Connie '– this lady would no more vandalise property than I would!'

'Why would you say that, sir?' There was an insolent disbelieving note in his voice that infuriated Will, but he answered with perfect calm.

'Why? Because she happens to be my fiancée.' He gave the policeman a brief, challenging look, then took Connie's arm. 'Come, my dear, or we'll be late for the theatre. Good evening, officers.'

As they walked out, Connie felt the policeman's eyes on her. Will's hand pressured her arm, and she heard him say under his breath, 'Slow march, and don't look back.'

They reached the Strand, and Connie fought the impulse to break into a run. At her side, Will flagged down a cab. They climbed in, and once settled, they looked at one another. She had been so impressed by Will's sangfroid that it surprised her to see him puff out his cheeks in exaggerated relief.

'That was a close one!' he said.

Connie, almost faint from the ordeal, said, 'What about your friends – your evening?'

'Don't worry about that,' he said. 'It was just a dinner in the grill room. I won't be much missed.'

He leaned back into the seat. They were returning along the Strand, and could see from the car's window the aftermath of disruption. Shopkeepers were sweeping up carpets of broken glass, and policemen had set up barriers in order to redirect the flow of pedestrian traffic.

'What an awful nuisance they are,' Will said, gazing at the littered pavements.

Connie felt herself bridle at this, but replied, in her lightest tone, 'Well, they wouldn't need to be if the government weren't so pigheaded.'

Oh dear, he thought, with a guarded look. Connie saw it, and, unwilling to let the mood of euphoria dissolve between them, clapped her hand to her chest.

'I can't tell you how grateful I am. You absolutely saved me!'

Will modestly held up his hand in a gesture of denial. 'Glad to be of assistance, Miss Callaway –'

'Please, it's Constance,' she said, and paused momentarily. 'After all, we are now engaged to be married.' They both laughed, perhaps more heartily than the jest deserved, because it had resolved a lingering awkwardness between them. Will, constrained by the recollection of their unhappy encounter last summer, was still bracing himself to raise the subject.

Their journey had been diverted into the Charing Cross Road, and Connie was beginning to wonder if the best way of thanking her rescuer might be to get out of the cab and leave him in peace. Yet she had no wish to part company; nor, it seemed, did Will, who took advantage of the lull to say, 'I don't know about you, but that little escapade has put me in a rare hunger. Would you care for a bite to eat?'

'Rather!' Connie replied, but as she glanced out of the cab she saw another file of policemen hurrying down the street. 'Though I'm afraid of being seen around here.'

Will smiled inwardly at the idea of Connie's photograph being pasted like some outlaw's on a wanted poster, but seeing her face clouded with worry he decided not to tease her. 'That's all right. I was thinking of a place just round the corner from me, near Baker Street.'

It took them another twenty minutes to get through the West End, where evidence of a concerted campaign marked one shop after another: glass twinkled on the pavements and boards were being erected to cover the broken windows. 'Good Lord!' cried Will as they passed a long suite of shattered picture windows on Regent Street, though he refrained from further comment. The cabbie, however, on depositing them in Marylebone Road, muttered something about the necessity of 'slingin' 'em all in prison'. As they walked away, Will turned to Connie and pulled a face that indicated an ironic sympathy.

'That won't be an uncommon view,' she said drily.

'Would it be your own?'

She paused before answering. 'Well, I do feel sorry for the shopkeepers. After all, it's not their fault women don't have the vote. Some of them might even be in favour of suffrage.'

'I don't suppose they will be now.'

They had stopped outside a small restaurant lit from

above by gas lamps bracketed along the wall. Through the glass door they could see that the place was heaving, and Will, having briefly consulted within, reported back that there wasn't a table to be had.

'Oh,' said Connie, feeling suddenly depleted by the adventure of the previous hour. Will must have sensed it, for he now said, 'You look rather tired. May I suggest we repair to my rooms?'

Connie smiled. 'Gladly. Do you perhaps have any biscuits?'

'I'm sure I can find some,' he said, amused. They turned into Devonshire Place and were soon outside his flat. It was a tall red-brick mansion block with mullioned windows. Connie looked up.

'The top floor, did you say?'

'Don't worry – there's a lift.'

At the top Will gestured her out of the lift's iron-wrought cage and across the corridor. Connie knew that a single lady visiting 'bachelor rooms' unaccompanied was still considered, in some circles, highly improper. But her father had never concerned himself over chaperones for his daughters – whether out of trust in their good sense or out of affectionate negligence she wasn't sure. The rooms she stood in now were very different to Brigstock's poky hideaway on Mornington Crescent. Where the latter had barely any furniture at all, Will's sitting room looked almost cluttered with it: a pair of club chairs conversed with an enormous sofa; a drinks trolley waited obediently in the corner; above the fireplace hung the portrait of a mutton-chopped worthy gazing blandly into the middle distance. The facing wall was adorned with cricketing memorabilia, plaques and shields and team photographs. Will returned from inspecting his larder with a packet of Jacob's crackers in his hand.

'Not really biscuits, I know,' he said apologetically, 'and possibly not the freshest either. But I do have some cold chicken. I could nip out and buy some bread.'

'That sounds lovely,' she said.

'Would you like a cup of tea before I go? Or something stronger?'

Connie eyed the drinks trolley. 'A sherry?'

'Of course!' Once he'd poured her a tot, he checked his pockets for money and told her he'd be back directly. She heard the door slam, and holding her sherry, she wandered over to the bookcase. With an inexplicable stab of disappointment she inferred that Will was not a great reader. There were tubby volumes on the law – remnant of college days, she presumed – a set of *Encyclopaedia Britannica*, an assortment of history books, some biographies, a small selection of classical texts. A set of Jane Austen was the single concession to fiction. The uniform coating of dust indicated how often their owner picked them up. The one redeeming feature, as far as Connie judged, was the blocky rows of *Wisden*s, a duplication of her father's shelves at home. On a side table in the hall, a packet of unopened post squatted expectantly. She surveyed the kitchen, then ventured further and looked into the bedroom. A lugubrious wardrobe inlaid with a thin slice of mirror. A mahogany dressing table, where sleek monogrammed brushes rested on their stiff bristles. Above the bed, a single cricket bat hung crosswise, like a trophy. On the bed, a huge travelling trunk lay open, its contents half unpacked. Or was he about to leave? The flat rather puzzled her. It was orderly enough, but it held a curious air of impermanence, as though its occupant were only passing through rather than settled there.

She heard the key clink in the latch, and quickly scurried out and back into the sitting room as the door swung open. Will entered carrying a loaf wrapped in striped paper and held it up with a look of triumph.

'I'll just be half a sec,' he said, and disappeared into the kitchen, returning a few minutes later with a tray on which a plate of chicken sandwiches, a large hunk of cheese and a dusty bottle of claret were balanced. 'I'm rather used to these pot-luck suppers,' he explained, as they sat facing one another, plates on their knees. The sandwiches weren't at all bad.

Connie dabbed her mouth with a napkin. 'Do you – live here all the time?'

'Off and on. I only recently got back to town, actually. From South Africa.'

'Playing cricket?'

Will swallowed a mouthful of wine. 'For Western Province. They offered me a contract last year – and I had nothing else to do in the winter.'

'You had a good season at M—shire, I noticed.'

'Eventually, yes,' Will admitted. 'It began rather badly, as you know. My deplorable batting . . .' They both sensed the moment had come. 'And you'll also recall my . . . deplorable behaviour.' Connie said nothing, but tweaked the side of her mouth in an expression of wry acknowledgement. 'You were quite right, of course,' he hurried on, 'what you said. I was just shocked that –'

' – that you should hear it from a woman?'

Will looked away. She was gratified to note that he was blushing. 'I really was the most arrogant – I'm sorry.'

'Well,' said Connie, with a faint smile, 'you've certainly earned forgiveness today. And how is Mr Tamburlain? Still thriving?'

Will frowned at this. 'Not exactly. He didn't have a good season, by his standards. The reflexes are slowing. You know he'll be forty-four the week after next?'

'But he wants to carry on playing?'

'Oh, by Jove, yes. It's just that he's not been his old self. His mother has been ill, and they're rather close, you know. I'm going down to see him, in any case, for his birthday.'

'To cheer him up,' said Connie approvingly.

'I'll certainly try,' he said.

They talked for a while about cricket, and the forthcoming season. It would be an important one for Will, who had picked up a rumour from the Priory that the captain, Dodds, was about to quit – and that Will was being mooted as his successor. The possibility of this was undeniably flattering, yet aside from Tam he hadn't breathed a word of it to anyone. Until this evening.

'Captain!' said Connie, wide-eyed with delight. 'Oh, how marvellous!'

Will held up his palms in panicked admonition. 'Only a rumour. Even if old Dodds does move on they won't necessarily pick me as replacement.'

'They'd be mad not to,' she said firmly. 'You're the best batsman they've got, including Tam.'

It pleased him to think she was right. Last season he had topped the club's batting averages, and while he would never admit it himself, he was beginning to eclipse Tam as their star player. Age would finally cede the laurel to youth. But more than that, it was an awareness that his supper companion this evening had advanced from an object of curiosity – a woman crazy about cricket – to a focus of admiration. It had dawned on him first back at the Savoy, watching her struggle to command her nerves in the ladies. Other women would have cracked – men, too, come to that. She did not. Now, with the glow of a second bottle of wine dappling her cheeks, and his own senses pleasantly blurred, he was more enamoured than he had first thought. It didn't even bother him that she smoked.

Moonlight was rearranging shadows across the room before either of them noticed the hour. 'Heavens, it's nearly ten o'clock,' said Connie, checking her watch. With a guilty start she thought of Lily, and asked Will if she might use his telephone. He gestured out to the hall, where it stood, and she rang Lily's parents' house in Ellington Street. Her mother answered, with the news that Lily had not returned home. Connie tried to allay her worries, though to her own ears the reassurances sounded less than convincing. Will read her expression as she came back into the sitting room.

'Bad news?'

'She's not at home. I can only think she's been arrested.' She picked up the veiled hat that Will had commandeered from the cloakroom as her disguise, and murmured, 'And I'll never see my hat again.'

Will silently wondered at a mind that could flit with no apparent effort from criminality to hats. He sighed philosophically.

'Is it worth it? I mean, all that you've been through today – for the vote?'

Connie looked incredulous. 'Of course it is. I believe the vote to be an entitlement. Years from now, people will look back in wonder to think we were denied it for so long.' She searched Will's face to gauge his reaction, and read there not disagreement but bemusement.

'I don't really understand why it's so important . . .'

Connie took a deep breath. 'Perhaps because you have it by automatic right.'

'Yes – but I don't use it.'

She stared at him. 'You mean, you've never voted?'

'Not once,' he said, shrugging. Connie fell silent, sensing that further pursuit of the subject would find no common ground between them. Will, on the other hand, felt he had blundered and now sought to make reparation. 'But, of course, if that's what they – you – want, then it should be open to discussion . . .'

'Open to discussion,' echoed Connie. 'You may have noticed how far that has got us.' She looked at her watch again. 'I'd better be going –'

'Won't you help me finish off this wine?'

She shook her head. 'No, I mustn't. You've been kind – very kind . . .'

There was an awkward pause between them. Will was annoyed with himself for accidentally hurrying their night to a close.

'If you give me your address I'll ring down to the night porter – he'll whistle up a cab for you.'

'No, there's really need –'

'Please,' said Will earnestly, 'it's the very least I can do.'

Connie, too tired to argue, told him her destination, and Will went off to make the call. On returning, he found her clearing up the detritus of their supper.

'Don't bother with that. My housekeeper will do it in the morning.' Connie paused, then continued stacking the tray and carried it into the kitchen. Will hovered in the doorway, wondering how he might delay her departure. He went off down the corridor and returned holding the cricket bat that Connie had noticed hanging above his bed. She tried to compose her features in such a way that suggested she'd not seen it before.

'I wanted to show you this,' he said, running his palm along the varnished blade in reverent absorption. 'It's the bat Tam was using when he hit that ball over the Lord's pavilion in 1905. Only been done once before.'

He gave the sacred relic to Connie, who hefted it in her hands. She looked up at him. 'I saw him do it,' she said.

'No! You were there?' Will's eyes widened in awe.

Connie nodded. 'MCC versus Sussex. I was with my father and Fred – my brother. I remember him saying it was like a golf shot. Did you know it dislodged a chimney pot before it went down the other side?'

'I read about that!'

'So Mr Tamburlain gave it to you?'

'Oh no. I bought it at an auction, before I knew Tam. He'd laugh to hear how much I paid for it.'

'Well, it's . . . a lovely thing,' she said, handing it back. She gave him a polite, end-of-the-evening smile, and Will knew their time was up.

'Allow me to see you out.'

On the street, their faces half in shadow, he was holding the door open for her when she turned. 'I won't forget what you did for me today. Thank you.' She extended her hand, which he clasped and then brought to his lips.

'Goodnight –' He wanted to say her name, but didn't quite dare. 'I hope your friend is . . . safe.' He closed the taxi door and looked at her through the window. The smile he offered in farewell felt starkly at odds with his mood: there had been so much more he wanted to say.

Lily had been arrested and taken to Bow Street Police Court, where she was charged with conspiring to commit damage in violation of the Malicious Damage to Property Act 1861. Connie, with a foreboding that felt close to a physical ache, had gone to visit her at the holding cells, and been refused admission. She was reading *The Times* over breakfast one morning the following week when her eye fell on the name – Lily Vaughan, 21 – under the headline suffragette militants sentenced. Connie stared at the column for some moments, unable to move. Her stricken look must have caught Olivia's attention, for the latter looked over the top of her ladies' periodical and said, 'What's the matter?'

'Lily. She's – they've given her two months' hard labour.'

'Oh, that foolish girl!' She gave Connie her mongoose stare. 'You can say goodbye to your cause now. After what she's done – and the rest of them – nobody will ever think women fit to exercise the vote.'

'I don't agree,' Connie replied quietly, though her heart was sinking. 'And I don't think Lily's foolish – she's brave.' But had she really advanced the struggle for suffrage? Connie had persisted in believing that the vote would be yielded to them on the basis of justice and common sense. Attempting to gain it by violence seemed precipitate, and the indignation it caused did perhaps play into the hands of the anti-suffragists. She returned to the letters of outrage in *The Times*. A few minutes later they heard the postman at the door, and their mother came into the morning room carrying a large parcel.

'It's for you, darling,' she said, handing it to Connie with a look of mild curiosity. The label was in a hand she didn't recognise, though the postmark indicated it had been sent within London. She unpicked the string and tore off the brown paper, revealing a cardboard box emblazoned with the name of a Scotch whisky distillery. None the wiser, she opened it and found, nestled in whispering layers of tissue paper, her navy cloche hat, with a piece of creamy card folded under its band. She read its text:

Portman Mansions,
Devonshire Place, W.,

5 March '12

Dear Miss Callaway,

Here it is, retrieved from the cloakroom at the Savoy. Your sorrowful air on recalling its loss was too hard to bear, so I poled over there the next day. Got an awfully queer look from the attendant, until I mentioned my personal connection to the hat's owner – a fiction you've already heard.

I don't claim a reward, though I would be very much obliged if you agreed to join me for luncheon down at the Priory when the season begins in May. If the company does not entice you, the cricket perhaps will.

With my respectful regards,
Wm Maitland

Connie felt her smile being scrutinised. She looked to the enquiring faces of Olivia and her mother, and clapped on her hat.

'I thought it was lost,' she said brightly, 'but some kind stranger found it.' She packed up the box and, still wearing the hat, tripped off to her room to look for writing paper.

6

The herring gulls were screeching for their midday feed, but to Will, sauntering along the esplanade, their unlovely ululations might as well have been Mozart. The sun glistened upon the pleated waves, and an April wind carried on it a salty spume to refresh the lunchtime promenaders. A little way out to sea a rowing boat bobbed tipsily on the waves, and he stopped to watch it. How delightful it was to feel at ease and savour the prospect of one's talent being rewarded. He first perceived his ascendant star from the moment last month when Tam, at his forty-fourth birthday dinner, had taken him aside and said, in a confiding tone, 'It's definite. Old Dodderer's walking the plank. They'll give him a testimonial but they want him gone. According to Du Boung, you're their man.' This utterance, impenetrable to an outsider, made Will quite light-headed with excitement.

He kept reminding himself it was still hearsay, but last week a letter had arrived from the Priory secretary inviting him to lunch, not at the pavilion but at the Royal Victoria. That venue could only have been fixed upon if there were a cause for celebration – such as a change of the guard – and when Will had informed Tam of this communication, the latter said merely, 'It's yours, Blue. Well done.' Out at sea, the little boat he had been monitoring bucked on a sudden swell and put one of its occupants on his back. Will chuckled, and walked on. The effort of tamping down his sense of achievement had proven beyond him. He had got his Blue at nineteen; had made his county debut at twenty-one and hit a hundred on the occasion; had overhauled Tam as the club's top scorer; and now, a few months shy of his twenty-fifth birthday, he looked likely to be made captain. Even his mother might deign to crack a smile once she learned of this elevation. Better still, he had received a letter from Miss Callaway – he kept testing the name 'Constance' on his tongue, in a tone (he hoped) of suave address – accepting his invitation to lunch on the first Sunday of May, the eve of M—shire's first home match of the season. He felt certain she would be persuaded to stay and watch him lead out the team as captain.

He had donned his plum-coloured Priory club blazer, light grey bags and deck shoes, but had left his shirt collar open, hoping to strike a middle note between formality and rakishness. A tram chuntered by, and as he crossed the Marine Parade he felt a large raindrop smack his shoulder. He frowned up at the sky. *Gah!* That moisture wasn't rain. A gull had swooped overhead and its load was now dribbling down the silk-faced lapel of his blazer. It looked as if someone had just thrown a small egg at him. He took out his handkerchief and began to wipe at it, distractedly wondering whether such a splattering augured good or ill. He couldn't remember. It was the sort of thing Tam would know. Like most sportsmen he was incurably superstitious, and harboured a knowledge of arcane folklore that never failed to surprise Will. He now recalled Tam casually telling him that you should never kill a seagull because it was the soul of a dead sailor, or something. Or was that an albatross? Either way, Will would happily have shot whatever bird had just deposited this muck on him . . .

Entering the foyer of the hotel he made straight for the gentlemen's cloakroom. The humiliation of facing the committee with a great streak of birdshit badging his jacket was not to be borne. He did what he could with his dampened handkerchief in front of the mirror, but a ghostly whitish crest was still discernible on the cloth. The more he thought about it, the more convinced he became that being used as a seagull's privy signified bad luck, not good. It had taken the wind out of his sails. He dumped the sodden kerchief in the bin and hurried out.

The Royal Vic prided itself on a 'better' class of clientele, but the polite murmur of talk among the early lunchers only put an edge on Will's nerves as he scanned the tables. Where were they? He asked a passing waiter, who informed him that a group of gents had taken one of the private luncheon rooms upstairs.

'Ah, William, there you are,' called Du Boung, the club secretary, rising from the table around which were gathered the three other committee members. Will already knew the expressionless treasurer, Leach, and the doughy, florid-faced manager, Colonel Pawley, who turned to the man on his right. 'I don't think you've met Lord Daventry, our new president?' Will shook hands with a sleek-looking, neatly bearded fellow in tails whose gaze seemed instantly to settle on his recently mortified lapel.

'Mr Maitland – how d'you do? I've been hearing great things about you.'

The colonel was soon running through a precis of those things for the general benefit of the table. Will, unlike Tam, thrived on praise, though he kept his head bowed shyly while his host mulled over which of his hundreds last season had been the most pleasing. Leach signalled for lunch to be served, and over cold salmon and potato salad they talked in a desultory way about the forthcoming season, the current repair work on the pavilion, and sundry other matters of moment. Will, though braced by the early gusts of acclaim wafting his way, could not quite relax while the subject of the captaincy hovered like an invisible guest.

As the plates were being cleared Du Boung, a drawling enthusiast whom Will regarded as his secret ally at the table, raised his voice and said, 'Well then, if it suits you, My Lord, shall we attend to business?' At Daventry's nod, Du Boung addressed Will across the table. 'I dare say you have already divined the purpose of our little gathering, William. We, that is, the committee, have accepted the resignation of Mr Dodds – after years of sterling service, I might add – and would like to offer the captaincy of the club –' his head made an ingratiating sweep around the table '– to you.'

Will sensed his face flush with pleasure and relief. Right up to the last moment he had worried that his intuition had been mistaken, that he had been invited to lunch simply to meet the new president, or to hear those expressions of gratitude for his performance last season, or – he hardly knew what. *The birdshit* – a good omen after all!

'Thank you, gentlemen, My Lord,' he said, looking at each of them in turn. 'I'm delighted to accept.'

'Bravo!' cried Du Boung, leaning over the table to extend his hand. Then the colonel, to his left, merrily patted him on the back, and even Leach, impassive as an owl, had minutely tweaked his mouth into the thinnest of smiles. As the congratulations dwindled in echo, Lord Daventry fixed a keen eye on Will and said, 'I'm sure you're going to make an excellent captain.'

'I hope so, My Lord.'

'I need hardly tell you,' Daventry continued, his tone more confiding, 'that the job will entail certain, ahm, responsibilities, off the field as well as on.'

'I'll try to do whatever's in the best interests of the club,' said Will, already enjoying the sound of his own seriousness.

'Of course, of course. Just so long as you appreciate that some of those responsibilities may be less . . . agreeable than others.'

'I understand,' replied Will, not quite sure that he did. Lord Daventry was now looking at Colonel Pawley to take up the conversation's reins. The latter cleared his throat and said, 'What we need, Maitland, is for a new broom at the club. M—shire has ambitions for the championship this season, as you know, but we are burdened at present by a fair bit of, well, *dead wood*. Dodds ought to have been released years ago, and there are one or two others whom the committee believes would best be – put out to grass.'

There could be little doubt as to whom he meant. Alfred Lunt, a veteran amateur, had lost whatever guile his left-arm spin once had, and his unathletic presence in the field had become a team joke. Will felt a little sad, but knew that the fellow had an upholstery business in town to see him through to retirement. 'Alf Lunt, I suppose.'

Colonel Pawley nodded. 'Mr Lunt is certainly one of them. Mr Jarrold, also.' He had named another amateur, the club's wicketkeeper, facetiously known in the changing room as the Ancient Mariner, because 'he stoppeth one of three'. Will replied that he would deal with both of those gentlemen before the season began, and looked around the table in the expectation that business was concluded. But the colonel had knitted his brow into an expression of earnest solemnity.

'There is one other whom we've talked about, just between ourselves, and have come to the conclusion that he's, erm –' he seemed embarrassed to say it – 'surplus to requirements.'

Will compressed his lips. He had no wish to play a guessing game. 'I'm sorry, I'm not sure who . . .'

There followed an awkward exchange of glances before Colonel Pawley said, with a little jerk of his neck, 'Tamburlain.'

No other name could have surprised Will more, and for some moments he was struck dumb. He could almost have believed it a joke, only the faces around the table were deadly serious. Du Boung, registering his shock, took a quietly conciliating tone. 'We all know what a superb batsman he's been, and we know, too, of your very high regard for him, William. This is a fearfully difficult decision for all of us. But –' he twisted his mouth into a rueful grimace '– sacrifices have to be made. And he's not getting any younger.'

There was some mumbled talk at this point as to how old Tam was, but Will, his mind racing, interrupted it. 'So . . . you appoint a captain without first telling him that you intend to sack the club's best player.'

'We're not "sacking" him. We're just not going to renew his contract. And he's *not* the club's best player any more,' said Du Boung, with a meaningful glance at Will, who now began to detect an ulterior motive behind this afternoon's blandishments. Knowing of their friendship, the committee must have reasoned that he, Tamburlain's friend and protégé, would be the best choice – the most sympathetic, that is – to break the unpleasant news to the man himself.

'This is madness,' Will said simply.

'Not at all,' cut in Leach, quiet up to now but listening closely. 'I'm afraid it's economic sense. Tamburlain's wages are the highest of any player at the club. From the money recouped we could afford another two men in his place.'

'Can't argue with the treasurer,' offered the colonel. The complacent finality of his tone seemed to induce a glandular reaction in Will. He felt about to combust with indignation, but strove to keep his voice steady.

'Let me make myself clear. First, I don't care how much he earns – he's worth every penny. Second, the club hasn't a hope of the championship this season if he doesn't open the batting. Andrew Tamburlain is the first name on the team sheet. That's it.'

The note of obstinacy was unmistakable. The atmosphere at the table, so recently convivial, was now dropping towards a distinct chill. Du Boung made one more effort at diplomacy. 'William, please, we understand your loyalty, and it does you credit. But we think young Revill could step in as opener – '

'Revill?!' Will couldn't believe his ears. 'He hasn't even made a first-class hundred. If you think you could replace Tam with *Revill*, you really have taken leave of your senses.'

Lord Daventry appeared to have heard enough. 'I must say, after what we've just been talking about, I'm disappointed by your attitude, Maitland.'

'And I'm disgusted by yours,' replied Will coldly. 'If I'm to be captain of this club, then Tamburlain stays. Otherwise, I must oblige you to find someone else for the job.'

An offended silence fell upon the table. Will folded his arms and fixed his gaze on the tablecloth, refusing to say more. He felt the blood throbbing at his temple, its pulse so insistent he wondered if the vein might pop. He supposed they would have expected opposition to their plan, but they surely hadn't envisaged anything quite so adamant as this. At that moment, a waiter arrived with champagne in a bucket, his timing off by only five calamitous minutes. Daventry dismissed him without a word, then turned to Will.

'Would you be kind enough to wait outside?'

Will rose from his chair, dropped his napkin on the table and made for the door. He felt his step to be mechanical, a little like the slow walk from the crease after you've got out, with that terrible sense of self-rebuke companioning you right back to the pavilion. Outside, he stalked up and down the corridor as waiters and chambermaids padded past, oblivious to the deliberations going on behind the closed doors. Pausing before the framed landscapes hung on the wall, he pondered the gamble he had taken: they could strip him of the captaincy, and get rid of Tam anyway. What would he do then? Behind him, he heard the door open and Du Boung calling his name.

He walked back in, a defendant returning to hear the verdict of the jury. Two of them had cigars in blast, their burnt chemical odour an affront to Will's nostrils.

'Sit down, Maitland,' said Pawley, with a kind of weariness.

'I'll stand if you don't mind.'

The decision of this court . . . Daventry, with the air of a man handing down sentence, looked sternly at Will. 'You've caused us great disappointment, sir – though it is yourself you have principally let down. I'm sorry to say that, given your intransigence, we must withdraw the offer of the captaincy.'

That didn't take long, thought Will. He swallowed hard. 'And Tamburlain?'

Daventry looked away, yielding the floor to Pawley. 'I'm sorry, old chap. He won't be kept on.' So there it was: the worst possible outcome. Will wasn't sure if it was the cigars or the impact of those words that were making his stomach lurch. There was one more bullet in the chamber. He knew then that if he used it he would have to mean it. And he did. 'Very well. I'm glad at last to know what manner of men run this club. If a batsman of Tamburlain's calibre is no loss to you, I can't imagine what difference my departure will make.' He walked over to the stand to take his hat, and his leave. Sensing their confusion, he said, 'That, in case you were wondering, is my resignation. Good day.'

He was almost at the door when he heard the scrape of a chair and Du Boung called, 'William, a moment please –' He had hurried to catch him at the door, and held up his hands in a gesture of placatory surrender. Pawley had also stood up. 'Come, come, Maitland. Let's not be hasty. We can discuss this further, like gentlemen.'

'I think the time for gentlemanly behaviour passed when you charged me with the sacking of my closest friend.'

'It's not a sacking –'

'Whatever you prefer to call it,' said Will, sensing the moment on a knife-edge. 'I'm sorry to present you with such a stark choice, but there it is. If Tamburlain isn't offered a contract for the season, I want nothing more to do with this club.'

From their uncertain glances he judged that they were taking him seriously, at least. And why should they not? His loss as a captain was a mere inconvenience to them, but they would think twice about sacrificing his runs. The seven centuries he had scored last season had been vital in hauling M—shire up to sixth in the championship table. They would not be able to replace him in a hurry, and they knew it. Will was not going to flinch. Taking out his watch, he glanced at it and said, 'I dare say you'll want to discuss it. I shall be outside – for another five minutes.' It was an arrogant touch, he knew, but his blood was up now. If this was to be his last association with the club he wanted to go down fighting. Back in the corridor he stood gazing once more at a heavily varnished picture of a stag hunt. As the minutes ticked on he became stoical: let them sack him, then, see if he cared. He moved to the window, where the afternoon light was sharpening the blue of the sky. The door opened again, and this time both the colonel and Du Boung emerged. The latter closed the door behind him; evidently Will was not to be invited back a second time. Oh well. With his record, some other county might pick him up, there was always a chance –

The colonel approached, stroking distractedly at his toothbrush moustache. His eyes drooped a schoolmasterly disapproval at Will. 'That was quite a gamble you took in there. Daventry thinks you're a damned insubordinate and wants rid of you.'

Will shrugged, as if His Lordship's opinion were of no consequence to him. He sensed there was more to come. Du Boung, with the air of a man exhausted by his own reasonableness, shook his head. 'I'm surprised at you, William, really I am –'

'Please tell me what you've decided, and I'll go.'

Colonel Pawley's rubicund complexion had deepened. 'My God, I never thought to hear such insolence –'

Du Boung made a tactical interruption. 'The committee is very eager not to lose you, and to that end we are . . . prepared to make a compromise.' Will cocked his head. The gesture asked the question.

'Tamburlain' – Du Boung's voice sounded weary of the name – 'will be offered a year's contract. But, in the light of your attitude, we can't possibly instate you as captain.'

Will listened with an expression as impassive as granite. He realised that Du Boung had probably worked harder than anyone to salvage his career with the club, but at this moment he felt no warmth towards him or any of his colleagues.

'Thank you for the lunch. I'll see you at the Priory next month.' He tipped his hat to them, and turned down the corridor towards the exit.

Back on the Parade, the bright innocence of the day Will had enjoyed not long before seemed to him now one of charmless banality. People still strolled along the esplanade, seagulls still wheeled and cawed, but he pounded the pavement with the distracted air of a man who had just mislaid his wallet. He must have been muttering to himself, because a couple of elderly promenaders looked askance at him as he stalked past. The further he walked the less real to him the previous hour or so seemed: the tumultuous interview he had just endured, the size of the gamble he had taken, and the shocking, wilful stupidity that had provoked it. Had he just dreamt the whole thing? The stink of cigar smoke on his sleeve argued that he had not. He turned off the Parade and began to roam the backstreets that sloped up from the seafront, the rows of early-Victorian terraces, the peeling stucco, the sudden boarding houses, the identical porches, the bay windows and their illusionless gaze. What a wretched, parochial, mean-minded place it was – no wonder the likes of Leach and Pawley lived here. That such mediocrities had a say in the running of a county cricket club! As for His Lordship, he should desist from poking his aristocratic beak into affairs he clearly didn't understand. Even Du Boung he thought of as a Judas, all smiles as he offered him the captaincy while hiding the knife with which he was to stab his friend in the back.

His aimless, fretful perambulation brought him eventually to the manicured gardens of Warwick Square, where the smaller of the town's two railway stations stood. He had made an arrangement to visit Tam at his lodgings that evening, but now the temptation of a swift exit called him on. He stopped at a tobacconist's next to the station, and picked a seaside postcard off the rack. He bought a pencil to go with it, and wandered into the waiting room. There was nobody else there but an off-duty signalman smoking a lonely cigarette. Will sat down, and after a few moments' reflection wrote on the card:

A false dawn. The proverb of counting chickens springs to mind. Purpose of the luncheon only to meet His Lordship (wdn't call it a pleasure). Hope you'll forgive if I cry off this evening. See you in a fortnight for nets, when I shall be in better spirits.
    Fondest,
    Will
PS Remind me to ask about seagulls.

Would it convince Tam? he wondered. The tone of breeziness mingled with disappointment seemed right, but Tam was shrewd: he might suspect something was amiss. Well, he would never hear the truth of it from him, and the committee would want to keep mum about it, too. Perhaps, in time, Will would feel proud of his noble stand, but at that moment all he could think of was the honour he had effectively denied himself. To think that he had for just those fleeting minutes actually *been* captain. He wondered if he had set some kind of record for the shortest tenure in the club's history. In the history of captaincy itself. A thunderous hissing at the platform outside and the irregular volley of carriage doors clunking shut interrupted his reverie. A question to the signalman revealed it to be the train to Charing Cross. Stopping to tip his postcard into the letter box he walked out and boarded a first-class carriage. He tried to rid himself of the preceding few hours as the branchline stations slid past his window, but as the outskirts of London began to thicken, the fateful confrontation was proving in his mind as tenacious and maddening as the peculiar stain on his lapel.

A train travelling in the opposite direction nearly three weeks later deposited Connie on the platform at Warwick Square. As the pall of steam cleared she spotted Will scanning the alighting passengers, glance by glance, and felt rather touched by his look of furrowed anxiety. He had insisted on meeting her off the train, though she had expressed herself perfectly capable of taking a taxi. He raised his hat on finally spotting her, and she realised he had perhaps not expected his guest to emerge from a third-class compartment.

'Miss Callaway!' he said.

'Constance,' she corrected, smiling. She allowed him to relieve her of her small suitcase, and followed him out over a footbridge and into the square.

'A change of plan,' said Will over his shoulder. He gestured her into the taxi.

'Oh?' She arranged herself on the seat as he climbed in after her.

'The good news is that we're not dining at the Royal Vic. We'll have luncheon at my mother's. The bad news – well, you haven't met my mother.'

Connie laughed. 'I'm sure she's not as bad as all that.'

Will smiled uncertainly, then said, 'I've invited Tam along, too, so the good news sort of outweighs the bad.' The taxi turned out of the square and along the seafront; Connie watched as the rows of shops and hotels reeled by. It was her first visit to the town since the week before the Coronation last summer. The taxi had temporarily stalled, as it happened, right by the Wellington, scene of their little difference of opinion. Strange to think of her contempt back then for his arrogant chauvinism, and now here they were, like a couple of fast friends. She turned and found him looking, slightly sheepishly, in the same direction.

'Happy days,' she said gaily.

Their journey took them a mile or so north-east of the town, down a winding road that suddenly offered a sharp turn up a narrow wooded lane. The first sign that they were approaching the Maitland home was a notice on a white gatepost announcing it as private property. A break in the thickly set cypress trees and poplars allowed a glimpse of Silverton House, grey-stoned, three-storeyed, and fronting a wide crescent-shaped garden. The patchy crimson colour on the facade gradually resolved itself into a Virginia creeper. It all seemed very grand to Connie, who had no acquaintance with the rural gentry, or their houses. As the car pulled to a halt, she had an idea that an aged retainer would totter from the house to greet the young master. The front door did indeed swing open, but the girl who ambled out to meet them was plainly no member of staff. Will was paying off the cabman, so Connie introduced herself.

'Hullo,' she said, 'are you by any chance –'

'Eleanor,' she replied brightly, extending her hand. 'And you're Constance. I hope you like fish pie.'

'I'm sure I do.'

'Good. It's Tam's favourite, you see.'

'I don't suppose he's here yet,' said Will, coming up behind them.

'Actually, he *is* here. He's on the terrace with Mother. I think they're yarning about horses or something.' She gave an exaggerated shrug, as if to absolve herself of responsibility for what the older generation talked about.

'I'll just show Miss Callaway round the place, then we'll join you.'

They proceeded into the entrance hall, their footsteps clacking on the tiled floor. In quick succession Will threw open doors, one revealing the dining room, another the drawing room, another a little lobby that led down to the kitchen. They lingered a while in the echoing hallway, where a grandfather clock croaked a froggy, metalled tut. Then they cut through a billiard room and up two flights of stairs, Will retailing the history of the house as they went ('They say Tennyson stayed here sometime in the 1860s') in a faintly responsible way. On a half-landing he paused, and they looked through a casement window onto the long back garden, with an old lead sundial in the middle and a brick path leading off to a tennis court and an orangery. A wild meadow could be seen straggling beyond.

'We should go for a walk later,' he said, 'if it stays fine.'

Connie raked her gaze over the aspect, then turned to him. 'So just your mother and your sister live here?'

'And the maid. It's much too big for them,' he said, picking up her implication, 'but she can't bear to sell it. It was her father's, you see.'

The final flight of stairs took them to a pair of attic rooms, one of which was to be Connie's for the night. Its window sat right beneath the eaves, and the lowering slant of the ceiling made it seem perhaps more cosy than was comfortable. The air felt musty and unstirred. Will placed her suitcase on the chaste single bed, with its faded floral eiderdown, and then pushed open the window. He cleared his throat apologetically. 'It was originally a servant's bedroom, I think.'

'It's lovely,' she said simply.

Having waited while she had a quick wash, Will then led her down again and through to the terrace, where a maid was depositing a jug on the table between Mrs Maitland and Tam.

'Um, Mother, this is Miss Callaway . . .' From the moment she stepped forward Connie was alive to the unsmiling scrutiny of this matriarch, who held forth her hand for the visitor to shake.

'Miss Callaway. A pleasant journey from London, I hope?'

'Oh yes, thank you. I had a smoker all to myself.'

Mrs Maitland's eyes just perceptibly widened. Will hurried on. 'And this, as you know, is Andrew Tamburlain.'

Tam had stood up to greet her. 'Miss Callaway. I recall you from last summer – at the Wellington?'

'Indeed, yes. How d'you do?' she said, covering her surprise. She now remembered passing him on her way out of the hotel, but she never thought for a moment *he* would remember. 'I happened to see *you* first at Lord's some years ago. Your big hit over the pavilion.'

'Ah,' said Tam, nodding, 'Will told me you saw that . . . you must have been very young at the time. Well, I always liked playing at Lord's – I scored my first county hundred there.' Now it was Will's turn to be surprised. In his experience Tam hardly ever responded so genially to strangers reminiscing about the Lord's hit: he always believed it had overshadowed his more deserving achievements.

'Some barley water, Miss Callaway,' Mrs Maitland cut in, 'or perhaps you would prefer a glass of wine?'

Connie sensed that the latter was offered in a rather ironic spirit, to go with her cigarette smoking. 'Some wine, thank you.' Will stepped forward to pour a glass of hock for their guest, and noticed the bottle was already half empty. Tam, the old toper. 'I do like your house,' said Connie, hoping to soften up her hostess. 'The meadow over there – is that yours, too?'

'Yes. Most of what you can see from the house is ours.'

'How nice to have a tennis court!'

'Do you play, Miss Callaway?' asked Tam.

'Oh no,' said Connie with a sad little laugh, 'I'm hopeless at sports. But I do love to watch.'

'Eleanor is a superb tennis player,' declared Mrs Maitland airily, as if the accomplishment admitted no contradiction.

'Lunch is ready,' said Eleanor, who from the slight flush in her cheeks had evidently been helping to prepare it. 'I hope you're all hungry – there's heaps.'

They repaired to a conservatory, where a fish pie was steaming at the centre of an oval table. A knocking sounded distantly from the hall.

'That'll be Mr Fotheringham – with immaculate timing.'

'I was wondering where he'd got to,' said Eleanor, who dropped her voice confidingly to Connie. 'Wouldn't be like him to miss a feed.'

The appearance at the conservatory door of a balding, bespectacled and unarguably corpulent gentleman explained her remark. It transpired that Mr Fotheringham was the family lawyer, and a regular guest at the Maitland table. Connie already felt a secret relief at his arrival, for his bulky placement to Mrs Maitland's right at the table (Tam was to her left) had put a saving buffer between herself and the hostess. Will, with a quick encouraging smile, came to sit by Connie, briefly introducing the lawyer and filling up their glasses in turn. He was beginning to wonder if he should have organised the lunch just à *deux*; it might have been more relaxing for her – and him, come to that – without his mother's wrongfooting approach to hospitality. But then he had wanted her to meet Tam, and he couldn't face the Royal Vic, so lunch at home seemed the sensible choice. As he watched her converse with his sister, he found that his susceptibility to her had by no means diminished since their encounter back in March. The intelligent, animated expression in her dark eyes, the swan curve of her neck and the generous fullness of her mouth were still working a spell. True, he hadn't noticed her hands before – long and bony, like a farmer's wife's – but that anomaly only made her seem more vividly human to him. He tuned back in to the conversation: Connie was recounting to Eleanor, with careful omissions, the story of her bumping into Will at the Savoy.

'I've been meaning to ask,' he said, lowering his voice, 'what became of your friend – that day?'

Connie glanced warily up the table at Mrs Maitland, who was busy talking to Tam and the lawyer. She said, sotto voce, 'She'll be out next week. Two months, hard labour.'

Eleanor, hearing this, leaned in excitedly. 'You mean, she's been – in *prison*?' It was unfortunate that this last word emerged on a rising note of scandalised interest, and could not fail to be heard at the other end of the table. Mrs Maitland, with the reflex of an eagle spotting a rabbit in open country, swooped down on this sudden titbit. 'Who's been in prison?' she asked sharply.

Will instantly stepped in. 'A lady Miss Callaway knows – she was involved in an affray some weeks ago in the West End.'

'So, this lady – she was wrongly arrested?' asked Eleanor.

How nice to be so innocent as that, thought Connie, who hesitated, then said, 'No. Not wrongly. She broke a shop window on the Strand – with a hammer.'

Mrs Maitland, a nerve twitching in her cheek, looked down the table at her. 'Are we to suppose this miscreant is

. . . a suffragette?' She said the word as if she were holding it, distastefully, with a pair of tweezers.

'I suppose she is.'

'And how do *you* know this . . . person?'

Connie felt her heart begin to thud. 'She's – Lily – is a friend of mine,' she said, then quietly corrected herself. 'Actually, my best friend.' In the short silence that followed she sensed her revelation exerting an almost physical pressure on the atmosphere. Tam was nodding philosophically over the rim of his wine glass, while Fotheringham, with professional impassivity, stared straight ahead. Still hoping to limit the damage, Will blundered in again.

'But Miss Callaway actually tried to stop her – and got a bloody nose for her trouble. She wanted nothing to do with it.' Connie obscurely resented this defence, even though she saw it was a shield against his mother's Medusa glare.

Mrs Maitland was very far from being mollified. 'These women . . . they simply bring disgrace on us all. Two months seems hardly adequate punishment –'

'It's the maximum sentence,' Connie broke in, 'for the cost of the damages.'

'Miss Callaway is right,' said Fotheringham neutrally. 'Under the Malicious Damages Act if the window broken cost less than five shillings, two months is all she could be given.'

'And it's only a broken window!' added Eleanor. 'It's not as though anyone was hurt – apart from Miss Callaway.' Connie could have hugged her for that.

Mrs Maitland's gaze narrowed. 'That's foolery, Eleanor. It may be "only a broken window" to you – to a shopkeeper it's his livelihood. What if everyone decided that their grievances required them to break windows and burn down buildings? What price democracy then? I'm sorry, but any sane state will allow that lunatics ought to be restrained.'

The tone of her voice did not invite disagreement. For

the next few moments all that could be heard was the soft clink of cutlery on plate. Eleanor took a deep breath, and for a second Will was seized by a dread that she was going to pursue the argument.

'More fish pie, anyone?' she said, looking around the table.

By the time pudding was finished the social temperature of the room had been restored to a level of civility, if not of jollity. Mrs Maitland seemed to have laid aside her aura of queenly displeasure for the time being, and was once again holding forth to Tam and Mr Fotheringham, both of them still content to play murmuring courtiers around the throne. Will, used to her sudden cold fronts and lightning flashes of temper, felt that it might have gone much worse, though he sensed beneath Connie's well-mannered constraint a brooding sense of hurt. And pluck, too! My God, he'd almost fallen off his chair when she'd spoken to his mother so candidly . . . He was coming round to the idea that the two of them would best be kept apart in future.

Connie's own thoughts were tending in the same direction. A natural sense of tact, and her nascent regard for Will, inclined her to maintain a blameless front, but she realised that her confessed association with Lily had put her, for the moment, beyond the pale. It was strange, though, for she had never encountered anyone she could not in some small way charm. To judge from Mrs Maitland's refusal to catch her eye, there was a first time for everything. The table had been cleared and they had drifted back onto the terrace when Tam suggested a walk. The prospect of escaping Mrs Maitland's presence appealed so strongly to Connie that her response ('Oh yes, let's!') betrayed perhaps more feeling than she had intended. Mr Fotheringham, settled into post-prandial torpor, declined such exercise, which effectively meant that his hostess would stay put, too.

The afternoon was offering hints of the summer to come, a certain sultriness in the air and a sun that kept playing hide-and-seek with the clouds. They started through the meadow, the four of them naturally splitting into pairs, with Connie and Eleanor setting the pace ahead of Will and Tam. Eleanor, in her final year at Roedean, had the same athletic ranginess as her brother, though with something more pensive in her demeanour. It seemed that she had recently been presented at Court, and described the fuss of the ceremony with a shrugging disregard.

'The courtiers chivvy and shoo you about as if you were a beagle. But once I'd made my double curtsy the worst was over. Now I just have to attend a lot of dances and hope some chap takes a shine to me.'

'You don't wish for a career, then?'

'I've not really thought about it. I suppose I'd like to play tennis, but I don't think Mother would stand for that. It was bad enough when Will decided he was going to play cricket.' As if reminded of him now, they stopped and settled on the grassy verge of a river to wait for the men. Eleanor said, in her straightforward way, 'Do you work, Miss Callaway?'

'Yes. In a bookshop near my home. But it's – not what I'd like to do.'

'Oh?'

'I've recently gone back to my medical books. I studied medicine for a year after leaving school –'

'So you wanted to be a nurse?'

'No. A surgeon.'

Eleanor gave a little giggle, which she stifled on seeing that Connie was quite serious. 'I don't think I've heard of a lady surgeon before.'

Connie pursed her lips wryly. 'If it were left to men you never would.'

Further discussion of this topic was curtailed by the arrival of Will and Tam, who were in the middle of a heated discussion. 'I haven't a *clue* why,' Will was saying in a defensive tone.

'What's the matter?' asked Eleanor, looking from one to the other. Will shook his head, saying nothing; Tam, holding his gaze, said, 'Your brother has been a damned fool –'

'Ladies, Tam,' muttered Will. Tam sighed, and apologised to Connie and Eleanor for his language.

'I'm just trying to get to the bottom of why Bluey hasn't been made captain.'

'Oh no,' said Connie with a look of dismay. 'How could they not?'

Will shrugged. 'Not for me to say. I fear I misconstrued the committee's intentions. The subject didn't come up –'

'I'd dearly like to know what you said to them,' Tam cut in. 'That job was yours for the taking. You know they've given it to Middlehurst?'

'I'd heard. Decent chap.'

'But no captain.'

Connie, sensing the burden of disappointment on both men, said, 'Well, it might be a blessing in disguise. Your only responsibility now will be to score runs.'

'Quite so,' replied Will, grateful for this defusing remark. 'I'll bear that in mind at the Priory tomorrow morning.'

'You'll be there to watch us, Miss Callaway?' asked Tam.

'Of course,' said Connie, standing up to smooth down her dress. She looked out upon the river while Eleanor and Will discussed what direction their walk should take. They would follow this path, it seemed, and skirt the border of the neighbouring farm. Just then a trio of swans hove into view, serene and inscrutable in their movement through the water, their heads so still and sculpted they might have been made of porcelain.

'Wouldn't think they were dangerous, would you?' said Tam, who was following her gaze. Connie looked round to catch his half-rueful, half-amused expression. The question didn't seem to demand an answer, so she smiled, and watched the birds glide on until they disappeared from view – three, two, one – at the willow-clogged bend in the river.

The next day at the Priory would become, in the long perspective of Connie's memory, one of near-Elysian bliss. The morning started fine, with a lemony sun peeking through the vast cathedral skies; M—shire's new captain, on winning the toss, had elected to bat. When the pavilion bell rang for the first time that season she craned forward on the bench to watch Tam and his fellow opener stride out to the crease. Will, who had reserved the seat for her in the members' stand, had considerately supplied a picnic blanket to ward off the late-spring chill, and sat with her until the first wicket went down. She had hardly dared hope to see the two of them batting at once, but the loss of another wicket did indeed bring Maitland and Tamburlain together. Their opponents, Yorkshire, were rusty from lack of match practice, and their quick men bowled fatally short all day. What stuck most enduringly in her mind's eye was the sight of the ball nearly disappearing – a black dot against the sky – before it dropped into the midst of the murmurous crowd, or else over the wall for a six. Tam started off the more briskly, thrashing anything loose on either side of the wicket and racing to the seventies by lunch. In the afternoon Will picked up the pace and overtook his senior partner; by tea they both had hundreds and were still going strong. Connie, thrilled as she was by this display of explosive hitting, could not help wondering if the two batsmen were, at times, stealthily competing with each other; whenever one of them had rattled off a few boundaries, the other would follow suit with a flurry of his own. She would have dismissed the observation as fanciful if she hadn't read the match report in the next day's paper making the very same point.

Will's own favourite moment was driving the final ball

of the day straight down the ground and not breaking stride until he was clattering up the pavilion's wooden steps, and saw Connie applauding them from her seat. He stopped, doffed his cap and grinned. He and Tam had put on an unbroken stand of 310. That was one in the eye for the committee! In years to come he would look back on this day – as perfect a day's cricket as he had ever had – with a yearning that squeezed on his heart. It was not that he wouldn't play so well again. But it was never to be with Tam as his partner at the other end.

7

Connie heard the meter click on as she continued to gaze out of the cab's window. Slanting needles of rain had just begun spattering across it. Her driver had parked opposite the unfriendly castellated front of Holloway Prison, the blank repetition of its institutional brick a kind of complement to what one imagined were the cheerless routines within. She had received a message from the Vaughan family's lawyer asking her to meet Lily at ten o'clock in the morning at the gates, and felt a flutter of nerves at the prospect of seeing her for the first time in over two months. Connie had written several letters to her in the meantime, and received nothing in reply, a silence due, she hoped, to the constraints of His Majesty's Prisons rather than to her friend's unwillingness to correspond. The authorities forbade prison visits to anyone but family. It was a weekday in the middle of May, and she had been obliged to take time off from the bookshop: 'a sudden illness in the family' was the excuse she had made to her two assistants.

At a quarter past, the door within the gatehouse heaved open, and a woman carrying a suitcase stepped out. Connie strained to make out her features: she was about Lily's height, but something in the colouring and tautness of her skin caused her a brief confusion. Could it be . . . ? She got out of the cab and took a few faltering steps across the road. The woman had put down her case, and was staring vacantly into the middle distance, as if trying to remember how she had come to be standing on this bit of pavement. She didn't seem to be aware of anything at all until Connie was almost in front of her, at which point her eyes swam into focus.

'Lil? It's me,' she said, trying to keep her voice gentle and steady – more difficult than it should have been, for she sensed her face betraying alarmed surprise at Lily's appearance. Her skin was the shade of uncooked dough, dramatically heightening the effect of the faded purple-yellow bruising around her left eye. Her lips were cracked and flaking, and when Connie leaned in to kiss her she smelt something faintly metallic and yeasty on Lily's breath.

'Connie,' was all she said, in a voice quiet enough to suggest a fear of being overheard. Connie intuited an estrangement even in the way she spoke her name. She picked up Lily's suitcase.

'I've got a cab waiting. Let's get you home.'

Lily nodded in spiritless assent, and allowed herself to be led across the road. They stepped into the car, and Connie called the address to the driver. As they sat together, Connie took Lily's hand in her own. She felt something strangely valetudinarian in her friend's demeanour; their separation was beginning to seem more like two years than two months.

'Did you get my letters?' Connie asked her.

Lily nodded, and searched her coat pocket for a moment. She brought out a little bundle of letters, tied with string, which Connie recognised as her own. None of them had been opened. 'They handed them to me this morning – the whole lot.'

'You mean you didn't get to read a single one?'

Lily shook her head, seemingly indifferent to the outrage expressed on her behalf, and stared out of the window.

Connie felt ill at ease. While she feared what prison might have done to Lily, she had still anticipated a wild relief on their being reunited, and perhaps a brave joke from the released prisoner to prove that she was unbroken. The wraithlike creature sitting next to her, however, was very far from reassuring. She had never thought to see her look so frail – so depleted.

'What happened to your eye?'

Lily looked puzzled for a moment, then lightly palpated the bruised skin with her fingers, as if it would help her to remember. 'One of the wardresses was holding me down, and I became . . . agitated. I think it was her elbow.'

It was not just the dark allusion to duress but the neutral tone in which she spoke that shocked Connie. Tears would have been preferable to this hollow-voiced calm.

'So you were on a hunger strike?'

Lily nodded, distantly. 'I think most of us were.'

Connie gave her hand a sympathetic squeeze as an image of tubes inserted into nostrils flashed unbidden across her consciousness. She had read reports of forcible feeding, and the detail contained in them had made her recoil: it seemed almost inconceivable that her own best friend had been subjected to it.

'Are you – all right?' said Connie, sensing the feebleness of the question.

Lily turned from the window to look at her. 'No. But I will be.' The ghost of a smile passed over her face. 'I've got to go to the dentist,' she added, fingering the inside of her mouth. 'They broke a tooth when they were – forcing my mouth open.'

'Oh, Lil . . .' She didn't know what to say after that. The cab had turned off Roman Road. The Vaughan house, on Ellington Street, looked stolidly unsuspecting of the return of its convicted resident. Connie tapped on the driver's window, and the cab pulled to a halt.

Lily hung her head, and said, 'You know that my parents wouldn't visit me the whole time I was there?'

'I suppose they thought it would upset you –'

'They were ashamed,' she said baldly.

'I wish they'd have let *me* visit you.'

Lily nodded thoughtfully, and they got out of the cab. The car's engine must have been overheard, because the front door opened and her mother was coming down the path towards them. Mrs Vaughan's was a bustling stride, suggestive of a comic matron in a Savoy Opera, but now she faltered on seeing her daughter – much as Connie had – and her plump chin began to tremble uncontrollably. But she had none of Connie's tact.

'Oh my good God – what have they *done* to you?' she cried.

'Hullo, Mum,' said Lily by way of reply, and was then swaddled up in her mother's embrace. Connie stood still, caught uncertainly between the roles of friend and witness to a familial scene that excluded her. Mrs Vaughan was clucking about her daughter with tearful endearments, stroking her hair and making the kind of fuss that Connie knew Lily would instinctively resist. But when she touched her friend's arm to signal her leave-taking, the face Lily turned to her was a surprise: her eyes no longer bore the dry, careworn tolerance she had shown in the cab, but a glistening sorrow that was just about to spill over the rims. Her mother's helpless abandon had proven too much. Connie silently raised her hand in goodbye, and bent her steps in the direction of Camden.

Will's reverie was interrupted by the clang of the Priory pavilion's bell. He had his feet up against the iron rail of the players' balcony, from which vantage he now watched Tam and his fellow opener start out to the wicket. He could always spot Tam a mile off from his casual, ambling gait.

The previous week he had watched him pace in rather different circumstances, shouldering the corner of a coffin down the aisle. The vicar conducting the funeral had not known the deceased. Tam's mother had succumbed, in the end, to pneumonia; the stroke of two years ago was the foreshadowing of a death which, he knew, would hit the son hard. Will, invited back to the family home a few miles out of town, found it barely more welcoming than the poky, miserable church they had just left. A relic of Victorian days, the house felt steeped in the crepuscular atmosphere of illness, dust and long-forgotten conversation. The room which was evidently 'kept for best' had been laid out with sandwiches and thimble-sized glasses of sherry, though even these meagre tokens of hospitality seemed to affront the dark, cumbersome furniture and heavy curtains, which stared in cold silence at those murmuring guests who had dared to help themselves. From the paucity of numbers, Will surmised that the late Mrs Tamburlain had either outlived most of her friends or else shed them through neglect.

He felt so unnerved by the melancholy of the old place that he was already rehearsing his excuse to leave when a middle-aged lady, gentle-eyed and diffident-looking, approached him.

'You're Mr Maitland, aren't you? Will?' He smiled and replied in the affirmative, sensing that he had seen her before. She held out her hand. 'I'm Beatrice – Drewy's sister.' It took him a moment to realise that 'Drewy' was Tam. He could not quite take in the fact that Tam's actual name was Andrew.

'I'm very sorry – about your mother,' he said. 'It must have been . . .' Will didn't really know what it must have been, but Beatrice filled in the blank.

'A merciful release. She'd not been able to get about, you know.' She offered this with a meekly apologetic wince. Will knew from Tam that his sister had nursed their mother in the final months, which perhaps explained her prematurely grey hair; he had assumed that she was the younger of the two siblings. She was now in reminiscent mood – '. . . had some happy times when we first moved here. She was an excellent swimmer, even into her sixties.'

Will made a bland remark about the convenient proximity of the sea, and Beatrice gazed towards the window, beyond which the grey line of the Channel could distantly be seen.

'Yes, she and Drewy would sometimes go for a dip when he was visiting from Brighton. I used to sit on the beach and watch them – they seemed able to swim forever. I would see their heads bobbing into the distance.'

'It must be a comfort to have him back here again,' said Will, trying to match her buoyant nostalgia with some optimistic reflection of his own. But now she stooped her head confidentially towards him and lowered her voice.

'He's putting a brave face on it, but it's been . . . dreadfully hard. I'd be very obliged if you'd, you know, buck him up a bit.' She paused, and again came that shy wince of regret. 'He doesn't have that many friends.'

Will, secretly taken aback by this unsolicited disclosure, nodded with emphatic sympathy and said, 'Count on it, Miss – um, Beatrice, I'll look after him.'

She beamed at him. 'I think he'd like to get back to playing, really.'

He had been pondering her words all week. It was now the last Thursday in June, and Tam was returning to the M—shire side a fortnight after his bereavement. Will suspected that his friend's insistence on getting back might have had something to do with the fact that Revill, the stand-in as opening bat, had made a big hundred in his absence. Will was only now beginning to admit to himself that Tam's game was in decline. His hundred on the opening day of the season – happily witnessed by Connie – had been his only major score of the summer. His eye, once snake-quick, was no longer dependable, he was troubled by a persistent knee injury, and his famous big hitting was more often landing in the outfielders' hands than over the ropes. His slow eclipse had caused Will to wonder if his showdown with the committee back in April had been altogether wise. Might it not have been better, after all, if Tam had been gently persuaded to retire rather than allowed to string out another season in pain? For heaven's sake, the man was practically middle-aged! Had he been less loyal to his friend and a little more hard-headed about his waning powers, Will would now be club captain instead of Middlehurst – who had just then plumped himself down on the balcony seat next to him. No word had passed between them on the matter, but a certain guardedness in his manner suggested that Middlehurst knew he had got the appointment by default.

'Maitland,' he said by way of greeting. Will noticed again his discomfortingly pale eyes and the determined jut of his chin; he had heard somewhere that the Middlehurst family owned half of Northamptonshire. They both stared out to the square, where Tam was cautiously seeing off the opening spell. *Please make some runs*, thought Will, *for my sake*. A couple of balls later his prayer seemed to have been heard. Tam had rocked back and slashed a loose one square past gully for four. The crack of the 'Tamburlain Repeater' resounded through the air.

'Shot!' shouted Will over the desultory applause. It was nearing midday, and the ground was still slowly filling.

'Let's hope he can get a few today,' said Middlehurst, looking sidelong at Will, who heard his implication: runs from Tam were overdue.

'He's just had a bad trot,' said Will, shrugging.

'I was sorry to hear about his mother,' he continued. 'They were close, I gather.'

Will only nodded. From his tentative manner he sensed that Middlehurst had something more he wanted to say. A minute or so later he was proven right. 'Odd thing, you know. I happened to be in the Fountain last Thursday, and I saw Tam drinking in the saloon. On his own.'

'No law against that, is there?'

'No, of course not –'

'And he *has* just lost his mother.'

'Yes, I understand,' said Middlehurst quickly, and waited for another broken volley of clapping – the end of an over – to subside. 'But I wonder if you, as his friend . . .' Will sensed what was coming, but a cussedness in him refused to help his interlocutor spit it out. Middlehurst gave a thoughtful sigh. 'I wonder if you'd agree he might be . . . in difficulties. With drink.'

'Difficulties? No, I wouldn't say so,' said Will, trying to keep his tone airy. 'Tam has always liked a beer or two – as do I. It has never impaired his batting.'

Middlehurst squinted in a way that withheld complete agreement. 'You see,' he began slowly, 'I take into account the fact that it's a sociable game, and of course a chap deserves a drink. But when I turn up to nets in the morning and smell alcohol on a man's breath, it inclines me' – his shrug was parsonical – 'to doubt his worth to the team.'

Will's chuckle sounded lighter than he felt. 'I imagine it's from the night before!'

Middlehurst closed his eyes and pinched the top of his nose to indicate he wasn't taken in. 'It won't do, I'm afraid. I cannot have a player – however well regarded – turning up drunk on a match day. It's entirely unprofessional.'

'He's never missed a game, though, has he?' said Will.

'Hardly the point. You know as well as I do that Tamburlain is not pulling his weight. Aside from that ton back in May he hasn't made a score over twenty. Now, either I must talk to him –'

'No – don't do that,' said Will, knowing that Tam would not respond favourably to any expression of authority, and certainly not from someone he regarded as unworthy of the captaincy. 'I'll have a word with him. If he is, as you say, in difficulties, I'll report back to you. But I think your concern is misplaced.'

He gave Middlehurst a tight smile of reassurance. He had absolutely no idea what he would say to Tam, but considered it imperative to let the captain believe he was going to take the matter in hand. A brief silence intervened, broken moments later when a collective shout went up at the wicket: an lbw appeal against Tam. Will helplessly watched the umpire's slow raising of the finger, and Tam, with a little shake of his head, began to walk. By the time he had reached the pavilion steps the scorers had changed the tins on the board: LAST MAN 14. Middlehurst looked round at Will, but said nothing.

Bicycling back to his mother's house after stumps that evening, Will felt at a loss. His volunteering to 'have a word' was not lightly undertaken, for Tam had always been the one he had consulted for advice – his elder and, in ways that mattered, his better. The idea of reversing roles on him seemed not merely impudent: it smacked of disloyalty. But who would do it if not himself? *He doesn't have that many friends.* His sister's observation had been haunting him ever since. Could it possibly be true? The 'Great Tam' was traditionally mobbed by admirers wherever he played; he had only to show his face at a pub in M—shire and someone would be at his side buying him a drink. He was a star, still. Yet only now did it occur to Will that Tam, while seeming to know everyone, was not actually close to anyone. Even he, who *could* call himself a friend, had never visited the family home until Mrs Tamburlain's funeral last week.

In fact, it was not his sole preoccupation at present. He had been wondering if Miss Callaway – Constance – would ever bestir herself to write to him again. He had received one letter from her thanking him for the weekend at Silverton

House and 'that glorious day's cricket' (her own words!) at the Priory, though he couldn't help noticing that she had avoided any mention of his mother. Not that he blamed her. He would wince each time he recalled the frosty matriarchal glare she had directed at Connie over the lunch table. He had written, aware of pressing the correspondence towards absurdity, to thank her for her thank-you letter, and since then – nothing. Now, as he cycled along high-hedged country lanes, past hay carts and the occasional trotting cob, he began to formulate a little scheme that might resolve two problems at once. A family friend, trustee of a gallery in King Street, St James's, had invited him to the private view of a group show – some loose gathering of 'urban realist' painters whom Will had never heard of – and would surely be amenable to his bringing a couple of guests. Remembering now the almost instant congeniality that had flowered between Connie and Tam that afternoon, Will realised he could extend an invitation to her on the pretext of 'bucking up' his recently bereaved friend: a noble and apparently selfless gesture of which Will would be the secret beneficiary. On arriving home he almost flung the bicycle against the wall as he hurried into the house and plucked a sheet of writing paper from the bureau, there to compose a casual (but actually very careful) letter to Miss Callaway.

Her reply was prompt.

Thornhill Crescent, N.

29th June 1912

Dear William,

Thank you for your letter of the 27th inst. I was very sorry to hear of Tam's bereavement – he talked so fondly of his mother during our walk that day. Perhaps you will be good enough to pass on my condolences?

I am obliged to you for your kind invitation to the Beaufort Gallery viewing next month. By cheerful coincidence I happen to have received that same invitation under my own name. An acquaintance of mine is one of the artists to be exhibited there, and he has been most insistent upon my attendance! But this should not preclude my dining with you and Tam afterwards.

Congratulations on your hundred – I read of it in *The Times* today, with great pleasure.

With my best regards,

Constance

It was progress, of a sort. But he paused over the allusion to that acquaintance – *most insistent*, indeed? He didn't care for the idea of any fellow insisting on her company, other than himself. It was a vexing conundrum to Will that the longer the lapse in time since their previous meeting the more alluring did Connie become in his mind's eye. He liked to recall the moment he saw her on the platform at Warwick Square, the expression of wry amusement playing across her features as she detected his anxious scouring of the other arrivals. That was one side of her. But even stronger was the memory of her in the ladies' room at the Savoy just after he had helped clean up her nosebleed. It was that look of alarm in her eyes, at once anguished and luminous, which appealed to his most chivalrous instincts – touched his heart, in truth. He wanted to ensure that she would never get into such a scrape again. Constance. *Constance*. And she had addressed him in her letter as William! It was really too stuffy of him to keep addressing her as 'Miss Callaway'.

Connie loved the garden seat of the motor bus's upper deck. True, not so pleasant when it rained, but during balmier days like this one it provided an incomparable vantage from which to survey the city streets. Her father used to say that the upstairs of a 'bus offered the best theatre in London. It was the chance to watch people unawares that fascinated. The one on which she travelled was just negotiating the evening rush-hour traffic around Regent Street, and the sight of a boatered gent risking his neck to dash across the thoroughfare, of a crossing-sweeper gently patting a cart horse, of a policeman on point duty showing off his repertoire of hand signals, of two elegantly attired ladies poised on the kerb and looking about them, plainly lost – she was beguiled by these fragments of life in simultaneous motion, hurrying on, heedless of one another. How could so many consciousnesses be contained in one world, she wondered, each of them believing themselves to be the centre of the universe?

She stepped off the 'bus just past Piccadilly Circus, and made her way down Jermyn Street. An early-evening sunlight dappled the plane trees in the garden of St James's Square, and she shielded her eyes against the dazzling lozenges of brilliance that were refracted through the leaves. Around the next corner a busy termitary of men in evening dress had formed around the porticoed entrance of a baronial Georgian house: the Beaufort Gallery, she presumed. A taxi pulled up, disgorging a trio of toppered gents with a lady whose bare shoulders were festooned in a dramatic white feather boa. For a moment Connie thought she knew her, but then dismissed the idea. Their social circles would not have overlapped. A residual shyness caused her to hang back while the toffs trooped in; she followed them half a minute later.

Brigstock had advised her to arrive early, and now she saw why. The rooms were already forested with people, their brayingly loud voices floating right up to the cornices. She accepted a glass of wine from a liveried waiter, and wandered upstairs in search of the painter. In the upper gallery she edged her way around another scrum; the walls of this room were mostly hung with dark-toned pictures of music halls and nudes disporting themselves in dingy bedrooms. The Brigstock signature. She had seen little of him since their visit to the music hall back in December. The embarrassing encounter that morning in his flat and his own aptitude for disappearing for months at a time had kept a distance between them, though the invitation to this evening's event had been couched in his familiar friendly way.

She had paused at another cluster of his canvases when her eye was drawn to a small painting of a woman, directly facing the viewer, her head propped against her fist and a faint smile tweaking her mouth. She stared, rapt, at the portrait for some moments. The paint had been applied in Brigstock's loose, free manner, but there could be little doubt as to the identity of the subject. Just then, a shadow at her side interrupted her scrutiny.

'Enjoying the show?' It was Tam, dressed in a sombrely immaculate suit with a pin carefully speared through his plump silk tie. His dark hair was oiled back from his forehead, and his salt-and-pepper moustache trimmed.

'Hullo there,' said Connie, recovering herself. 'I'm sorry, I was just rather absorbed by . . . *this*.' She gestured at the painting of the woman. Tam leaned in to take a closer look, and Connie smelt a musky, sweetish cologne on him. He craned his head round at her, and then back to the portrait. He squinted.

'It's you, isn't it?'

'I think so. He didn't tell me he was . . .'

They both stared at it again in silence. Eventually, Tam drew back, and said with an approving nod, 'He's got your expression just right.'

'D'you think?' she asked, trying not to sound too delighted. He was peering at the signature at the corner of the picture.

'DAB?'

'Denton Brigstock. He lives near to the shop where I work. In Camden.'

Tam nodded, considering. 'He's good. But then, the sitter would have inspired him.'

Connie laughed at his grave gallantry. Then, remembering, she dropped her voice to an undertone. 'I was very sorry to hear about your mother. William told me –'

'Thank you,' he said, bowing. She saw his jaw tighten. 'I thought I was prepared, but these things still . . . give you a shock.'

'I know they do,' she said, fixing on him a look of earnest sympathy. 'I lost my father nearly four years ago, and hardly a day goes by when I don't think of him.' Tam looked down, and Connie felt she had said the wrong thing. After a respectful pause, she continued. 'I did so enjoy that day at the Priory – seeing you and Will make all those runs!'

Tam narrowed his eyes in reminiscence. 'What a day that was. I got to thinking you were a lucky charm for us. The next morning, after you'd gone, I got out in the first over.'

'But still – you'd made about 130 by then.'

'Aye. The one decent score I've made all season.' He shrugged, as though it didn't especially bother him. He plucked fresh drinks for them from a waiter's tray. Connie, sensing the need for cheerfulness, tried a different tack.

'It must be wonderful to earn a living at something one loves. Were you – did you always think you'd be a cricketer?'

'Not really. I liked all kinds of sports as a boy – football, tennis, swimming. Cricket just happened to be the one I was best at. I turned pro when I was eighteen.'

'You must still enjoy it,' said Connie, not sure whether she was asking or encouraging. Tam gazed ahead, and gave a helpless little grimace

'P'raps. But I've no choice in the matter. There's nothing else I can do.'

Connie decided not to enquire about his plans for retirement. She looked about the room, and said, 'Have you seen Will?'

'I left him talking to some fancy-looking types. We could go and look for him,' he said, proffering his arm, which Connie gladly took. As they moved on she noticed one or two of the older men glance at Tam, as if wondering where they might have seen him before. On their way down the balustraded staircase Connie passed within inches of the woman in the white feather boa, whose face, at this different angle, she now recognised. The woman looked right through her.

'Ah, there you are,' called Brigstock, detaching himself from a group of well-wishers. He was dressed in a rakish velvet frock coat Connie had not seen before. He took her gloved hand and raised it to his lips.

'Hullo,' she smiled, inclining her head. 'Allow me to introduce Mr Tamburlain. This is Denton Brigstock.' As the two men shook hands, Connie saw Brigstock's face stiffen with surprise – the first time she could recall such an expression on it.

'*Andrew* Tamburlain? The cricketer?' Tam nodded, and Brigstock blinked furiously, as though his eyes were playing tricks. 'I'm deeply honoured, sir. I had no inkling our little show would bring in a celebrity.'

Tam laughed, in a slightly mechanical way that suggested to Connie he was used to such blandishments. 'I'm honoured to be here,' he replied. 'I've just been admiring your picture of Miss Callaway.'

Brigstock's eyes brightened wickedly as he looked at her. 'Indeed? And does it also please the lady?'

Connie raised her eyebrows ambiguously. 'I'm still reeling from the surprise, to tell the truth – but it *seems* quite well done.'

'Hmm,' said Brigstock, eyeing her archly, 'not exactly the hosanna of praise I was hoping for . . .'

'Give it time,' interposed Tam, and clinked his glass against Brigstock's.

The clamour of the surrounding throng had intensified, and they had to raise their voices to be heard. Connie leaned towards Brigstock and said, 'That lady wearing the white feather boa – d'you know her?'

Brigstock shook his head. 'Ought I to?'

'She's Meredith Foulkes. You've heard of her husband, Greville Foulkes?'

'The MP? The suffragette flogger?'

'The same,' replied Connie, 'and his wife cheers him on from the sidelines – heaven knows why.'

Brigstock shrugged. 'Perhaps in the privacy of the marital chamber she enjoys a spot of flagellation herself.'

At that moment, Will was approaching from the across the room. He had been watching Connie and Tam talk with the frock-coated fellow – an oldish type, who plainly fancied himself a card – and felt rather put out that his latest remark had stirred them to mirth. Connie, still laughing, was now greeting his arrival with a friendly lift of her chin.

'Hullo,' said Will, aware of his mistimed entrance. 'I seem to have missed the punchline . . .'

Connie shook her head, as if to indicate the unimportance of the joke or, worse, his unfitness to appreciate it. Without waiting to be introduced, Will tried to catch the jocular mood with a sally of his own. 'Well, I'm not much of an art critic,' he said, 'but frankly these paintings are a shambles. Never seen such unfathomable daubs!'

As soon as the words were out of his mouth he realised something was wrong, though he couldn't for the life guess what it might be. Tam had averted his eyes; Connie looked simply appalled. The fellow in the frock coat, however, was grinning at him in undisguised delight. Well, at least *he* was showing a sense of humour, thought Will, and seeing that neither Connie nor Tam would introduce him, he thrust out his hand.

'How d'you do? I'm Will Maitland.'

Brigstock, accepting the handshake, replied urbanely, 'How do *you* do? I'm . . .'– he gestured at the walls – 'an unfathomable dauber.'

A beat passed, and Will felt an inward chill that manifested itself in a paradoxically warm blush. *Ah* . . . He looked away, and stuttered out a few words of apology, but Brigstock had taken his faux pas as a glorious joke.

'Don't fret, Mr Maitland. I've always said – to be great is to be misunderstood.'

'And as you admitted, Blue,' Tam added drily, 'you're not much of an art critic.'

Will, embarrassed into silence, would like to have withdrawn at this point, but a chafing curiosity about the painter induced him to stay. Judging from their ease in one another's company, he sensed rather more than acquaintanceship existed between him and Connie. The fellow was old – possibly even older than Tam – but he had austere good looks and an air of chuckling suavity that could find amusement even in a stranger's affront. Talent, too, allegedly – not that Will could discern it. He had made a chump of himself, and Connie's reluctance to catch his eye was a merited reproof. As she continued chatting with the two men, Will was reduced to the role of spectator, bow-tied and tongue-tied. He caught the attention of a waiter ferrying about a tray – he could now feel sweat beading on his neck, the night was that warm – and liberated a bottle of wine from him. Meekly, he began to fill their glasses.

Connie, in fact, was not annoyed with Will. Brigstock had laughed off the insult to his work with characteristic nonchalance – he had seemed genuinely tickled – but it had left Will looking foolish, and she felt for him. She had accepted his offer of more wine and now, out of the corner of her eye, saw him talking to a couple of men who emanated an air of unsmiling self-importance. Then, in an awkward little gavotte, Will shepherded the men forward to be introduced. 'Would you allow me? – Tam, I think you know Lord Daventry, and this is, um, Mr Greville Foulkes . . .'

The name sounded on the air with a convulsive twang, a tiny barometric pressure felt by all but Will, who had not heard of the MP before this evening. Foulkes was a man of about forty, short, stockily built, with tight-curled reddish hair that extended to whiskers; his eyes gleamed marine blue, with a slow, disconcerting droop to the lids. Connie caught Brigstock's look of suppressed, or perhaps antici-pated, hilarity, while Tam, hesitantly polite, had extended his hand. It was Tam they wanted to meet, she could tell, but the proximity of Brigstock and herself now obliged Will to include them in a general introduction.

'. . . and this is Miss Callaway . . .' said Will, still unsus-pecting. Foulkes bowed his head briefly in her direction. After a moment's deliberation she said, in an even voice, 'I notice you have a cane. Do you find it easier to wield than a horsewhip?'

Foulkes jerked his head slightly to take a different angle on her. 'I beg your pardon?'

'Well, according to the newspapers, you've been encour-aging men to horsewhip any woman caught damaging property. I thought you might lead by example.'

'I hardly think this is the time –' began Daventry, but Foulkes raised a tolerant hand to quieten him.

'Regrettably, Miss –?, we live in a time when decent citizens are under attack from militant elements – who do go out armed. So we must in consequence be prepared to defend ourselves.'

'But I'm confused,' said Connie. 'When Nationalist mili-tants in Ireland demand Home Rule, the Liberal Party supports them. Yet when suffragists demand the vote they are thrown into prison and subjected to torture. Can you explain this?' She sensed around her a shocked bemusement that she was bandying words with him – that a 'scene' was being made. Will, she noticed, was frozen to the spot.

'That is *quite* different,' replied Foulkes. 'The women to whom you refer belong to no recognised political party. They are merely a mutinous rabble of individuals. They have no remit to break windows and destroy property. They are criminals, and deserve to be treated as such.'

'Criminals?' cried Connie scornfully. 'What gives you the right to call a woman "criminal" who acts out of the highest ideals of truth and justice?'

Foulkes was shaking his head in a mime of impatience, as if it were useless to argue with this lunatic firebrand. 'Young lady,' he said, 'if by the "highest ideal" you intend to signify the enfranchisement of women, then I can only think prison is the safest place for you.'

Daventry chuckled at that. Will, a bystander up to now, was at last moved to speak. 'I do think this is neither –' The sentence was left uncompleted, for Connie had taken a step forward and dashed the contents of her wine glass directly into Foulkes's face. Time hung suspended for a few moments. Nobody could quite take in what had happened: only Connie looked unfazed by the sight of the doused MP, whose incredulous response ('What in *God's name* –') came out at a volume that turned heads. Deeming her empty glass to be no longer of use, she flung it down where it crashed ecstatically on the tiled floor in front of Daventry, who took a couple of mincing steps back. The noise pushed a little ripple of alarm through the onlookers.

'There's your broken glass,' Connie said, invigorated by the noise. 'Are you going to have me arrested?'

Foulkes, brushing the drops from his cheeks, advanced on her. 'Right after I've dealt with you –' he hissed. Connie expected him to strike her, but Tam had stepped protectively across and was warding off her opponent with his pugilist's bulk. It was convenient that Foulkes reached only to Tam's armpit in height.

'I don't think that's advisable,' was all Tam said to him.

Connie heard Daventry mutter to Will, 'Get that woman out of here, Maitland.' Will, the colour quite drained from his face, shouldered Connie away through the gawping crowd into a side corridor. Once they had gained a private space, he turned on her a look of mingled outrage and disbelief. She had seen that look before, the night they had first met and she had offered him the benefit of her wisdom on his batting.

'What on earth d'you think you're doing?'

'I should think it perfectly clear to you what I'm doing,' she said coolly.

'No. Please explain. All I saw was a chap who'd got on your nerves, so you threw a glass of wine in his face.'

Connie looked at him pityingly. 'That "chap" is the most notorious anti in Parliament. He's also a double-dyed brute who would sooner have women flogged than granted an equal footing with men.'

This only further exasperated Will. 'So what if he is? I fail to see how it could possibly justify making a scene like that. One meets all sorts of men one dislikes, but one doesn't go assaulting them in the middle of a conversation. It's absurd!'

'You don't understand, do you?' said Connie, searching his face. 'Everything has come so easily to you. The privileges you've had, the freedom you've had. This isn't just about being denied a *vote*. You've never known what it is to feel helpless – to feel ignored simply because one isn't a man.'

Will stared back at her. Somewhere, buried deep, he could perceive the justice of her words, could even admire the conviction with which she spoke. But he could not square that with the egregious behaviour he had just witnessed. For a long minute they stood there, gazes unmeeting, until they heard approaching footsteps. It was Brigstock, who stopped and looked from one to the other, seeming to take in the strained silence between them. He removed from his pocket a slim cigarette case and held it open for Connie, who took one, and then for Will, who shook his head. 'I don't, thanks,' he murmured, sensing another apology due to the painter, so quickly after the first: this was his night, after all, and it had come unhappily close to being upstaged. Brigstock, however, was blithe about the recent turbulence.

'I think that should get us a mention in the *Daily Mail*,' he said brightly.

Will, at a loss before such urbanity, said, 'I'm most terribly sorry about this. She didn't know what she was doing –'

'*What?!*' interrupted Connie, not quite believing her ears. 'What did you say? "She" is right in front of you, if you hadn't noticed – and I knew exactly what I was doing. How dare you apologise for me? How *dare* you?' She was now face to face with Will, so close he could feel tiny flecks of spittle feathering his cheek, an involuntary result of her savagely emphatic consonants. Her eyes flashed with cold fury; she looked even more riled than she had been with the MP. Will was so startled he took a step back. He had been trying to help! In appeal he looked to Brigstock, who had tactfully dropped his gaze, as though reluctant to take sides.

'I seem to . . .' Will muttered, and gave up. Farcical to apologise again. He nodded briefly at Brigstock, and with the merest glance at Connie, he walked off. Still fuming, Connie hardly trusted herself to speak.

'May I presume that you'd – like to leave?' asked Brigstock. She nodded, and he held out his arm for her to take. As they traced their steps back through the gallery's main room, she kept her eyes to the floor, though her ears picked up stray voices above the conversational hum ('That's her'). Then they gained the entrance hall, and left the hive of talk buzzing in their wake. Out on the street, where the soft July night was pulling down shadows, Brigstock sighed and took a drag of his cigarette. He allowed himself an abrupt laugh.

'Well, I know whom to invite *next* time I want to create a stir.'

Connie's lips formed a defiant moue. 'I could tell you I'm sorry –'

'– but you would be lying,' he cut in. 'No need, in any case. I wouldn't have missed that for the world . . . though there's one thing I regret.'

'Oh?'

He paused for a moment, looking quite wistful. 'I do wish it had been *red* wine in that glass of yours.'

8

A few days later Connie received in the post a note from Brigstock, to which was appended a scrap of newsprint untidily torn from the *Mail*. His prediction had been correct. Beneath the headline LATEST SUFFRAGETTE ATTACK she read of an incident:

> at the opening night of an exhibition at the Beaufort Gallery in King Street, St James's. Among the invited guests were Lord Ernest Daventry and the Liberal MP Mr Greville Foulkes, whose implacable stance on the female suffrage question has been widely reported. The MP happened to be in the main hall when he was approached by a militant suffragette. Having cried 'Votes for women!' she seized a bottle of wine to discharge over Mr Foulkes's head and then hurled a glass at Lord Daventry. Neither man was seriously injured. By the time the police arrived the assailant, her identity unknown, had fled.

Quite the desperado! Brigstock had written in his flowing cursive. *Forgot to say at the time, but I was very pleased to meet the 'Great Tam' and your other cricketer. Don't be too hard on the young fellow! DAB.* Connie was not inclined to be so forgiving. Each time she recalled Will's behaviour that evening she felt almost faint with anger. At the lunch with his mother, she had already sensed his unease around mention of the cause, but on that occasion he had been trying to protect her. To have apologised as he did to Brigstock, however, on *her* behalf – 'She didn't know what she was doing' – the arrogance of it! But then, she considered, it was not so surprising. William Maitland was at heart a conventionally minded fellow, from a conventionally minded class. Not so different from her own class, in truth, only she had been born with some stray gene of independence that had rendered her wholly unsuited to such a man. She would not play the second-rate, subservient creature he expected a woman to be, and she would absolutely not be someone he felt obliged to apologise for.

Yet the fire of righteous indignation could not wholly cauterise her disappointment. Ever since the encounter at the Savoy back in March there had passed between them a number of those fleeting but unmistakably interested looks that might have been thought to invite – she could not deny it – the possibility of romance. She had remembered liking his face from the very first time they met. It was hard to reconcile that pleasing countenance with his overweening presumption of superiority.

Saturday was always lunchtime closing at the bookshop, and once Connie had cashed up and locked up, she hurriedly bent her steps homewards. Fred, her brother, had returned the night before from a sojourn in Italy with college friends, and the two of them had vaguely discussed the idea of going to watch the final day of Gentlemen vs Players at Lord's. Less than two years her junior, Fred had been the closest companion of Connie's childhood until he disappeared to public school at the age of thirteen, and thence to Cambridge at eighteen. Their relationship was then limited to visits home in the holidays, when Fred would be his unchangingly agreeable self, but those firm bonds that had existed between them – a shared love of cricket and reading, and his curious brotherly deference towards her – were less easily sustained during his long periods of absence. Fred had inherited his father's attractive gregariousness, and it ensured that he was a regular house guest on Continental holidays that would have been quite beyond his own means. It took him away for weeks at a time, so the unusual prospect of his staying at Thornhill Crescent for the rest of the summer strengthened Connie's determination to make the most of it.

It was Fred's laughter she heard first on entering the hall, where a huge bouquet of fresh flowers dominated the sideboard. The mid-July temperature, less scorching than the previous summer, had enabled the family to have lunch in the garden, from where the voices were wafting. Discarding her hat and gloves on the way, she sensed from the somewhat heightened volume that they had guests – a surmise which proved correct on her spying Lionel, loud enough for two, through the open French windows. Olivia's wedding was several weeks away, and as Lionel's presence in the house became more frequent Connie found that she faced the coming event less with dread than resignation. Taking the quite steep steps into the garden, she saw that the far end of the luncheon table, invisible to her from the doors, was occupied by another pale-suited guest, and for a fraction of a second thought it might be one of Fred's swarm of 'chaps' down from Cambridge. As she approached, the man rose, and his shape startlingly resolved itself into Will. He offered his hand with a shyly hopeful smile.

'Hullo,' said Connie, a not quite friendly note of puzzlement in her greeting. Her mother gaily supplied the explanation.

'Mr Maitland called by with those flowers, darling – did you see them?'

'And your mother very kindly allowed me to barge in on lunch,' added Will, clearly embarrassed to have surprised her.

'Oh, please! We're delighted to have you. Constance, we've kept a place for you there,' continued Mrs Callaway. 'Fred, help Constance to the fish, will you?'

Connie sat down next to Fred, who scooped a portion of cold poached trout onto her plate. He nodded over at their guest. 'Mr Maitland's been telling us about your visit to the Priory in May. Three hundred-odd runs in a day!'

She looked to Will, who would not, she knew, have volunteered that information himself. On the subject of his own batting feats he maintained a modest reticence. Olivia, who had no interest in cricket, was nevertheless directing a look of open curiosity at Will.

'You live in London, then, Mr Maitland?' she asked him.

'Yes, part of the time,' Will admitted. 'During the season I tend to stay at my mother's place.'

'Constance told us what a *beautiful* house it is,' Mrs Callaway chimed in.

'We're – very fond of it,' he said, with a meek glance to see if Connie's face registered any favourable memory of her visit, but she was bent over her plate, not catching his eye. He felt once again the liberty he had taken in pitching up, unannounced. 'Will you be holidaying on the south coast this summer?'

'We might have a run down there,' said Olivia grandly, 'though there's so much to do before the wedding.'

Lionel squinted at Will, as though he had recalled something. 'I say, Maitland – that name . . . you're not one of the wine and spirits people, by any chance?'

'I am. The company was started by my grandfather.'

'Doing pretty well, I dare say,' Lionel speculated further, at which Will nodded politely. For an awful moment Connie thought that Lionel might be about to ask him for 'a deal' on the wine for his wedding. She could sense around the table a concerted enthusiasm for Will, whose gift of flowers only she knew had been brought in contrition rather than courtship. His show of interest in the forthcoming nuptials was making Olivia almost purr with approval, and even their mother seemed strangely coquettish in his presence. Will himself, aware that Connie had hardly said a word to him since sitting down, had taken to charming the family instead. Mrs Callaway had perhaps noticed, too, for she now addressed her directly.

'How was it at work, darling?' It secretly annoyed Connie that her mother would never refer to it as 'the shop'. It was always 'at work'.

'Fine,' said Connie, picking a tiny bone out of the fish.

Mrs Callaway turned to Will. 'Constance always loved to be around books,' she said, as if she were offering a courtroom testimonial.

'She used to write them, too,' added Fred. 'D'you remember, Con?' Sniggering laughter followed from Olivia and her mother as they heard the door to a favourite family story creak open. Connie sighed long-sufferingly at the imminent prospect of being teased. Will had leaned forward, head cocked in interest.

'Did you really?'

Before she had time to answer, Olivia had jumped in. 'Oh yes! She got through huge heaps of paper. And when she finished one of these great loose-leafed tomes she would make Fred sit down and listen to her read it out. The poor boy was only about five!'

'I remember rather enjoying them,' Fred said with loyal promptness. 'Though I did used to wonder whether dragons *really* had the power of reason. Or indeed of speech.'

Even Connie couldn't help smiling at that. She thought now of Fred as a boy, his darkly serious eyes staring into the distance as he listened – or seemed to listen – to her youthful epics of storytelling. It was some years after that, when Connie was about fifteen, that Fred had repaid the gift and told her something *she* didn't know. Her curiosity, inflamed by whispered schoolgirl conversations about where babies came from, had prompted her to supplement her small store of physiological facts from close reading of the Bible, Keats and *Adam Bede*, but it was Fred, home from school, who one afternoon during a walk down Upper Street had bluntly recited to her the precise details of the sexual act. It seemed to her that his eagerness to impart the information came not of an instinct to shock but of an excessive wonderment: he wanted to know if Connie could possibly believe it either. She concealed her own surprise at the time, though months, perhaps years, elapsed before she deduced that the procedure Fred had described could be more conveniently practised while lying down.

Lunch was being cleared. Will was talking with Lionel in the warily appraising way that men tend to do on brief acquaintance. Connie carried the remains of the ravaged trout off to the kitchen, where her mother and Mrs Etherington, the cook, were stacking the plates.

'Darling,' said Connie's mother over her shoulder, 'a little parcel arrived for you this morning. I left it on the seat by the telephone.'

Connie went out to the hall and picked up the slim package, but she hadn't started to open it before Olivia came hurrying in after her, her expression lit with conspiratorial excitement. 'What a charmer!' she said, keeping her voice low. 'Nicer than I remembered. And he's absolutely spoony about you!'

'You think so?' said Connie unconcernedly.

Olivia's brow darkened. 'Yes – so please tell, why are you being so stand-offish with him?'

'I wasn't aware of it.'

'He's always looking at you, and you've barely said a

word to the poor man. Just buck up!' She gave Connie's arm a schoolmarmish tap. 'Lionel thinks he's a capital fellow, too.' Nothing could have been less likely to endear a man to Connie than Lionel's approbation, but she held her tongue: like it or not, he would soon be a member of the family. Baffled by this continuing cool, Olivia dipped her head towards Connie's ear. 'You do realise how much he's worth?'

So there it was, thought Connie. The eager, almost fawning attention Olivia and her mother had paid Will, Lionel's impudent enquiry as to the Maitland fortune, and now these whispered exhortations: it all came down to money. Will had it, and Connie, as far as she could tell, was being encouraged to pursue it. But unlike her sister, she revolted at such calculation. If she were to marry at all it would not be for the sake of financial security. She would find a man she loved and who loved her, and once established, at a time of her own choosing, she might consent to marry him. Not before. To explain this, however, would effectively cast Olivia's own rationale in a very poor light; it wouldn't do to impute mercenary motives to her sister, no matter how obvious they appeared.

'I'd rather not discuss this,' said Connie quietly.

Olivia pursed her lips, then said, decidedly, 'I've an idea. I think it would be a friendly thing if you invited Mr Maitland – William – to our wedding.'

Connie blinked in surprise. 'Why? You hardly know him.'

'But *you* know him. And wouldn't it be agreeable to have a man walk you in?'

'Not especially.'

Olivia gave an irritable sigh. 'Just ask him.'

'No,' said Connie, turning away and making for the stairs. She heard Olivia's footsteps tick irritably over the parquet back towards the garden. Once in her bedroom she took out her sewing scissors and cut through the string on her

164

package, revealing a slim white box embossed with the Garrard's marque and the royal warrant. It was itself secured with purple and green ribbons. Intrigued, she untied them and raised the lid: as the light gleamed on it, her instant reaction was delight that someone had given her silver. Only when she plucked it from its cushioned bed of purple velvet did she realise that it wasn't a paperknife, as she first thought. It was a silver brooch in the shape of an arrow, with 'Votes for Women' minutely engraved upon its flight. An ivory-coloured envelope, creamy to the touch, had been inserted with the package, and she read the note inside.

18 Sumner Place, Kensington, SW.

Friday, 19 July 1912

Dear Constance,

News has reached us of your 'sharing a drink' with Mr Foulkes the other night. I need hardly tell you it has roused feelings of admiration and even envy among certain Union members – such a forceful and public rebuke was long overdue. To speak personally, your boldness has been a source of considerable pride to me, for I recall your misgivings as to the efficacy of militant action. But you have splendidly upheld our old motto: *audere est facere*. As a token of my warm regard please accept the enclosed gift, and may it encourage you to higher degrees of daring in this great cause of ours.

Believe me, very affectionately yours,
Marianne Garnett

A postscript appended the address of a hotel in Belgravia, and a date in September on which a deputation of the WSPU were planning to assemble. It did not require any great intuition on Connie's part that another campaign was about to be launched. She looked at the date again: three days after Olivia's wedding. As she gazed at the slim shaft of silver, she considered Marianne's letter. On the one hand, she felt a pleasurable glow in having won the respect of a woman whom she personally revered; this heroine of independent womanhood had taken the time to write, warmly, *affectionately* – to her. On the other, she detected the sly hand of opportunism steering her, somewhat against her will. Connie did indeed have 'misgivings', not just over the efficacy of militant tactics but over the morality, and, if she were being honest with herself, they had not been resolved. Marianne's blandishments hid an agenda: her expressed delight in Connie's boldness subtly implied that the Union had won a new recruit, one who would moreover be moved to 'higher degrees of daring'. Tipping a glass of wine over an MP was a beginning; now she would have to take a step up to breaking windows and risking imprisonment. But was she ready to do that?

Below she heard laughter and the clink of china in the garden. She went to her window and looked down, where Olivia was just depositing a pot of coffee on the lunch table, while the men yarned on among themselves. Fred, she noticed, had a cigar in blast. She watched as Olivia seated herself next to Will, his body weight shifting around towards her in an accommodating effort of politeness. There was something so appealing about good manners, she thought, particularly in men, from whom she expected very little. Her father, while not ill-mannered, had been domineering, and was apt to put people on the spot – a consequence, she supposed, of the frantic pace of business in the City. Fred, less worldly than his father, was sometimes thoughtless, but he had an unaffected geniality that was more cherishable than social forms. There was about him an air of wanting nothing more than to enjoy the company of whomever he was with. As for Will, he *did* have beautiful manners, she had to concede; it was the reason he had been a hit this afternoon. She didn't wonder that Olivia and her mother suddenly had her matrimonial eligibility in view. More fluttery laughter drifted up from below. She could only imagine their commotion on discovering what had prompted the gift of the brooch she now weighed in her hand, and the identity of the sender.

Her mother was calling her. Hiding the box and its gift in a drawer, she descended the stairs and walked through to the garden. As she approached the table she saw Olivia vacate the chair next to Will, thus obliging Connie to take it. Had he noticed that they were being forced together? In fact, all that bothered Will was not being able to talk privately with Connie. He would have endured another half-hour of Lionel's droning monologues if she would only favour him with a look of – what? Forgiveness, he supposed. Yet his mood consisted in more than simple penitence. Smarting from her furious outburst at the Beaufort, he had tried to convince himself in the following days that she was half mad, unstable, absolutely to be avoided. And then he had woken one morning to a palpitating sense of alarm that he might never see her again. This in turn compelled him to acknowledge the possibility that he was – it seemed preposterous – growing attached to her.

Connie, stirring cream into her coffee, glanced surreptitiously at her watch. It was nearly three, too late for a trip to the Gentlemen vs Players match. The letter from Marianne was making her feel skittish. She had to get out and walk.

'I have an errand to run,' she said to her mother.

'Oh . . . can it not wait?'

'No. I promised to call on Lily this afternoon.'

She heard Olivia click her tongue in exasperation, but didn't say anything.

'Your friend – lives nearby?' asked Will.

Connie nodded. 'A ten-minute walk.'

'I wonder if you'd allow me to accompany you – some of the way?'

Softened by the meekness of his request, she said, 'As you wish.'

'I can come too, if you like,' said Fred innocently. Connie caught Olivia's flint-eyed look of warning at their brother, who took the hint. 'Or not . . .' he shrugged.

A few minutes later Connie was coming down the stairs from her room, where she had retrieved her navy cloche and gloves, and saw Olivia and her mother almost simpering over Will in anticipation of his departure.

'*So* nice to meet you again,' trilled Mrs Callaway, 'and thank you for those beautiful flowers!'

She then overheard Olivia say, 'I look forward to seeing you at the wedding.'

'That's very kind of you,' said Will, with a nervous glance at Connie – he could tell that the invitation was not at her prompting.

Out on the street they walked for about a minute in awkward silence. Connie looked straight ahead, satisfied that the conversational onus rested upon Will for imposing his company on her. He cleared his throat at last.

'I hope you liked the flowers. They were meant as an apology.'

'I did. Thank you for them.'

'So may I venture to hope that I am . . . forgiven?'

Connie kept walking. After some moments' delay, she said, 'In truth, I'm quite surprised by the question. When we last met you took so very decided a view of my behaviour. First you were indignant against me, then you condescended to make excuses for me. Which of these two do you wish to apologise for?'

Will compressed his lips, then said, 'Both. I was wrong on both counts. And that's why I called, to ask your pardon.'

Connie stopped, and turned to look at him. Her gaze was so disarmingly candid that he bowed his head.

'Well, if you mean it . . .' she said. They were standing by a row of shops on Roman Road, and over his shoulder Connie saw a little bakery she occasionally visited for treats. She knew that Lily would love a cake. 'Would you mind waiting here a moment?'

As she hurried over to the shop Will followed her at a distance. Coming to a halt on the pavement where he could see her through the window, he was rewarded when she turned her head and, spotting him there on the other side, proffered a smile. At last! He continued to watch as she handed her money over the counter, picked up her purchase and walked back out, swinging two neat striped boxes on a string. 'For you,' she said, handing one of them to Will with an arching of her eyebrows. Will peeked inside the box: it was a jam tart. 'They didn't have any humble pie, I'm afraid,' she added. Now it was his turn to smile.

'Much obliged,' he said with a little bow. They walked on, listening to the leaves of drooping sycamores shiver beneath the light breeze. Connie, with a sidelong look, said, 'So . . . you've been invited to the wedding.'

Will did not hear enthusiasm in her tone. 'I wasn't angling for an invitation, I assure you,' he said. 'Your sister rather took me by surprise.'

Connie nodded slowly. 'Well . . . you've probably earned it, what with having to listen to Lionel the whole lunch.'

These last words, delivered in an eerily accurate imitation of Lionel's nasal drawl, caused Will almost to yelp with laughter. 'I take it you aren't thrilled by the prospect of your brother-in-law.'

'Do you blame me? I've never known a man so enchanted by the sound of his own voice. Olivia is only –' She stopped herself. However much she believed it, it would be indiscreet, not to say grossly disloyal, to put it about that her sister was marrying for money. Nobody would emerge from such gossip looking well, including the gossip-monger. Will sensed something withheld, but didn't press her.

'The heart has its reasons,' he shrugged, attempting a note of airy indulgence. 'And I'm sure you'll be happy for your sister on the day.'

'Of course,' said Connie. 'Don't worry, I'll be all sweetness and light.'

By now they had turned into Arundel Square. A carriage drawn by two horses rattled past them as they walked, prompting Connie to muse aloud.

'D'you ever wonder what they'll do with all the horses? I mean, with so many motor buses and cars nowadays, one sees fewer and fewer of them on the street. Will they simply be – retired?'

Will hadn't really considered the equine life after obsolescence, but now that he did, he envisaged a somewhat darker fate than retirement awaiting them. He said, 'I'm not sure. Perhaps they'll find something useful for them to do. In the country?'

Connie half smiled at his vagueness, though she felt sad about the horses' gradual disappearance; it was hard to imagine the roads without the castanet rhythm of hooves any more. The advent of something useful always seemed to entail the loss of something cherished. Her steps had slowed as they approached the Vaughan residence. Will, experiencing a lurch of regret at their imminent parting, felt moved to keep her a few moments longer, but couldn't think of a suitable diversion.

'This is Lil's house,' she said with a valedictory air.

'Ah. She's recovered, I hope?'

'I think so. She was quite ill in the weeks after her release, but . . . getting back to her old self.'

Will nodded seriously, as if he were a doctor digesting the latest news about a troubled patient. 'I'm glad. Well . . .

goodbye, Constance.' He felt himself blush on seeing Connie's flinch of surprise.

'I don't think I've ever heard you call me by my name before.'

'Would you prefer "Miss Callaway?"' he said anxiously.

Connie smiled. 'No. I asked you to call me Constance that day at the Savoy. But I couldn't *keep on* telling you.'

'Sorry. It's just that I'm rather slow to – absorb things.'

They shook hands, and with another exchange of smiles, took their leave of one other.

Brigstock held the door open for Connie, and she entered the saloon bar at the back of the pub. It was a gloomy high-ceilinged place just off Whitechapel Road, with sawdust scattered on the floor. Even in the dim glow of the gaslight, she could tell within seconds that this was a haunt of the less privileged classes; a few women, shawls about their shoulders, deep in conversation, one of them smoking a clay pipe; the rest were men, attired in dun-coloured jackets, collarless shirts and caps, wearied by their day's labour and now nursing their reward in pints of dark ale and bitter-smelling tobacco.

'I dare say you'll welcome a drink after that,' said Brigstock, shouldering up to the bar. They had come away from the operating theatre of the London Hospital on Whitechapel Road, where Connie had just witnessed her first ever surgical procedure. While she watched the surgeon, Mr Cluett, make busy with his scalpel and scissors and clamps, Brigstock looked about the theatre with his air of abstracted concentration, making sketches of the raked seating, the staring faces of the medical students, and the little knot of activity centred upon the operating table. Apart from Cluett's occasional muttered instruction, the only sound to be heard in the room was the hiss of the gas jets.

Settled at a table with their gins, Connie fished out a

Sullivan from her packet and accepted a light from Brigstock. She blew the first plumes down her nose.

'Well! A profitable few hours?' he asked.

'It was . . . instructive,' she said. 'The surgery was fascinating, from what I could see of it. But I was alarmed by the standard of hygiene.' She had noticed that one assistant, apparently in charge of Cluett's instruments, sometimes sucked the thread before inserting it in the needles, and then handing them to the surgeon. 'One would have thought Lister's teaching had been heeded by now.'

'But you found none of it – upsetting? Those gouts of blood?'

Connie gave a small twisted half-smile. 'I was too absorbed in it to be upset. Do you really think us women so terribly squeamish?'

'Not in my experience,' said Brigstock. 'And I suppose I ought to have known *you'd* not quail. Been cornering any MPs lately?'

She shook her head. 'How are sales going at the gallery?'

'Capital, since you ask. Three-quarters of my lot have been bought.'

'Congratulations,' said Connie warmly. 'I wonder, did that little painting of me . . .'

'Get sold? No, it didn't,' he said, waiting to see if her face betrayed offence. 'Though I had a few offers for it – good ones, actually.'

'Oh?'

There was a faint sadness in his smile. 'I couldn't bear to part with it.'

A few moments later the saloon door opened and Cluett himself entered, as previously arranged with Brigstock. The latter hailed his friend, who joined them at the table. He was tall, heavily bearded, with a noticeable stoop exacerbated by the demands of his profession, though in his placid grey eyes and casual manner one couldn't have discerned any hint of his power over life and death. Cluett bowed neutrally to Connie when Brigstock introduced her, then pointed to the portfolio of sketches resting by the artist's chair.

'Did you get what you needed?' he asked in his deep lugubrious voice. For answer, Brigstock took up the case with its blunted edges and untied the black silk cords that secured it. Pulling out five or six sketches of the surgeon's workplace, he passed them over to Cluett, who eyed each one impassively before handing them back without comment.

'As you see,' Brigstock drily explained to Connie, 'Cluett is one of my most ardent admirers.'

Cluett rocked forward in a mime of silent, straight-faced laughter. Connie sensed that these two had been friends for many years. Once Brigstock went off to the bar, Cluett turned to her with a look of distant enquiry.

'So – how long have you known old Dab?'

'Oh, not that long,' she said, amused at the mention of his nickname. There was a pause while Cluett rummaged around for more small talk.

'Hope he's been treating you well.'

Not sure of his meaning, she said, 'Erm, perfectly well, thank you.'

He nodded bleakly, as if he'd heard the same answer often before. 'Been at the modelling game long?'

'I beg your pardon?'

He perhaps heard something genteel in her tone, for he now looked confused. 'You're one of his models, yes?' At that moment Brigstock returned to the table, and over-hearing his friend's question, gave out a long-suffering sigh.

'Good heavens, Henry! Not every woman of my acquaintance is a model. Constance is the budding student I told you about – a first-rate mind, prevented from studying medicine by an untimely financial misfortune. I invited her for the purpose of fieldwork.'

'Oh,' said Cluett. 'I didn't expect someone – so young. Pardon me.' Connie sensed in him a sudden coming to attention, as if she had been mistakenly dismissed and now had to be reappraised; and in the next instant realised that 'model' was quite possibly his codeword for 'mistress'.

'I did a year at the London School of Medicine,' Connie explained, 'but my mother had to put my brother through Cambridge.' She had been careful not to resent this, though she sometimes wondered at the tacit assumption that Fred's education took precedence over hers. Cluett asked her what she had read, and Connie reeled off the titles of some medical textbooks.

'You're familiar with *Surgical Applied Anatomy*?' he said.
'Of course.'

'That should be your guide. It contains everything you need.' There was a pause as he narrowed his gaze. 'Why do you think you could be a surgeon?'

Connie heard the challenge in his voice. 'I can't be sure until I try,' she said, 'but I'm as clever as most of the college men I know, I learn quickly and I have steady hands.'

'You sew, I presume?'

'I do. This dress that I'm wearing, I made myself.'

Cluett glanced at Brigstock, as if to say, hark at this one. He considered her for a few moments. 'Would you be able to tell me what operation I performed just now?'

'It looked like – an excision of the tongue?'

He nodded, then said, 'And could you perhaps explain the pathology?'

'I would hazard that it was some form of wasting disease that had attacked the jaw and mouth. Given the number of match factories in this area, perhaps an occurrence of phosphorous necrosis?'

'Good Lord,' Cluett murmured, and from his blink of surprise she knew she had guessed right. Brigstock filled the silence between them.

'I warned you, Henry. Sharp as a tack, this one.'

Cluett raised his eyebrows in acknowledgement, then looked shrewdly at Connie. 'I regret to say that it will be a more arduous journey for you, as a woman . . .'

'I have no illusions in that regard.'

'Surgery is a profession – one of many, no doubt – that barely takes women into account. But I know one or two institutions that offer training. With your leave, I could make enquiries.'

'That would be very kind,' said Connie, wondering how reliable such an offer might be. He had no need to help her, after all – few men did.

Lights were beginning to glimmer on Whitechapel Road by the time they emerged from the pub. As Connie accepted Cluett's hand, he held hers for a moment longer to examine. With a thoughtful look, he said, 'What a surgeon requires in his hands – the delicacy of a lacemaker, and the grip of a seaman. Goodbye, Miss Callaway. I hope we'll meet again.' Hat raised, he turned and crossed the road back towards the hospital.

Brigstock accompanied her on the 'bus towards Islington. 'Good man, Cluett. He studied under Treves, you know – the King's surgeon. He's quite enlightened, for a medical fellow.'

'It was kind of him to – take an interest.'

'Hmm. I think you rather intrigued him,' he said, adding slyly, 'no surprise there, of course. And talking of enlightened fellows, how's your young cricketer? Has he stopped *apologising* yet?'

Connie smiled wryly. 'He's been contrite. My sister was so taken with him she invited him to her wedding.'

'Ah, well. I like a fellow who can admit he's wrong – it shows humility.'

'He was very wrong about your paintings, as I remember.'

'Ha! That was priceless, wasn't it? There's a gallery in Paris eager to put on a show of mine. You can tell your young man I'm considering his words for a title – *Unfathomable Daubs!*'

'That's twice you've referred to him as "my" young man. May I assure you – he's nothing of the sort.'

Brigstock responded with a slow, ironic nod of acquiescence that Connie found rather maddening. She turned her face to the window, determined not to rise to his bait. The 'bus was passing over Holborn Viaduct, thronged at this hour by office workers on their way home. After a while, Brigstock spoke again, in his familiar musing way. 'In any event, I do hope you'll come and visit.'

'Visit where?' she asked.

'Why, Paris! I'll be moving my studio there while I prepare for this exhibition.'

'How long do you intend to be gone?'

'At least six months,' he said casually. 'Possibly longer.'

'I see,' said Connie. Though she encountered Brigstock at only irregular intervals, it was a strange source of comfort to her to know that he was in London. She had always felt him to be on her side. For a moment she was tempted to say so, but then, with a quick glance, noticed him gazing interestedly at a young woman seated opposite them, and the urge to confide withered on her tongue. No doubt he would find plenty more to absorb his eye in Paris. 'You set off – soon?'

Brigstock, interrupted, looked round at her. 'Hmm? Oh, in a week or so, once my digs there have been settled. You know, the devil of it is –' an expression of amused regret was legible on his face '– you're the one person in this city I'm actually going to miss.'

Connie returned his look, but said nothing. The painter merrily beguiled the remainder of their journey with talk of his plans. At the junction of Pentonville Road and

Caledonian Road he jumped up in a sudden show of decisiveness, kissed Connie's hand in farewell and alighted
from the 'bus. She watched his lean figure recede and
disappear into the crowds.

9

Will knew something was wrong the moment he walked into the pavilion at stumps. He had had a good last hour at the crease, pushing on to eighty-odd and saving a match that might have been lost. The Priory had looked especially beautiful in the late-August light, with the pavilion brick a soft rose colour against the waning sun and the shadows closing in around the ground. While M—shire's bid for the County Championship had been knocked off course with three defeats in July, Will at least could look back on another season of achievement. He had scored steadily all summer, and would again top the club's batting averages by a distance.

Once inside the dressing room, however, he sensed no great relief that the game had been drawn. Instead, the handful of players sitting around looked as though they'd just had their match fee docked. Then he noticed a long crack running down one of the large back windows. At that moment, a raw-boned young bowler named Cadell sidled in, and on seeing Will, said, 'Smashing knock, that, Maits.'

Looking about the room, Will said, 'What's wrong? Where's Tam – and Middlehurst?'

'You haven't heard? They had the most fearful row.' This was baffling: Tam had at last managed to make a fifty, and Will, on his way out to the square, had congratulated him as they crossed. All had seemed well. Cadell continued: 'Middlehurst comes into the room and starts moaning, says Tam should have batted on and not thrown his wicket away. Well, Tam didn't like that at all, and proceeds to tell Middlehurst exactly what he thinks of him – in some pretty ripe language, too. Then it got quite out of hand, I couldn't follow everything that was said, but it ended with Tam hurling his bat across the room. And, as you see, that window got the worst of it.'

'So where are they now?'

Cadell shrugged. 'I think Middlehurst is sulking in the committee room – like Achilles in his tent. Don't know about Tam.'

Will packed away his kit and, carefully avoiding the committee room, went to retrieve his bicycle from the shed. Ten minutes later he was cycling down the Parade, and, obeying an intuition that Tam would avoid the Fountain, a rowdy pub favoured by the other players, he turned up London Road and made for the Durham Arms, one of the haunts where his friend was less likely to be recognised. There was no sign of him in the lounge, but on passing through to the saloon he discerned the familiar outline of his back, hunched over the bar. He pulled up a wooden stool and joined him there.

'How many windows *have* you broken in your time?' said Will, keeping his voice light. Tam turned his head, and acknowledged Will's drollery with a rueful snort. Then, with an indifferent flutter of his hand he invited him to have a drink.

'A beer, but no chaser, thanks.' He suspected Tam was on his second or perhaps third of the evening. A table of locals were carousing at the other end of the bar. Tam stared at them while the barman pulled their pints. Will sensed a need to tread softly.

'Some innings, today. Vintage Tamburlain, I thought.'

Tam's expression remained morose. 'Not everyone was so appreciative.'

'You shouldn't allow Middlehurst to bother you.'

'He had the nerve to claim I threw my wicket away. Another couple of yards and that ball would have been over the ropes.' Tam had been caught at deep square leg by a fielder who had only just been posted there.

'It was desperate luck. But you'd got your fifty at least.'

More booming laughter sounded from the far end. Tam turned again and stared, then called down to the coven of drinkers. 'Keep it down, would you?' It was not a friendly request. Will had noticed of late that Tam was becoming intolerant of noise. The drinkers, briefly silenced, fell to muttering.

'Anyway,' said Will, keen to divert his friend, 'as you once said to me, talent is luck. You just have to wait for it to turn –'

'Hmm. At my age the wait gets longer and longer.'

'How's the knee feeling, by the way?'

'Like it's on fire.' He shook his head and, perhaps hearing his own glumness, half smiled at Will. 'Don't ever get old, Blue – not if you're a sportsman.'

The affable set of his mouth vanished as another mad hoot of laughter echoed from along the bar. It was followed by stifled sniggers as a couple of the locals looked round in mock apprehension of their disapproving neighbour.

'Just ignore them,' said Will quietly, but his words found no heeding ear. Tam had stood up, and was taking heavy but purposeful steps towards them. Will's heart sank; he seemed increasingly to find himself in the company of people spoiling for a fight. There were four of them, flat-capped working men, house painters by the look of their smudged overalls; one of them, a stocky bantam, rose to face the wide-shouldered presence suddenly looming over them.

'I asked you to keep it down,' said Tam.

'We 'eard you,' said the bantam. 'We got as much right to drink 'ere as you.' He sounded much too cocky to Will's ears.

'It's not the drinking that bothers me. It's the noise you're making.'

'Oh. Sorry, I'm sure. Maybe you want to take this outside?'

'No need,' said Tam, who had imperceptibly altered his stance in a way that enabled him to send his fist flying arrow-straight at the man's face. It connected with an explosive smack. For a fraction of a second the man stood, as if amazed at its impact, before he crumpled back over the table; glasses crashed to the floor and chair legs screeched sharply as his fellow drinkers hauled themselves out of the way. Will examined their reaction: one of them seemed about to offer a fight, but shrewdly perceived that a man who could throw a punch with that kind of strength and speed was perhaps best left alone. Instead he turned to help his stricken mate off the floor. The latter's nose looked like a squashed strawberry.

The publican had come from behind the bar, his jowls quivering with indignation. He had started ranting, and was wagging his finger so close to Tam's face that Will, for the man's own safety, stepped in between them.

'It's all right,' he said, holding out his palms in conciliatory fashion, 'we're just leaving.' He began gently to shoulder Tam out of the fight's immediate blast area, glass tinkling beneath their feet.

'You'll pay for them breakages, 'n' all!'

Will put his hand in his pocket and fished out a sovereign, flipping it onto the bar counter. The publican seemed in no way appeased. 'Fuckin' 'ooligan! You come in 'ere again an' I'm callin' the pleece.'

Tam, stung by this, began to push past Will, muttering, 'Not if I break your fucking neck you won't . . .' The man flinched and took a step backwards, like one who had been baiting a bear and fatally miscalculated the reach of its chain. Will, fearful of catching a roundhouse himself, nevertheless clung to Tam's arm, dragging against his forward momentum and repeating, almost crooning, his friend's name in a tone of entreaty. Tam stopped suddenly and thrust his livid, glowering face at Will's, so close Will could see the tiny broken capillaries of his mottled complexion and smell the downdraught of his drinker's breath. In his eyes gleamed a terrible disgust, at what was unclear. With a brusque jerk he shook off Will's restraining hand, and, taking a few slow steps back, he turned and pushed out through the saloon's swing door.

Wheeling his bicycle down the slope of London Road, Will followed at a distance, reckoning that Tam should have some time on his own to calm down. The early-evening warmth was touched with an eager little bluster coming up off the sea. Gulls wheeled over the front calling plaintively, each to each. Tam's hulking figure could be seen crossing the Parade and ambling alongside the rails of the esplanade. Then it disappeared as he took the wide steps down onto the beach, where the last few stragglers were packing up for home. The bathing huts had been hauled up and parked beneath the wall; some fishermen were fixing their nets for tomorrow. Tam slowed as he approached the point where a jagged corridor of coarse grey sand had opened up between the shingle and the sea. Across the horizon a soft blue sky had melted into blushing-pink striations, and the melancholy sun was withdrawing by reluctant degrees. Will, at the foot of the steps, stood watching the motionless figure staring out to sea.

Although Tam glanced behind on hearing footsteps crunch over the pebbles, he said nothing. He continued gazing out, listening to the surf as it fizzed and seethed over the sand then slid back again. In the distance the head of a solitary swimmer rose and dropped on the grey-blue swell.

Will began, 'Your sister said you used to swim right out there – you and your mother both.'

'She told you that?' His voice was mild, musing. The violence in the pub might have been a lifetime ago. 'I still love listening to the waves – last thing at night 'fore you drop off to sleep. Every other sound just gets on my nerves.'

Will, trying to brighten his mood, cast about for another exception. 'Come on. What about . . . the sound of a woman's voice?'

Tam looked at him curiously, as if there were some ulterior meaning in the suggestion. When he realised that Will had meant it quite innocently, he said, 'That would depend on the woman . . .'

Another silence lengthened, until Will casually nodded towards the horizon. 'There's a proper Turner sunset, don't you think?'

Tam didn't reply. To judge from his thousand-yard stare he seemed to be ruminating on something else, and after a long delay he spoke. 'You oughtn't to have done it. Really you oughtn't.'

'Done what?' asked Will, though he all but knew what.

'Fallen on your sword. Not for me. I knew it near for certain, soon as I heard you hadn't got the captaincy. If I'd known what you were –'

'What makes you think I did?' said Will, feigning ignorance.

'Please don't pretend,' Tam said quietly. 'I only wish it hadn't been Middlehurst. That superior look as he told me – "You're only playing because of Maitland" . . .'

'Tam, I'm sorry. I just couldn't captain a side that would treat you like that. You know I'd rather watch you make twenty than anyone else make a hundred.'

A little smile twitched beneath Tam's moustache. 'It was a loyal thing to do. But maybe not a wise one.'

Will wasn't sure about it either, but saw no use in lamenting his quixotic behaviour. He had gambled with the committee to secure another season for his friend, and won – for what? Now that the cat was out of the bag, he couldn't even enjoy the satisfaction of his sacrifice; indeed, it seemed he was being rebuked for it again. Tam, as if overhearing these thoughts, said with a chuckle, 'Sometimes you can't do right for doing bloody wrong. You're a good man, Blue, you stuck by a friend. Too bad I couldn't repay you. But they'll make you captain one day. I'm only sorry I won't be there to see it.'

'What d'you mean?' said Will.

'Well, this time I'll walk before I'm given out. I won't give them the pleasure of sacking me. We've one match left – after that, I'm gone.'

'To play somewhere else?'

Tam shook his head. 'The game's up. I should probably have called time a couple of years back, but I couldn't bear to. Pride, I suppose.'

'But another club will sign you up in a trice.'

'P'raps. But I could only enjoy it if I were making runs. There's no good in fooling myself – the eye isn't there any more.'

The dying rays of the sun had baked the waves to a molten gold. Will had a sudden intuition that this scene would be imprinted on his consciousness forever: the wobbling sun, the pink-hued sky, the platinum glint of the sea, these he would recall as the moment Tam announced his retirement. There must have been an expression close to shock on his face, because he now heard Tam's flat, dry chuckle.

'Look at you. It's like someone's died.'

'Sorry. It's just – hard to believe –' Will was struggling to command his voice, so heavy was his heart. The truth was, it *did* feel a little like a bereavement. Once the sun had set on a great sportsman's career it seemed, eerily, that the life itself was over, too. The wind off the sea was making his shirt ripple, and he felt a sudden shiver. They started to walk back along the beach. From the Pier they could hear the distant oompah sounds of a brass band tuning up. Tam stopped for a moment to light a cigar, and Will caught a noseful of its charred aroma in the breeze.

'What will you do?' he said suddenly. 'I mean, what are your plans?'

Tam exhaled a fiery cloud of smoke, and shrugged. 'Haven't made any. I'll write a resignation letter to the committee tomorrow, and then – who knows?'

'Well, there'll have to be a testimonial, of course. And a dinner, a slap-up dinner . . .'

Tam nodded, though he seemed hardly enthused by the prospect. 'I was thinking, p'raps, of a little fishing, the first Saturday after the season ends. We could hire a boat, if you like.'

'Capital idea,' cried Will, whose face fell the next moment on recalling a prior engagement. 'Dash it – I can't, I'm afraid. There's a wedding in London I've been invited to. Miss Callaway – Constance, I should say – well, her sister's to be married.'

'Ah, Miss Callaway,' said Tam, thoughtfully. 'So you're back on friendly terms?'

'It would seem so. I had to grovel rather, but she forgave me in the end. Wilful girl, that.'

'She's got strength of character,' said Tam, seeming to endorse his judgement yet subtly correcting it.

'To tell the truth,' said Will shyly, 'I've grown awfully fond of her.' The phrase sounded inadequate to his own ears – 'fondness' wasn't telling the truth of it at all.

Tam stared at him for a few moments, then said, 'And does she return this feeling?'

Will puffed out his cheeks. 'I hardly know. Most of the time we get along quite amicably . . . but if the conversation turns to a woman's rights, or whatever, you have to play pretty much on the back foot.'

'Ah . . .'

'I mean, you saw her that night at the gallery,' Will said, with an air of clinching the matter.

'D'you not admire her pluck?'

'Well, yes, I suppose so. But that sort of behaviour, it's dangerous – for *her*, I mean. I don't care a rap for the fellow she soaked.'

They had mounted the steps to the esplanade and were now heading towards the centre of town. Will talked on dreamily about Connie, until he noticed how quiet Tam had become.

'Sorry, old chap. Here I am jawing on . . . Look, why don't you come back for dinner? My mother would be glad to see you.'

Tam shook his head absently. 'Thanks, but – I said I'd call on Beatrice.' His words had the ring of a carelessly improvised excuse, and Will thought better of pressing the invitation. The dusk light was turning grainy as they reached the end of the Parade. They parted with a handshake and Will was heading towards the tram stop until he suddenly remembered his bicycle, parked up on the front. Having doubled back he was hurrying along the Parade when, out of the corner of his eye, he spotted Tam sitting on a bench facing away from the sea. His head hung down, and he was staring fixedly at his joined hands, as though in prayer. If he had looked up he would have seen his recent companion walking past, but he did not. Will was tempted for a moment to cross over and interrupt Tam's solitude, but then felt daunted by the sadness of it. *He doesn't have that many friends*. Will wished he'd never heard that line, because now he couldn't get it out of his head.

*　　*　　*

Connie could not have been less beguiled by the wedding ceremony. From the moment the church organ vigorously pealed out *Die Meistersinger*, she had tried to settle herself into a trance of dispassion from which she could watch the proceedings unfold. It was not providing a very reliable screen against reality. She had kept telling herself that it was Olivia's day, that the groom had been willingly chosen, that their match might prove to be as felicitous as any other. Fred had slow-marched Olivia up the aisle with a sweetly nervous air of propriety, but Connie had only to think of whose place her brother, perforce, was occupying and a hot tear welled in her eye. How dearly she wished their father were alive today. Would a man of Lionel's narrow character and plump self-importance ever have survived the humorous scrutiny of Donald Callaway, or dared to ask him for his daughter's hand? She thought not. However wedded to the ideas of prosperity and security Olivia might have been, Connie imagined that a bracing dose of their father's plain talking would have withered Lionel's prospects on the spot: he would have seen right through him. Too late, too late.

She found that this line of thought was upsetting her, and decided to concentrate her gaze on the trio of young cousins – Alice, Jecca, Flora – sporting bridesmaids' veils and myrtle wreaths. Their exuberant scattering of rose petals along the aisle had provoked a little pant of laughter from Connie's aching throat. Next to her, she felt her mother's tense monitoring of the wedding service, like a circus spectator hypnotised by the precise step of a high-wire artist. The officiating cleric droned on over the obedient heads of the bride and groom. During one of the hymns, Connie cast a glance back through the forest of congregants in search of her cousin Louis. He was three or four rows behind her, unnoticingly roaring out the words; but she felt a little jolt of pleasure on seeing his neighbour, Will, who hoisted his eyebrows in silent communion. She smiled in reply, then returned her attention to the nuptial inevitabilities.

Will spotted the glistening in Connie's eyes and ascribed it to an onrush of sisterly affection. He had arrived at St Andrew's, the parish church in Thornhill Square, with the helpless air of an intruder, and spent some awkward minutes loitering in the churchyard pretending to be absorbed by the inscriptions on the lichen-coated gravestones. Relief came on hearing a voice hail him from across the way.

'Fancy seeing you here!' cried Louis, his friendliness carrying a note of enquiry. They had not seen one another since their encounter at the Priory the previous summer. Will shook hands, and gestured in a vague way that seemed to cover the entire unpredictable nature of guest lists.

'How are you?'

'Oh, tolerably well,' said Louis, thumbs in the pockets of his waistcoat. 'Things don't change a great deal in East Molesey,' he added, with a satirical twang on the name of his native suburb. 'I don't need to ask how *you've* been getting on.'

Will was nonplussed for a moment, wondering how far the report of his friendship with Connie had spread. But Louis turned out to be referring to his recent successes at M—shire.

'It's not been too bad,' Will shrugged.

'"Not too bad?"' Louis echoed incredulously. 'Hang the modesty, old fellow. You topped their batting averages *again*! The hundreds this season – five, was it?'

'Six,' Will admitted. 'I suppose you heard about Tam retiring?'

Louis put his hand to his head mournfully, like a music-hall mime. 'Sad to think of him going,' he said. 'But it must have been hard for him these last seasons.'

'Yes. He was struggling with a knee injury.'

'Hmm, I'm sure, but that wasn't what I meant. I dare say Tam's real soreness was watching *you* day in, day out. Tough for any sportsman, I suppose, to be eclipsed by his protégé – particularly when your style is so similar to his.'

Will was taken aback by this casual intuition, and would have pursued it further if another of Louis's friends hadn't at that moment interrupted them. Had it really been painful for Tam to watch the young pretender emulating his batting feats? He had never seemed anything but delighted by Will's success.

This ambiguity preoccupied him for most of the service. Only the sudden climbing peals of Elgar's 'Imperial March' finally woke him again to his surroundings. Olivia and Lionel were returning down the aisle, arms linked, casting anxiously proud glances on either side. The bridesmaids stepped in their wake, followed by the two families. As Connie passed close, Will felt an unaccustomed hollowing-out of his chest. The hat she wore, trimmed with tiny roses, was pretty enough, but her face beneath it seemed to have taken on a complicated new lustre; her jaw looked softer, her skin paler, while the circumflexes of her eyebrows were a poignant frame to the chocolatey-dark eyes, still gleaming from her staunched tears. She had also done something with her hair that made the ends curl up in girlish scrolls. The concerted effect was almost cartoonishly beautiful. She was gazing determinedly ahead, allowing no one to catch her eye. Only her mouth, fixed in a distant smile, might have suggested that the ceremony just gone had not been an unalloyed delight to her.

As Will joined the shuffle of exiting congregants, he sensed a quickening in his blood, and deeper within a headlong lurch, like seasickness. The sight of her just now had been the final push overboard. He was falling – no, he had fallen, irretrievably – in love. *I love Constance Callaway*. He said the sentence in his head, and repeated it. The tender shock of

189

this realisation both panicked and spurred him. But to what? It wasn't only that he desired her, though the physical yearning that had ambushed him just then was powerful enough. He also felt an impulse (a noble one, he thought) to protect her against the perilous inclinations of her temperament – to save her from herself!

Out in the churchyard more rose petals were being flung around by the giggling bridesmaids. He found himself in a jostling scrum of guests all trying to offer their congratulations to the happy couple, Lionel's metallic voice piercing the air ('*So* kind of you . . .'). Will raked his gaze over them in search of Connie, but beneath the unwitting disguise of their headwear it was difficult to distinguish one lady from another.

'Hullo there.' Will turned to find Fred, who appeared somewhat dazed by his recent duties *in loco parentis*. They shook hands, and Will saw a brief glimmer of Connie in her brother's dark brow. He made some blameless compliment on the bride's radiance.

'Yes, she looks jolly happy,' Fred agreed, then looked earnestly at Will. 'I say, in the absence of . . . do you suppose it's my job to give the groom a bit of a man-to-man about, you know, taking care of my sister?'

Will, unaccountably touched, assured him that a man-to-man at this stage would be of doubtful utility. Fred nodded, puffing his cheeks out with relief. 'That's what I thought.'

'I wonder where your sister's got to – Constance, I mean.'

'Oh, she's gone ahead to the reception – make sure everything's shipshape. But we've arranged carriages to take the guests. You're coming, I hope?'

'I wouldn't miss it,' said Will, who had privately begun rehearsing what he should say to her.

The house, which had been lent for the occasion by one of Lionel's banking colleagues, was a large, stolidly unattractive red-brick mansion off Holland Park Avenue. Connie paid off the cab and hurried up the steps through the wide double doors. Large potted palms stood sentinel within. Liveried staff were scuttling around the entrance hall, and on enquiring she was given directions to the cloak-room. Her footsteps clopped echoingly over the glazed parquet of the ballroom, where a string quartet were just setting up their stands. Without an audience, the room seemed to crouch in a deferential hush of anticipation. At the top of the staircase she found a wood-panelled corridor, and the WC. The windowless closet was gloomy, but she saw to her relief the nacreous gleam of a mirror on the wall. She dipped her face to it enquiringly, and winced at the sight of her tear-smudged eyes. She attended to them with a handkerchief for some minutes.

There was a useful ambiguity about tears at a wedding, she thought; they were by tradition interpreted as an over-flow of happiness. Lionel, on the church steps, had accepted her kiss with an airy complacency, little suspecting the pangs of doom that were afflicting his new sister-in-law at that moment. His induction into the family felt to her more like an invasion. Connie had then looked searchingly at Olivia, her face now liberated from her veil and flushed with nervous excitement. About Lionel she didn't wish to specu-late, but she knew, almost for a certainty, that her sister was a virgin. Did Olivia have any idea of what she was commit-ting herself to? Their parents' marriage had been more or less a mystery to her. She recalled her father once quoting, out of his wife's earshot, the words of John Stuart Mill on matrimony. Connie had later read the passage for herself and recorded it in her diary: 'Marriage is really, what it has been sometimes called, a lottery: and whoever is in a state of mind to calculate the chances calmly and value them correctly is not at all likely to purchase a ticket.'

Her tears had lent her eyes the unforeseen benefit of a

liquid gleam. She felt a little calmer now, and practised a smile in the mirror, as if readying herself for a taxing performance. It was Olivia's day; whatever she thought of Lionel was, for the moment, immaterial. From the top of the stairs she could hear the deep bowed notes of a cello warming up, and the violins' stuttering pizzicati. She spotted a door slightly ajar at the end of the corridor, and, still nursing her sense of solitude, she approached and pushed it open. The room was dark within, dominated by a billiard table and its long hooded shade, fringed with little tassels; a thick, unvisited stillness clung to the air. She walked over to the shutters and released a catch, drawing back the double panels with a creak. Motes of dust shimmered in the light, which flung an almost electric sheen upon the green baize of the table. A huge fireplace stood in blackened disuse, and a stuffed stag's head protruded mournfully above. The dark panelled walls had been so deeply varnished that Connie could see the blurred outline of her reflection. She walked around the billiard table, stroking its smooth felt surface as she went. A painting in an elaborate gilt frame showed, to her surprise, an aristocratic lady against a feathery pastoral setting; she wouldn't have imagined such a portrait – a Gainsborough, was it? – in this clubby, masculine atmosphere. A coquettish hauteur beamed from the woman's face. Reaching the other set of shutters, Connie unfolded them, too, and now this new source of light revealed what she had missed on the opposite wall: the answering portrait of a country gentleman, a rifle in his crooked arm and a hound at his heels. The lady's husband, evidently. His unillusioned gaze seemed to rebuke Connie for her naivety – no lady, for all her position and wealth, would occupy such a room without her lord and master. Down below she heard voices, and looking out onto the terrace she spied the earliest guests, laughing and drinking and already forming their own little groups. At that moment the door opened and a young maidservant walked in; she jumped in fright on seeing Connie.

'Beg pardon, ma'am, I was told to open the shutters . . .'

'That's all right,' replied Connie, gesturing at her job already done.

'Very good, ma'am,' said the maid, blushing. 'Will that be all?'

Connie had a sudden inkling that the girl had perhaps mistaken her for a daughter of the house, and rather than correct her into further blushes, she simply smiled and nodded. The girl bobbed a quick curtsy and withdrew. It was time to join the fray. Just before she closed the door she considered the room again, and imagined the sort of life that would offer one the leisure to play billiards. A married life, it would have to be.

Her descent into the hall coincided with the rowdy entrance of several men, toppered and tailed and so loud-voiced they could only be Lionel's friends. In the ballroom the musicians had settled into a polite minuet. She proceeded out through the garden doors; the sun, invisible up to now, was idly communing with the high wispy clouds. At the end of the terrace Connie saw a familiar stooped figure, and, led by a tug on her heart, she sidled up to him. On hearing her salutation, the old man turned and offered a crinkly sort of smile. She bent down to kiss his papery cheek and smelt cigars mingled with Penhaligon's cologne. His dark-hued morning suit, mutton-chop whiskers and watch chain were so unconstrainedly old-fashioned he might have passed for a representative of the mid-Victorian gentry in a street pageant.

'Ah, my dear girl,' he said in his friendly, hoarse-throated voice. 'I was just asking feller-me-lad where you'd got to.' Feller-me-lad was Fred.

'How are you, Grandpa,' she said, giving his arm a companionable squeeze. Roger Callaway was Connie's only surviving grandparent, and since the death of his only son – her father – he had drifted to the very periphery of family life: nobody quite knew what to do with him. A widower for many years, he lived in a remote manor house in West Sussex with a lady who was formerly his housekeeper and now de facto his spouse, though no official announcement had ever been forthcoming. When Olivia had been compiling the wedding-guest list, she had paused over the problem of 'Grandpa's helpmeet' (their late father's droll soubriquet) and asked her mother, 'Ought we to invite Mrs Rhodes?' Mrs Callaway gave a moue of uncertainty, and as the silence lengthened Connie said, with a disbelieving gasp, 'Of course you should! She's been living with him for however many years.'

'That doesn't make her his wife. We don't even know this . . . *woman*,' said Olivia.

'Try to consider it from Grandpa's point of view. Think of the discourtesy to him.'

Olivia frowned, and said, 'I suppose,' but in such a reluctant tone that Connie suspected the helpmeet would have to whistle for an invitation.

Now a vicarious guilt needled her as she asked the old man, 'Is Mrs Rhodes keeping well?'

'Oh, very well. She asked to be remembered to you,' he added, with no trace of irony. Connie felt so awful then that she was suddenly tempted to explain her abortive efforts on the lady's behalf, but her grandfather had forgivingly moved the conversation along. 'Doesn't seem a moment ago,' he said, his eyes glazed in faraway reminiscence, 'we saw Donald and your mother at the altar. Eh?' Connie smiled patiently at the interrogative note, forbearing to mention that she was not alive to witness her parents' nuptials.

'I suppose they were very much in love,' she said, thinking again of her father's amused but rather disobliging quotation from Mill.

'Oh, yes, yes,' he replied, with the accompanying *nyuff-nyuff* sound his mouth made when in ruminative mood. 'Though he married late, Donald. Thirty, at least, I should say.' Connie tried to imagine her father at thirty; the odd thing was, he had never seemed very old to her even at fifty. His energy, always formidable, lent him the slightly impatient air of a man who had to slow down for everyone else, including his wife. In a friendly, even a loving sort of way, he had bullied her. Her grandfather was still revisiting old scenes. 'I used to argue with him about it. I'd say, "You *cannot be* without a woman."' He spoke with remembered emphasis, and clenched his gnarled old hand to hammer the sentiment home.

'Why d'you say that, Grandpa?' she asked.

'Why,' he replied, with a bemused pause, 'because without a woman it's only *half a life.*'

Connie was so moved by these words that she sensed again how close to the surface her tears were. She was saved by the arrival of Louis and Fred, who both chorused 'Hullo, sir!' to the old man. She looked on approvingly as they made respectful overtures, like schoolboys with an indulgent housemaster, asking after his health and whether he'd got up to Lord's this summer. Louis had casually lit a cigarette in the meantime.

'May I have one of those?' Connie said, dropping her voice.

'Better not let Ma see you,' said Fred. She had ceased to chafe at the absurdity of her mother's disapproval, though she conceded that secrecy would be tactful for the moment. With a sly bit of legerdemain that again reminded her of the schoolroom, Louis slipped her a cigarette and a box of matches.

'*Nyuff, nyuff,* don't so often see a gel smoking,' murmured her grandfather, who had perhaps a beadier eye than his doddery demeanour suggested. Connie raised an admonitory finger to her lips and went off in search of a hideaway.

The terrace had filled up by now, and guests were spilling onto the wide crescent-shaped lawn. Through the doors she could hear the party's rising babble. Without looking back, she trotted the fifty yards to a rambling vegetable garden where a decrepit greenhouse seemed to provide cover. A trellis had been raised over the narrow cinder path between a row of pear trees and the aged brick wall that demarcated the garden from Holland Park. A small cane love seat hid beneath, and with a grateful sigh she sank down on it. She had just taken her first rasping lungful of the cigarette when she heard the giveaway snap of a twig announcing footfall on the path. Her seat, situated at a right angle to the trellis, made her invisible to passers-by, and she held herself still in the hope that whoever it was would not cast a glance sideways. The footsteps approached, and stopped.

'Er . . . Constance?'

She let out her breath, and bent her head around the seat's enclosure. Will was standing there, looking slightly bewildered.

'Hullo,' she said with a mock-rueful grin.

'Are you hiding from someone?'

She shook her head and held up her cigarette in explanation. 'Only my mother.'

'May I . . . join you?'

She smiled her acquiescence and moved along the seat to give him room. He looked somewhat preoccupied, she thought.

'I don't suppose you know many people here,' she said.

'Oh, one or two. There's Louis, of course . . .' He hesitated, sensing a guest's obligation. 'The wedding service was splendid, really.'

'Do you think so?' she said non-committally, drawing on her cigarette.

'Yes,' he blundered on. 'Weddings always make one rather sentimental. Don't you agree?'

Connie frowned, considering. 'They exercise some effect on me, but I'm not sure precisely what. My grandfather's just been reminiscing about my parents' wedding, and it made me wonder . . .'

'Yes?' Will leaned forward slightly.

Connie hesitated, realising it might not be the moment to start lecturing on the moral infirmities of marriage. 'Oh, nothing – I'll tell you another time, perhaps.' Will felt cheered at the mere suggestion of a time when he might again be a recipient of her confidence: on such scraps does the hopeful heart feed. Her eyes were narrowing on him. 'But you surprise me. Why do weddings make you – susceptible?'

'Oh . . . I suppose it's the idea of two people committing themselves, you know, *absolutely* to one another, with all their friends and family standing witness – willing them on, as it were.'

While he was talking he had picked up one of her gloves, discarded on the seat while she smoked, and was now absently tracing his fingers over the buttons. Connie watched him curiously; the distracted way in which he had spoken, and his nervous fiddling with the glove, inclined her to think he might be hiding something. At that moment he looked up, and said, apropos of nothing, 'That's an amazingly lovely dress you're wearing, by the way.'

Connie plucked at the lavender silk, an extravagance from Selfridges, and canted her head in thanks – though his little gallantry had been awkwardly bestowed. 'Are you quite all right?' she asked him. 'You seem rather agitated.'

Will smiled weakly, and dropped his gaze. 'I do beg your pardon,' he said, haltingly. 'It's not easy – under such – circumstances . . .'

Connie looked puzzled. 'What circumstances?' she began, and then her face cleared as her speculation finally clicked into place. She pulled back to take a measuring look at him.

'Would I be correct in thinking you've – formed an attachment?'

His stricken expression confirmed it. But why had he been so circumspect in confessing it? She spoke again, more lightly. 'So – may I ask the lady's name? Would I have met her?' She fleetingly recalled Will introducing certain female acquaintances during her weekend on the coast. Now he was staring at her.

'Would you have met her?' he said, repeating her words with a disbelieving scowl. Did she really not understand? He watched her as she raised the cigarette to her mouth, and just as it touched her lips he plucked it out of her hand and threw it to the ground. Then he leaned forward and abruptly pressed his mouth to hers. She was so startled that an indistinct exclamation (*unnph!*) escaped her lips, which adjusted and then, slowly, yielded to his own. He had never cared for tobacco, but the taste of her mouth, smoky and sweet at once, was enrapturing. After some moments she detached herself, not unkindly, and gave him a look that mingled doubt and astonishment. He still held his face close, and his eyes searched hers, avidly, imploringly.

'Have I made a mistake?' he said in an undertone.

Connie felt herself colouring. 'I – I'm surprised –'

'I know that I haven't,' he broke in immediately. 'I know that in some way you felt it, too.' She wasn't sure what 'it' might constitute, but she didn't quite trust herself to ask. Will took her hand in his, and said, very seriously, 'I love you, Constance. I love and admire everything about you. I love your face, and your clothes and your hair. I love the way you gaze at things, and the way you smile – as if you're forgiving someone. I love –' he shook his head, briefly confounded, and saw her hand in his '– I love your very hands!'

These hands? thought Connie, splaying her long fingers uncertainly. 'Really?'

'Really and truly. I love everything about you.' She returned his gaze, still at a loss, though the warmth that rose through her seemed to answer his passionate avowals. Other men had been amorous with her before, had kissed her – in the case of poor Mr Nairn had even gone on bended knee to her – but none had ever come close to stirring her as Will was doing. Tentatively, she leaned into him, eyes half closed, and found his mouth again with hers. The dry firmness of his lips caused her body to tremble; it was a giddying sensation, like sitting in a motor car when it suddenly accelerated, and one's stomach took a leap to catch up. He had put his arms about her. There didn't seem quite enough air to breathe, and yet the constriction within her chest felt madly, intoxicatingly pleasurable.

'Connie,' he whispered, so close she could feel his breath on her skin, 'please tell me it's as true for you.'

She put her hands on his shoulders, and nodded. 'It is. It is.'

They were still gazing earnestly at one another when voices drifted into earshot. She jumped away from him, as if something had scalded her touch, and cocked an ear. The voices were coming this way. She stood up and smoothed down her dress, composing her features into a look of businesslike indifference. Will watched her, half amused by this dissemblance and half exasperated by the intrusion that had prompted it.

'There you are!' cried Jecca on spying Connie from the end of the path. 'We've been looking *every*where.'

'What are you actually doing here?' asked her younger sister, Flora, with disconcerting directness.

Connie gave a shrug, and gestured casually at Will. 'You remember Mr Maitland from last summer? He was playing cricket?'

Will bowed as the girls looked at him neutrally. Then Flora bent down to pick up the end of a cigarette, still smouldering. 'Someone's been smoking . . .' she said, in an imitation of disapproval.

'Oops! Mine, I'm afraid,' said Will, gently plucking it from her fingers and swapping glances with Connie: both of them registered its confused symbolic resonance from the previous scene.

'Aunt Julia sent us to fetch you,' said Jecca in a responsible voice. 'There's a lady going to sing.'

'A fat lady,' supplied Flora helpfully.

'That will be Olivia's friend,' Connie explained to Will. 'I ought to go.' Her eyes silently expressed regret at this untimely interruption.

'May I accompany you?' asked Will, reading her look.

They all walked back across the lawn towards the house. Connie heard herself conversing with her young cousins as they went, but had little idea of what was being said. She could only think of what had just passed between herself and Will, ghosting at her side. He had said he loved her, and with such meaning in his eyes that she could not doubt him. He loved her! She felt quite dazed by the knowledge, the surprise of it. That she could speak her mind and yet still be . . . *irresistible* to him.

They entered the hall and joined the excitable press of bodies crowding towards the ballroom. Will, his own nerve ends thrumming, felt a swagger that was almost vertiginous in its illusion of power. He was observing Connie as she walked slightly ahead of him, musing on how queer it was that people could be so unheeding of her presence. Didn't they notice how beautiful she was? Even now there was a guest, a presentable fellow of about his own age, who glanced at Connie – and then unconcernedly looked away. How? How could that man have failed to swoon at the woman he had just set eyes upon? How could anyone? As they filed into the ballroom, where the quartet had been joined by pianist and soprano, he saw Mrs Callaway beckon to Connie across the room, where a seat had been reserved for her. Connie turned back to Will, and gave a helpless shrug – familial duties, it seemed to say.

He returned an understanding smile, and edged his way through the crush; he found a spot from where he could continue to gaze at her unnoticed. A hush had settled. The first slow notes of the soprano's aria began, and Will listened to her voice as it floated aloft, pure and crystalline.

Ombra mai fu . . .

He had no idea what the words meant, but the aching sweetness of the melody seemed to play on his own heart-strings and plunged him into another reverie. Loving Connie as he had never thought to love, he still brooded anxiously over her absolute surrender. He admired her independence of mind, yet he also feared it, and while she was still fired up with the righteousness of her cause there was no telling what troubles she might bring on herself. He had cornered her, but not caught her – not yet. He had to make sure. As the soprano warbled on, Will watched Connie whisper something to the ancient cove with mutton-chop whiskers sitting next to her, who beamed back a look of almost blissful agreement. *Ah*, thought Will, approvingly – that old man knows he has the best seat in the house.

Another aria came to an end, and gave way to a shuffling interlude of exits and entrances. Connie rose and, after a reassuring word to the old fellow, made for the door. Will's gaze, and then his footsteps, followed her. She crossed the hall past loitering guests, smiling at this or that one, before mounting the staircase. He waited until she passed out of sight, then began climbing the stairs himself. At the top, he gravitated down the wood-panelled corridor towards the door at the far end, and tried the handle. It admitted him to a billiards room, where the green baize of the table immediately flooded the eye. Light fell in slanting bands through the pair of tall sash windows, and there, seated on a bottle-green chesterfield, was Connie. She did not look surprised to see him. Her eyes had returned to the brimming pathos he had seen at the church.

He came to sit by her. 'Something's upset you.'

Connie gave a half-laugh and shook her head. 'I seem unable to stop crying today. The Handel just set me off again.'

'I told you – weddings make us sentimental!' He illustrated his remark by taking up her hand and holding it to his lips. A tear bulging at the corner of her eye now rolled down her cheek, but the sobbing laugh that followed it assured him all was well. He moved closer and noticed, to his delight, a pale dusting of freckles across the bridge of her nose. There seemed to be no end to how beautiful she was.

'What you said before,' Connie almost gasped, her voice gluey in her throat, 'did you mean it?'

'How can you doubt it?' he replied gently, holding her gaze. 'It is why I want you to be my wife.'

She inwardly froze at this. In truth, she had wanted only to hear him say again 'I love you' – she had not expected the traditional consequence so precipitately. Will, construing her silence as maidenly modesty, tightened his hand around hers, and said, 'So . . . will you, Connie? Will you marry me?'

The uncertainty that had clouded his features when they sat in the garden was gone. He spoke as one emboldened by love. Catching his mood, Connie's impulse was to yield – but she checked it. Quite apart from the misgivings about marriage which had oppressed her at the church, she realised that her involvement in the cause could only be distracted, if not altogether dashed, by bonding herself to a husband. Will was as eligible a man as she could hope to meet, but she was under no illusion as to his *understanding* her. If she now informed him, for instance, that on this coming Tuesday she was due to join a window-breaking delegation of suffragists in Belgravia, would he be quite so sanguine in his proposal of a life together? She looked at him now, his face alight with encouragement.

'I – I hardly know what to say.'

'What is the difficulty? You believe that I love you.'

'Yes, I do.'

'Then – you are doubtful of your love for me?'

She paused. 'No. If I understand what love means, I love you. But I'm afraid of making an agreement I can't honour.'

Will squinted at her. 'I don't quite follow . . .'

Connie looked down, deliberating. 'You said before that you loved everything about me. But there was an occasion not long ago when it became clear that not *everything* about me delighted you – indeed, you may recall, I was the cause of considerable embarrassment and exasperation. Now, as we've heard today, a woman must pledge to love, honour and obey her husband. Of the first two you would always be assured from me. But of the last . . . knowing that our sympathies may not be entirely compatible, would you place me under such an obligation?'

Will might have taken offence that his proposal had not been received with quite the ardour he thought it merited: instead of falling into his arms, she was querying the small print. Yet his determination to win her overrode any slight puncturing of his self-esteem.

'I'd hope to be able to count on your *loyalty*,' he said, carefully, 'just as you would count on mine. I have a respect for your . . . causes and so on. But if you love me as you say, I cannot imagine your doing something that would violate that.'

It was a fair answer, but she doubted him still – 'your causes and so on' did not suggest a very thoughtful engagement with the fight for equality. She longed to feel his arms about her once more, but an instinct goaded her to resist. 'William,' she began, earnestly, 'I'm very conscious of the honour you've paid me . . . I feel grateful that –'

'I don't want your gratitude,' he cut in impatiently. 'I only want your consent.'

'I can't answer you at once,' she said, her eyes cast down.

'And I must insist that you do – at once.'

Connie, freeing her hand from his, stood up and walked over to the window. Outside, guests were still swarming over the lawn, the light twitter of female voices mingling with the odd hearty boom of male laughter. She kept silent while she examined the options before her. She *was* grateful for Will's offer, but she was wary of accepting now what she might have cause to regret later. *To calculate the chances calmly and value them correctly* . . . She saw his reflection loom behind her. If she rejected him he might never ask her again, and she would be left to ponder a future without him. She thought again of the appointment with her suffragist comrades on Tuesday. An idea began to take shape in her mind. What if –

'For the moment I must ask you to wait. Only allow me a little time, and I will give you an answer.' Her tone was decisive, and Will, though chafing at the delay, sensed her heart was his. As she turned to him, he took her in his arms and fixed her with an appraising look.

'A little time, you say. How long?'

She met his look unflinchingly. 'This time next week. Wait until then, and you will have an answer.'

The slow pardon of a smile began to play over his face, and he nodded. His eyes gleamed as he bent to kiss her unresisting mouth.

10

Stirred from sleep by the grainy half-light, Connie wondered why her bedroom felt so chilly. Barely opening her eyes, she clutched the blanket tightly to her, and started in surprise at its coarse, scratchy texture between her fingers. This was not her blanket, and this, she now realised, was not her bedroom. Peering through half-closed lids she began to discern the unfamiliar accoutrements around her: a wooden chair, a table fixed into the angle of the wall, a washing basin. Above her the dawn was seeping wanly through a high barred window. Her cell; and this her third morning in Holloway Prison. Outside she heard a pigeon cooing, and for some reason thought of Olivia, who would by now be en route to Venice, the second stop on her honeymoon, presumably oblivious of her sister's disgrace back in London. She hoped that her mother would resist the impulse to telegraph the happy couple's hotel with the news.

The cell, airless during the day, got cold at night. A few minutes later she heard a metallic clunk at the door, and a face appeared at the spyhole. It was a wardress checking on – what, exactly? That the prisoner hadn't hanged herself, perhaps. In the distance Connie heard a bell being rung; the prison reveille. She swung her legs out of the bed, shivering like a greyhound, and removed the linsey nightdress. She put on the underclothes issued to her on arrival, patched and stained, though reasonably clean, then the drab serge dress with its shoulder adorned with a broad arrow. Her bed sheets had these arrows, too, like the footprints of birds in the snow. The dress felt horrible, prickling against her skin, but at least it provided some warmth. Her boots were cracked and worn, the insoles lined with hard little ridges from their previous owner, or owners. She hoped she would be able to have a bath today, though she was beginning to realise that personal hygiene was not something the prison authorities set much store by. On the table were the prison-issue brush and comb, but without a mirror there seemed little use in trying to arrange one's hair. When Connie had asked about this a sour-faced wardress had sneered at her, 'Who's going to look at you in here anyway?' She blushed at the woman's rudeness.

Breakfast arrived about an hour later. There were no clocks here, so Connie would listen out for the church bells to mark the time. She spooned the lukewarm, lumpy porridge into her mouth, and swilled it down with the unspeakable beverage from the tin mug. (She assumed it was some kind of skilly – the taste made it difficult to tell.) Then, as she had been instructed, she folded up her bed-clothes into a roll, stowed them away, and laid her plank bedstead against the wall. After that she cleaned her tin plate and mug and spoon with bath-brick. Another hour of waiting, and a wardress arrived to lead her and other inmates in the wing down to the chapel. Aside from a half-hour of exercise in the afternoon, it was the only time in the day she was allowed to step out of her cell. As they were filing down the corridor in silence, she caught the eye of a young wardress whose features had a shy affability she had not encountered in anyone since arriving. In an undertone, Connie said, 'Excuse me, is it Saturday today?'

The wardress looked so surprised she might have thought a statue had spoken, but before she could shape her mouth to reply, another voice boomed close behind them. 'No talking!' This was Mrs Tarrant, the ward matron, whose pinched face and rebarbative gaze had overseen Connie's introduction to prison life some days before. On emerging, handcuffed and dazed, from the swaying interior of the Black Maria, she had been escorted up to an office whose brick walls were painted a sickly underwater green.

Mrs Tarrant sat writing at her desk, and without looking up said, curtly, 'Name.'

'Constance Callaway.'

'Occupation.'

'Bookseller.'

'Sentence.'

'Six months. For breaking –'

'I know what you've done. Take off those clothes and step onto the scales.'

After being weighed, and measured, Connie was handed a prison uniform by an orderly. Another one was sorting through a box of boots. Nobody deviated from the strict impersonal mood of the room – she felt queerly like some farm animal that was being processed for sale. She remembered her advice from the delegation. 'I gather I'm entitled to be put – in the first division?' she said, trying to make it sound like a reasonable request. Mrs Tarrant stopped writing and, for the first time, looked closely at her.

'You *gather*?' she said, her voice steely with sarcasm. 'Understand this. You are a convicted criminal. You have forfeited the freedom to choose. You will spend your sentence in whichever part of this prison we see fit to put you. Miss Boyle – take her down.'

Nothing like getting off on the right foot, thought Connie, as she was marched off to solitary confinement.

Now she was shuffling into one of the chapel pews, within touching distance of prisoners on either side, but nobody spoke. At one point Connie looked round at her neighbour, a thin, rheumy-eyed woman who seemed afflicted by a nervous tic; she kept jerking her head sideways as if trying to shoo a fly from under her nose. Her skin was wrinkled, pale as mushroom stalks, and so unhealthy-looking that Connie had to stop herself staring. As she lowered her weight onto the unforgiving wooden kneeler, she winced from the abrasions to her knees she had sustained on Tuesday afternoon.

She had met the other two, by arrangement, at a small hotel in Victoria. One of them, Laura Scott, was a cheerful, clear-skinned, athletic-looking woman with mischievous eyes whom Connie took to immediately.

'You know Marianne Garnett?' Laura almost squealed, on learning of their mutual friend. 'We're near neighbours in South Kensington,' she continued breezily, as if they were members of the same coffee circle rather than a cabal of suffragists plotting sedition. She glanced at her watch. 'While we're waiting for Ivy I suggest we have a drink. It might be the last enjoyable one we have before –' She raised her eyebrows in wry complicity.

Connie replied with a tense smile, which Laura was quick to read. 'Your first time? Well, don't fret. We'll be shoulder to shoulder all the way through. So what'll it be – gin?'

They had moved on to a second glass by the time their tardy companion arrived. Ivy Maddocks offered an apology, though in a tone of such martyred exasperation that Connie felt it was somehow their fault for imposing on her time. Small and compact, Ivy had a beaky sort of look; her eyes were as bright as a bird's, and her unsmiling face was all angles and points. She seemed to peck at her words, though in her brief moments of repose she was perfectly still. Connie was fascinated by her, and perhaps a little frightened.

'A drink, Ivy, before we set off?'

Ivy shook her head vigorously. 'No, no. I've taken the

pledge,' she said, adding proudly, 'henceforth, my body is a temple.'

'Oh. Any particular denomination?' replied Laura teasingly. Connie giggled, but Ivy looked blank.

'What do you mean?'

Laura, draining her glass, said, 'Nothing, just a joke. Well then . . . shall we?'

Connie rose unsteadily. She had been too nervous to eat, and now the effect of two large gins was making her head swim. She was halfway to being drunk, which she supposed might be a blessing in view of what lay ahead. Outside the hotel, the afternoon sky had turned a strange, glowering grey-white, as if reeling from some meteorological sickness. Clouds of starlings swarmed overhead. Ivy was walking with a cane, prompting Connie to ask if she was injured. Ivy's expression turned crafty.

'No, but *someone* might be,' she said, and showed Connie a little mechanism on the cane. She clicked it, and a small blade protruded at its end.

'It's a dagger-cane,' Laura explained. 'To be used only in self-defence. Isn't that so, Ivy?' It was lightly spoken, but there was a warning in Laura's tone.

'Of course,' said Ivy, who fixed Connie with a significant look. 'Though I've dealt with our constabulary often enough to know it pays to be armed.'

As they proceeded through the seemly hush of Belgravia, Connie felt the weight in her bag bumping against her calves. It felt such an odd thing to be doing, and she had a fleeting sense of hovering above her own steps along the pavement, as though watching someone else walk abreast of these two strangers. Twenty yards ahead a policeman turned the corner and began strolling towards them. Ivy, who had been quietly humming 'Onward Christian Soldiers', stopped mid-note, and then resumed. Laura glanced at Connie and murmured, 'Don't say anything.'

The policeman, quite unsuspecting, tipped his helmet at the trio of respectable young ladies. 'Af'noon,' he muttered.

'Good afternoon, Constable,' Laura said, 'I wonder, are we going the right way for Chester Square?' While she was speaking Ivy had kept on with the hymn. The policeman stared at her for a moment, then turned to Laura.

'Next turn right, ma'am – you can't miss it.'

Laura inclined her head graciously, and they walked on. Just as he was out of earshot, Connie heard her say under her breath, 'Oh, we shan't, Constable.'

A few minutes later a navy tin plaque fixed high on the gable wall announced their arrival at Chester Square. Laura took out a little pocket-book and checked the address. 'So, if that's number 4, we should be . . .' She walked on, counting off the door numbers, until she stopped in front of one of the identical porticoed fronts. 'Here we are,' she said, with the brightness of a house agent about to show prospective tenants around. 'It's the residence of one of Asquith's junior ministers,' she added musingly. The sash windows of the house gleamed black as oil. There seemed to be not a single other person in the vicinity. Connie, light-headed, put down her bag and opened the clasp. Inside were three bricks taken from a pile she had spotted at the front of a builder's yard in Camden. Laura peered at them, and said, 'Best to wrap them up. We don't want to kill any servants who might be lurking about.' She handed over some rags, which Connie took and began to wind loosely around the bricks. Ivy, in the meantime, had unbuttoned her coat to reveal a wide sash of green, purple and white across her chest. Having abandoned the hymn she was now humming the Marseillaise. She removed a large smooth stone from her own bag, and hefted it in her hand.

'I brought this from the beach at Sidmouth,' she said, almost wistfully. 'It would have made a lovely paperweight.' She looked up and down the street, then turned to Connie and Laura, who were still wrapping the bricks. 'No time like the present,' she said, and taking a step back launched her stone, quite gracefully, at the ground-floor window. It flew over the railings and went clean through the top half-pane, like a letter posted through the mouth of a pillar box. For some reason Connie thought of Tam smashing the ball over the walls of the Priory, and the distant tinkle as it fell through a window. The applause he would get! She felt the dumb weight of the brick muffled within the cloth. Up above, they heard the scrape of a sash being opened: someone had heard the crash, and as a face appeared, Connie shouted, 'Votes for women!' and heaved her ragged missile at the next window along. It broke against the glass with an outraged unmusical *clang*.

'Oh, fine shot,' cried Laura, who herself took a step back and, like a fielder in the deep aiming for the wicketkeeper's gloves, she found the window above with a high, hard throw. Connie found herself laughing, rather giddily, as Ivy sent another stone skimming through the pane below the one she had previously holed. They might have been competing at a coconut shy. The noise by now had attracted some onlookers; a man had dismounted his bicycle and stood watching, hands on hips. A few doors along an aproned charwoman had stepped onto the street to investigate. Beyond her, Connie could see the policeman they had passed some minutes before hurrying towards them. He had started to blow his whistle.

'Let's keep at it,' called Ivy, and Connie obediently picked up her second brick and hurled it forward. It made another satisfying explosion against the startled pane. She had envisaged herself at this moment being quite terrified, and yet it was not so; perhaps the gin was to blame. She really did seem to be having the *most tremendous fun*. The policeman was now upon them, and had unwisely chosen Ivy as the assailant to wrestle down. She responded by beating him about the head with her stick. From round the other corner two mounted policemen came trotting, and Laura gripped Connie's arm.

'I think it's time to make a run for it!'

The constable trying to restrain Ivy now bellowed in pain, and fell clutching the foot which Ivy's hidden blade had just speared. Connie, seeing the private garden gate open, hurried through and gained the opposite kerb when two more policemen came bolting along the street. She turned back round the corner and found one of the police horses galloping straight at her. As she swerved out of the way and dodged along its flank, she saw the rider raise his arm and a thin shadow descended towards her. The blow which caught the side of her head surprised her with its force, and then she was tumbling down, down, her stomach heaving violently. As she retched onto the cobbles, the last thing she remembered before the blackness closed over was the taste of juniper in her mouth.

Connie joined the listless file of inmates traipsing out of the chapel, the scuff of their boot soles on stone the only sound to be heard. The corridors outside echoed with the muffled din of the prison cranking into life. She was becoming used to the smell of the place – a rank compound of ill-washed bodies, unclean hair, stale breath, boiled cabbage, lime-washed walls, gas and damp, though far more oppressive than any of these constituents was the almost tangible atmosphere of defeat. It was no surprise to Connie that the women she passed looked so miserable and cowed; what was truly disconcerting were those faces that were empty of any expression at all. It was a curious blindfold look: the eyes were glassy but opaque, like a dead rabbit's. She could not yet tell whether their blankness was the evidence of an inner crisis or simply a mask of animal indifference that had stuck fast through habit.

As each prisoner was conducted to her solitary cell, Connie braced herself for the slam of the door, so harsh at times it would make her jump. She had stepped over the threshold of her cell when she heard an uncertain step behind her. She had not even noticed that the wardress in charge of her was the same one she had addressed earlier. In a hushed tone, the woman said, 'It is Saturday.' She hadn't forgotten Connie's question. Caught off guard by the unexpected courtesy, Connie was about to thank her when the door was closed fast, and another long spell of solitude began. Saturday, then. This was the day she had set as her deadline to answer Will's proposal of marriage. Before they had parted on the night of Olivia's wedding he had asked permission to call at Thornhill Crescent to receive her answer. From the gleam in his eye she could tell that he was confident of a favourable outcome.

And she would have obliged him, she felt sure, but for her needling doubts as to his true character. While she believed in the sincerity of his love, and returned it in full measure, she sensed that a future together would very soon provoke a test of loyalty beyond Will's command. His anger at her disobliging treatment of Foulkes had later occasioned an apology, but she nonetheless felt that Will's remorse was the result of a change of mood, not a change of mind. He was, at heart, a traditional fellow who would not take kindly to forthright displays of independence on the part of his wife. Or would he? Connie, mindful of her date with suffragist destiny on the following Tuesday, had decided to take the risk. Knowing there would be little chance of escaping arrest and a conviction, she would go to prison. If Will should renew his offer of matrimony after *that*, she would rejoice; the proof of his love would be incontrovertible, while the assurance of his solidarity would be her comfort through the dark vale of incarceration.

In the first hours of her arrival at Holloway she had

been too disorientated even to consider his reaction, or anyone else's. She had not yet recovered from the shock of the sentence – six months had winded her like a punch to the stomach. Now, with the hours beginning to slow, she sensed trackless swathes of dead time in prospect, like an Arctic explorer looking out upon a tundra and suddenly daunted by the isolation.

A few hours later on this same Saturday, Will was strolling north from King's Cross, rehearsing in his head the scene to come. He had slept poorly that week, distracted by his endless replaying of what had occurred at Olivia's wedding between himself and Connie, and the suspense she had provoked by deferring her answer. It was, he felt, a quite delicious suspense, rather like being not out overnight on ninety-odd, knowing that one boundary and a dashed single or two would take him to a hundred the next morning. Her demeanour, the very softness in her eyes, had instilled in him a certainty that she would consent to be his wife. If it pleased her to be coy and to pretend at indecision for a few days, well, then – so be it. Her footling over the matrimonial contract scarcely worried him. Once they were wed she would no longer have to query his entitlements, still less to make a public nuisance of herself. Her life would instead be consumed with the duties of a wife and hostess, and soon enough, perhaps, the joys and cares of a mother. An involuntary chuckle escaped his lips; only think, Mr and Mrs William Maitland! *Request the pleasure of . . . will be At Home . . . are pleased to announce . . .*

Tickled by these rapturous novelties, Will quickened his pace along Caledonian Road, a thoroughfare he found quite hilariously tatty. Two o'clock, she had said. Crisp low sunlight hung over the September afternoon, gilding leaves that were just beginning to lose their green. As he approached the Callaway home he was puzzled to see the shutters closed and the blinds on the upstairs windows still down. It gave the house a prim look of mourning. Composing himself, he trotted up the front steps and, rather than pull the bell ring, applied a respectful double knock. A maid answered his summons, but on hearing his request she flushed deeply and stuttered out a few words to the effect that 'Miss Constance' wasn't home at present.

'Oh . . . out shopping, perhaps?' he said lightly, but the girl frowned as if he had made a rather tasteless joke. Behind her, a door opened, and Fred put his head out. On seeing Will at the door, he gave an awkward little wave and said, 'Thanks, Maggie, that'll be all.'

He invited Will through, and ushered him into the room from which he had emerged. It was a study, with a cliff face of books on either wall. Fred, unshaven and without a collar, gestured Will to the couch, and resumed his own place on a leather-backed chair. Newspapers lay open on the desk. Will sensed his host's preoccupied air.

'I'm sorry if I've disturbed you. Constance appointed this hour to call upon her . . .'

'Ah. Then . . . you haven't heard.'

The seriousness of his tone caused Will a moment of horrific dread. 'What – is she ill?' he said.

'No, no, not that . . .' Will felt relief flood his senses, though Fred's countenance remained sombre. 'She's – she was arrested, on Tuesday. Breaking windows. She wouldn't pay the fine, so . . . she's in prison.'

Will stared at him, too stunned to speak. In the silence that followed, Fred picked up a cigar cutter and began toying with it. After some moments Will found his voice, though it sounded strange to his ears.

'In prison – where?' He sensed his mind playing a trick, for this wasn't the question foremost in his thoughts.

Fred gave a slow, brooding nod. 'Holloway.' He could

see that Will was struggling to digest this. 'I'm sorry . . . It's been rather a shock for us all.'

'What – what did they give her?'

Fred looked down, and said quietly, 'Six months' hard labour.'

Will felt his hands shaking as he tried to steady himself. His thoughts, like a ragged army in retreat, were flying in vain towards any refuge that might hide him from the terrible pounding of these bare facts – that the woman he loved had been guilty of criminal damage, that she had gone to prison rather than pay a fine, that she had dealt his proposal the most belittling rejection. Had she meant to wound him? It seemed inconceivable, given their mutual avowals the last time they met, and yet her request for a week's grace now seemed a mockery of his hopes. Fred had been talking on in the meantime, explaining how Connie would do four weeks' solitary confinement before she was to be allowed a visitor or a letter, and how their mother had taken to her bed, while Olivia didn't even *know* about it yet . . .

'I say, old chap, are you – ? You've gone awfully pale.'

Will couldn't speak. He lowered his head until it was cradled in his hands. Gazing at the Turkey carpet at his feet, he heard Fred rise from his chair and leave the room. Will was thinking of her, alone in a cell, and the terrible clench of pity it caused him overrode the shock of his humiliation. For a moment he sensed a mysterious nobility about her. She had sacrificed herself for a cause, a *thing* . . . He had never had that sort of belief himself – not in anything. That he had not suspected her capable of it was almost frightening. Did he really know her, this woman to whom he had poured out his heart? He heard Fred's footsteps returning, and felt a nudge on his shoulder.

'Here, down the hatch.' Fred put the glass in his hand. Will smelt the soothing, nutty fumes of brandy, and, too wretched to object, he tossed it down his throat. The burn of it made his eyes water. When he finally looked up, Fred was sitting on the edge of the desk, his eyes trained anxiously on his visitor.

'Thank you,' Will croaked, handing back the drained glass. He wondered if his reaction to the news might look peculiar, for Fred would have no clue as to how matters stood between him and his sister. He had no clue, come to that. They talked for a brief while about what might be done for her, though neither of them had friends in Parliament, or in any other sphere of influence.

'*Six months*,' Will said in an appalled undertone. 'Isn't that . . . a bit stiff?'

'I thought so, but then it came out in court that it was the house of one of Asquith's cronies, and the magistrate apparently decided to make an example of them.'

Another gloomy silence fell between them. Fred went pacing around the room, then eventually sighed: 'To think of the fun we had at the wedding – this time last week! Poor Con . . .' He stopped, and frowned. 'I wonder if she was planning it *then*?'

Will, staring into the distance, gave a non-committal shake of his head. He would like to have been open with Fred, to have recounted the peculiar course of his relationship with Connie, but he hardly knew the fellow. And any prospect of intimacy between them had now disappeared behind a prison door. He took up his hat, and rose hollow-legged from the couch.

'I'm very sorry to have intruded,' he muttered. 'Be kind enough to pass on my condolences to your mother –' He stopped, and looked Fred in the eye. 'If you do get to visit Constance, would you tell her that – I called?'

Fred gave a suspicionless nod. 'Of course I will,' he said. At the door a grave handshake was exchanged, and Will took his leave of the forlorn house. He retraced his steps around the crescent and onto Richmond Road, remembering the last time he had walked down this way, the afternoon he had come to her bearing flowers and an apology. Then he tormented himself further by retrieving the image of her face at the wedding, her eyes agleam, the lashes dark with tears. She had not intended to be so heartless towards him. Had she? *You will have an answer*, she had said, and this was it – she preferred a prison sentence to betrothal. He had just reached Matilda Street when he was seized by a dreadful sweating faintness. Grasping hold of a railing he half crouched, and had a couple of seconds to groan before he vomited onto the pavement.

When the magistrate handed down his sentence Connie had wondered what might constitute hard labour, so it came as a relief to discover that the burden, so far, consisted in darning prison clothes. She was at work on a rough old stocking one morning when she heard the rattle of keys and her cell door being unlocked. She stood up, preparing for an inspection, but her visitor turned out to be a short, pudgy-faced man with a watchful gaze and fine, sandy-coloured hair. She recognised him as the prison chaplain. He introduced himself, in a gentle, faintly impedimented voice, and they sat down. He asked her how she was getting along.

'Quite well,' replied Connie, 'apart from the light burning outside my room all night. And not having a book to read.'

He picked up the cell's prayer book from her table. The volume was unpromisingly titled *The Narrow Way*. 'I have known inmates who have found great comfort in this,' he said, riffling the pages.

'I know quite enough already about "the narrow way",' she replied equably. 'It rather describes the policy that put us in here.'

He paused, watching her. 'Have you faith in the Lord, Miss Callaway?'

Connie gave a shrug. 'As little as makes no difference.'

'And yet the wardresses tell me they have heard singing from this cell – hymn singing.'

She nodded. 'I find it brings a certain . . . solace. When one is alone. Which is most of the time.'

'And what hymns do you sing?'

'Oh . . . I'm rather fond of "When I Survey the Wondrous Cross" at the moment.'

'It's a beautiful one,' he agreed, and spread his palms. 'Would you care to sing it now?'

'No.'

'Why not?'

'Because I'm not alone.'

His shoulders slumped in a little mime of disappointment. He drew his hands together, fingertips brushing his nose. 'So you are confident of surviving this ordeal without the help of – a higher power?'

'I'll take my chances,' she replied mildly.

'Miss Callaway – may I speak candidly? Most of the women in this prison have not enjoyed the advantages that you have. They have strayed into criminality through hard circumstances, or through vicious influences – or because they scarcely know any better. You, on the other hand, have been privileged by birth and education to understand the concepts of good and evil, to make moral discriminations and to act accordingly. Have you never considered it your duty to set an example?'

'My duty, as I see it, is to support the principle and justice of women's suffrage. And in submitting myself to imprisonment I *am* setting an example – to women and to men, who will one day come to understand what the sacrifice of a few has done for the many.'

'But that is absurd. All that you are sacrificing is your self-respect.'

Connie narrowed her eyes at him. 'I cannot agree. The

absurdity is the government's – to think they can crush an idea by shutting hundreds of us up like this.'

'Your sentence is six months, I gather. Are you really prepared to serve that? Prison time will seem far longer than time spent outside.'

She paused, considering. 'A woman gives nine months of her time to the creation of a life. What is six months to give to a great movement like ours?'

'Yes, but the waiting –'

'Birth always means waiting.'

The chaplain looked away, and sighed. He picked up the prayer book again, and seemed rueful. Eventually, he said, 'I will endeavour to obtain other books for you. Is there anything in particular . . . ?'

Connie smiled at last, acknowledging his concession. 'Some poetry? – if they have any.'

He nodded, and his voice took on a musing tone. 'I used to write a little, in that line. Before I was called to this . . .' He looked about the cell, almost as if he were an inmate himself. 'It was . . . mostly poor stuff. But you oughtn't to think that all persons employed by the government are incapable of – lyric feeling.'

She heard the slight defensiveness, and felt sorry for him. 'I don't think that,' she said in a softened voice. He stood up to leave.

'The life here can be grievously hard. Should you ever be in need of help, I will be at hand.'

Connie waited until he had called for the wardress, then cleared her throat. 'There *is* something I'd like to ask you.'

'Yes?' he said, leaning forward.

'The hot drink they serve us here, with the meals. What is it?'

The man looked puzzled. 'The drink? Why, it's tea.'

'Tea?' She blinked in surprise. 'Well – thank you for telling me! I would never have guessed it from the taste.'

It was evidently not the question he had hoped for. He bowed briefly at her, and withdrew.

The window of her cell was three bars across, six bars down. Twenty-one squares of grimy glass. The bottom two panes opened, and Connie would stand on the stool to look out at the yard below, where ordinary prisoners took their daily exercise. They walked in a single file, one behind another, unspeaking. A cheerless brick building was all that she could see opposite her; the young wardress, whose name was Miss Ewell, had told her it was the infirmary. Today Connie was putting out a few breadcrumbs for the pigeon that had alighted on her ledge. It pleased her to think she was feeding the birds of Holloway at the government's expense. The pigeon had paused, its gaze magisterial. Sometimes she would stare back into its marbled jet eyes, imagining she could hypnotise the creature and bring it under her control. But just when she seemed to have locked its eyes on hers, it would jerk its head aside and resume its silly pompous strut.

Across the lower portions of the window names, dates, had been etched into the glass by the cell's previous occupants. Was it mere idleness that had prompted them to scratch their names here, or was it an urge to memorialise, to remind future inmates that they had once passed through here? HELEN o8. SD. MIM. ANN. MAISIE. One artistic hand had carved her initials, EHW, with the first two letters floating daintily inside each cone of the W. Then Connie spotted one etched into a higher pane, quite on its own. R LOVES ALICE MARCHANT 1907. Something about the declaration surprised her; she had assumed that the prisoners would record only their own names. Why? Were they not just as likely to be the names of their sweethearts? She stared at the words again: 'R', whoever she was, had been tall, since Connie, even with her height, had to stand on tiptoe to touch the glass. It moved her, for some reason, that R had limited herself to an initial, yet had patiently carved out the whole name of the girl she loved. Lucky Alice Marchant. She wondered if the love had survived imprisonment. How strong would it have to be? The pigeon she had been feeding had moved off, probably to scavenge outside another's window. She felt in the pocket of her dress, and found her darning needle. Still on tiptoe, she began – an inch below R's message – an inscription of her own. The point of the needle was less than sharp, so she couldn't be as ambitious. But, heedless of the time, she scratched away at the glass until the initials were clearly legible. There were only two.

WM

11

As the cab drew to a halt outside Silverton House, Will stepped onto the gravel and held open the door for his mother and sister, both of them muffled in their winter coats and hats. It was ten days before Christmas, and they were returning late from one of the soirées that constituted Mrs Maitland's seasonal round. Will's present mood had inclined him against such gatherings, and this evening had become a particular trial once he realised that he was to be part of a matchmaking experiment. He had barely shaken hands with the host before his mother was imperiously summoning him from across the room and almost forcing him into the company of a young woman, who looked no less startled than he must have. Ada Brink was delicately pretty, with a mass of blonde curls, a pert mouth and a tinkling girlish laugh that Will found pleasant on the ear, if a little too easily provoked. He would no sooner offer some pale witticism than she was giggling behind her hand and calling him 'a card'. When she told him that she had recently been to Court, he enquired as to her offence.

'Not that court, silly,' Ada gasped, following another paroxysm of mirth. 'I mean, *presented* at Court.' Will asked her how she liked being 'out' in society, and she replied that she liked it very well, though the scarcity of young men who could dance was *very* dismaying.

'Do you dance?' she asked him, her large delft-blue eyes candid with interest.

'Er, rather poorly, I'm afraid,' he had said, and on seeing her face drop, added, 'but I'm quite willing to learn.' She had smiled broadly, as if he had just given the correct answer. They had chattered on in this fashion for a while; Will had looked around the room at one point and caught his mother's vigilant eyes upon them.

Now, back at home, Mrs Maitland was enumerating the accomplishments of Miss Brink: '. . . *and* I gather she plays the piano to a high standard.' Will made no comment, hoping his mother would drop the subject. 'You seemed to be getting along very nicely with her,' she continued. 'I thought we might invite her to lunch over Christmas.'

'I don't think that's necessary,' said Will. 'She probably has plenty of other engagements already.'

His mother, divesting herself of coat and scarf, turned a sharp look on him. 'What was wrong with her?'

Will shook his head. 'Nothing at all. Quite a pretty girl, I suppose –'

'Then I wonder what the matter is with *you*. Really, William, you could make more of an effort. Your expression this evening suggested you were suffering a violent . . . *toothache*.'

'In which case, Miss Brink made an excellent chloral.'

They had moved into the living room, where Mrs Maitland clicked her tongue in vexation. 'Oh – the girl's forgotten to set the fire, when I specifically asked her to.'

'At least she remembered to draw the curtains,' said Eleanor, picking up two split logs from the basket and crouching at the grate. Their mother had paused, momentarily confused by the shifting targets of her indignation. 'Well, I shall invite Miss Brink in any case. It will at least guarantee some lively company.'

Eleanor looked round with a mock-affronted expression.

224

Will bent down next to her and took the firelighters and wood from her hands. 'Allow me.'

He felt his mother's gaze glowering behind him as he made up the fire. When she realised he was not going to argue, she huffily announced that she would retire for the night, and asked Eleanor to bring her some tea, and left with a brusque goodnight. Will continued heaping twists of newspaper in the grate, miserably amused by his own obstinate nature; he wondered, not for the first time, if he were the only person his mother had not bent to her will. Even while his father was alive, there existed little doubt as to who had the whip hand in their marriage. As a boy he could remember loving his father and fearing his mother; when his father died, the fear went, too, for some reason. He wasn't sure what he felt for her now. Pity, perhaps, with smaller measures of love and irritation blended in.

The fire had begun to kindle by the time Eleanor returned from attending to their mother upstairs. Will registered a look from her that provocatively mixed shrewdness with curiosity. She was discerning, like their mother, but without her abrasiveness, having inherited an equable temper from their father. Will was secretly thankful for it.

'Mother despairs of your making a match with anyone,' she reported, rubbing her hands in front of the fire.

Will continued staring at the flickering licks of flame. 'Really,' he said, in a tone as lifeless as ashes.

'You might at least . . . humour her. I thought Miss Brink looked very presentable.'

'Oh, more than presentable. I just don't –'

'– have an ardour for Ada,' Eleanor said neatly, and Will gave a quiet laugh. After a pause, she spoke again. 'May I ask – whatever happened to the admirable Constance?'

Will felt a twist on his heart. He stood up from his crouch and flopped back on one of the sofas. 'Did you think her "admirable"?' he said, toying with her question.

'Of course. And you seemed to find her rather more than that. I wondered why you never asked her down again.'

Will's mouth twitched in a rueful grimace. 'Well, there was one good reason not to –' he raised his eyes in the upward direction of their mother's brooding presence '– but I might have done if – it's a long story.'

Eleanor nodded her willingness to listen. Inwardly he hesitated; he had a sincere but guarded affection for his sister – the six years' difference in age and their respective boarding schools had distanced them. Fixing his gaze on the fireplace, he haltingly related the story of his burgeoning relationship with Connie, his proposal, and the sudden rupture back in September. Its conclusion drew from her a look of horrified surprise, much as it had when he told Tam.

'Six months? *Oh . . .*' She asked if there was anything to be done, and Will shrugged. 'So you've applied to visit her?'

He pursed his lips, and slowly shook his head. Eleanor looked puzzled, and asked why ever not.

'I'm surprised you need to ask. A fellow asks a girl to marry him, and the girl responds by getting herself arrested and thrown in jail. Surely you must see the insult of it?'

She furrowed her brow. 'Why an insult? She asked for time to consider your offer, which only suggests to me how seriously she took it. And then . . . events may simply have got in the way – does anyone plan to be arrested?'

'She knew the risks, I'm sure. She could have given me an answer *before* her little . . . escapade.'

Eleanor looked measuringly at her brother. 'And if she had warned you of what she intended to do – would your proposal have stood?'

Will scowled and fell silent. He had asked himself the same before now, and the very fact that he wavered on the matter had stirred in him a creeping sense of doubt. It came down to this: would he tolerate the idea of his betrothed being a militant suffragette – of her being jailed for it? He knew, but couldn't quite admit to himself, that he would not. His pride wouldn't stand for it.

'I don't want a wife I have to make excuses for,' he said eventually.

Eleanor shook her head, puzzled. 'But you told her – Constance – you told her you loved her. Perhaps that was why she felt able to go through with it, having the assurance of your love.'

'I don't know why you're so keen to defend her,' he said, irked by this imaginative line of reasoning. 'All I know is this – I made her a proposal of marriage, and it was rejected in the most mortifying fashion. Am I not entitled to feel aggrieved?'

'As I see it, she hasn't yet been allowed to *give* you an answer. It's possible she hoped you would visit her.'

'That's rot, Ellie. Her answer was plain enough in her actions. Why on earth should I humble myself to visit her in prison?'

'Because she *is* in prison! Only imagine how wretched it must be – how alone she must feel.'

'She chose it. She can suffer the consequences.'

Eleanor looked at him sadly. 'Too harsh, William. It is unworthy of you. If you no longer wish to marry her, so be it. But she was also your friend. Does she not at least merit the kindness of a visit?'

Will closed his eyes and pinched the bridge of his nose between forefinger and thumb. It was vexing to argue with someone whose good sense and sympathy would not yield to him the comfort of being in the right. Perhaps it was affinity with another woman that had distorted Eleanor's view of the matter – women so often stuck together. He felt the heat from the fire on his face, cooking his blood. Kindness, yes; a simple draught of human kindness was what he should offer her.

'We were friends,' he said with a bitter little laugh, 'until

227

she saw fit to humiliate me. It would be weak, preposterously weak, to go chasing after her.'

Eleanor stood up, shaking her head. 'To be kind – that is not a weakness. I'm sure, in time, you will recognise the difference. Goodnight, William.'

She stepped quietly out of the room, leaving Will to a solitary hour of fireside brooding.

In her dream Connie could feel herself drowning, whelmed in gulfs as dark and viscous as treacle. Every time she tried to catch her breath she would swallow down another terrible mouthful of it; she couldn't call for help, and yet she sensed that there were others *watching* her while she struggled, refusing to pull her to safety from the choking fathoms. How could that be? And then someone did call to her, softly, coaxingly, and she felt her hand being taken. She surfaced with a start into consciousness, and looked about her. This was nowhere she knew. The smell of Holloway was there, but the mattress, the very linen beneath her felt different, and the light in the room was not the dingy light of her cell.

'Connie? It's me.' She squinted through her bruised eyes at her old friend hovering by the bedside.

'Lil . . . – where am I?' Her voice sounded parched and cracked in her throat. Lily, her face tender with concern, said, 'You're in the infirmary. You've been very ill, Con, but you're getting better.' She drew back to mumble a few words to someone just behind her. Straining her eyes Connie made out Laura, the woman she had been arrested with in Chester Square.

'Darling,' she said, with a tentative little wave.

'I'm awfully thirsty,' Connie said weakly. At this, Laura stood up and went off to fetch a jug of water. 'How long have I been here?' she asked Lily.

'Four days. You've been sleeping most of the time.' She

put her face closer to Connie's and dropped her voice. 'D'you not remember what happened?'

Connie could remember, but she didn't want to think about it just then. She still felt the soreness in her joints that had forewarned her of the trial to come. A ward matron had stopped at the foot of the bed, and told Lily she had five more minutes. Laura returned carrying a tin jug of water, from which she filled a glass and went round to the other side of the bed. Gently, she lifted the patient's head to an angle at which she could put the glass to her lips, but as soon as Connie realised what she was doing she jerked her face away.

'No – please, not like that.'

Lily understood the problem almost immediately. 'It's all right, Con. Don't fret.' As Laura backed away, Lily helped Connie into an upright position against her pillows; as soon as she was settled, Lily put the glass in her friend's pale hand. Connie flicked grateful eyes at her, and shakingly raised it to her mouth. As she felt the relieving trickles of water on her tongue, she heard Lily whisper to Laura, 'She doesn't want anyone pouring liquid down her.'

Laura nodded, and in a gesture of apology she smoothed Connie's hair from her brow. 'So sorry, dear girl.'

Connie drained most of the glass, and handed it back. She moved a finger to her lips and felt their dry flakiness. She supposed she must look an awful fright. Lily had taken hold of her hand again.

'Everyone's been asking after you. They've suspended the doctor because of what happened.'

'I seem to remember collapsing. What then?'

'That throat infection you had led to a fever. You probably caught it from one of the tubes. They say the doctor should have known about your condition.'

Laura said, 'Well, those devils will never do it to you again – there's been such an uproar about it.'

The matron's footsteps sounded behind them. 'Scott, Vaughan. Back to your wards now.'

'We'll come again tomorrow,' said Lily, who bent over and kissed Connie on the forehead. 'Get some rest.'

After they had gone, Connie drifted back to sleep. When she woke again it was evening, and the bars of the infirmary windows cast shadows across the ceiling. Her throat and sinuses still ached, but the awful sweating fever had abated; she knew that she was recovering. When was the moment she knew she would have to join the hunger strike? It was not because she felt an especial injustice at having to wear prison clothes. Whether they put her in the first or the second division of this place seemed hardly to matter; it was still *prison*. Nor was it because she wished to become a martyr. No, it was a strange compound of reasons. Solidarity had proved stronger than dread; she would not shrink from the ordeal that Lily and the others had endured. Natural defiance played a part. And something else, odd to think of now – an inexplicable conviction that *they could not harm her*. They would mark it in her eyes, that 'courage never to submit or yield', and know that their infamous tortures were nothing to her. Nothing!

So she had waited there, like a condemned woman, listening to the scenes of violence as the doctors went from cell to cell. On first hearing them outside, she had quickly checked the makeshift barricade piled up against the cell door. It was frightening to hear such a number of wardresses accompanying the doctor – she heard their low mumble, and then they began to force open the door. Fear gave way to rage: 'If any of you so much as dares to take one step inside this cell, you'll pay for it.' The sound of splintering wood rent the air. In spite of her faintness Connie had fought like a maenad when they had tried to restrain her ('Got a wild one here') and the *language* that had boiled up like poison

230

from her throat as they grappled with one another was a shock even to her. She had coped with the indignities of prison life better than she had expected – it was astonishing how one could adapt – but the cold and the smells and the wretched food and the lack of privacy were as nothing to this, this brutal screaming struggle with hands and arms too many and too powerful for her. Faces loomed above her, their expressions closed, like gates. Was it worse to know what was coming, as she lay pinioned to the bed, to know the physical damage that might be wrought by having an unsterilised tube inserted into a nostril? As she felt the cold rubber snaking up into the nasal cavity, she tried to imagine that it was happening elsewhere, that the aproned doctor with his funnel and the nurse standing on a chair with the jug of liquid were operating upon a body not her own; this was not *her* body going into convulsions, not her eardrums that seemed about to burst, not her throat and breast that heaved against this violation. On and on, it went, she could hear the blood pulsing in her ears until it was no longer possible to dissociate the agony from her own traumatised self. The pain was beating on the walls of her chest so fiercely she thought they would crack.

When it was over, she lay there, shivering, eyes streaming. Mucus clogged her nostrils, and her mouth felt sour from the vomiting she had endured immediately afterwards. Her cheeks felt sore and swollen in a way that reminded her of when she had the mumps as a girl. She felt tearful, but her throat already hurt too much to give way. Some hours later, she jumped at the rattle of the keys at her door, and tensed herself against the return of her tormentors. The figure of a woman was silhouetted against the doorway.

'It's only me, dear,' said Miss Ewell, who had been kind to her these past months. She had brought her an extra blanket.

Connie slumped back onto her bed. 'I thought –' She

laughed in spite of herself. 'I thought it might be them again. With pudding.' Miss Ewell didn't laugh. In the fading light Connie saw that her eyes were glistening. She watched as the wardress opened the blanket and laid it over her. 'Were you there?'

She sensed Miss Ewell stiffen at the question. 'I've asked to be – excused that duty.'

'Why?'

'Because it is barbarous,' she said, casting her eyes down. After some moments she spoke again. 'You're shivering still.'

'I think . . . I'm not quite well. Would you fetch a doctor?'

Miss Ewell nodded, and put a hand to Connie's burning forehead. She had turned for the door when Connie, propping herself on her elbows, called to her.

'One thing – not that doctor.'

By the following morning a throat infection had been diagnosed, and Connie was transferred to the infirmary.

A few days after Lily and Laura had been, Connie had another visitor. Though she had not seen Marianne Garnett in several months, that lady had seldom been far from her thoughts. Even as the WSPU began to break up, Marianne was making her name an increasingly bitter pill in the mouth of the Liberal government. Connie was pleased to see that her aura of glamorous defiance also remained intact.

'How's our brave soldier?' said Marianne, bending down to kiss her. Connie suddenly felt aware of her own smell: the sweetish odour of corruption that always accompanied a recovering hunger-striker.

'The better for seeing you,' she smiled.

'Your illness has caused quite a scandal. It seems incredible that the doctor didn't check your medical records. Lily told me that you probably diagnosed it before he did.'

'Rheumatic fever,' said Connie. 'I had it quite severely as a girl. It resulted in heart trouble – a "murmur" they called it.'

'A murmur? Sounds almost romantic – except that it might have killed you. Well, a letter has been sent to McKenna, and another to *The Times*. We have some eminent names from the medical profession on our side now. We'll make them pay for this.' She looked almost transported by the prospect, but then seemed to recall that this was not the purpose of her visit. 'Forgive me, my dear. That is for another time. Here, I've some things for you.'

She had brought with her a small cardboard box, from which she produced a bottle of cognac, a packet of Lipton's tea, a bar of chocolate, a bag of tangerines and an old edition of Emily Dickinson's poems.

'What a bounty,' Connie said. 'It's very kind of you.' She picked up the Dickinson and riffled its pages. On the flyleaf Marianne's own name was girlishly inscribed.

'To improve the shining hour,' said Marianne with a smile. 'I used to read a good deal myself, before I had children.'

Connie looked up at her. 'You must miss them terribly – in here.'

Marianne shrugged philosophically. 'It's hard, of course. But it will seem a small sacrifice to have made in the long run. And they're not abandoned, in any case – they have their father, and a nanny.'

'Do you suppose we'll get visits over Christmas?' Connie asked.

'Oh yes,' said Marianne. 'Even those blackguards at the Home Office wouldn't refuse us that. I dare say your family will be eager to see you.'

She nodded, reluctant to speculate on the matter. Only Fred had visited her since her sentence began; she had received fretful letters from her mother; from Olivia she had heard nothing. She was surprised to find how much that upset her. She and Lionel were now at Bayswater, in a large house with four servants, a cook and a gardener – 'They're awfully grand,' said Fred, who looked mortified when

Connie had asked him if Olivia intended to visit her. On his second visit it wasn't mentioned. But it was another's absence that had most preoccupied Connie these last months. She now looked upon her initial hopes of a letter from him as merely naive. Fred had told her about Will's visiting the house back in September, and his thunderstruck reaction to the news. Give him time, she thought. When his silence began to lengthen she was compelled to admit to herself that her gamble had been a failure. She supposed that the offence to his pride had been too severe; perhaps he had given way to resentment, to indignation. At times, she could understand why – her behaviour could be construed in one light as the most callous rejection of him. At others, she grew reproachful and thought him irresolute, cold, unfeeling. If kindness were beyond him, wouldn't simple curiosity have induced him to write? It seemed not. He was not going to yield an inch.

Her visitor had risen from the chair at her bedside. Connie held her hand for a moment.

'I'm sorry to presume further on your kindness, Marianne, but could you find me some writing paper?'

Christmas had come and gone by the time Connie was strong enough to get out of bed. She had heard carols being sung by suffragettes outside the walls, but she was still too feeble to partake of the small festive cheer that smuggled its way inside the infirmary. Her mother had sent gifts of a woollen shawl and soap. Fred, permitted a fifteen-minute visit, had also brought in a plum pudding, which she didn't feel up to eating and had passed on to Miss Ewell. Her brother had looked so mournful on seeing Connie in bed that she found herself having to cheer him up.

'Mother and I have been invited to spend Christmas with Olivia and Lionel,' he sighed, picking at the wax candle on the bedside table. Connie gave a grimacing expression.

'That makes me almost grateful to be in here,' she said, and was pleased to hear Fred's tittering laugh. Then he looked suddenly serious again.

'We won't half miss you, Con – really.'

'We?'

'I think even Olivia's softening. She said the other day it was high time she had a talk with you.'

'She knows where to find me,' said Connie drily.

'I wish there was something I could do for you.'

Connie looked down the ward to check the matron's whereabouts. 'There is one thing, actually,' she said, feeling under her pillow and drawing out a thin letter. 'Deliver this for me.'

Fred had a quick look at the envelope before secreting it in his breast pocket. 'Maitland? Has he written to you?'

Connie shook her head. Fred looked nonplussed.

'He once – he once fancied himself in love with me.'

Fred nodded slowly, and when Connie looked away he took the hint that she didn't want to talk about it. A few minutes later the matron came round to call time on his visit.

Will did not return to his flat in Devonshire Place until the new year. He had spent Christmas on the south coast, and had managed to appease his mother by inviting Miss Ada Brink to lunch in the restaurant at Gildersleeves, the town's venerable department store. Will had reasoned that this would be more congenial than a lunch at home, where he and the young lady would be under his mother's scrutiny. They had a table by the window, overlooking the seafront and, beyond it, the swaying grey expanse of the Channel. He found it no imposition to let Ada do most of the talking, for over the years he had learned an eye-contact technique whereby he could appear to be good-naturedly attentive to his interlocutor while communing exclusively with his own thoughts. He felt guilty, sometimes, about the use of this counterfeit social polish, but reckoned that feigning interest in another's conversation was more gracious than showing none at all. He could tell that Ada was quite beguiled by his expressions of involvement – his *hmm*s and *is that so?*s were carefully timed – and while he watched her talk his mind returned to that fireside conversation with Eleanor. They had not spoken of Connie in the days since, but Will realised that his sister's gentle rebuke had made a tiny hairline crack in the carapace of his righteousness. At first he ignored it, and clutched his grievance to him as tightly as a miser to his coin. Then he began to probe at it, and once he had, infuriatingly, he couldn't stop.

Ada had almost reached the end of an intricate anecdote whose point Will was still trying to determine when she broke off, her gaze distracted by something just beyond his shoulder. In an undertone she said, 'There's a gentleman with a large moustache who's been staring at us . . .'

Will shifted round in his chair and there, seated at a distant table, were Tam and his sister Beatrice. Feeling a sudden jolt of embarrassment, he waved to them. He hadn't seen a great deal of Tam these last months, having holed up in London for the autumn; he now remembered that he owed him a letter. Yet his stab of conscience was related to something quite different. As his friend rose and ambled towards their table, Will, arranging his features into a mask of cheerfulness, made the introductions.

'Compliments of the season,' said Tam, after shaking hands with Ada. Something in his expression prompted Will to explain his relation to Miss Brink; he would have liked to assure him that he barely knew the lady, but of course there was no opportunity for such candour. They talked briefly of their respective families, and Will, displaying an ease he didn't feel, invited Tam to bring Beatrice over to Silverton House one evening soon. He hoped the mention of his sister would compel Tam to return to his table, where she still waited, but there was in the older man's eye a gleam of enquiry, and Will knew too well what it concerned.

'I wonder if you've had any news of Miss Callaway?'

'I'm afraid not,' Will replied, pursing his lips. Tam looked puzzled, and his gaze flicked to Ada for a moment before it settled back on Will.

'I thought p'raps you might be curious,' pursued Tam, who knew nothing of what had passed between Connie and Will in the days before her imprisonment. Will, beginning to blush, could only offer a weak shrug; for some reason he felt very reluctant to make reference to Connie in front of Ada, or to discuss her present whereabouts. He could not quite trust himself to speak of her. Tam, who had perceived the awkwardness without understanding its cause, looked at Will searchingly. 'Well . . . I'd best make my own enquiries, then.'

Will canted his head slightly. 'As you wish.' He knew he was handling it poorly, but he wanted this little encounter done with. 'Do pass on my regards to your sister.'

Tam nodded, and with a bow to Ada, he withdrew.

Will had shuddered on recalling this scene in the days following. What a cad he must have appeared to Tam. Now he was back in Marylebone, pulling back the concertinaed metal door to the lift at Devonshire Place when the porter put his head round the door of his office. He offered Will seasonal greetings, and handed over a letter.

'Young feller called with it. He was very pertickler about me handing it *personally* to you.'

Enclosed in the clanking lift, Will examined the envelope. He didn't recognise the handwriting, which was unsteady, like an old person's – and who but an old person or a child would write in pencil? Opening it, he took out the single folded sheet, and flinched as he saw the two words at the top of the page. *Holloway Prison*.

20 December, 1912

Dear Will,

It has become evident that you don't intend to write. It grieves me to presume, therefore, that my arrest and incarceration have only provoked your disapproval, perhaps even your disgust. If so, I am sorry for it. I write not from a wish to pain you further but from the feeling of a debt unpaid – a debt of gratitude. I suppose you might just cast this letter into the fire, but I hope your sense of fairness will allow me a brief hearing. When we last met in September (how long ago that now seems!) we made avowals that could only have been spoken by people who loved one another. I don't regret a word of them. That day you also made a proposal which even now, even *here*, I can't recall without feeling the great honour you did me, and, conversely, the great injustice I did you. While I could make an excuse of the turbulent emotion which my sister's wedding day had brought on, or of the suddenness with which you offered your hand, I ought to have recognised the duty of answering you directly instead of obliging you to wait. In the light of what happened you might suppose that I disdained your proposal, or thought light of it, or – I dread to think what. Believe me, Will, when I say the opposite was true. My comrades and sisters would be astounded to hear it, but I went to prison not only in the assurance of a great cause to sustain me – I went emboldened by the secret solace of *your love*. This, I knew, would lend me the courage to endure. To live, even. You'll probably think me deluded, but I had imagined the day when you would visit me in this place to seek an answer, at last, to the offer you so generously made me. I now see that I asked too much of you.

Perhaps you're wondering why I bother to write this

now. For a time I wondered myself. The hours of prison life pass slowly, and solitude renders the habits of contemplation inescapable. I would have resisted the temptation but for a recent experience that forced me to acknowledge the fragile tenure we hold on life. It seemed suddenly vital not to leave unsaid all the things I ought to have said. Since that day we last spoke I have changed in ways I could hardly have conceived; but the love I had for you then I have for you still. Of your feelings for me I daren't guess. Your silence would indicate that I have wounded you deeply, and for that, again, I most humbly beg your pardon. Please know it was never my purpose to do so.

I hope that your sister and mother are well, and that your Christmas is a peaceful and joyous one. I will only add – God bless you.

Constance

He stood in the cage of the lift, staring at the letter, unable to move. He read it again, and would have remained there still had not another resident on the way out interrupted his trance by pulling back the folding door. With the mechanical step of a sleepwalker Will exited the lift and gravitated across the landing to his flat. Once inside, he threw his travelling case on the bed and sank into an armchair. As one compulsively touches a wound, he returned to the quavery pencil-written text again and felt – it could not have been otherwise – horribly moved. He could not quite take in the meekness of spirit that seemed to inflect every line, and her noble reluctance to accuse or even to complain induced an unwelcome flush of shame at his own indignation. She had not betrayed him, after all. As for the 'recent experience' that had prompted her to write, he could only make conjecture. Had there been a death in the family? He stood up and wandered to the window, from which he gazed down upon the sluggish traffic tooling along Devonshire

Place. He remained standing there, ruminating, until the lamplighter could be seen on his rounds, bringing little points of illumination to the January afternoon's encroaching shadows.

12

Outside the gatehouse at Holloway Prison he stamped his feet to keep the circulation going. It was another unforgivingly cold January morning, the sort when everybody's breath plumed like a dragon's in front of them, and Will was trying not to catch the eye of any of the other visitors waiting there. They were a piteous assembly: a raw-boned young woman in a shawl whose face was pinched and careworn; a couple of dowdy-looking loafers in flat caps and jackets too thin for the cold; and a brawny older woman, her grey hair pulled back in a ragged bun and a pipe clenched in her mouth. Will felt uneasily self-conscious in his grey topcoat and Balmoral boots. His first concern on waking that day was to decide upon the appropriate dress. How ought a man to present himself at one of His Majesty's prisons? He had discarded the black overcoat and respectable homburg on the grounds that they made him look like a hired mourner at a funeral. But among this company he still felt indecently prosperous.

Behind him he heard the iron-studded door creak open, and the porter stood there in soundless invitation. The castellated gatehouse with its battlements and turrets reminded Will of the entrance to a medieval fortress, an effect heightened by the carved winged griffins flanking either side, each bearing a key and shackles. Once inside the prison grounds any such whimsical associations fell away. The walls rose forbiddingly tall and gaunt, their stern Gothic brick interrupted by sequences of mean barred windows. He walked at a slight distance behind the others along a narrow path towards the central concourse, where they were again obliged to wait. Presently a wardress approached him to check the name of the prisoner he was to see, and then he was following in her wake, stopping at doors that sounded to the screech of a bolt and the shivery rattle of keys. As they proceeded up the clanging staircase to a first-floor gallery, Will could hear, from somewhere above them, a choir singing the Marseillaise. The wardress announced, over her shoulder, that the song was a regular favourite of the suffrage prisoners.

'Are all those . . . ladies kept on the same ward?'

The woman nodded. 'As far as possible we try to separate them from the rest. They make a nuisance of themselves, you see, and excite the ordinary prisoners to troublesome behaviour.'

The rousing sweet-voiced anthem sounded incongruous to his ears; this was not at all like the 'shrieking sisterhood' demonised in the press. There seemed almost an innocence to their singing. Holloway itself, on the other hand, had measured up to his gloomiest foreboding. The atmosphere alone would have been offensive enough, a sour, unwashed stench mingled with blocked drains and boiled vegetables that transported him, reluctantly, back to the dinner hall of his public school. His own experience of an enforced institutional life had not been happy, and he felt sometimes that only his cricketing prowess had enabled him to survive it. He recalled his first days there – the sudden shouts, the peremptory bells, the implacable thunder of footsteps, the noxious odours – and the sickening realisation that this would be his life for the next five years. Yet it now seemed positively benign in comparison with the infinite drear of this vast, echoing enclosure, and he felt a hollowing sensation in his stomach that this – *this* – was the place she had been shut up inside for the last four months.

The wardress had come to a halt outside a cell whose door stood open, ready to receive him; she tilted her head, and said, 'You have half an hour.' Will looked through the doorway and saw a woman sitting on a bunk, her face in profile. At first he thought that there had been a mistake, and he turned to explain to the wardress that this was not the prisoner he had come to visit – when he heard a voice call his name. Her voice. He looked into the cell again, and saw, with an inward shock, that it was Connie. He stepped across the threshold, and she stood up to greet him. In those first few moments he took in her sallow skin, the sunken eyes, the visible depletion of her frame, though it was the cropped hair, seemingly cut by a blind man, that had caused his initial failure to recognise her. It sprouted unevenly on her head in tufts and spikes, and even the colour appeared to have changed from its natural chestnut to a dull, nondescript brown. She was wearing her own clothes, which was a mercy, though even they had lost most of their colour and shape.

'Hullo,' she said, shyly extending her hand. Will wondered if he should kiss her, but did not. Her hand felt bony in his. He was mute and motionless, with the air of someone not quite sure what he was doing there. 'There's a little chair behind you,' she added, sensing that it behoved her to establish some small impression of hospitality on the proceedings. She now sat down opposite him, with her hands in her lap. They looked at one another in silence until Connie said, 'How are you?'

Will, swallowing, found his voice at last. 'Your hair . . . what – what happened?'

Connie instinctively ran her hand over her scalp. 'Oh . . .'

she sighed, and grimaced. 'Head lice, I'm afraid – caught from the hairbrush that was here. I didn't realise – it was difficult to get them out, so one of the girls cut it for me.'

He nodded, and looked about the cell, uncertainly. Then he returned his gaze to her. 'How are you?' Given her unhealthy pallor, he sensed the awkwardness of his question.

She smiled, and shrugged. 'Better than I have been. I was quite ill, just before Christmas – did I mention it in my letter?'

'No, you didn't. What was wrong?'

'I caught an infection –' She paused, and decided that it would be kinder to spare him the details. 'A throat infection, which led to rheumatic fever. It became quite severe . . .'

She watched his brow darken as he digested this information. 'You wrote something about a "recent experience" – I thought you were referring to a bereavement . . .' He looked at her almost in panic. 'How ill *were* you?'

Connie looked down for a moment, then lifted her eyes to his. 'As you can see, I survived.'

Something horrific had now begun to insinuate itself, and he felt torn between conflicting urges to know and not to know. She read his perturbation in the sudden draining of colour from his face. 'Am I to understand . . .' he said, in a voice barely audible, 'you've been forced . . . ?'

She only looked at him, and Will lowered his head into his hands, the same appalled attitude he had last adopted, unknowingly, when Fred had told him of her prison sentence in September. He remained in that position for a long minute, unmoving. When he finally raised his face again she saw that his eyes were glassy and red-rimmed, and it seemed possible that he would cross the narrow space between them and take her in his arms. That was her hope. But he remained seated, his expression frozen with pity while, within, he tried to master a shiver of fright. For in spite of the love that still scrambled for a hold on his heart, he could no longer pretend to himself that he was not scared by her. Some terrible derangement must have brought her to this pass – how else could she have exposed herself to such a violation? He stared at her, at her poor shredded hair, and recoiled. A woman must indeed be graciously endowed if her outward appearance can defy the toll of prison life. He might have anticipated her condition, and armed himself to face it, but his imagination was not sufficiently developed to do so.

Connie, perceiving some of his dismay, said, 'I suppose you must have been very angry with me, or else you would have written.'

Will nodded. 'Yes, I was. I took it very badly. I'm sorry.'

'No, no – I should be the one to say sorry. After what passed between us you deserved far kinder treatment than I gave you.' His head was turned away, and she didn't know if she was more disheartened by his silence or by the odd mechanical way he had spoken.

'So, you didn't mean to – humiliate me?'

'Of course not. How could you think me capable of such a thing?'

'When I first learned of what had happened, I thought you'd been possessed by some kind of . . . madness. I couldn't see how else to explain it.'

Connie looked at him sadly. He really was that far from understanding her, it seemed. She stood and leaned over to the little shelf of books. His remark had triggered a memory of something she had lately read, and she took up the Emily Dickinson poems which Marianne had lent her.

'D'you mind if I read something to you?'

Will made a little gesture of assent with his hands. She found the page she was looking for, and read aloud:

'Much Madness is divinest Sense
To a discerning Eye
Much Sense the starkest Madness
Tis the Majority
In this, as All, prevail
Assent and you are sane
Demur you're straightway dangerous
And handled with a Chain'

She closed the book, and gave him a level look. Will, feeling as if he were sitting a viva, only nodded; he supposed it had been written by a woman, but he said nothing. Connie tried a different prompt. 'Have you never fought for something you believed in, even when you knew that doing so might be harmful?'

Will considered this. What, really, *did* he believe in? He took no interest in politics or in the controversies of the day, and he had never been one for causes – unless one deemed cricket to be a cause. 'I once – a friend of mine – I defended him when he faced . . . dismissal. But there is a world of difference. I didn't go to prison for it.'

'But it was to your disadvantage that you helped him?'

He gave a small shrug. 'I suppose it was. In the end it profited neither of us.'

'That is beside the point. You saw an injustice and stood up for him. The principle remains the same.'

Will looked away, shaking his head. 'The two are in no way comparable. You broke the law – you willingly went to jail. And you did so knowing that it would destroy any chance of a future we might have.'

She heard a bitterness in his tone. The rift had widened between them, and it was by no means certain that Will wanted to help repair it. A kind of calm despair settled upon her. It was better to know how matters stood between them than to foster the illusion of hope.

'William – please look at me. I make no claim on you, don't be alarmed. I have forfeited the privilege of accepting your offer, and I don't expect another. I only wish to know –' here she paused '– have you no love left for me?'

Will flinched at the word, and let his gaze stray over the room. The agony of it was that he did feel love, yet the woman to whom he had declared it was so very different from the one seated here before him. He wanted that one back, the Connie who had beautiful bright eyes and a gay laugh, not this pale, half-demented wretch. He shifted in his chair, discomfited by his own delay. 'I – I hardly know what to say. The woman I loved was not one I ever imagined visiting in prison.'

'You see me here nonetheless. I am still that woman you held in your arms. Is it perhaps *you* who have changed?'

Will, pierced by the suggestion, decided that going on the offensive would be the surest way to get out of this corner. He gave an exasperated sigh. 'I'm sorry, I should have known it was a mistake to come here,' he said, coldly swallowing down the shame of his evasion.

'It wasn't a mistake, Will,' she replied, trying to keep hold of her voice.

'Tell me,' he said, sharpening his wronged tone, 'why should I trust you after what you did? How do I know that you won't go and break more windows on getting out of here?'

His blustering words had spared him the courtesy of an honest answer, and the growing suspicion that he no longer loved her reduced Connie to silence. She absently drew her hand over her head, as if to check that her long dark hair really had gone; the pity of the gesture touched him so painfully he had to look away. He knew at an instinctive level that he could have asked her forgiveness, just as meekly as she had sought his, but the guilt he felt was being dissolved by the quick-acting acid of self-righteousness. She watched him stand up, but couldn't make herself catch his eye.

His voice sounded hard and businesslike. 'You will be out in – two months?'

Connie nodded, her eyes fixed to the floor, while he lingered there, turning his hat in his hands. He cleared his throat again. 'I hope – I hope it passes quickly for you.' He waited for her to raise her face to him, but she didn't move from where she sat, and after a few moments he turned on his heel and walked quietly out of the cell. As she heard his footsteps recede down the corridor the first tear rolled from her chin on to her lap; she did nothing to staunch the steady *plip* of the ones that followed.

One morning, some days later, Connie was idling in the exercise yard with Laura when one of the wardresses emerged from the administration wing.

'Callaway,' the woman called, crooking a finger at her like a headmistress to a naughty pupil. 'Visitor for you.'

Laura, her arms held across her chest against the cold, turned an inquisitive expression on Connie, who gave a shrug, then followed the wardress in the direction of the visitors' room. She had not been expecting anyone. Fred, faithful Fred, had been to see her the previous week, and any further visits would have had to be arranged in advance. She smoothed her hand over her tufty hair, a gesture which had unwittingly become a tic, and entered the hall. The wardress, not troubling to speak, nodded in the direction of a large gentleman seated at one of the far tables. As she walked towards him, she tried to recall where she had seen him before. He was bald, and his girth, unabashedly spherical, was adorned by a gold watch chain. Thin-rimmed spectacles perched on the end of his nose. He stood up to greet her.

'Miss Callaway? George Fotheringham,' he said, holding

out a hand. 'We have met once before . . .' And now Connie did remember: he was the Maitland family lawyer who had arrived at lunch on the weekend Connie had gone to stay.

'Yes – hullo,' she said, still nonplussed. 'How are you?'

Fotheringham spread his palms expansively. 'Very well indeed, I thank you. But it is about *your* health I have come to enquire. Please – sit.' His gaze, shrewder than it had been when tucking into his food, seemed to interrogate Connie's appearance and then offer a sorrowing verdict. He joined the tips of his stubby fingers to make a steeple. 'I have been apprised of recent events via one means or another. I gather you were forcibly fed on several occasions last year, as a result of which you contracted a quite severe rheumatic fever. I've not read the report of the doctor responsible, but if my information is correct it seems that you have a very good case.'

'Case – for what?'

'Why, for an early release, my dear. The matter stands thus: the doctor failed to check your medical history. He then suffered you to be forcibly fed, thereby exacerbating a heart condition and endangering your life. One could sue on a charge of negligence, of course, but that would entail gathering witnesses, testimonies and so forth. It would take too long to come to trial. If, however, His Majesty's Prisons agree to settle out of court – which would be to their advantage – the remainder of your sentence will be waived, and you will walk free.'

Connie was taken aback, first by the prospect of sudden deliverance; second, and more piquantly, by the implication behind Fotheringham's presenting himself here. Will must have commissioned this esteemed legal gentleman to visit her, which in itself suggested a remorse for his previously unyielding attitude. Did that mean . . . ? She couldn't allow herself to hope such a thing. Perhaps it was a gesture of conciliation, which would in itself be remarkable after their last encounter. But there was a practical consideration to discuss.

'Mr Fotheringham, I am very grateful to you for coming here, believe me, but I must tell you, my finances are in no fit state –'

'All taken care of,' he broke in, holding up his hands like the stage magician who has just made his silk handkerchief disappear. 'Your benefactor has underwritten all of my fees, so let it not concern you. Now, to business. I am obliged to take a statement from you, so if you would be good enough to recount precisely what happened . . .' Having removed paper and a pen from his briefcase, he proceeded for the next half-hour to question Connie on the circumstances of her hunger strike and the brutal measures HMP Holloway had taken to thwart it. Aside from an occasional harrumph or a clarifying question, the lawyer's demeanour remained steadily dispassionate: he might have been compiling a list for his grocer. It was oddly reassuring, Connie found, to describe what had befallen her without having to endure a listener's sympathy. While they talked, she wondered what Mrs Maitland would say if she ever found out that her lawyer had been co-opted to the defence of a suffragette. It spoke highly of Will's nerve that he had gone behind her back.

When he had completed the transcript to his satisfaction, Fotheringham carefully replaced the cap on his fountain pen and folded away his papers. He fixed Connie with a rueful look of reminiscence.

'The last time I visited this place, my client was facing a life sentence.'

Connie hesitated before she spoke. 'In truth, Mr Fotheringham, to anyone who has been here, all sentences are life sentences. The experience of this place will stay with me for as long as I live.'

'Well, then, I shall make it my business to ensure your speedy liberation.'

'Speedy?'

'I envisage no longer than a week, once we set the wheels in motion.'

'You must be a very good lawyer,' she said, confounded.

'Oh, more than good, Miss Callaway – the best!' And he permitted himself a complacent chuckle. Which meant that he must be expensive, too, thought Connie, preparing her expressions of gratitude.

'I shall write a letter in due course,' she said, 'but in the meantime, please do pass on my thanks – my sincere thanks – to William.'

Fotheringham frowned at this. 'William? I don't quite –' For the first time since their interview began the lawyer appeared at a loss.

'William Maitland?' she prompted. 'I presume he sent you.'

He slowly shook his head. 'I've heard nothing from young Maitland. Forgive me, I should have made it clear. I am here at the behest of Mr Tamburlain.'

Connie was stunned. 'Tam?'

'The same,' he replied. 'I thought you would have known . . .' He proceeded to explain the circumstances of Tam writing to him. 'I *am* a little surprised he didn't write to you also, but then Mr Tamburlain has a delicacy about him – as I'm sure you know.'

Connie nodded, merely to hide her confusion. Tam, of all people. That he knew about her imprisonment might have been expected; that he had put himself out to help her was beyond comprehension. She barely knew him. They had met one another only a handful of times. As she adjusted to this unforeseen beneficence she felt a simultaneous plunge of her heart: Will would have nothing to do with her, after all. Fotheringham had risen from his chair and was hitching up his trousers. He looked about him, sniffing the air as he might have done a corked bottle of wine.

'I am sorry that you have had to brave this place, Miss Callaway. Be assured that it will not be for much longer.'

She smiled as they shook hands, and studied his slow, waddling gait as he left the room, her roly-poly redeemer dispatched from out of the blue.

The lawyer proved as good as his word. Five days later Connie had gathered together her modest rubble of possessions and was tidying up her cell when a knock sounded on the open door. It was Miss Ewell, who, Connie realised, had come to say goodbye in spite of being off duty this day. There was a fond glimmer in her eye.

'I find myself quite torn,' she began, blushing slightly. 'On the one hand, I'm very glad to see you getting out of this place, and on the other – I'm sorry, because . . . you'll be missed.'

Connie looked down. 'You've been so good to me, Miss Ewell –'

'Faith. My name – I'd rather you remember me as Faith.'

Connie made a little bow of compliance. 'Faith, Constance – what a pair we make!'

'My father is a minister. I suppose that's why he thought the name . . . I'm afraid my conviction in most things has been – unsteady.'

'Even in your . . . calling?'

'Especially in that. I started at prison work so hopefully – I thought I could do some good – but my high ideals have been worn down.'

'You *did* do some good,' said Connie, gently. 'I wish that all the wardresses had been as kind as you.'

But Miss Ewell looked sad, and shook her head. 'I can't help thinking what has been done here, to you, to others – it's – wicked. Which is why –' at this she checked the door, to see that no one was about '– I'd like you to take this.'

From her pocket she drew out an envelope, on which she had written Connie's name in brown ink.

'You have nothing to apologise for,' said Connic.

'Maybe not. But I'd like you to have it anyway.'

'What is it?'

'You'll see. Open it when you're gone from here. Please?'

Connie thanked her and hid it in the breast pocket of her coat. Then she put on her hat, the navy cloche with the flame-coloured band, which Fred had brought in for her last week. She stood before her jailer.

'How do I look?'

'As neat as a new pin,' said Miss Ewell, and shyly offered her hand. Connie pressed it between her palms.

'Goodbye, Faith. And thank you for . . .' she hesitated, not sure if the words would ring true, but she said them anyway: 'for being a friend.'

A quarter of an hour later, Connie heard the choir practising on the gallery above, and she asked permission from the wardress who had come to escort her for a few minutes' leave. She quickly climbed the stairs and there, conducting the women as usual, was Ivy Maddocks. Unlike Laura, to whom she had become close during their months of incarceration, she had not enjoyed more than a remote cordiality with Ivy. Connie was impressed by her zealous adherence to the cause – it was difficult not to be – but she found it impossible to converse for long with someone so deficient in a sense of humour. In fact, there were moments when a light flared in her eyes that Connie found quite disconcerting. Even in a ward bristling with the militant spirit there were a handful of women who seemed to live the struggle more intensely than their sisters. Ivy caught sight of her now; with a sudden flick of her baton she silenced her choir, and came along the gallery to greet her.

'I'm going today, Ivy. I just wanted to say goodbye.'

'Oh!' she said, narrowing her aquiline gaze. 'Your singing

will be missed, Constance. Perhaps you'd like to join us for "The March of the Women" before you leave?'

Connie laughed, until she realised that Ivy was being quite serious. 'Thank you, but – the wardress awaits.' That she also cheerfully loathed the song she decided to keep to herself.

'I dare say we'll see one another soon enough – at the meeting in April?' There was a WSPU reunion planned for those suffragettes who had served time in Holloway.

'Yes, of course,' said Connie, 'Laura told me about it. We three shall meet again – like the weird sisters!'

Ivy blinked at her uncomprehendingly. 'Weird?'

'Yes . . . like *Macbeth*?'

'Oh, I see,' said Ivy, in a frowning way that made Connie regret the humorous allusion, and wonder indeed if it were humour at all. One simply couldn't be frivolous with certain people. She held out her hand, which Ivy took in a surprisingly fierce grip.

'Remember, Constance,' she said, moving her face so close that Connie could see her light-coloured eyelashes, 'no surrender to tyranny. *We must win this war.*'

Connie nodded, and was about to conclude with a 'goodbye', but Ivy had already turned away and stalked back to her spot in front of the choir. As she descended the stairs, the familiar words echoed along the gallery.

> *March, march, swing you along,*
> *Wide blows our banner and hope is waking.*

She left by the same gate she had entered the place, though she hadn't seen it back in September, immured within the jangling dark of the Black Maria. Up to the very last moment, having signed for the return of her possessions and walked across the courtyard, she had to suppress an irrational anxiety that a clerical error would come to light, and that she would be obliged to serve out her sentence after all. But as the gatekeeper drew back the bolts and pushed open the studded door she knew at last that there had been no mistake, for there, loitering by the outer railings, stood Fred. Never had she been so glad to see him, even she, who had always held her brother the dearest companion of her life. She had envisaged this day often enough to believe herself prepared for it, yet who can really know the violence of relief a prisoner experiences at the moment of liberation, but that prisoner herself? Flinging herself into his arms, she hugged Fred so tightly that he was at length moved to loosen her embrace by small degrees.

'Just let me – if you wouldn't mind – catch my breath,' he said, with laughing gasps, though she could not for a long time lift her face from his shoulder. Nor was she able to form a coherent sentence, so Fred did the talking for both of them, and merely the sound of his voice – with nobody there to interrupt it – assured her that she was, incontrovertibly, a free woman. A policeman on duty at the gates was looking on in idle curiosity; she wondered how many such reunions he had witnessed at this spot. To him she was just another member of the criminal classes.

Fred had picked up her suitcase. 'We could wait here for a cab, if you like –'

'No, let's just walk,' she said. 'I'd rather not spend another minute around this place.' They started up Hillmartin Road, and Connie linked her arm through Fred's. A low sun glistened over the rooftops. To tread this pavement, to feel the nipping February air on her face – these things she would never take for granted again. On Caledonian Road they caught a 'bus heading south, and sat on the top deck. Fred took a packet of Sullivans from his pocket, and they lit one each. She watched an aproned waiter sluicing down the pavement outside one of the poky dining rooms that lined the way, and noticed the bill of fare in its window. Chops, steamed pudding, cocoa; what a treat in store after five months of Holloway's food. Would she ever be able to banish the taste of that tea?

Fred meanwhile was praising the good offices of Mr Fotheringham, who had called at Thornhill Crescent in person to tell them the news of her imminent release. 'Very decent of Mr Tamburlain to hire him, wasn't it?'

'Yes . . . astonishingly decent,' she said thoughtfully. 'He's a friend of – William Maitland.' She suffered a sharp little pang as she said his name, and wondered how long it might take her to forget him. Fred glanced warily at her.

'Heard anything from him?'

She shook her head. 'I don't expect to. He made his feelings quite plain when he came to visit.'

Fred nodded, and gave a slight grimace. 'I should warn you – there'll be a reception committee waiting at home. Ma says that the family needs to pull together in a crisis –'

'A bit late for that, I would have thought. And if she really believes in pulling together, why did she never visit me?'

Fred looked embarrassed, unable to defend his family's negligence yet unwilling to be disloyal. 'Well, I suppose it was hard for her –'

'No need to explain, Fred,' she cut in, not wishing to hear about her mother's delicate nerves. 'I'm only glad that I had you to rely on.' And she hugged him fiercely again.

'Steady on, old thing,' he said, blushing. Fred was never quite at ease with public displays of affection. They alighted from the 'bus and turned into Lofting Road. The streets looked the same to Connie, yet felt subtly different; they had taken on a queer new vivacity in her absence, she thought. Life had been going on as usual while she was away. It would go on as usual when she was dead. On past St Andrew's Church they walked, and she felt a hollowing nervousness as they rounded the crescent towards the house.

At the front window a face appeared, and then withdrew – Olivia's? At the steps she took a last drag of her Sullivan and extinguished it beneath her heel. She realised she had been holding Fred's hand, something she'd not done since they were children.

The front door opened, and her aunt Jemima stepped onto the porch, and Connie walked into her embrace.

'Welcome home, dear,' she said, patting her back like a child. 'I'm so glad to see you again.'

'Not as glad as I am to see you,' said Connie, trying to keep her voice steady. She walked into the hallway, and Fred took her coat and hat while she wondered where the rest of the family was. Jemima gestured silently towards the drawing room, and Connie followed her in. The first person she saw was her mother, swathed in blankets on the couch; her face looked pale, waxy and drawn. Olivia and Lionel, both stationed by the fireplace, seemed rooted to the spot. Seated near the piano, his knobbly hand resting on his cane, was her grandfather, with his 'helpmeet' Mrs Rhodes, and next to them Louis. It was almost as if they were all waiting for her to do something. Then, amid the dithering, Louis sprang forward to plant a kiss on her.

'Hullo, Con,' he said, and taking courage from his gesture she went around the room offering her hand to shake and her cheek to kiss. She sensed a wariness in their reception, but also a sort of pride, as though she were a notorious royal returning from exile. She supposed there had never been a jailbird in the family before. Folding herself onto her knees she kissed her mother, who, still supine on the couch, said in a broken voice, 'Oh, darling, what have they done to your lovely hair?' And with a trembling hand she stroked Connie's shorn head.

'It'll grow back, Ma. You'll see.' On her way home she had promised herself that, having succumbed to tears on seeing Fred, she would not cry again that day. But the tenderness of her mother's touch proved too pathetic to bear, and Connie fell against her, eyes flooded and unseeing.

Later, encouraged by the benign midwinter temperature, she drifted out to the garden and held her face to the thin silver brilliance of the sun. She had made a particular point of talking to Mrs Rhodes, who seemed pleasantly surprised to have been invited to the house after being excluded from Olivia's wedding last September. Connie knew it must have been Fred's unthinking generosity that had secured her invitation. Louis had just lit a cigarette for her when she saw her grandfather tottering towards them.

'My dear,' he wheezed, 'splendid to have you back in the land of the living.' His eyes were rheumy and rather bloodshot.

'Grandpa,' she smiled.

'I'll have you know I wrote to *The Times* about that black-guard doctor,' and he proceeded, with pauses and many *nyuff-nyuff*s, to recount the burden of his outraged missive. 'Didn't print the damned thing,' he concluded vaguely.

'It was good of you to take the trouble,' she said, patting his hand.

He eyed her worriedly. 'You're looking a bit scrawny, my dear. What say I take you and feller-me-lad to dine at the club one of these days?'

'No ladies permitted, I think . . .'

He looked confused for a moment. 'Oh . . . well . . . Verrey's, then. We'll have a good feed at Verrey's.'

Out of the corner of her eye Connie saw Olivia coming down the garden towards them, Lionel and Fred in tow. Her sister's greeting in the drawing room had, not untypically, lacked warmth: she had a habit of leaning in and offering her cheek, while keeping her lips firmly pointed away from the recipient, as if in fear of a contagion. Connie could not recall the last time they had embraced. Even their long separation had not inclined Olivia to soften her glacial manner. She was staring at the cigarette in Connie's hand.

'I suppose it barely matters inside a prison, but it *is* rather common to be seen smoking on the street.' So it *had* been her face at the window. Connie looked hard at her, then shook her head.

'Is that really the first thing you wished to say to me after five months?'

Olivia, flinching, pursed her lips. 'I'm – very glad you've recovered from your illness. Fred kept us informed. But I'm appalled that you could have put your life at risk in that way. Your behaviour . . . I sometimes wonder how we could possibly be related to one another.'

'I wonder about that, too,' said Connie, surprised to find herself so quickly on the defensive. 'I suppose you think I'm a danger to myself.'

'As a matter of fact I do,' Olivia replied, 'though short of having you put away somewhere there's not much we can do about that.'

Fred interposed himself at that. 'Olivia – please. How can you talk of putting Con away when she's only just *got out*?'

Lionel, whose thunderous brow was writ large with disapproval, now began to address Connie. 'I do think you might start with an apology to your mother.'

'Oh, really – an apology?'

'Yes. For bringing disgrace on the family.'

Connie gasped out a little laugh at this, and then stopped. She fixed Lionel with a gaze of incredulous scorn, and said, very coolly, 'I'm sorry, but I haven't the smallest notion as to why you feel qualified even to *speak* to me, let alone advise me.' Lionel made to reply, but Connie was now addressing herself to Olivia. 'I'm quite prepared to continue this conversation, but I'm afraid it must be without . . . *him* at my elbow.' Olivia looked to Lionel, who seemed to rear back as though his face had been suddenly slapped.

'Of all the impudent –' he began, until Olivia cut him short.

'Lionel, *that's enough.*'

Connie, her arms folded, would not even deign to look in his direction, but she knew from the sharpness of her sister's tone that Lionel had overstepped. Some moments passed, and then, following some heated whispers between husband and wife, Connie heard Lionel turn sullenly away and recede from earshot. She looked round at Fred, who had gone pale. The air felt abruptly charged, and the three siblings stood there waiting for the tension to subside.

'So – am I to be awarded the official role of the family's black sheep?' mused Connie.

'It pleases you to jest,' Olivia replied. 'But it is our misfortune that you are blind to any sense of shame.'

'Well, that's not entirely –' Fred began in objection, but was cut off by Olivia, whose face seemed to tighten with hostility.

'From what I've heard Mr Maitland was also appalled by your behaviour –'

'Who told –' Connie glanced at Fred, who had let his head drop guiltily. With an answering coldness she said, 'Whatever passed between Mr Maitland and myself is none of your business.'

'Perhaps so. He has had a lucky escape, one might say. But it becomes my business –' and here she dropped her voice to a threatening undertone '– when your pursuit of notoriety impinges on Mother's health.'

'What are you talking about?'

'You must see how ill she is! Do you suppose she rejoices in the knowledge that her daughter tried to starve herself to death?'

'But Ma has been like that ever since Pa died. She has made herself a martyr to her nerves – you know that.'

'You selfish girl,' Olivia hissed, colouring angrily. 'You

have no *idea* what she has been through. What Pa did she will never be able –'

'That's enough, Olivia,' said Fred, whose interruption this time was so decisive that Connie sensed something afoot. Olivia herself looked suddenly discomfited, as though her reference to their father had been quite involuntary. Something ominous, glimpsed from the corner of Connie's eye but never comprehended, was gathering into view. But what it was she still couldn't say.

'I think, perhaps, you ought to explain,' she said. 'I know how hard it's been for her – but we lost a father, too, remember.'

Olivia now paused, and looked around to check that their conversation was not being monitored. Her voice sounded different. 'I never wanted to have to tell you this, but your behaviour compels me to. This cannot happen to Ma again – it must not.'

'What do you mean, "again"?' said Connie, who felt her dread stirring into certainty. She knew what was coming. It was like burning your hand on the stove; the accidental touch warned you, but it took your brain a fraction of a second longer to register the pain. Olivia's mouth trembled as she spoke.

'Another suicide in the family – it would destroy her.'

Connie felt the shock of the words, and yet it wasn't a surprise. If she had thought about it long enough, it would have been obvious, and so she had never dared to think about it. Her father had been brought to ruin by a financial speculation. Had she never suspected the convenience of his being felled by a heart attack so soon afterwards? She looked at Fred, whose face was averted. She could tell from the hang of his shoulders that he already knew.

'How?' Her voice sounded hollow in her chest.

Olivia stared down as she spoke. Their father had stayed late in his office on the evening that news of the scheme's failure had broken. One of his business partners by chance had seen a light under the door and gone to investigate: he had found Donald Callaway slumped at his desk, his throat leaking from the blade he had taken to it. It seemed that he had used a razor instead of a gun so as not to disturb any of his colleagues with the noise. Connie pictured her father now, the lifeblood pooling out of him, his skin still warm when he was discovered. She shuddered, and looked to Fred.

'When did you know?'

He lifted his face, taut with misery, and glanced at Olivia. 'About two weeks ago.'

'Why did you keep it from us? *How* could you keep it from us?'

Olivia, dabbing at her eyes, shrugged. 'You were both young. The company was trying to hush up the story, so we thought – I don't know what we thought.' And at that she looked to Connie, who discerned in her sister's face not the resentment of old but something closer to anguish. Olivia and her mother had wanted to protect them from the knowledge, yet they had obliged the whole family to live a lie. A bankrupt was bad enough; a suicide was beyond the pale.

They could hear Mrs Etherington calling them into lunch. Connie suddenly felt sick to her stomach, and the thought of being the centre of attention in the dining room was not to be borne.

'I'm afraid you'll have to make an excuse for me,' she said. 'I need to go . . .'

'Where?'

Connie shook her head. 'I don't know. I just need to gather my thoughts.' She realised that the colour must have fled from her face, because Fred had his anxious look again.

'Connie,' said Olivia, 'please don't say anything to Ma.'

Connie nodded, then slipped round the far side of the

house and exited through the garden gate. On her way down the crescent she ran into her cousins, Jecca and Flora, returning from an errand.

'Hullo, girls,' she said with all the brightness she could manage.

'You've got short hair!' said Flora unarguably. Connie touched her hand to her head, as if reminding herself. Both girls were staring at her, their infamous cousin, the jailbird.

'Where are you going?' asked Jecca.

'Oh, just for a walk. I need some fresh air.'

Flora was still fascinated by her new haircut. 'It looks nice.'

Connie bent down and kissed her, catching the girl's sweet breath – so different from prison breath. 'I'll be back shortly,' she called over her shoulder. On the other side of Thornhill Square she stopped in front of the new public library; they still called it 'new', though it had opened in 1907. Her father had taken them there – it must have been the summer before he died – and Connie remembered his remarking upon the classical ornamentation within. He had delighted in the architect's modelling of the motifs on a Greek temple, she couldn't recall which. Her father, the enthusiast, the showman, who could cajole anyone into a good mood by sheer force of his personality. She entered the place now, and went up the stairs to the reading room, as quiet as a church on this cold, crisp morning. She settled at a desk by the window with a view across the square. How could a man so much in love with life have shown so little regard for it? Was it a failure of reason that induced him to take his own life, or was it something worse – a failure of love? Did he ever pause to wonder what it would do to them, to her? She had been his favourite it had been a joke among them. A shocked little gasp escaped her, and she looked about the room. No one had noticed. *Another suicide . . .*

Connie felt a sudden lowering hopelessness. What use had been the strike? What use had been any of their protests?

Then she remembered the envelope which Miss Ewell had given her earlier that morning. She opened it, and drew out a crisply folded ten-pound note, with a card attached to it. The handwritten text was brief.

HMP Holloway, London, N.

25 February 1913

Dear Miss Callaway,

The enclosed is a gift to the Women's Social and Political Union. I know that you will ensure it reaches their treasurer via the appropriate conduit. I hardly need explain why I cannot be seen to make the donation in my own name. I pray for you and your perseverance in the cause – a good and courageous one, as it now appears to me. God bless you in all of your future endeavours, and permit me to call myself,

Your friend,
Faith Ewell

13

In the weeks following her release, Connie frequently found herself at a loss, so disabling had been the habits of prison life. Things that she had once been inclined to do almost without thinking now required a careful negotiation. Even the simple process of leaving the house gave her pause: she would tell her mother that she was about to go out, and then would look for a reply, as if awaiting her permission. In her bedroom at night she found the quiet unnerving, and would stay awake listening for a wardress's footfall that never came. At mealtimes she was distracted by the absence of the prison grace she had heard recited daily, and would mutter it under her breath. She had also become neurotic about the laying of the table, and would surprise Fred and her mother by suddenly standing up and rearranging plates and cutlery before anyone was allowed to eat. She thought of this repetitive behaviour as 'Holloway-itis'.

Yet Connie was not the only one to have changed. Mrs Callaway seemed at last to slough off the lassitude of her widowhood, put aside her phantom illnesses, and devoted herself to her daughter's recuperation as though in apology for her own habits of neediness. Nothing was said on the matter between them, but Connie wondered if her mother had sensed that the dark secret of her husband's demise was now shared equally among her children. It was as if they had pledged one another to a vow of silence. Whenever his name was mentioned, they would tread carefully and watch each other like spies in possession of the same terrible knowledge. And yet it seemed to Connie that they behaved this way not out of fear, but out of love.

Olivia also appeared to notice this change, and some weeks after their momentous encounter at Thornhill Crescent she did something quite out of character by inviting Connie to dinner. No mention was made of her heated exchange with Lionel, though Connie sensed that Olivia at some level approved of her sister's refusal to be cowed by him: perhaps she had belatedly recognised a strain of defiance that reflected well on the Callaways. She shook her head at the pompous invitation card Olivia had seen fit to send, but she was pleased by it nevertheless. The spirit of conciliation was not everywhere apparent. At the bookshop her position as manager had been usurped in her absence, and Mr Hignett's letter in response to Connie's enquiry about her old job was, though polite in tone, unequivocal in its rebuff.

Yet no sooner had one door closed than another quite unexpectedly swung open. Among the stack of correspondence that had gathered during her detention at Holloway was a letter from Henry Cluett, the surgeon to whom Brigstock had introduced her last year, expressing a hope that she may wish to act as his assistant – unofficially, of course – in his new post at St Thomas's Hospital. He regretted that the emolument would be small, but it would afford her useful experience in 'theatre'. Connie was thrilled by the offer, though she fretted that her less than prompt reply might have injured her chances: Mr Cluett's letter had arrived in January, six weeks ago, and, reckoning that a full disclosure of her whereabouts was inadvisable, she wrote explaining her tardiness as 'an indisposition' and hoped that his invitation still stood. The surgeon replied forthwith, admitting puzzlement at the delay but assuring her that the job was hers. She would start in April, if it suited.

Hardly able to believe her good fortune, Connie now discharged another debt of gratitude. Having obtained his address from Mr Fotheringham, she wrote a letter of thanks to Tam for his kind offices, not only in hiring the lawyer but in settling his fees, too. It was small recompense, she knew, but would he allow her to thank him personally over lunch when he was next in town? Her letter went unanswered for some weeks, a delay explained on her receiving a reply care of a hotel on the Isle of Wight, where he had gone for a month's fishing and sailing. She briefly wondered if Will had accompanied him. In any event, Tam accepted her thanks, expressed relief that she was well again, and assented gladly to the prospect of a luncheon when he next came up to town.

The early months of the new year had seen the Union stepping up its campaign of civic disruption. It was no longer enough to set fire to pillar boxes and break windows. Now there came attacks on municipal buildings, railway trains and pavilions; golf links and bowling greens were cut up or scoured with acid. At a house being built for Lloyd George at Walton on the Hill in Surrey a bomb was detonated, an outrage for which Mrs Pankhurst herself claimed personal responsibility and was subsequently arrested. The language of war bristled in the air, and the militants began to see themselves as guerrilla fighters operating in enemy territory. Connie sensed a turning in the tide of public opinion. The outlaw glamour of the suffragettes, once treated with a wary respect, had begun to provoke impatience, and sometimes outright hostility. One afternoon late in March she and Laura were selling copies of *The Suffragette* news-sheet outside the Strand Tube station. Most passers-by ignored them, though Laura's natural good cheer was beguiling the sluggish trickle of sales. She was squinting at the 'Votes for Women' brooch on Connie's coat.

'What a lovely thing!' she exclaimed.

'It was a gift from Marianne,' Connie said. 'I had a letter from her yesterday, as a matter of fact. She said that since she got out of Holloway last week the police have been watching her house.'

'Oh, really?'

Laura sounded insouciant, so Connie continued. 'Actually, I've wondered myself – perhaps I'm mistaken . . .'

'About what, darling?'

'It's just a feeling, but – I think I'm being followed.'

'*No*,' said Laura, raking her gaze across the street. 'By the police?'

'I can't be sure. There was a man I caught looking at me on the tram –'

'Ooh, lucky you!'

Connie shook her head. 'No, I mean it, Lau. I think I saw him again on my way here. I've heard that as soon as we leave prison they put spies on us.'

Laura frowned. 'Well, that might be true – but only if they think we're going to explode a bomb!'

As they were talking, a young man, elegantly dressed in topcoat and highly polished boots, stopped to stare at the news-sheet they were selling. His saturnine gaze and sharp cheekbones lent him a severely handsome aspect. Laura noted his hesitation and, with a little wink at Connie, took a step towards him. In her most convivial tone she said, 'Hullo, sir. May we interest you in purchasing *The Suffragette*?'

The man, visibly offended to have been mistaken for a potential buyer, said in a low, unfriendly voice, 'You must be joking.'

Laura flinched, too genteel to respond in kind. 'I'm sorry, it's – I just thought you were showing an interest –'

'What?!' He shot them a look of disgust. 'In a pair of toms

like you?' He began to walk off. Then, changing his mind, he retraced his steps and put his face close to hers. 'I know what you lot need,' he hissed – and sent a glistening arc of spittle at her face. Laura's sudden intake of breath matched Connie's own. She turned away in shock.

'You brute!' Connie called after him as the man stalked off. She honestly wished at that moment that she'd had Ivy's dagger-cane to hand. Laura, stunned by the insult, was wiping the slimy deposit from her cheek when Connie spotted a pair of policemen strolling along the Aldwych. She hailed them loudly, and they turned.

'Excuse me – would you help us?'

The two bobbies, exhibiting no particular urgency, crossed the thoroughfare to meet them. As they approached, Connie saw them eyeing the militant news-sheets, and sensed a sceptical reflex in the look they exchanged.

'Officers, that man has just grossly assaulted my friend,' she said, pointing up the street at the receding figure. The taller of the policemen, hands on his hips, looked over at Laura, who was balling up her handkerchief in her fist.

'Miss? D'you want to tell us . . . ?'

Laura, colouring, shook her head. 'Please, it's nothing –'

'He spat in her face,' said Connie. The taller one nodded, and looked for a contribution from his partner, a stocky, pugilistic type. 'Spat at her, you say? What had she said to him?'

The question confounded Connie. 'What d'you mean?'

'I mean – what did she say to provoke him?'

Connie gave an incredulous half-snort. 'Nothing. *Nothing!* She only asked him if he wished to buy one of our news-sheets.'

The tall one picked up a copy of *The Suffragette* from the stack on the pavement, and ran a critical eye over its front page. He handed it to his companion, who made a show of examining its contents.

'What d'you reckon, Alf?'

'This what you've been selling?' said Alf, riffling its pages.

'Yes,' said Connie, with a note of impatience. 'Excuse me, but – are you going to stop that man?'

They were not listening to her. From their muttered exchanges it was becoming apparent that Laura's assailant didn't interest them at all. The one who wasn't Alf now cleared his throat.

'May I have your names, please?'

Connie and Laura looked disbelievingly at one another. '*Our* names? Why?'

Alf, taking out a notebook from his breast pocket, puffed out his cheeks and said, 'This newspaper of yours. You know its distribution is illegal?'

'Constable, really – it's just a newspaper,' said Connie, alarmed by the sudden prickle of confrontation.

'That's as maybe,' said Alf, 'but I still require your names.'

Connie shook her head. 'No, I'm sorry. You've no right to ask – we've done nothing wrong.'

'I'd advise you to reconsider.'

'Or else?'

'We'll be obliged to arrest you.'

At this point a man who had been hovering just outside Connie's eyeline interposed himself. Connie knew that she had seen him before, but couldn't immediately place him. 'That's all right, gents,' he said, with almost a chuckle in his voice. 'I can supply their names. This is Miss Laura Scott, and this –' he nodded politely to Connie '– is Miss Constance Callaway. Both recent detainees at His Majesty's Prison, Holloway.' He took out a badge and flashed it before the two policemen. 'Relf, Special Branch. I'll look after them from here, thank you.'

The bobbies tipped their helmets in brief salute and walked on. Connie studied the man's face again: his melancholy eyes and silvered moustache reminded her a little of Tam.

'The last time I saw you was on a tram in Upper Street,' she said.

Relf lifted his chin in acknowledgement. 'Yes, I wondered if you'd marked me,' he said, narrowing his eyes at her.

'Are we under arrest?' asked Laura.

'Not as yet,' he replied casually. 'But you should take this as a warning. There's a new bill proposed for lady militants who've been released before completing their sentences – they can later be arrested and taken back into custody. To serve their full term.'

Connie blinked at him. 'Do you mean that you wait for us to recover and *then* put us back in prison?'

'That's about the size of it. "Prisoners' Temporary Discharge for Ill Health" is what they're calling it.'

'Iniquitous is what I'd call it,' said Connie flatly.

Relf shrugged. 'Better take it up with the Home Secretary. I believe it's his idea.'

Connie looked at Laura, and then back at Relf. 'So – may I ask why you've chosen to be a gentleman? We don't encounter many such among the police force.'

He creased his mouth into a mirthless smile. 'Perhaps it's just that I don't like seeing young ladies spat upon.'

'Well, that's jolly decent of you, sir,' said Laura warmly, as she gathered up her bundles of *The Suffragette*.

'You'd better leave them with me, miss,' Relf said. 'The constable was right on that score. Its sale is illegal.'

Connie clicked her tongue. 'Really, Mr Relf, hasn't the Special Branch more urgent business than confiscating newspapers?'

'We're employed to uphold the rule of law. Don't forget it, because I won't.' Relf's tone was suddenly grave. 'And don't depend on my present lenience. If you're caught in unlawful activity, under any circumstances, I *will* arrest you.'

271

A silence fell between them after he had spoken. Connie would have liked to engage him in argument – he seemed quite reasonable, for a policeman – but she sensed that discretion would be the better course.

'Then we'll thank you for the warning,' she said, linking her arm through Laura's. 'Are we free to go?'

Relf nodded impassively. Laura offered him a sweet smile in departing, to which he did not respond. They crossed through the Strand's unceasing traffic and made for the crescent of the Aldwych. As they were about to turn the corner, Connie looked back. Relf was standing on the spot where they had left him. His eyes were still on them.

Connie could not recall the full name of the parliamentary bill Relf had quoted, though by the middle of April it had become law and earned itself swift notoriety. Suffragist hunger-strikers were let go until they had recovered from the effects of malnutrition, whereupon they were promptly rearrested and thrown into jail to complete their sentence. It was soon known by a popular soubriquet: the Cat and Mouse Act. Detectives and police spies were now being deployed to watch militants, and on waking each morning Connie would peek through the drawing-room curtains to check the street. Sometimes she saw a figure loitering on the pavement outside St Andrew's Church, though she could never be sure if he were engaged in surveillance or not.

A more agreeable distraction came her way when she received a note from Tam, informing her that he would be in London on Friday week. The promised luncheon was confirmed. Connie, eager as she was to offer her thanks in person, anticipated their meeting with a tiny quiver of trepidation. She didn't know Tam well – he was Will's friend – and she wondered if they would have sufficient funds of conversation to carry them through a lunchtime together. An energetic spring wind was rioting about Piccadilly as she dodged the crowds and pushed through the revolving doors of the Criterion. Voices echoed off the marbled walls and lingered around the high azure-and-gold-tiled ceiling in a way that recalled the noise at the local swimming baths. Portrait-length mirrors threw back flattering profiles of the clientele. Aproned waiters strode with Napoleonic decision about the room, attending to diners whose aura of leisured entitlement caused Connie a moment's mischievous reverie. The last time she had dined among so many was in the prison refectory. The comparison amused her. How would these people have taken to the lumpy potatoes and the greasy, gristly meat slopped on the plates at Holloway?

'Constance.' It was Tam. She had walked right past his table without noticing. He stood up to greet her, and gave a little bow.

'Hullo, Tam,' she said, smiling and blushing at once. They sat down. Tam was handsomely turned out in a navy worsted suit, its peaked lapels cut dandyishly wide. He had a flushed, well-groomed look which Connie couldn't help remarking on.

'Ah. I called in at the Turkish baths on Northumberland Avenue. They gave me a wash and brush-up.'

'You look very . . . spruce,' she said, and sensed him looking closely at her with a view to returning the compliment. She knew how very different she must have appeared to him. Her hair had grown back a little, but her skin was pale, almost translucent, since her incarceration, and she had failed to put back much of the weight she had lost. Her grandfather was right: she was scrawny.

'You look –' he began, and in the slight pause she feared some politely crushing word would follow '– quite lovely.'

'Oh,' she said, pleased, and rather flustered by the sincerity of his tone. To hide her embarrassment she made a little gesture about the room. 'I've always wondered what this place would be like. You – know it well?'

He nodded. 'Whenever we were playing at Lord's, we'd catch the number 13 'bus outside the ground – took us right to the door.'

Connie inwardly marvelled, again, that she should be on friendly terms with a man whom she used to watch batting for Sussex and England. She could remember the time her father had shown her a cigarette card – it must have been during an England–Australia Test series – with the little painted portrait of A. E. Tamburlain in blazer and cap. And here he was, her lunch companion.

'That reminds me,' said Connie, looking in her coat pocket and drawing out a small package emblazoned with the Hatchards marque. 'This is for you.' She watched as Tam unpicked the string and folded back the layers of brown paper. It was a new cloth-bound copy of *The Poems of Francis Thompson*. 'There's a very sad one he wrote about cricket,' she explained. 'It's called "At Lord's".'

Tam blinked at the book in his hand, and for a moment Connie wondered if he was about to break down in tears. Into the silence she added, 'It's hardly adequate, I know, but it's a gift of thanks for – well, for all that you did.'

Eventually he raised his eyes to her and said quietly, 'Nobody's ever given me a book of poetry before. Would you – dedicate it for me?'

'Gladly,' she smiled. She took out a stubby pencil, and held it up. 'A little souvenir from Holloway. Strictly forbidden, of course. I can't bear to get rid of it.' As she paused over the title page of the book, she gave him an impish look. 'Shall it be – "For the Great Tam"?'

He shook his head. '"For Andrew".'

'Who calls you that?' she asked gaily.

'Oh, only my sister . . . and one or two others. "Tam" is just the name I got stuck with.'

Connie wrote her dedication, and handed the volume back. A waiter was hovering at their table, and they both ordered the lamb cutlets. Tam also asked for a pint of champagne, which duly arrived in a gleaming bucket. When the waiter popped the cork Connie noticed Tam flinch, though he waved away her concerned look. 'I'm apt to get a little jumpy around noise, I don't know why.'

They talked for a while about his sojourn on the Isle of Wight, and about his plans now that he had quit M—shire. He had been offered work as an umpire – 'but it didn't appeal', he added slyly, and they both laughed. 'I've had an invitation to play in the Lancashire leagues. It's club cricket, back where I started . . .'

'But you don't sound very keen,' observed Connie.

Tam sighed. 'This game . . . the trouble with it being a profession is that you reach the top too young. The rest of your career is a long slide down. D'you know, I think it can send a fellow mad.'

Connie smiled uncertainly. 'Not *actually* mad,' she demurred.

But Tam's expression was in deadly earnest. 'Don't you think there's something odd about spending so much time almost motionless in a field?'

'I've never thought of it like –'

'Cricket's so much about nerves,' he continued. 'I once knew a fellow, name of Usher, he used to open the batting with me at Sussex. Quite a solid player, but he scored slowly – and the crowd would give him gyp. It began to prey on his mind. Meanwhile I'd be at the other end blasting away, which only made things worse for him.'

'He must have seemed *very* slow next to you.'

Tam nodded. 'It was painful to watch, but it was the only way he could play. I remember *Punch* ran a little satirical verse about him.' He paused, and stared into the middle distance while he retrieved the words. '"Oh nice for the bowler, my boy / That each ball like a barn door you play! / Oh nice for yourself, I suppose, / That you stick at the wicket all day!" Poor old Usher.' He laughed as he said it, but he looked sad.

'What happened to him?'

'Ah,' said Tam with a shake of his head. 'He retired, as we all must, but he didn't settle to anything. I used to see him now and then. The game was all he knew, and he couldn't cope. At least when you're on your own in the field you know you're there for a purpose. Anyway . . .' He seemed to have drifted into a reverie, and at length his gaze came back into focus. He looked at Connie. 'He moved to Eastbourne in the early nineties – and killed himself in his lodgings. A shotgun, they said.'

Connie's hand flew to her mouth in shock. The sudden tragic conclusion had caught her off guard.

'Suicide among cricketers is more common than you might think,' added Tam, who spoke with no inkling of his story's effect upon Connie. 'You didn't know?'

Connie shook her head, and said nothing. Their food had arrived, and Tam poured them another glass, though the interruption had not diverted him from his sombre theme. 'Aye, I've known a few who've . . . gone that way. P'raps the game attracts them. You need the strength up here –' he tapped his temple '– if you're going to survive as a player. I could always tell which ones had it – Will, for instance –'

It was the first time his name had been mentioned, and Tam broke off in the manner of one who had blundered. But Connie had already prepared herself for this moment, and with a self-conscious calm, said, 'How is Will? Did he join you on the Isle of Wight?'

'No,' Tam replied distantly, 'I think he was – elsewhere.' He didn't look her in the eye as he spoke.

'He came to visit me in prison. Did he tell you?'

Tam nodded, and shifted awkwardly in his seat. She suspected he was not much disposed to talk about matters of the heart. 'I think he was quite shocked,' he said tactfully. 'Seeing a friend in distress . . .'

'Well, a true friend would have offered to help,' she said, and Tam took the oblique compliment with a small tilt of his head. They had finished the cutlets and paused for a smoke – Tam had a cigar in blast – when a shadow loomed over their table. It was a fashionably dressed young man – a 'nut' – with a monocle gleaming in his eye and a grin as toothy as an alligator's.

'Hullo again!' he cried and offered his hand to Tam, who looked nonplussed by the stranger's greeting. If the man suspected that Tam didn't remember him he betrayed no sign of embarrassment. 'Pardon the interruption, just spotted you across the room. Coronation Day, two years ago? Though I'll always recall it as the day the Great Tam was guest of honour at my flat!'

Tam's brow slowly cleared as the memory began to surface. 'Er, yes . . . is it . . . ?'

'Reggie – Reggie Culver,' he supplied cheerily. 'I think we have a mutual friend – Will Maitland. Saw him the other day, as a matter of fact, out walking with a young lady –'

'It's a pleasure to see you again,' Tam cut in, glancing at Connie, who now understood his awkwardness when Will's name had come up. So . . . it had not taken him long to form a new attachment. She could tell from his distracted manner that Tam wanted rid of their intruder, but Reggie plainly had no intention of letting his catch slip away; he had begun, like so many others, to yarn through his personal memories of the batsman. Connie had the disagreeable sensation of having met the man before, but she couldn't exactly recall where. The drawling voice, that monocle . . .

'. . . never seen such a hit!' Reggie was reminiscing over the shot they always talked about, the one that cleared the pavilion at Lord's. Tam took this moment to gesture in

Connie's direction, saying, 'This young lady was there, too – saw it with her father and brother, I think . . .'

Connie smiled, touched that Tam should have remembered this out of all the hundreds of people who had bedevilled him with their recollections. Reggie, glancing briefly at her, offered a stiff tweak of his mouth before resuming his descant of blandishments. Connie might as well have been invisible for all the interest he had displayed – and she realised in that instant where they had met before. This was the bumptious creature who had accosted her and Lily on the suffrage march during Coronation week ('Don't you wish you were a man?'). Reggie plainly had no memory of her; perhaps he asked every woman he met the same question. Good Lord – to think he was a pal of Will's! He might have jawed at their table all lunchtime but for the intervention of a waiter and his pudding trolley.

'Oh well!' said Reggie, as if his imminent removal were a cause of regret for all concerned. 'Nice to run into you again. Good luck for the new season, sir!'

As he strolled off back to his own table, Tam muttered under his breath, 'He thinks I'm still playing, the jackass . . .' He seemed upset by his recent idolater.

'He was very enthusiastic about the Lord's hit,' said Connie, trying to coax back his good mood.

'Yes, him and a thousand others,' he said gruffly. 'They seem to assume it's the only thing I ever did. I scored 23,000 runs in a career, made the quickest championship hundred in the game, played for England – but all they want to talk about is *that shot*. It makes me –' He checked himself, as though hearing his own disproportionate irritation, and looked at Connie. 'I'm sorry – must seem very graceless of me. I've just been brooding about things . . .'

'You mean your retirement?' she asked.

He let his head drop. 'It'll take some getting used to.'

Connie reached across the table and patted his hand. 'I'm sure you'll find fulfilment in other ways, Tam,' she said gently. 'You still have your life ahead of you.'

Tam surprised her by clasping the hand she had laid on his. She felt his gaze so searchingly upon her that, in slight alarm, she cast about for a diversion. With a brave laugh, she said, 'So Will has found himself a young lady, it seems. I'm curious – I confess it!' Her voice was light, but her words contained a question that Tam couldn't ignore.

'I've met her the once,' he said, shrugging. 'She seemed – perfectly nice. But she couldn't hold a candle to the previous one,' he added.

She smiled at his nervous gallantry, and murmured, '"'Tis not a year or two shows us a man . . . " Never mind. There are worse fates than being alone.'

Tam looked at her searchingly. 'What could be worse than that?'

'Oh . . . to be mistakenly joined to another person. I dread that more.'

'D'you really?' he said, giving her a curious look. He leaned back in his chair. 'I've known both states, and I'm not sure.'

Connie stared at him, astonished. 'You were – *married*?'

'Is that so surprising to you?' he said with a hurt expression.

'No, no – I mean . . . you never talked about it, so I assumed . . .'

'There are some things I don't talk about,' he shrugged. After a pause, he said, 'We married young – too young. I was playing cricket six days a week, trying to earn a crust. We'd hardly see one another. Dora, that's the wife, she got upset about it, and for a while I tried to set things right. We took more holidays. But once my career was on the up it just became harder and harder. The final straw was going to Australia with the England team in '94. I was away for four months. By the time I got back, it was all over. She'd moved out, found someone else.'

Connie said quietly, 'I'm sorry, Tam.'

'It wasn't all bad, though – when we were together, I mean. We had some happy times . . . The marriage failed, but I wouldn't call it a *mistake*.' He seemed to be debating the matter with himself. Connie sensed, not for the first time that afternoon, that Tam's odd mood might have its source in something other than professional disgruntlement. There seemed a tentativeness in his manner with her, as though he were gauging how much intimacy could exist between them. It occurred to her again how little she knew him. The more he revealed of himself – and this disclosure about his marriage was certainly a surprise – the less she felt she understood. The 'Great Tam' she had read about in the newspapers, the loud, gregarious sportsman who gambled and caroused late into the night, was very different from the vulnerable fellow before her now. A suspicion, unformed but troubling (the way he had clasped her hand), was prompting her to wonder if he might be rather lonely.

They talked about their future plans. Connie spoke of her excitement at the prospect of assisting Mr Cluett at St Thomas's. Tam looked startled by her ambitions, and said so.

'Why? Do I seem such a feeble feminine creature to you?' she said jestingly.

He shook his head. 'Far from it. I only wonder at the terrible responsibility of it. To have someone's life in your hands.'

'Perhaps,' said Connie. 'But then it's a terrible responsibility to do anything useful at all.'

There followed some argument as to who would have the honour of the bill. Connie eventually insisted over Tam's alarmed protests. 'You paid for my lawyer. You will not pay for my lunch as well.'

He looked quite unhappy about this, but brightened on conceiving another opportunity to meet in the summer. The Priory would stage a benefit match to salute his retirement, he explained, and, scheduled during Festival Week, huge crowds were expected to attend. 'There'll be a dinner for me at the pavilion, with various worthies of the town. I'd be very honoured if you agreed to attend.'

Connie bit her lip. 'It's very kind of you, Tam, but there's a certain mutual friend I would prefer to avoid . . .'

Tam nodded slowly, and looked so crestfallen that Connie held back from a firm answer. She knew almost for a certainty that she wouldn't go, but asked Tam for a little time to consider the proposal. It seemed to mollify him. They emerged from the restaurant into the blustery spring day they had left behind. Connie clapped her hand on her hat to prevent it from blowing away, and offered her other hand for him to shake. As he did so, he said, 'I'm sorry about what happened with you and Will, but . . .' He paused, and looked more anxious than she had ever seen him. '. . . but I hope it won't prevent our being friends.'

'Of course it won't,' she said, wondering how she could soften the eventual refusal of his invitation to the Priory. He offered her his arm, and they began walking towards Piccadilly Tube station. On a news-stand was blazoned the shrill headline:

LATEST SUFFRAGETTE ATTACK ON GOLF COURSE

Tam caught her eye, seeing that she had read it. Connie returned a sidelong look, and laughed. 'Nothing to do with me.' She glanced behind, nevertheless, mindful of strangers tracking her steps through the uncomprehending crowds.

14

'Dead?'

Will had just cracked the top of his breakfast egg, and laid down his spoon. The gesture felt like a mark of respect. Eleanor, with *The Times* unfolded across the table in front of her, nodded gravely. For some moments a hush fell over the room, distantly punctuated by the metronomic *tunk* of the grandfather clock, before she spoke again.

'In hospital at Epsom yesterday afternoon. She never regained consciousness. "Two visitors had draped the screen around the bed with the WSPU colours . . . A sister of the patient and a lady friend of her mother stayed at the hospital for many hours, and on Saturday night her brother arrived at the bedside. Only members of the staff, however, were present when the end actually came".'

Dead. It was that odd conjunction of something that was shocking yet not surprising. The lady whose final hours the newspaper described was Emily Wilding Davison. In common with many others, Will had become uneasily preoccupied by her fate. On the Wednesday of the previous week, Miss Davison had taken the train to Epsom Downs racecourse with a suffrage flag wound about her middle, concealed beneath her coat. During the Derby Stakes, as the horses rounded Tattenham Corner, she had run out onto the course and, attempting to grasp the reins of the King's

horse, had fallen beneath its hooves. She was rushed unconscious to a nearby hospital where a surgeon tried to relieve
the bleeding inside her head from the fracture. For the last
four days her life had hung in the balance. The Queen, who
had seen the incident, was reported to have enquired about
her condition.

Incredulity mingled with outrage in the newspaper
reports, which Will had read in a state of sickened fascina-
tion. He couldn't comprehend the wilfulness that had
induced the woman to destroy herself. To hunger-strike
was one thing; to throw yourself in front of a galloping
horse quite another. He supposed, vaguely, that there must
be causes worth dying for – King and Country, of course
(one had to say that) – but it seemed inconceivable that
female emancipation could be one of them. She *must* have
been a madwoman; her middle name, 'Wilding', almost
confirmed it. Yet as news of the incident became clearer,
details of Miss Davison's preparations on the fatal day
appeared to undermine the assumption of suicide. It
emerged that she had bought a return ticket to Epsom,
indicating that this was not to be her last journey. Eyewitness
reports at the course suggested she was quite in control of
herself. After the first race, she had marked on her card the
winner, Honeywood, and in second place King's Scholar.
The next race came and went – she marked that, too. The
third race was the Derby.

For as long as Will relied only on newspaper reports,
Miss Davison's act of martyrdom remained an abstraction;
unsettling, of course, but essentially elsewhere. It was upon
seeing it for himself that the full horror overtook him. He
had been walking down Baker Street when he noticed a
queue outside a dingy little music hall. It was now the
fashion for such places to show Pathé newsreels of recent
public events – royal weddings, society gatherings, popular
demonstrations. Will would have passed right by the hall

but for his eye snagging on that day's bill of entertainment: SUFFRAGETTE INCIDENT! His curiosity piqued, he bought a ticket and entered the frowsy darkness of the auditorium, full to the door even this early in the evening. He sidled through the crowds in the back gallery, heads silhouetted against the flickering screen as the projector whirred laboriously on. The only film Will had watched for any length of time had been the report of an MCC game at Lord's, and that principally because he knew Tam featured in it. As it transpired, the reels were so imperfect that it rendered the images of the cricket near-meaningless – the players moving at that jerky, farcical speed – and Will had seriously wondered if this craze for cinematography could last.

He sensed a murmurous hum of anticipation: a title card announced DERBY DAY, 4 JUNE 1913. The audience seemed to close in around him. It started, the camera silently, almost primly, surveying the Epsom crowd, an unsuspecting sea of hats, then a switch of angle to the horses bunched together, pounding across the turf. They turned Tattenham Corner, a racing blur of equine sinew and muscle, until nearly all had passed the camera's static gaze. Then Will saw a figure materialise, as in a dream, in front of the last rider but two and in the blink of an eye caught the drastic impact and the tumbling havoc that followed. In the dark around him he heard a protesting intake of breath, though the moment had come and gone so suddenly he wondered if he had really seen it at all. But here it came again, the same sequence played on a loop, and now he began to piece it together. It was horrifying to mark how the figure ducked beneath the rails and stepped, quite daintily, around the oncoming horses; then, an extraordinary thing, she dodged one as it thundered towards her, as if to say, No, you're not the one I came for. She seemed to stand in the midst of them for an eternity, waiting for Anmer, the King's horse, until it was almost on top of her, and then raising her hand to stop it. Will stood there shaken, appalled. The collision had sent Miss Davison somersaulting over the ground; the horse struggled to its feet, but she and the jockey lay motionless as the crowds began streaming onto the course.

He had watched it again, and again, nine or ten times, until the sequence seemed burnt onto his retina. It was that deliberate sideways step the woman made which haunted him, the calculation of it. She knew precisely what she was doing. In the days following Will had made no mention of the Derby film to anyone, though he could not help himself thinking about it, and he waited for news of the injured woman in a private agony of suspense. If she died, would others follow her lead? Or would the government finally yield to the women's demands? He looked across the table at his sister, still absorbed in *The Times*. Eleanor was a rational, educated, trustworthy sort of girl . . . it did not seem so terrible to him that she might one day have the vote. Indeed, he suspected that she might know a great deal more about the political processes of the country than he did.

Now she raised her eyes from the paper. 'I wonder if Constance knew her . . .'

'I've no idea,' he said, after a pause, rather nettled. He regarded her continuing interest in Connie as rather tactless, though he added, casually: 'Tam would be the man to ask about Miss Callaway. He saw her in London.'

'Tam? Are they friends?'

'Hardly. But for some odd reason he's invited her to his benefit match at the Priory next month.'

When Tam had informed him of this development, Will sensed that he was being asked, implicitly, for his permission. He had heard nothing more of the matter since, and trusted that Connie would stay away – for the sake of all concerned.

'Perhaps Tam enjoys her company,' mused Eleanor. 'And she does love cricket.'

At that moment their mother sailed into the room, and in unspoken agreement brother and sister dropped the subject they had lately discussed. Mrs Maitland looked at the fractured head of Will's boiled egg and said, in peremptory fashion, 'Something wrong with the breakfast?'

Will shook his head. 'My appetite seems to have deserted me.'

'Oh? I hope you're not sickening,' said his mother. 'You haven't forgotten about dinner with Ada and her parents this evening?'

Suppressing a sigh, he said, 'Of course not. Would you excuse me? I have practice at the ground in an hour.'

With a meaning look to Eleanor, Will discarded his napkin and retreated from the table.

The sun was hidden beneath rolling banks of cloud, and the atmosphere had become muggy. Will, sweating astride his bicycle, was unsettled by the recent conversation with his sister. Bad enough to have that unfortunate woman at Epsom on the brain; now she had become, maddeningly, entangled with the memory of Constance, whose face still rose unbidden before him in his dreams. Whenever he thought of their last interview in that wretched prison cell, with iron doors clanging in echo, he suffered a blinding spasm of shame; it literally caused him to close his eyes for a moment and bow his head. Hitherto he had salved the conscience-needling discomfort by reminding himself that they were never likely to meet again. It was shabby, but it would be endurable. And then Tam had nonplussed him with the news that he had invited her to the Priory for his testimonial match. Of all the – He could only presume that Connie would have as little inclination to see him as he did her.

And yet his dissatisfaction went deeper than he would admit. His courtship of Ada Brink, now into its sixth month, had been perfectly agreeable, its steady rather than scintillating progress apparently suiting the different temperaments of both of them. Lately, however, Will had felt renewed vibrations of enthusiasm for their match emanating from his mother, who had taken to organising dinners and lunches and outings that would bring the young couple unavoidably into one another's company and indicated, with ominous clarity, the ultimate destination Mrs Maitland had in mind for them. While he felt strong enough to resist the pressures of maternal manipulation, it did incline him to make a serious appraisal of Ada's suitability as the prospective companion of his life. Of her beauty he could make no complaint; as the days lengthened and the sun stayed longer, colour touched her cheeks and her blonde hair turned flaxen. She looked lovelier than ever, and he didn't mind telling her so. She was possessed of exemplary manners, and a natural affability that drew people to her. All of this was encouraging. It was the idea of a *lifetime* together that gave him pause. She was young, of course, and relatively unformed, but there seemed little hope of passions and pursuits that might unite them in time to come. She had no interest at all in cricket; he had none in dances and riding, unless it were a bicycle. Neither of them liked the theatre. She had even less interest in books than he did, though she was a keen reader of ladies' magazines and she laughed at the cartoons in *Punch*, which only made him wonder at the quality of his own jokes – she giggled no less delightedly at them.

But what worried him more, surprisingly, was Ada's placid, almost bovine temper. Most of the time he thought this pliancy quite wonderful, and enjoyed the manly prerogative of deciding where they would eat, which concert they would attend, whose friends they would invite (his, usually). On occasion, however, the novelty of making all the decisions palled, and he would ask her whether there were something in particular *she* wanted to do. She might then offer a suggestion, but with no great enthusiasm; more often she shrugged and smiled and said, 'You decide.' Will knew that most men of his acquaintance would take this to be the natural order of things and rest complacent in their own dominion. He felt less certain, and the more passive and biddable Ada seemed to him the more he found himself hankering for a show of spirit, of independence, of simple curiosity. He wanted someone beautiful, but with a mind of her own. Someone like – no, he would not say her name, but . . . someone *like* her, only without the criminal tendencies. Was that too much to ask?

These troubling ruminations were still a weight on him as he guided his bicycle through the players' entrance at the back of the Priory pavilion. Middlehurst, the M—shire captain, was recovering from injury, so Will, as one of the senior players, had agreed to supervise Monday-morning nets. As he approached the changing room he could hear a competing medley of male guffaws, and on entering found the players trading jokes whose topicality he wasn't slow to grasp. Someone had been reciting the headline story from the *Daily Mail*.

'I 'eard she was very short-sighted and mistook the creature for the Queen – she was only tryin' to curtsy.' More laughter.

Another voice piped up. 'Nah, she had ten bob on Anmer to win and was telling the jockey, "Oi, get off – I can ride this nag quicker meself."'

Revill, the cocky young opening bat, was red-faced and short of breath from cackling. He spluttered out, giddily, 'No, no, she knew it was a good each-way bet – she just wanted to hear it from the horse's mouth!'

Will, steering his gaze around the room, saw that he was

the only one there not hooting with laughter. He dropped his kitbag on the floor and walked over to Revill, who was knuckling tears of mirth from his eyes. He looked up unguardedly as Will's shadow towered over him.

'So you regard it an apt subject for comedy, Revill?'

'Beg your pardon?'

'You heard me. A woman is trampled to death by a horse, and you think it appropriate to entertain the fellows with your so-called wit?'

'The woman was a lunatic –'

'And that makes it permissible to mock her?' snapped Will, his voice cold with disgust. A silence had fallen as suddenly as a slammed door. 'You say a lunatic. I realise it might be incomprehensible to oafs like you, but sacrificing oneself for a cause takes courage – real courage. Instead of making tasteless jibes you might try considering what *you* would die for.' He shook his head, and cast a baleful glance around his teammates, who looked stunned. 'What that woman did . . . she was braver than the lot of you. I mean it.' He could almost feel his lip curl as he spoke. He paused for a moment, then walked out of the room.

For the rest of the morning he batted at nets without interruption. Nobody caught his eye and, aside from the groundsman, who had no inkling of what had occurred in the changing room, nobody spoke to him. Having thrashed ball after ball in a trance of fearsome concentration – the players seemed too cowed to bowl him anything above military medium – he tucked his bat under his arm, discarded his gloves and pads, and walked off alone towards the pavilion. Revill was loitering, with the hesitant air of one who had prepared an apology, but Will didn't look at him as he passed.

Connie had taken the Tube to Holborn, but on gaining the street outside she found herself unable to move more than a few steps at a time, such was the press of bodies heaving around Bloomsbury. Wheel traffic had been halted, and crowds of people surged along the streets. She had been in surgery all morning with Cluett, assisting as he performed an appendectomy; she still had the smell of gas and blood in her nostrils. She had eventually been obliged to ask his leave for the afternoon off. He didn't enquire as to where she was going, though it wouldn't have entailed a great deal of guesswork: Miss Davison had become the nation's cause célèbre, and today was their final opportunity to salute her. The police looked overwhelmed by the numbers which had followed her coffin from Victoria through the West End. St George's would provide a funeral service, one of the few churches willing to accommodate the deceased. Connie had accepted the impossibility of securing a place inside, but it seemed that the size of the crowd might actually prevent her getting within two hundred yards of the church itself. They swarmed on, and every side street and byway disgorged yet more bodies to swell their number. She had not seen a public bereaved in this way since the day Queen Victoria died. She vividly remembered that day, hearing the news on the street and rushing indoors to tell her father. He had looked at her and said: 'I'm glad it was you who told me.'

She had at last got to the turning of Hart Street. From here she could see the church, with its Hawksmoor steeple, incongruously surmounted by a statue of George I in a Roman toga. As she inched through the crush, she heard rising from within the church the strains of 'Nearer My God to Thee', and instantly thought of Ivy Maddocks conducting the choir in Holloway. Standing on tiptoe, Connie could see the draped coffin being shouldered under the portico; it was festooned with flowers of all kinds, though their colours were only green, purple and white. The police were clearing a space so that the pall-bearers could manoeuvre the bier down the steps and onto the open carriage, which was also decorated with flowers. As this was happening Connie noticed the hush that had fallen around her. Women – men, too – stood in rapt silence, tears in their eyes; a man standing next to her had taken off his cap and was mouthing the words of the hymn. What an extraordinary thing was the British public, she thought. It hurled missiles and broke up meetings of law-abiding suffragists, spat in the face of blameless newspaper vendors and openly rejoiced in the arrest of demonstrators. But now it turned out in its thousands to mourn the passing of the most rabidly militant suffragette who had ever lived. It seemed the people loved nothing more than a renegade who flouted all reason and addressed them in the unanswerable language of self-destruction.

An hour later she had found a suitable vantage on the steps of St Pancras Station from which she could see Miss Davison's funeral cortège approach its terminus at King's Cross. Her earthly remains would be borne hence to the family home in Northumberland and a private burial at her local church. Marching bands had maintained a strident serenade in her wake. As the bier finally disappeared amid the teeming crowds, Connie stood there for some moments, sensing the anticlimactic deflation of the afternoon. She had witnessed a spectacle, and had paid her tribute – but she felt no catharsis. The deceased was already being hailed as a martyr, even among those who had previously shown no interest in the suffragist cause. Yet the revelations about her own father still touched Connie too rawly for her to regard Miss Davison's suicide as anything other than a tragedy. She was descending the steps towards Euston Road when she heard her name being called, and looked round to see Ivy Maddocks approaching, wearing a wide black armband and a face exhilarated with misery.

'Hullo, Ivy,' she said, offering her hand and a smile of

honest sadness. She knew that Ivy had been on friendly terms with the dead woman. Her eyes were red-rimmed behind her spectacles, though a light shone in them.

'A famous day, Constance. From now on they'll know we shall stop at nothing. Only look at our support!' She gestured at the crowds milling loosely around them.

'It's remarkable –' Connie began, but Ivy wasn't listening.

'They can't hurt her now. She's going to a better place,' she said, her voice choked with feeling. '. . . a better place,' she repeated with breathy emphasis.

'You mean – Northumberland?' said Connie, unable to resist mischief.

'No,' said Ivy, as deaf to teasing as ever. 'I mean the Lord's kingdom. This act will be her monument.'

'I hope you're right,' Connie replied uncertainly.

'How can you doubt it, dear? Emily knew she was on a mission. "Fight on," she said, "and God will give the victory."'

Connie thought the quotation was from Joan of Arc, but she decided not to quibble with this determined apostle. Ivy had been present at the church, and was recalling the service in reverential detail, from the flowers on the coffin to the funerary prayers and the choice of hymns. For want of something to contribute, Connie said, 'I thought of you, actually, when I heard "Nearer My God to Thee" – one of your favourites, wasn't it?'

Ivy nodded in a childlike way, apparently pleased that her tenure as Holloway's choirmistress had left its mark. They had been walking down the Gray's Inn Road alongside straggling groups of mourners, most of them in black and adorned with laurels or purple irises.

Connie was about to turn north when Ivy, still with purpose in her step, said, 'I have a meeting just near here – would you join us?' Ivy belonged to a tight-knit clique of militants whose zeal for the cause was underpinned by an evangelical Christianity. Miss Davison, as their most cele-brated member, was likely to be the exclusive subject of conversation.

'It's been rather a long day, Ivy. I should be getting home —'

'Oh please, Constance,' she said earnestly. 'Can you really not spare the time? It's only a few like-minded friends.'

Connie had met some of Ivy's friends before, and guessed that her mind was less 'like' than her companion assumed, but some deep-lying gland of pity reacted to Ivy's plaintive tone. She had lost a friend, after all, not just a comrade.

'Well, perhaps for half an hour . . .'

Connie failed to guess, however, that the meeting would be held in a temperance hotel. She would have enjoyed a glass of something after footslogging behind the funeral cortège, but the only refreshment provided was cucumber sand-wiches and tea. The upper room to which Ivy had led her disclosed a dozen or so ladies, all of them righteously flushed from the afternoon's proceedings and eagerly gabbling over one another, as if to claim their own little share of history in the making. Connie, as the only one of them not to have been in the pews at St George's, or indeed to be sporting a black armband, was regarded with an air of polite puzzle-ment. To hear them talk, one would imagine the funeral service had combined the eloquence of the Book of Psalms and the majesty of the Sermon on the Mount. One lady, still in a transport of idolatrous fervour, kept murmuring, 'So beautiful . . . so beautiful.'

The one to whom the rest of the assembly deferred was a lady of imposing handsomeness, thin-faced, green-eyed, with a tightly coiled bun of russet hair. Her name was Edith Aitken, and as soon as Connie entered the room she felt this queen bee's gaze alight upon her. At first she wondered if it was disapproval for not wearing an armband, but on being introduced she perceived herself to be an object of interest to the lady, who took her aside.

'I see you were on the strike, Miss Callaway,' said Edith, glancing at the Portcullis medal pinned to Connie's jacket, a decoration awarded to every hunger-striker at Holloway. 'A tribute to your mettle, I should say.'

'Yes – though it nearly killed me,' Connie replied, in a light but rueful way.

'Well, the blood of the martyrs is the seed of the church. Sacrifice of the self is the noblest of all, do you not think?'

'I'm not sure that I do,' said Connie quietly, sensing the heresy on her tongue. 'I would be sorry to see anyone following Miss Davison's example.'

'Oh?' said Edith, with a not unfriendly curiosity. 'So you object to the idea of martyrdom?'

'In that form – yes. I cannot regard her in the same spirit of admiration as your friends here do.'

'Then . . . how *do* you regard her?'

Connie paused, hearing the steel in Edith's tone. 'As a very unhappy woman who had lost the balance of her mind. Please don't think I deny her courage – she did more than I would dare –'

'Yes, she did,' Edith broke in sharply.

'– but martyrdom was the result, not the cause, of her action. As you know, she had tried to kill herself twice before, in prison. She may have been predisposed, mentally, to do so, I'm not sure. But I feel certain that Miss Davison was in grave need of medical help.'

Edith looked at her with a challenging gleam. 'Are you suggesting she was mad?'

Connie held her gaze. 'I believe that, to one degree or another, all suicides are mad. And I have observed the effect on their loved ones enough to know that they destroy more than their own selves.'

At this point a discussion which had begun elsewhere in the room was now being foregrounded, and Ivy, eager to invite Edith's participation, interrupted them.

'Edith, we've been putting our heads together. We must take up the sword that has fallen from Emily's hand. Our conclusion –' here she gestured at the half-dozen ladies assembled around her '– is that we intensify our campaign against the enemy.'

'And so we shall,' said Edith coolly. 'With or without the approval of Mrs Pankhurst. It is a matter of taking the initiative – I propose a series of "spectaculars" that will seize public attention in the same way that our dear Emily has done. We will have this government on the run.'

There followed a debate about the most immediate way of inflicting damage. Government buildings were now too heavily guarded to be viable targets, while incendiaries at railway stations had drawn down too much popular opprobrium. It seemed that sporting events remained their best option, guaranteeing both huge publicity and ease of disguise: faced with large crowds, the police could not always be vigilant as to who were militants and who law-abiding citizens. The women's arsenal of matches and kerosene and hammers could be concealed about the person. Connie, having listened in dutiful silence, was about to make her excuses when she heard someone talking about Festival Week on the south coast. Ivy, eyes glittering behind her spectacles, made one of her sudden bird-like turns in her direction.

'Constance knows all about cricket.' All eyes now focused on her. 'I recall a little postcard of a pavilion on your cell wall. Where was it?'

Connie, put on the spot, smiled wanly. 'It's . . . a place called the Priory.'

'Ah, we've all heard of that,' said Edith. 'And Festival

Week would ensure the crowds. Miss Callaway, is this a mission you would lend yourself to?'

She felt herself blushing guiltily. 'I'm not sure how . . . useful I could be.'

Edith squinted at this hesitation. 'Well, you seem to *know* the place. Perhaps you have information about access, about escape routes. Come, my dear, you are a soldier of this volunteer army, are you not?'

Connie had to think quickly. Lord Daventry, President of M—shire CC and his friend the MP, Greville Foulkes, were scheduled to attend. Yet the thought of damage being done to the Priory appalled her, and her immediate instinct was to refuse them flat. Sensing the fanatical mood in the room, however, she realised it would be more politic to assume the guise of support. And it might be to the Priory's advantage if she were there to keep an eye on these potential saboteurs.

'I have a friend down there . . .' she said with a meaning look.

'Excellent,' said Edith, not taking her eyes off Connie. 'We have three weeks to prepare. We will need to have a plan of the building, and then determine on which day we should make our attack.'

'What exactly would be the nature of this – attack?' asked Connie, holding her voice steady.

Edith's expression was Delphic. 'That's to be decided. But it will be something worthy of our fallen comrade – be sure of it.'

This was said in a tone that made Connie afraid. But she betrayed not a hint of her anxiety when, some minutes later, she picked up her hat and bade the good Christian women farewell. On her way out Ivy leaned across her conspiratorially.

'I knew we could depend on you,' she said, almost in a whisper.

* * *

That evening, back at Thornhill Crescent, she sat down to write a short letter, though its brevity belied the agonising that was spent in its composition.

14 June 1913

Dearest Tam,

I have been pondering the very kind invitation to your testimonial match which you extended the last time we met. You will recall my hesitancy in accepting it, and perhaps also the reason why. I can't claim that my estrangement from Will has been easy, nor that any future association with him would be greatly relished – yet such feelings on my part seem trivial, and perhaps egotistical, when set against the prospect of your farewell appearance at the Priory. Please don't think it impertinent that, after several weeks of silence, I write in the hope that your offer still stands. If it does, I would most gladly accept.

I did so enjoy our lunch at the Criterion.

Believe me, affectionately yours,

Constance

There was no word of a lie in it, yet Connie read the letter through with an unpleasant feeling of duplicity. She imagined Tam reading it, and the lift of pleasure it would give to his dark brow. Keener than that, however, was a sense of foreboding. Connie had taken her own commitment to suffrage further than she had ever anticipated, but Edith and her band of zealots, operating beyond any constraints imposed by the Union, made her worry that the cause was being fatally retarded. The woman whose funeral carriage they followed today had, by her action, apparently entrained a new spirit of violent opportunism. Connie had been shocked by the Epsom Derby film, like everybody else. But pondering it later she was moved not by the bravery of a 'soldier' who had found something to die for: it was the loneliness of a woman who had run out of anything to live for.

15

Connie could smell and hear the place before she could see it as the train shuddered and slowed into Warwick Square station. She had not visited since Will met her on the platform here more than a year ago, his anxious gaze only brightening when it had settled on her. There was nobody to meet her now, though the seagulls still shrieked in their importunate way. The carriages had disgorged a flood of holidaymakers, day-trippers and other rowdies, and Connie, jostled along, felt a spasm of sadness to have arrived alone and unheeded. She had just gained the station's little concourse when a shadow rose at her side and Tam was there, doffing his hat, a smile beginning to pull at the edge of his mouth.

'May I take this for you?' he said, releasing her hand from the suitcase.

'Hullo!' she said, laughing her surprise. 'How did you know I'd be on that train?'

'I didn't. But you'd told me you'd arrive this morning, so it was no trouble to wait. I had a pot of tea and the *Daily Mail* to keep me company.'

'So you've been here all morning?'

'As I say, it was no trouble.' They emerged from the station into Warwick Square, its public gardens ablaze with summer flowers, its white stucco and uniform canted bays sloping gently towards the seafront. Tam suggested they walk into town, to which Connie assented; the day was fine, and he was evidently eager to play the host. 'I hope you don't mind,' he said, 'but I've taken the liberty of asking my sister to join us at the ground.'

'Not at all,' she replied agreeably. They had turned onto a road, Prospect Place, neatly lined with beech trees and mid-Victorian boarding houses of a kind usually damned as 'respectable'. Tam had slowed to a halt.

'Which reminds me – I promised Beatrice I'd take a brolly along. They said there might be rain this afternoon.'

Connie looked up at the tall sandstone terrace with its wrought-iron balconies. 'You live here?' She had imagined something more secluded.

He nodded, and seemed to register her surprise. 'Top floor. Carefully chosen, I should add. High enough to blot out the traffic, but still hear the waves against the sea wall at night.'

He excused himself, and hurried into the house. While she waited on the pavement Connie raked her glance casually along the road, and froze on seeing a figure who, she realised, had been tracking them from the station. Relf. She hadn't encountered him since the day they had met outside Strand Tube station. A minute or so later she heard Tam closing his front door and descending the steps with the promised umbrella. He sensed her dismay almost immediately.

'Is something the matter?' he asked. Relf, keeping his distance, hadn't moved. His concentrated stillness reminded her of a fox she occasionally saw in the garden at home.

'That gentleman,' she replied, 'I'm – I believe he's followed me from London.'

She noticed Tam's neck stiffen as he stared out the man. 'P'raps I should go and have a word,' he said, but Connie held his arm.

'No, please. Let's just go.'

'Who is he?' he said, his eyes still fixed on the stalker.

'I'll tell you on the way,' she said. As they walked on, Connie told herself not to panic. She could not believe that Relf had any inkling of why she had come here, but his shadowing presence made it more imperative than ever to be careful. She explained to Tam her brief and unsought acquaintance with Relf, and why she might be in danger; but she made no mention of her rendezvous with Ivy later that evening. Her mind racing, she asked him if they might make a quick stop at the Royal Victoria, where she was staying: her pretext was to leave her case, but while Tam waited she also sent a telegram to London, hoping that she wasn't too late. Outside again, the sun was poking through broken clouds in a diffuse way. Connie peered up at the sky.

'Is it really going to rain?'

Tam considered. 'They might just be summer clouds – hard to tell.'

As they approached the Priory she saw flyposters announcing Festival Week, and bunting that sprouted along the walls and windows of the narrow old streets. Tam was explaining the line-up of entertainments. Today they would watch a few overs of a local club match, a 'tee-up' for the main event tomorrow: M—shire, captained by Tam for the occasion, would play the MCC, followed in the evening by his benefit dinner. Connie, voicing a tentative enquiry as to Will's whereabouts, was assured that he would definitely not be at today's match: county players seldom watched 'the small fry'. He would, however, be at the dinner. She was puzzled that Tam had invited her knowing of the awkwardness between them, and she felt sure Will would have asked him to reconsider her inclusion on the guest list. But here she was.

Outside the players' entrance a small knot of schoolboys

were loitering, and on spotting Tam they surrounded him, autograph books at the ready.

'Duty calls,' he said to Connie with a little sigh, though she sensed that he rather enjoyed this ritual show of homage. Cricketers needed the proof of the public's affection, she thought – and retired cricketers perhaps most of all. Once the signing was done, Tam led her through the players' gate and thence around to the members' pavilion. Out on the square play was under way, though the stand was still only a quarter full. A woman, seated on her own at the end of a row, gave them a diffident wave. Connie responded with a smile, and then, on Tam's introduction, she was shaking hands with his sister. Beatrice had none of her brother's imposing physicality, but she did have his melancholy grey eyes and the same faint dimple in the chin.

'Constance. I'm very pleased to meet you. Drewy says that you're a *proper* cricket lover – his words.'

Connie had never heard anyone call him Drewy before. 'I'm honoured to learn it,' she said, settling on the wooden bench next to her. They talked for a little while about Tam's benefit the next day, the prospect of a large crowd, and the hope that the weather would stay fine. Beatrice opened the small hamper at her feet, and handed Connie a napkin, a fork and a little bowl of potted shrimp. She was about to do the same for Tam, but he waved it away and rose to his feet. He wanted to check on the preparations, he said, and disappeared through the tall double doors of the pavilion.

'He's nervous about tomorrow,' said Beatrice with a shy little smile.

'I should think half of the passengers on the train from London will be here to see him,' said Connie. 'He'll never stop being the Great Tam.'

'It's good of *you* to come. I know how much it means to him.'

The earnest tone of her gratitude caused Connie a jolt to her conscience. She dropped her gaze, and noticed in Beatrice's picnic hamper a library book: the gilt lettering on its spine asked, with unknowing pertinence, *Can You Forgive Her?* A glance at Beatrice's unadorned hand confirmed her initial impression of someone too meek for marriage. Yet she looked more settled with her singleness than her brother did. Their conversation, in Tam's absence, had kept so closely to a path of amiable vagueness – they had like-minded views on Trollope – that Connie was taken quite by surprise when Beatrice, in a moment of sudden particularity, remarked, 'You really are very beautiful, after all.' Connie blushed, stumped for a response (*after all* what?), but without seeming to heed the embarrassment Beatrice continued to scrutinise her. 'I begin to understand –'

Whatever that might be was left unresolved, for at that moment Tam returned along their row.

'I've put you two beside one another,' he said of the seating arrangements for the following night's gala dinner. 'I'm obliged to sit next to the mayor. It seems they're going to make me a freeman of the town.' He didn't look enthused by the prospect.

'It's meant to be an honour, Drewy,' Beatrice reminded him gently.

Tam shrugged, then turned to Connie. 'I've placed our mutual friend at the other end of the table, by the mayor's wife and Lord Daventry.'

A smile passed between them. 'I'm sure he'll enjoy that,' said Connie.

The rain started just before tea. The sky had been glowering all afternoon; slowly at first, then more insistently, a thin grey curtain of drizzle swept over the ground. When it began to thicken, and they could see fat drops ploshing onto the lower steps, the umpires pocketed the bails and called the players off. Tam stood up, and sniffed the damp air like a gun dog.

'I reckon we should call it a day,' he said with casual authority. 'This rain's not going to stop.'

They gathered the detritus of their lunch and retreated up the steps into the pavilion. Tam had suggested a drink in the long bar, and they were dithering in the hallway when Connie saw the door swing open and Will emerge, with a young woman in attendance. They all momentarily froze at once, though Connie was slightly better prepared for this untimely encounter, half believing that, the stronger the assurance of a thing not happening – the *Titanic* being sunk, for example – the greater seemed the inevitability that it *would*.

Will, visibly discomfited by this unforeseen social iceberg, was mumbling his way through the forms. '. . . and this is Miss Callaway – Miss Ada Brink.'

He did not dare lift his gaze as she and Ada exchanged handshakes. Nor did he listen to the polite talk that followed, Ada twittering on to the strangers in her amiable and uninhibited way, until he realised he had missed a conversational cue – from *her*.

'I'm sorry?' he said, coming to attention.

Connie, leaning forward slightly, as one might to a dotard, said, 'I was just asking about your family. Your sister is well?'

'Indeed, yes, she's very well – thank you,' he replied disjointedly, obliged now to look her in the eye. This caused him a severe inward turmoil. She had changed again since he last saw her at Holloway. Gone was the sallow complexion and the depleted physique; she was still thin (her cheekbones were expressively taut) but a gleam danced in her eye, her back was straight and her hair, though short, had recovered its lustre of old. Her beauty was, if anything, the nobler for having outfaced its traumatic assaults. This much he had taken in at a glance. What utterly confounded him was her self-possession, her readiness to deal with this highly awkward encounter as though it were a happy coincidence.

'I trust we'll meet again tomorrow,' he heard himself say, and Connie replied in a manner that could not have been better calculated to pierce him. She smiled – and not in a merely social way; it was a smile that seemed to encompass both agreement and acknowledgement of their former familiarity. This was more than Will could bear. With a stiff bow to them, he steered Ada away and out of the pavilion.

The rain, pittering thinly on their umbrella, had cleared the beach and most of the esplanade in front of them. Beatrice had caught a bus in the opposite direction, leaving Tam to accompany Connie back to the Royal Victoria. Tramcars made a whooshing sound as they passed along the promenade. A few hardy bathers were still braving the slate-grey sea.

Connie, pondering the recent encounter, said very little as they walked. She had not failed to register Will's embarrassment, and it had amused her to assume graciousness in the face of it. But it was the lady he was squiring who occupied her thoughts. She had seemed very comely, vivacious, youthful, and – Ada, was it? – would make someone an excellent wife, she supposed. Yet was it possible that someone so young, not much more than a girl, could truly sustain Will's interest? Or was it rather that she had seriously misjudged Will all along, and that Ada might be his ideal companion?

'Very pretty, wasn't she?' she said, after such a length of silence that Tam seemed to twig the deliberation that had preceded it. He murmured in assent, though when Connie pressed him for information he hadn't much to add.

'I barely know the girl. I haven't seen a great deal of Will since he took up with her.'

'D'you think they seemed – very close?'

Tam shrugged. 'He looks rather tense about her, 'sfar as I can tell. Not like he was with you.'

Connie gave a rueful little snort at this last remark, though a keen reader of her face might have discerned an ambiguous satisfaction flit across it. Tam himself was such a reader, but he didn't say anything else until they had reached the entrance of the hotel. He looked back in the direction they had been walking.

'No sign of that fellow who was stalking you.'

Connie nodded. 'All the same, I should be on guard for Mr Relf. He seems . . . tenacious.'

Tam enquired as to her dinner arrangements, and Connie sensed that he would have liked a part in them. But matters lay in such a state of uncertainty that she dared not venture out of her hotel that evening. She offered Tam a regretful smile and the excuse of tiredness.

'But I'll be champing at the bit for the start of play tomorrow. Eleven thirty?'

'Eleven thirty. Come to the players' entrance. I'll be there.'

He took her gloved hand and pressed it close to his mouth; then he turned away down the promenade.

Once inside, she went to reception and asked whether any telegrams had arrived for her. The desk manager reported none. So she couldn't be sure if Ivy had already left London and was on the train down here. Were Relf to get wind that Ivy was in town, it would not take him long to deduce that mischief was in the offing. For now, Connie would simply have to follow instructions and wait. Up in her room, she opened the windows and listened to the rain pattering outside. Along the front she could see the pier, its lights beginning to wink on as the evening paled to grey.

It troubled her that she had yet to be told her part in whatever scheme was afoot. Militants had got wind of the fact that police were intercepting their mail, thus enabling them to anticipate campaigns and arrest the suspects. Connie was told not to write to any suffragist associate in the weeks following the Davison funeral, but to wait until someone made contact with her. A note had come through the door at Thornhill Crescent, hand-delivered, not posted, instructing her to be at the Royal Victoria on the evening of 9 July. Her liaison was codenamed 'Hedera', which Connie knew was Latin for 'ivy'. She had a sudden comical image of Ivy turning up at the hotel and checking in a suitcase full of bricks.

Ivy had been due to arrive at eight this evening. It was now quarter past. Connie had been pacing her room for so long she felt like a circus lion before showtime. She was about to go down for a fresh box of Sullivans when there came a knock from outside. Opening her door she found two entirely unexpected visitors. One of them was Edith Aitken herself. The other was a younger woman Connie did not know.

'Miss Callaway,' she said, with a brief smirk on seeing Connie's bemused expression. 'May we – come in?'

Connie held the door open and stepped aside.

'This is Miss Webster,' said Edith, introducing her companion, a pale, somewhat prim-faced woman of about Connie's age, who gave a businesslike nod by way of greeting. Hers was the demeanour of the exceptionally clever but plain girls Connie had known at school. Edith was checking her watch. 'Typical, I suppose. Punctuality has never been Ivy's forte.'

'I'm not sure Ivy will be coming,' said Connie. 'I sent her a telegram earlier today warning her off.'

'Why?' asked Edith sharply.

'A Mr Relf has followed me here. Special Branch. If he sees Ivy and me together, the game's up.'

Edith exchanged a look with Miss Webster. 'Might he be waiting down there?' she asked Connie, who crossed to the window and took a long look over the darkening parade. She could see only the black blooms of passing umbrellas and an occasional motor cab. She turned back into the room.

'I don't see him. He may not know I'm staying here. Are you certain that *you* weren't followed?'

Edith shook her head. 'I don't think so.'

Miss Webster spoke directly to Edith. 'Whatever happens, it wouldn't do to get caught with this.' She gestured at a small leather briefcase which Connie had only just noticed. Edith was frowning, her eyes hard with calculation, and Connie now felt it was time to ask: 'May I know why you're here?'

Before she could reply there sounded a sharp rap at the door. They stood where they were, reluctant even to make a sound. Only when she heard a voice outside say 'Hullo?' did Connie let out her breath and open the door. Ivy entered, and with a quick birdlike survey of the room, greeted each of them, plainly innocent of any alarm she had caused.

'You didn't get my telegram?' asked Connie.

'Oh, I did. No time to reply – I spent the whole afternoon trying to throw the police off my trail. I made a roundabout journey to Charing Cross, only to find another bevy of detectives waiting there. So I took a cab to Victoria, announced *loudly* in the booking office that I wanted a ticket to Chatham, then sneaked onto the Brighton train. From Brighton I came here.'

'That was clever thinking, Ivy,' said Connie.

When Ivy had dispensed with her umbrella and rain-damp coat, they settled around a table. Edith said, 'To business, then. We know for certain that Daventry and Foulkes will be at the Priory for a dinner tomorrow evening. Miss Callaway, you have a contact there?'

Connie nodded. 'Actually, I'll be there, as the guest of a friend.'

'And who would that be?'

'Andrew Tamburlain.'

Edith almost reared back at this name, and widened her eyes at Connie. 'Tamburlain – the famous . . . ?'

'The one and only.'

Edith began to smile slowly. 'I see. My understanding was that your friend was a woman, who might be able to smuggle us in, so to speak. But if you're on the inside already . . . this makes it even better.' She looked at Miss Webster, who nodded in silent agreement. Connie, prickling with unease, decided that enough nods and winks had passed between them.

'I'd be very unwilling to see tomorrow night's occasion disrupted.'

Edith raised an enquiring eyebrow. 'Oh. Why, may I ask?'

'Because the dinner is in honour of Mr Tamburlain. It's his farewell to the club – to cricket.'

'I'm sure it is. And it will be attended by Daventry and Foulkes. We'll never have a better opportunity to get at them.'

'Only think of the stir it will create,' said Ivy.

'Foulkes and Daventry are attending tomorrow's play,' Connie replied. 'Why not then? I'll break the windows myself, if necessary.'

Edith gave her an arch look. 'Who said anything about breaking windows?'

Connie hesitated, realising she had assumed too much. 'I thought – well, please to say what you do intend.'

At a sign from Edith, Miss Webster picked up her briefcase and undid its clasp. Her expression remained impassive as she drew out a slim package, wrapped in brown paper, and laid it on the table. It was roughly the size of a book. Connie stared at it for a moment, and began to feel a cold turbulence rise within her. She had never seen such a device before, but she knew instinctively what it was. Edith, who had been watching her narrowly, now took the package in her hands.

'It contains about five pounds of coarse-grained gunpowder,' said Miss Webster, with the stolid air of a professional. 'I only need to prime it.'

Connie paused before speaking. 'Do you expect me to help you with this?'

Edith made a little gesture of appeal with her hands. 'It's why we're gathered here. Ivy and I will be on hand to create a diversion. Your job is to facilitate Miss Webster's entry into the building.'

She could not quite believe what she was hearing. 'And what of the Union's principle to hold life sacred?'

'We intend to honour it.'

'But with a bomb – you understand – there can be no guarantee.'

Edith gave a nearly imperceptible shrug. 'We do not seek to injure people.'

Connie, keeping herself quite still, returned an appraising look. 'What you're proposing . . .' She very slowly shook her head. 'It cannot be. Your plan is – monstrous. I want no part of it.'

Ivy, in a hurt voice, said, 'Constance, think what we have suffered for the cause. You can't let us down now.'

'I'm as loyal to the cause as I ever was,' she replied. 'But I'll not have anyone's blood on my hands.' Her body had begun to tremble. She felt suddenly in need of a cigarette.

'With or without you –' Miss Webster began, but Edith held up a hand to quieten her. Then, in a tone of conciliatory patience, the latter spoke again.

'I must remind you, Miss Callaway, we are engaged in a war. We do not *want* to burn down houses or to set off bombs, any more than we *want* to go to prison. But the position the enemy puts us in – their refusal to yield what is rightfully ours – has made it necessary to take up whatever weapons are at our disposal. Consider it this way. If men were to find themselves bent beneath such a yoke as ours, and compelled to fight, do you imagine for a moment they would hesitate to use gunpowder and paraffin?'

'Heaven help us if we are to be considered on *that* footing,' said Connie. 'Who knows what enormities men are capable of? Our job, if anything, is to set them an example – not compete with them in infamy.'

'Then you are handing them the victory,' said Edith, jutting her chin.

'On the contrary,' replied Connie. 'We are asserting our superiority. Sooner or later they will simply have to concede that we are as deserving of responsibility as they are.'

'"Sooner or later,"' repeated Miss Webster with a sneer. 'And what do you propose we do in the meantime? Simper and smile and make polite petitions to the government? I wish you joy of it.'

'Ladies, please – remember we are on the same side,' said Ivy, the plaintive peacemaker.

'Are we?' said Edith, fixing Connie with a sceptical look.

Connie sighed, and looked away. In the silence the rain could be heard spattering against the window. 'Does anyone have a cigarette?'

None of them did, so she would have to go down to reception. She asked the others if they cared for drinks to be sent up. Ivy requested a cocoa. Edith and Miss Webster said nothing. A minute later Connie was exiting the lift and crossing the hotel foyer. The night manager offered to fetch her cigarettes from the restaurant – they sold Woodbines and Gold Plate, but not Sullivans, it seemed. The man said he could send a boy to the tobacconist, but she insisted on going herself.

'It's still raining, miss,' the man said doubtfully.

'Then perhaps you could lend me an umbrella. I don't mind a walk.'

The manager led her to the back entrance, where he recited directions to the shop via a short cut. It would take her five minutes. She set off along the rain-slicked pavements, wondering how she might possibly counter Edith's incendiary purposes. There would be at least a hundred people in or around the Priory's Long Room tomorrow evening. Could she really stand by, knowing that some might be seriously injured, or worse? The glimmer of a gas lamp alerted her to the tobacconist's, where she bought Sullivans and a box of matches.

She had retraced her steps to the hotel and turned down the corridor leading to the foyer when she stopped, suddenly. Twenty yards ahead of her, stationed by the lift, two policemen were talking to the night manager. Holding her breath, she softly reversed until she had gained the safety of the corridor turn. Then she bolted through the back door again and onto the street, her heart beating a furious tattoo. They must have been discovered – there was no other explanation for those policemen being there. She tried to calm herself. She would check round the front of the hotel, just to make certain. If what she feared proved correct, then she may just have taken the most providential cigarette break in her life. Her circuit of the building had brought her to Marine Parade, where she could hear the waves bashing against the sea wall. She approached the hotel entrance, the palpitations in her chest now so agitated she wondered they could not be heard. A smartly dressed couple had just emerged from a cab and were heading up the hotel steps. As they did so, Connie took advantage of their cover and looked beyond them into the foyer. What she saw there froze her blood: the place was aswirl with police, and right in the midst of them stood Relf, bowler-hatted, hands on hips. Now there was no doubt. Dipping the umbrella to shield her face, Connie walked on past the entrance, trying to keep her steps at a steady, unpanicked pace. She was putting it all together in her head. Relf must have been waiting for them to gather in her room; she supposed he had distributed police photographs of each of them, and had checked at every hotel reception in town. She had escaped for the moment, but her occupancy of that room was unarguable – a room in which a bomb had been found. She would be implicated with the plotters, however she might protest her innocence. Another prison sentence would follow – a longer one this time.

She had been walking, almost blindly, along the Parade, glancing back every so often to see if anybody had followed her from the hotel. She must press on – but to where? To London? Even if she eluded the police at the railway station, they would be waiting for her at Islington. Lily? Marianne? They too were under surveillance. She knew of one suffragette safe house in Holborn, but with Relf on the warpath she could not depend on it remaining safe for long. Away, away . . . it was frightening to be so abruptly a fugitive. Never mind. Keep walking. A taxi chugged by, its tyres hissing in the rain. She should have hailed it, but then you only took a taxi if you had a destination. A line from a book came to her: *When you don't know where you're going, every path takes you there*. She was now in the vicinity she had walked through that morning with Tam. And in the same moment she realised – he was her only refuge. It would shame her to tell him, after all that he had done for her, but she would have to bear it.

After several wrong turns she arrived at Prospect Place. Under cover of dark the street seemed less friendly, and the tall houses with their trustworthy chimneys all looked the same. She hurried along the row until she came to the one she thought was his. At the top of the steps she paused; there were bell pushes, but no names to distinguish them. Then she remembered him saying that he lived on the top floor. She tried the bell, and waited. If Tam wasn't there then she truly was alone. In a moment of madness she had even considered Will, and then dismissed it. He was more likely to turn her in than respond to a plea for help. Through the frosted glass of the door she saw a lamp swim in the dark, and then the door swung back to reveal Tam. As his eyes focused upon her, Connie sensed his reaction turn from surprise to pleasure: it was as if presenting herself at his doorstep like this was something he had expected – or hoped for. He stood aside to let her pass, and once she had stepped into the hallway, she turned to him.

'Tam, I'm so sorry. I –' Where to begin? She had dragged the ghost of her seeming treachery across the threshold, and now stood there, obliged to explain it. Tam had turned up the gas lamp.

'You're soaked through,' he said, and took the dripping brolly from her hand. 'Come upstairs.'

She followed him up the darkened staircase and into his rooms, rehearsing what she would say. All of it sounded wrong – horribly, grievously wrong. Tam put down the lamp, and turned to her. Moonlight leaked narrowly through the sash windows, and she felt grateful at least for the shadows in the room.

'Let me take your coat,' he said, but she shook her head. 'A drink, then?'

It was intolerable that he should be so unwitting. Her words came out in a rush: 'Tam, I've something to say, and please don't offer me a drink and be nice because you won't want to after what I've told you, in fact you'll probably show me the door, and be perfectly justified in doing so.'

Tam cocked his head. 'What d'you mean?'

She began, distractedly, to stumble through it: the chance meeting with the Christian militants, the proposed attack on the Priory and her reluctant rendezvous, the unexpected arrival this evening of Edith Aitken and Miss Webster at her hotel, and the subsequent raid on the room.

314

'I swear to you, I had no idea about the bomb . . .' She now raised her eyes in appeal to Tam. He had been standing by the fireplace, listening in silence, lost in shadowy profile. She took a half-step towards him, needing to see his expression, and he turned his face to her. It wasn't congested with anger, nor could she read any sardonic gleam of disapproval. It was only very sad, and that seemed to her now the hardest thing of all.

'Please say that you believe me,' she said in a broken voice, and Tam, with a nod, replied that he did. He went to a drinks table, and poured each of them a finger of Scotch.

'Drink that,' he said, putting the glass into her hand. She swallowed a mouthful, and felt the smoky liquid burn down her throat. For some moments she watched him as he stood at the window, facing away from her. 'You're not safe in this country,' he said presently. 'Do you have people – abroad?'

Connie shook her head. 'Could I go to Ireland – Scotland?'

'You'd still have to go by the railways. And they'll be looking for you.'

After another silence she said, 'If I could get to Paris – I have a friend –'

'That's good.' He took out his watch. 'You need to start out now.'

She felt a recoil within her. 'But I haven't got – all my clothes, my case –'

'You know you can't go to the hotel.'

'But I've no money!' she heard herself almost wail. 'Only what I have in this purse.'

'I have money,' he said. 'Now, give me a moment.' He left the room, returning half a minute later in his bowler and mackintosh.

Connie, distraught, shook her head. 'Tam, I don't know what to say –'

'Then don't say anything,' he replied, handing her the umbrella. 'Come, you need to get to the station. There's a ferry crossing at twenty to midnight.'

Down in the hallway he told her to wait. She watched him hurry down the steps onto Prospect Place, where he looked up and down the street. The rain had thinned into a drizzle, a gauzy veil against the gas lamps. Within minutes Tam had flagged down a cab, and beckoned her from the shelter of his doorstep. He ushered her into the vehicle, and stepped in after. As the cab descended through the narrow streets towards the front, Connie said, 'Won't there be police posted at Warwick Square?'

'Yes – that's why we're going to Roe Street instead.'

His forbearance was heroic, given everything she had told him. Instead of throwing her out of his flat, he had taken pity on her, again. She stole a glance at him as he sat there, bands of brightness and dark falling across his face from the road's lamplight.

'You'll tire of saving me one day,' she said in a half-joking undertone. The words hung in the air, until Connie wondered if Tam hadn't heard, or else wasn't bothering to reply. Long moments passed before he did say, quietly, 'Why would I?'

They encountered no one at Roe Street. In the compartment of the train to Folkestone they exchanged barely a word. Connie, in a stupor of fatigue, had nothing of use to say, though she sensed Tam's gaze on her as she stared out of the window. She imagined the scene back at the Royal Victoria, the police searching the room, upending the contents of her case, sifting through her personal effects for incriminating evidence – as though they needed any more. She could scarcely yet take in the stroke of good fortune that had enabled her to escape, and at the same time she berated herself for having allowed Ivy to co-opt her into such a cabal. The naivety of it . . . but how could she have anticipated consorting with a bomb-maker?

They alighted at Folkestone, and Tam directed her to the tea room before heading to the ticket office. She thought of sending her mother and Fred a telegram, but realised that this would betray her movements should Relf intercept it. She took off a glove and rubbed her eyes, itching with tiredness. Moments later she heard someone call her name, more than once, and jerked back her head suddenly – she had fallen asleep. Tam was now sitting opposite her.

'Constance – put these in your handbag.' On the table before her was a ticket for the night ferry to Boulogne. So it was irrevocable: she was leaving. There was also an envelope, unsealed, which crackled with banknotes when she picked it up.

'Tam, I really –'

'Do you have any French?' he said, cutting short her attempt at a thank-you.

She nodded. '*Un petit peu* . . . I'm going to pay this back to you. I mean it.'

'Write to me with your address, when you have one,' he said. 'I'll try to recover that case for you.'

She looked intently at him, and in doing so felt a memory tug at her. She opened her purse, and picked out a cigarette card, perfectly preserved but for a tiny tear at one corner. It was a sepia portrait of A. E. Tamburlain, Sussex and England.

'I found it in my father's desk. I'm going to keep it with me.'

Tam looked at it for a few moments, then with a wry shake of his head he handed it back. 'It seems that they're boarding.' She followed his gaze across to the landing stage, where a ferry was moored. Passengers were straggling up the gangway. As Connie looked back at him, she felt her eyelids involuntarily begin to brim. She had not thought that a day which began with Tam meeting her off the train would end with this melancholy goodbye at a Channel port.

'I did so want to see you batting tomorrow,' she said with a choking sob. 'I hope the rain –'

'There, there,' said Tam, taking her gloved hand and holding it reverently to his lips. 'There won't be rain tomorrow. And that ticket's a return, you know.'

She nodded her comprehension, her heart so swollen it seemed to have blocked her throat, making it difficult to speak. She took out a handkerchief and blotted her eyes. Then, raising herself on tiptoe, she kissed his cheek – and walked away. She didn't turn round even as she reached the foot of the swaying plank, and allowed one of the steamer's crew to help her on. She grasped the sodden rope and walked across. Not until they had cast off the mooring ropes and she felt the engine's deep, slow throbbing underfoot did she go to the stern and stand against the passenger rail. Below her the black waters had begun to churn. She raised her hand, and Tam, still standing there, answered it with his own.

16

Will stared out at the wintry view below, where a few brave promenaders staggered against the buffeting winds off the Channel. He was sitting at one of the window tables at Gildersleeves, one ear cocked to the distant thrash of the gale outside, the other distracted by an anxious inner voice: he did not have a third to spare for the waiter's recitation of the lunch specials. But as usual Will had nodded and given a fair impersonation of having understood. What he had once forgiven in himself as a social duplicity – to seem to be listening while communing with his own thoughts – had, over time, hardened into a habit. Even Ada, who wasn't especially alert to the currents of social chitchat, had started to catch him out. After yarning away she would come to a sudden halt, and Will would slowly surface from his private burrow of thought ('Hmm?') to realise he had just been asked a question. 'William, have you been listening to me?' she said the first time it happened, more amused than offended, and he had stammered out an apology. But her tone had become sharper as she perceived that his attention could not generally be trusted for periods exceeding three minutes.

This negligence had provoked a small crisis two weeks before, whose astonishing outcome he was still barely able to comprehend. He had taken her up to London for a new year party, on Reggie Culver's invitation, and they had sloped off with a group of friends to the Savoy for a sharpener. Will had not been inside the hotel since the evening he had saved Connie from the police, and revisiting those same corridors he had drifted off into a sad reverie of her. Their accidental encounter at the Priory in July was the last time they had spoken, and only when he asked Tam did he hear the full story behind her disappearance abroad. He gathered that she was working at a hospital in Paris. It was unfortunate that Will was still imagining her life there when Ada broke in: 'You've not listened to a word I've said, have you?' He could not deny it. She fell morosely quiet, and he had spent the rest of the night devising a desperate stratagem to appease her.

Too galling to think of where *that* had led. He had won her round, in the end – and that was how he had found himself, at the turn of the year, betrothed. *Betrothed.* It was almost inconceivable – but most definitely incontrovertible. His mother, triumphant, had wanted to put an announcement in *The Times* immediately, but he resisted. He needed to tell Tam first, and had arranged today's lunch for that purpose. As their meeting approached, feelings of dread had gathered over him like snipers at an ambush, and he half thought about cancelling. His unease was twofold. They had always been bachelors together, and a confession that he was leaving those noble ranks might sound to Tam's ears a kind of betrayal. But what felt worse was the gradual erosion of their camaraderie, which marriage would only hasten. Tam's retirement had already driven a wedge between them; no more would they be partnering one another at the crease, or chatting in the slips, or sipping ale, feet up on the pavilion balcony. Tam had entered the exile of the former player, from which there was no return. They had gone from seeing one another nearly every day to meeting once every three or four weeks. And those hiatuses would doubtless extend, once he and Ada set up life together.

He took out his watch. Where was Tam, as a matter of fact? He was now three-quarters of an hour late, and in the meantime Will had exhausted his rereading of the menu; the beef Wellington being served at the adjacent table was making him hungry. He pulled out his pocket diary, and riffled its pages in search of Beatrice Tamburlain's telephone number. Tam would not countenance having his own telephone installed because the ringing sound irritated him; in fact, the last time they had gone fishing together he had confessed that even the rustling of a newspaper could infuriate him these days. Will left his table and went to the telephone booth just outside the restaurant's entrance. Beatrice picked up on the fourth ring, and after a brief exchange of new year felicitations he asked her if she knew of her brother's whereabouts. She had not seen Drewy since the weekend, she said, though there had been talk of his running down to the Isle of Wight for a few days. Will conceded that he may simply have forgotten their arrangement. He thanked her and replaced the earpiece on its cradle.

An hour later, fortified by his beef Wellington and a half-bottle of burgundy, Will exited Gildersleeves and bent his steps towards Warwick Square. The walk took him by coincidence along Prospect Place, and he thought he might as well call by Tam's lodgings to check that he really had gone. A landlady answered the door, and said that she had heard Mr Tamburlain returning to the house last night, though she didn't think he had stirred from his rooms today. 'I believe he was the worse for wear,' she added, shrugging. Will, looking up at the house, saw that one of the topmost sashes was open. Puzzled, he passed in and took the stairs to the top floor. No response met his knock, yet some unaccountable instinct told him that Tam was at home, probably lying helpless in an alcoholic stupor. He hurried downstairs and asked the landlady to let him into his friend's flat; the anxiety in his expression did not incline her to hesitate.

'Tam?' he called out on entering the hall, the woman close at his heels. He turned into the living room, icy cold from the open window, now shivering in its frame. In the kitchen an array of bottles had congregated over the table, not all of them empty. The landlady picked one up, and gave a prim told-you-so moue. He came at last to the bedroom, and turning the doorknob he craned his head within. The curtains were drawn, but he could see Tam lying on the bed, still in his clothes, sound asleep, his right hand apparently wrapped in a bandage. A stale, burnt odour suffused the air. Will called his name again, softly, then walked to the window. As he pulled back the curtain, he saw something had spilt on the pillow by Tam's head – then he took it all in at once. The reddish-brown stain was drying blood, the turbaned bandage on his hand was in fact a towel, from whose tapering end poked the pewter-coloured barrel of a pistol. The charred smell, he realised, was cordite. Behind him he heard the landlady step into the room, and a sudden dismayed 'Oh' escaped her lips. She stood there, a hand across her mouth, until Will came round the bed and said to her, quietly, 'Fetch the police.' Her eyes, round with horror, flicked briefly up to his, and she backed out of the violated room.

On hollowed legs he moved along the bedside, and, swallowing hard, sat down. He took Tam's wrist in his shaking hand, and felt its cold, pulseless weight. Without letting it drop, he stared at the half-closed eyes, at the mouth hanging open, as if he had been about to speak. The towel would have muffled the report of the gun, perhaps to spare the landlady a fright. From down below he heard a door slam, and footsteps hurrying down the path. For long minutes he stared at the contours of his friend's face (the violet-coloured

322

lips, the slackened mouth) and the glistening soot-blackened hole at the temple which had emptied it of expression, forever. Then, placing the left arm gently across his chest, Will stood up and walked to the door. He was going to step out of the room when an impulse stayed his hand on the doorknob, and he returned his gaze to the bed: nothing had ever made him feel so alone as the sight of that mute, untenanted body lying there. He felt a single, anguished sob break from his throat. It would have to do as his farewell.

Three days later Connie turned her bicycle into Place Dauphine, a triangular-shaped cobbled hideaway off the Pont Neuf. She had been living here, in a tiny third-floor apartment, since her precipitate flight from England last summer. On reaching Paris she had applied to Brigstock, who had gallantly put his studio at her disposal while she searched for a place of her own. She sometimes imagined that the oils and white spirit that permeated the room still clung to her clothes even now; they would always remind her of those early weeks of exile. Her only obligation had been to feed his cat, less imperious than Maud, the creature he had kept at Mornington Crescent, though her equal in selfishness. She didn't really mind, finding the cat a useful listener for her French, which, learned from the schoolroom, was sufficiently archaic to make Brigstock hoot with laughter ('I don't think they've used *that* word since about the time of Corneille'). She had been grateful to the painter these first few months; having arrived at his doorstep without a suitcase, he had provided 'the outlaw' with clothes and dresses left by – he made no pretence about it – the parade of models who passed in and out of his studio. The garments were mostly clean, which she regarded as a bonus. Brigstock's circle of acquaintance proved inexplicably wide, and not exclusively racy, either, which was how he had secured her a nursing job at a hospital run by an order of Catholic nuns near the Sorbonne.

He had arranged to meet her that afternoon at the cafe opposite her apartment, and as she propped her bicycle against one of the impassive plane trees standing sentinel around the Place Dauphine she spotted him, wreathed in cigarette smoke, at a window table. It was a kind of reunion, for Brigstock had spent Christmas and the first week of the new year in Venice. He rose from his seat as she entered the smoke-fugged establishment. His dark double-breasted overcoat with astrakhan collar seemed to invite comment.

'Greetings, m'dear,' he cried, with a flamboyant bow. 'And belated felicitations. I trust the new year finds you well?'

'Very well, thank you.' As one used to solitude, it hadn't occurred to him that Connie might have preferred some company over Christmas. But she was too proud to say so. 'Is that a new coat?'

He stroked its sleeve admiringly. 'Indeed it is. They're all wearing them in Italy. Makes me look rather *un homme serieux*, d'you think?'

She considered him. '*Serieux – et vieux*,' she added, to tease him.

He frowned at this. 'Good Lord, what a thing to say!' He glanced anxiously at his face in the mirror behind her. 'You shouldn't joke. You know, I'll be fifty this year?'

'But I *was* joking,' she said consolingly.

'Sounds a nasty word, fifty,' he murmured, still testing his reflection. 'Sort of stiff and dusty . . .'

'How was Venice?' said Connie, carefully changing the subject.

'Hmm? Oh, filthy – and beautiful. Hasn't changed much in the twenty years since I was last there. The food is appalling, but you could forgive a lot else for those views. Ruskin was right – "it is the Paradise of cities".'

'I'd like to visit. To be poled around in a gondola . . .' she mused.

'Ah. You'll see a fine armada of them at the Danieli, all black and gleaming. Like floating coffins.'

'That's a little morbid.'

He curled his lip sardonically. 'Well, at *my* time of life . . .' He was not going to forget her jibe too soon. Once coffee arrived at their table she managed to cajole him into a lighter mood, and he showed her some of the loose sketches he had brought back. 'While I remember, I should nip to the shop round the corner for some charcoal,' he said, rising. 'Would you mind these for me? Oh, and here's a *Daily Mail* to pass the time.'

While he was gone Connie idly flicked through the paper, which was a day old. She found that she did not greatly miss English newspapers, partly because her job at the hospital preoccupied her, and partly because she had grown sick of the press, the recriminations, and the hysteria targeted at the Union. In the reports of the arrest of Edith, Ivy and Miss Webster, the tone of self-righteousness complicated her private relief that the bomb plot had been thwarted. That wasn't all: she had received a letter from Lily concerning a rumour that Connie herself had tipped off Special Branch detectives, who had subsequently allowed their 'spy' to escape abroad. At first she was astonished by this hearsay, and felt certain that nobody in the Union would give it credence. Then *The Times* picked up the story and ran it as though her treachery were now an accepted fact. She was briefly tempted to write a letter defending herself, but then felt too disgusted by the charge to give it even that much dignity. People who knew her, who knew what she had been through, would damn it as falsehood in any case.

She was turning the pages of the *Mail* in a brisk, careless sort of way when her eye was snagged by a name, and she narrowed her focus. It was an account of the career of A. E. Tamburlain. Realising the column had begun on the previous page, she turned back and saw the story's headline: SUICIDE OF FORMER TEST CRICKETER.

She stared at it for some moments, unable to move. Her eyes coursed rapidly, disbelievingly, over the newsprint, alighting on phrases whose finality jolted her – *found at home . . . a single bullet to the head . . . depressed at retirement . . . lived alone . . . a great loss to the game of cricket*. She had to catch her breath from the sudden shock of it. She began to read the story again, trying to digest its terrible truth, and baulking at the attempt; her resistance to it felt almost physical. Her heart seemed to have retreated to her stomach in sympathy. She raised her eyes and looked about the cafe, at its unheeding walls and murmuring clientele, as indifferent to her distress as the birds of the air. Oh, Tam, what madness or despair could have driven you – She was trying to recall now the last time he had written. When she had first arrived here they had corresponded in quick succession. She had sent him her temporary address and he had replied with a letter of such kindliness and concern that she felt the dreadful weight of her solitude almost crushing her. Some weeks later her suitcase arrived, with a note from Tam apologising for its tardy liberation from the local constabulary. Once she found her footing in her new abode she became less assiduous a correspondent, though there was no hint of reproof from him if weeks elapsed before she managed to write. When *had* she last written to him?

Connie found a second article on Tam in the sports columns. Its spirit of lamentation was keener, and one phrase in it cut her deeply.

One wonders in how many houses a portrait of Andrew Endall Tamburlain at this moment hangs with those of other great sportsmen of the day. Had his admirers but known of his private difficulties would they not gladly have ended them? It is unfortunate that something – pride, perhaps – made him unwilling to ask for help. It is all too sad for words.

She felt a sudden spasm of guilt flash through her. *Private difficulties* . . . The phrase unavoidably recalled an earlier bereavement. Ignorance of those difficulties besetting her father had not assuaged the pain of his suicide, but it had at least excused her any personal blame. With Tam the case was different. While their friendship had not been intimate, she had been close enough to know that he was, essentially, quite lonely – The scrape of a chair interrupted her reverie, and Brigstock, returned from his errand, was staring at her with an expression of dismayed enquiry.

'My dear, you look as though you've seen a ghost.'

Connie, benumbed, nodded slightly and handed him the newspaper. Without looking up, she waited while he perused the story. Presently, with a soft sigh of resignation, he laid down the paper on the table between them. When at last he spoke, the tenderness in his voice was palpable.

'I'm so very sorry, Connie,' he said, and the words, dissolving the composure she had struggled to maintain, forced helpless tears to run down her face. Only afterwards did she realise that the last time such weeping had overcome her was that rain-blurred night she left Folkestone, and England – which was the last time she had seen Tam, or would ever see him.

Later that day, as the light faded in her bedroom, Connie lit another of the acrid-tasting cigarettes Brigstock had given her, and pulled out the drawer of her bedside table. In among the letters from Fred, her mother and Lily, she located one that bore Tam's handwriting, its postmark dated 6 November 1913. She withdrew its single sheet and read:

My dear Constance,

Thank you for your last. I am glad to learn that you are finding the work less troublesome at the hospital. You make fun of your alleged inadequacies as a French speaker, but I imagine the comfort and cheer you bestow upon your patients would transcend any limitations of language – it is your gift. (I still recall the sweetness of your condolences to me on the death of my mother.)

You remarked upon the 'troubled' tone of my previous letter, for which I must offer apology. Retirement does not sort well with me; formerly the winter would have been occupied with a club tour to Australia or South Africa, and I feel the absence of the game hanging heavy. It is the price one pays for choosing a young man's profession – after one's brief spell in the sun there seems to be too much time to fill.

Sometimes I fear that I have devoted myself to cricket at the expense of making a life. Yet I chose the game willingly, so there is nobody to blame but myself. Such dismal ruminations! I beg your pardon.

Beatrice asks after you, and sends her regards. She was sorry to hear that your period of exile must be indefinitely extended – as was I. Please to be assured that, whenever that period should end, there will always be a welcome for you here. Until then, believe me sincerely,

Your friend,
Andrew

Connie read the letter a second time, and felt again that obscure but insistent needling of her conscience. She discerned now an appeal in his words, and a sense of regret

– *there is nobody to blame but myself* – that required a friend's consolation. Given all that he had done for her, ought she not to have been more solicitous of his troubles? Perhaps – though in what manner she might have helped him she didn't know, and now the chance had gone. *Your friend, Andrew.* The sign-off had become a valediction, and pierced her to the heart. The newspaper had it right, for once – all too sad for words. Turning up the gas lamp, she found a sheet of writing paper and her pen. She crushed out her cigarette in a little saucer. *Dear Beatrice*, she began the letter, *I am at a loss to express my sadness* – and several hours of sorrowing meditation would intervene before she could bring herself to finish it.

It was another day of rain-washed skies and scuttling, wispy clouds as Will followed the coffin out of the church and down the path, thronged now with beady-eyed men in overcoats and bowlers. The press were out in force. He felt Ada's hand resting lightly in the crook of his arm as they stepped beneath the dark cage of ancient yews. His mother and Eleanor walked just ahead of them. Nearly hallucinating with sleeplessness, he had spent the last few days in a determined frenzy of activity, helping Beatrice to organise the funeral, arranging the caterers for the wake at Silverton House, fielding enquiries from the newspapers – anything, in short, that would prevent him brooding too much on his late friend. He dreaded breaking down, in public or in private, and had decided that his best chance of self-control lay in a willed benumbing of his senses. The struggle of it must have told on his face, however, because when he had collected Ada at her house that morning he saw her eyes widen in alarm.

The recessional hymn was still ringing in his ears as they went through the lychgate and began walking up the hill towards the cemetery, where Tam was to be buried in the plot alongside his parents. A flood of speculation had poured forth from the press as to why a man 'once hailed as the country's most popular cricketer' had destroyed himself. Some said that he could not endure the ex-player's slow fade into obscurity; that he drank too much; that his nerves were plagued by an irrational hatred of noise; that he had money troubles; that he had never recovered from the death of his mother eighteen months before. Will was surprised by the conviction of these obituarists and editors, who pronounced on the matter as if they had been on terms of intimate familiarity with the deceased. He, who actually *had* known him, was utterly in the dark as to what might have prompted him to take his own life – or, as one paper put it with dubious flippancy, 'to walk before he'd been given'. And how well did one know one's friends in any case? Outside the church, while waiting for the funeral cortège, someone had introduced him to a lady named Dora Lambert, who, astonishingly, turned out to be Tam's ex-wife. In the five, nearly six years they had known one another Tam had never once mentioned the fact that he'd been married. Will mumbled out his condolences, unable to guess how recently the former Mrs Tamburlain had seen her late husband, or what circumstances might have caused their sundering in the first place. Her appearance had winded him. If he didn't even possess the verifiable facts of Tam's life, how could he begin to understand the shadowy motivations that might have led to his death?

They were assembling around the grave, the black-clad mourners lining the open maw of the trench like crows along a branch. Will half listened to the vicar reciting the exequies, the words rubbed serenely smooth from use. Then, at a signal, they were invited to pitch a handful of earth into the excavated rectangle. Blindly, he scooped up some dirt and let it fall through his hand; it crackled on the wooden face of the coffin. He took a step back, catching nobody's eye.

Earlier he had nodded to one or two players, staff from the Priory, the mayor and his wife, but he did not look at Beatrice for fear of the desolation he might read in that gentle countenance. Avoid, avoid. He must have been so tightly coiled that the light tap on his shoulder made him jump. Eleanor had leaned towards his ear.

'Have you seen who's over there?'

Will followed her gaze past the throng to a spot a little distance beyond, where a woman stood, her figure straight and oddly stern. She was dressed in a long black coat, with a high fur collar. Her face was covered by a dark veil, but he knew her instantly. Once the mourners began to melt away from the graveside, he detached himself from Ada and, steering a path between the tilted grey headstones, approached her. Connie pulled back her veil by way of greeting, and he took the hand she held forth. They looked at one another for a few moments, uncertain of how to begin.

'Beatrice sent me a telegram,' she said, as though to justify her presence.

Will nodded. 'It's good of you to come – I mean, such a long way,' he said, wondering if he sounded proprietary. 'You're still living in Paris?'

'Yes. I'm only here to –' The droop of her eyes completed the sentence.

'When I saw you in the veil I thought of that time – d'you remember?'

The ghost of a smile passed across her face. 'Of course I do. The Savoy. You rescued me.' It was kindly said, but the mention of rescue stirred in Will confused feelings of regret and hopelessness; he might have saved another, if only he had been more vigilant.

'He told me – Tam told me – about what happened. That night.'

Connie, eyes downcast, paused for a moment. 'He was – so desperately kind. After what I'd told him he might just have turned me over to the police. But instead he helped me . . .' There was a tremble on the last two words that squeezed at Will's heart.

'Tam would never have turned you in, even if you'd been guilty. You know that. He regarded you as a friend.' The mood had become fragile between them. He sensed the next question coming before she asked it.

'I just can't help thinking about – *why*. He once told me that there was a high susceptibility . . . among cricketers. Did you know . . . ?'

Will stared off, his gaze not quite focusing on the line of poplars beyond the low cemetery wall. 'I'd heard of certain cases. But I never thought Tam would be one of them. He didn't leave a note – anything.'

Distress had welled up into her eyes. 'I feel –' she swallowed back a sob '– I feel I should have helped him – but I don't know how –'

Will wanted to say something – anything – to comfort her, but misery had stopped up his throat, and no words would come. She turned away, gathering herself, for at this moment his sister and Ada had broken from the main body of mourners to join them. Ada shook hands with Connie, though gave no sign of having remembered her from the summer. Perhaps it was just as well. Eleanor's conversational sympathy ('Awfully sad, isn't it?') was a relief to them, though to Connie it seemed to mark the end of any further intimacy between her and Will. They had begun to walk down the hill, back towards the town.

'We'd better go and find Mother – she'll be worrying about the caterers,' said Eleanor presently.

Will turned to Connie. 'There's a gathering at the house,' he explained. 'Would you join us?'

Connie shook her head. 'I'm sorry – I have to get back to Folkestone.' She decided not to make mention of the police presence in town; it would not have been a surprise to see Relf and his detectives waiting at the station for her. With their mutual connection now gone, it suddenly occurred to her that this might be the last occasion she and Will would ever meet.

'Goodbye, Constance,' said Eleanor, shaking her hand. 'I'm sorry we couldn't have met in happier circumstances.'

'I am, too,' she replied, exchanging a nod of farewell with Ada. Will realised what he should do.

'Ada, I'll see you at the house. I'm going to accompany Miss Callaway to the station.' Ada nodded, and joined Eleanor in the cavalcade of mourners heading out of town.

As they walked through the narrow streets leading to Warwick Square, Will was oppressed by an agitated sense of things unsaid between them. The loss of their friend had brought them together, yet he felt that the opportunity to redeem himself and their shared past might tempt him into unwise confessions. So he kept silent, hoping that Connie would take the responsibility of clearing the air. Perhaps she intuited his wretchedness, because she was at last moved to speak.

'She's very pretty – Miss Brink, I mean.'

'Yes, I suppose she is,' he replied. He realised the moment had come. If he told her now and she betrayed some inadvertent feeling, he would know that it might not be too late. He could explain to her about that new year's night at the Savoy, when he had been squiring Ada but thinking about her – Connie – and how that had caught him off guard, and the calamitous mess he had then made of mollifying Ada's hurt feelings. How in heaven's name had he turned an apology into an offer of marriage? Too impetuous of him. Swallowing hard, he added, 'As a matter of fact, I've asked her to marry me.'

He glanced at her, half expecting her to break step from

the surprise, but she walked on, nodding slowly. Her expression, in profile, gave nothing away.

'And the lady has consented?' she asked, in a tone that made Will's heart sink. It was not cold, not at all, only casually inquisitive, as though this were a matter of mere curiosity.

'Yes, she has,' he replied – *but I'd been thinking of* you *the night I proposed*, he wanted to say. But of course he did not. Now she turned her face to him.

'Then I offer you my congratulations,' she said, with a calmness he found almost intolerable. She doesn't care, he thought. She really doesn't care. 'Have you set a date?'

'We've thought about September,' he said, trying belatedly to sound a note of pride. 'Once the season's finished.'

'Ah, yes. Another disadvantage to living in France. No cricket.'

They were nearing the forecourt of the railway station, and Connie drew down the hat's veil over her face – a precaution, she explained, against being identified. Will nodded. The subject of his betrothal seemed to have been dismissed. They had come to a halt, and the atmosphere between them seemed abruptly heightened by their imminent parting. He could see her hesitate for a moment.

'There's something I'd like to know. Did the rain keep off that day – I mean, the day of Tam's benefit match?'

Will, wrongfooted by the question, frowned into it consideringly. 'Um – yes, it was fine, as I remember. No rain at all. The players made an archway of bats on the pitch for Tam to walk under. He didn't tell you?'

Connie shook her head. 'I always meant to ask him, and I never did.' She was about to ask if Tam had made any runs, but then couldn't bear to know, in case he hadn't. 'Well . . .' she said, holding out her hand to him. Will felt a panicky compression in his chest, and looked earnestly at her.

'I can't help feeling this may be, I don't know, the last time we'll meet – and that you'll forget all about me.'

He expected her to reply in the same nonchalant tone she had used in discussing his marriage plans. But he was mistaken. 'I shall not forget you,' she said. 'I've never forgotten anyone I once knew. My acquaintances have not been numerous, and in my present situation they are unlikely to increase. If we don't meet again – then I wish only a happy life for you.'

Will was stunned by her words, and by the unaffected way in which she had spoken. He wanted time to parse them and pursue their implications, but already she was backing away from him, joining the general footfall heading into the station. He took a step towards her, and she raised her hand in a gesture that seemed half-farewell and half-admonishment: this far, and no further.

'Goodbye, Will,' she said, and was on her way. Had he taken that extra step he would have been close enough to notice that, behind the veil, her eyes glistened. It was the moment she had wished him a happy life that had almost undone her, because she knew now that it would never be a life with her in it.

PART TWO

The Shadowy Coast

17

I

Squinting into the gloom, Will held the shirt over his knee and began to examine the coarse fabric. Along the inside seam of one arm he could see a beaded line of tiny insects, like white translucent lobsters. These were the lice that had been feeding on his skin all day. He had felt them moving about first thing this morning, but had not had time to deal with them until now. He knew from Bailey that the men were infested more or less permanently. Will had imagined that having his kit laundered regularly would spare him, as though it were an officer's privilege to be exempt, but he had succumbed like the rest. Lice were no respecters of rank. With a sigh of disgust he pressed his thumbnail against the first until he heard it crack, then moved on to the next. When he had finished this part of the operation he lit a candle and carefully ran it along the seams. The trick was to coagulate the blood of the louse without burning a hole in the shirt. At his request Eleanor had sent him over a bottle of Harrison's Pomade ('Sorry to hear that you've become *lice*-ntious,' she wrote) and for a while that seemed to deter them. But with hydra-headed tenacity another colony would sprout up, and he had resorted once more to the candle. He had just dropped another louse into the flame when Bailey, a junior subaltern, came into the dugout.

'Oh – sorry to interrupt, sir,' he said as he took in what Will was doing. 'Should I come back later?'

Will shook his head. 'Come in. Have a seat.'

The seat was an empty ammunition box. Bailey plumped himself down on it with a distantly preoccupied air. He was a slight, fair-haired fellow of about twenty-one with unnaturally blue eyes and a laugh that became almost falsetto on its upper notes. In civilian life he had been a bank clerk in Deptford and still lived with his parents. Here he had become known as the chief distributor of nicknames, and enhanced his popularity by making sure that the rum ration got to the men in time. Now he had taken out a penknife and was paring his nails thoughtfully.

'How was London?' asked Will. Bailey had just returned from a week's leave.

'Better than here,' he replied with untypical glumness. He looked slyly at Will. ''Scuse for asking, sir, but have you heard . . . anything?'

'About the push? Nothing for certain.'

Bailey ducked his head despondently and sighed. 'You know, when I was home I kept being asked by people, When's the Big Push? Even me mum had heard about it!'

Will picked off another crushed louse and dropped it on the candle flame, where it fizzed. He had heard Bailey's complaint from others. Everyone seemed to know about the impending offensive, including, by now, the enemy. In London, the government had negotiated a settlement with disgruntled munitions workers, who wanted to know why the May Bank Holiday had been postponed. Lloyd George, minister for munitions, had explained that output from the factories should not be interrupted at least until the end of July. The implication in the delayed holiday was taken up by the newspapers the next day; the deduction was there for anyone to make.

Will had decided that the only way to endure the days and weeks of uncertainty was to assume a blank impermeable stoicism: why fret about what was inevitable? The euphoria of 1914 and all the talk of a war that would be over by Christmas seemed now to belong in another era, though it was less than eighteen months since he had left the Officers' Training Corps near Oxford, his head brimming with lectures about gas attacks and the deployment of the Mills bomb. Then he had been awarded his commission to serve as a lieutenant in the 1st M—shire Rifles. He shuddered to recall his excitement on the eve of sailing from Folkestone, when he had booked into a room at the Metropole and written a brief letter reassuring Ada that the deferment of their wedding would only increase his – he was going to write 'ardour', but then wondered if she would understand the play on words. He wrote 'devotion' instead. And how proud he had been of his new riding boots, his service revolver, his Sam Browne belt, whose dark leather he had polished till it gleamed like a conker.

Having long felt the absence of a cause in his life, Will had taken this one to heart. They would wipe the floor with the bloody Boche. For King and Country! His patriotic fervour had suffered its first small cooling on arrival at Etaples, the base camp that lay a hard day's march from Boulogne. He immediately felt dwarfed by the sheer size of the encampment, a huge grassless paddock on which hundreds of dirty white tents stretched as far as the eye could see. The smell of old sweat, stale food and creeping dread had assailed his nostrils, while the brutish voices of NCOs bullying the men on platoon drill made him wince. Its atmosphere was closer to that of a prison than a military encampment. The OTC back in England seemed a model of civility in comparison.

He had missed the spring offensive of 1915, and for a while took to wondering if he would ever look a German in the face. He had made out spectral figures on night patrols, heard their voices and, occasionally, been shaken by a detonating shell; there had been skirmishes, raids, false alarms, but he had yet to be involved in battle. That changed in the last week of September, when the 1st M—shires went up the line at Loos. As the minutes swooned down to zero hour, Will realised with a terrible lurch how close he was to conflict, and how dearly he wanted to survive it. He remembered his foot touching the fire step and the odd sensation of weightlessness on finally hauling himself over the top, as in a dream when you fall down a precipice and see the rocks at the bottom rushing headlong towards you. He woke from the dream without being crushed; other men at his side did not. Hypnotised, he moved forward into the roar of the barrage, like a swimmer wading into a tumultuous sea, its waves breaking over his head. Just below that noise he could hear the jagged metal patter of a machine gun, though he could see no more than ten yards through the drowning curtain of smoke. He kept walking, encouraged by the voice of the company commander nearby, chivvying the line along. 'Not so fast on the left,' he heard. *Not so fast*. That was the amazing thing, the steady mechanical pace at which they were advancing, like walking out to bat, when deep within he could hear a countervoice urging *hurry*, *hurry*. But hurry to where, and into what? He cast a quick glance behind him and saw the ground writhing, hideously, with wounded bodies. 'Keep the line straight,' he heard, and continued walking. About his ears Will could hear a high whirring, like a mosquito, charging the air; only afterwards did he realise that these were individual bullets passing inches from him. Directly ahead he saw a man kneel suddenly, as though in prayer; Will thought he should warn against such casual behaviour, but on putting his face close to the kneeling man saw that a bullet had perforated his throat. The man's face wore an expression of crumpled vacancy. He left him in that supplicant posture, and wondered, again, why he still stood when so many others were falling. The line had become more ragged now, yet still they staggered into the blinding storm. Then of a sudden the earth beneath his feet convulsed, the side of his helmet took a monstrous clang and he was pitched forward through the air. The next thing he knew he was prostrate in the smoking black jaws of a shell hole with two kilted Highlanders, who had dragged his body in with them. He had been partially deafened by the blast. For perhaps three hours he lay there, drifting in and out of consciousness, a fragment of shell lodged agonisingly in his hip, until stretcher-bearers ducked into the hole to retrieve him. The Highlanders had disappeared, and he hadn't caught their names to be able to thank them.

And now here they were in June, waiting in a support line three miles south of Mametz, with a push in the offing. In January Will had been promoted, though he felt certain that this had less to do with his fitness as a company commander than with the BEF's need to make good the drastic loss of officers. At Loos, in a not untypical example, the 1st M—shires had started on 25 September with 670 men and twenty-one officers. Two days later at roll call 190 men and three officers answered to their names. That he had finally secured the designation of captain was an irony that didn't escape him. Sometimes, when he heard a rifle crack, his thoughts would drift back to the Priory and the sound of cover drives popping off Tam's bat. More than two years dead . . . Will felt obscurely relieved that Tam had been spared any of this – that he had 'walked before he'd been given'. The phrase had stayed with him. On that day at Loos it seemed they were all walking before they'd been given.

There came a knock at the door and Meadows, Will's batman, poked his head into the gloom.

'Message from headquarters, sir,' he said, holding up a letter. Will called him in. Meadows was a stout, neatly groomed fellow with a Yorkshire accent so broad that for the first few weeks of their acquaintance Will had been obliged to pause at roughly every third sentence and say, 'I beg your pardon?' Gradually his ear had attuned to his extravagant vowels and dropped aitches, until they were able to hold an almost coherent conversation with each other.

Will opened his letter and read the contents. 'From Lieutenant Colonel Bathurst. He's paying us a visit after rifle inspection this evening.' He offered a significant look to Bailey, and then turned back to Meadows. 'Tell the sergeant major to make sure the trench is tidy. That parapet needs repairing. I don't want Bathurst moaning about "slovenliness" again.'

'Will you be wanting – ?' His eyebrows were hoisted enquiringly.

'Yes, a bottle of Dewar's, if you can.'

'Very good, sir,' said Meadows with a nod, and withdrew. Will returned his attention to the shirt he had been delousing, and, satisfied, threw it down on his cot. He glanced again at Bailey, whose face looked tight with apprehension.

'Well, it looks like you'll have your answer by tonight, Mark.'

Bailey nodded. 'We're all looking forward to this stunt,' he said, though his voice argued the contrary. He was one of the younger men who had not yet been tested in a major action, and Will, touched with pity, wished he could spare him the necessity. He was only a few years older than Bailey, but he felt more like his father than his commanding officer. He unbuttoned his pocket and took out a pack of cigarettes, proffering it to him.

They smoked meditatively for a while, then Will rose to his feet. 'And now I must oblige you to leave, Lieutenant, unless you care to watch me delousing these breeches.'

'Oh – of course, sir,' he said. 'Will you, erm . . .

'Just as soon as I know,' Will said quietly. Bailey held his gaze for a moment, saluted, and left.

An hour later Will sat at his desk, his pen poised, his mind as blank as the sheet of paper in front of him. He knew he should write to Ada, but he was damned if he could think of anything remotely appropriate to tell her. *Dearest Ada, All well here, aside from the rats and the lice and the mud and the smell of dead bodies. How are you?* He sighed, and recapped his pen. Deciding to stretch his legs, he stepped out into the trench. The day was closing in, the late-afternoon light a greyish white, the colour of old batting pads. It was the quietest time of the day, though the toing and froing continued even now, as purposeful as an ants' nest. As he clumped along the duckboards, he checked the wire and the revetting along the lip of the trench, and was pleased to note that the CSM had got the men tidying up the place. He proceeded along the line, past ordnance parties, ration parties, engineers, signallers, sappers, gravediggers, runners, the whole microcosm of ancillaries that enabled an army to function. At one point he overheard a group of men joshing one another as they stacked sandbags against a parapet wall. One of them had come to the punchline of a story and cried, 'Wouldn't ya know – the fuckin' five-bobbers!' and the others burst out laughing. Will was continually astonished at how the men kept as cheerful as they did through the discomfort and boredom of waiting in reserve. He had once nursed a sullen hostility towards them – their pilfering, their sloppiness, their insolence, their complaints about pay, their repulsive language. How would this lot make soldiers? And yet, as he had got to know the men, they came to seem more vulnerable, and more admirable, than he could ever have imagined. At their first 'show', under a barrage of screaming artillery fire, they had

345

looked sick and ashen-faced, but it was the quiet gravity of their demeanour that moved him. Having arrived at the last extremity of hope, they would put their hand on their mate's shoulder and whisper assurances that all would be well, though they had nothing to trust in but themselves and each other.

He came to a dog-leg in the line. Around the sharp corner the floor was heaped with litter – used tins, broken boxes, bits of discarded equipment, a splintered wheel from a gun carriage – though quite empty of human activity; he couldn't see a single soldier in this part of the trench. Puzzled, he retraced his steps until he met a private coming the other way, his arms loaded with a box of empty shell cases. He stopped him and, on enquiring, learnt that the battalion that were occupying this sector had gone up the line this morning. The sergeant major, the man explained, had told them to dump any litter around this corner, thus making it the problem of whichever lot took their place. Will could see the pragmatic aspect of this, even as he admitted its cynicism: he himself would have been furious to arrive at a support trench that looked like a rubbish tip. He muttered a brief 'Carry on.' As he walked back towards his dugout, Meadows caught up with him, and thrust a small package into his hand.

'Hope that does the trick, sir,' he said, holding open the door for him. Will went inside and, pricked by curiosity, undid the wrapping on the package. It was a tin of lice powder, bearing the legend 'Kill that insect, Tommy!' He smiled in spite of himself. Good old Meadows. On his desk lay a sheaf of the men's pay books, and with another half-hour to kill before stand-to and inspection, he sat down and began signing them.

By the time Lieutenant Colonel Bathurst and his adjutant arrived, Meadows had also secured a bottle of Dewar's and a couple of folding chairs for Will's guests. The dugout itself looked neater than usual, though nothing could be done about the damp, frowsy smell or the sweating walls. Bathurst was a strapping career soldier, keen-eyed and waveringly tall, so tall that he had to duck his head as he walked in. Captain Otway was a man of about Will's age, with a quizzical gleam in his eye and a pencil moustache so trim it might have been pasted on. They both accepted a glass of Scotch from Meadows, who then sidled out.

'Glad to see you've kept the place in good order, Captain,' Bathurst began. 'All well with B Company?'

'They're a spirited lot, sir,' Will replied. 'I don't think they'll let us down.'

Bathurst nodded deeply. 'Good, good. Operation orders will be circulated tomorrow, but I thought I'd tip you the wink. Zero day will be Thursday the 29th. As part of the Seventh Division, we will join the offensive on the enemy line south of Mametz. With any luck most of the Boche in our sector will be either dead or running for their lives.'

Will coughed politely, and said, 'Sir, when you say "with any luck" . . . ?'

'Ah, well, we start our bombardment on the 24th, which should blow their front line to blazes. I talked with Brigadier-General Culver last week and he's quite confident that in certain sectors we'll be able to stroll into the enemy trenches.'

At this, Will checked to see if Otway's expression registered the hubris of such a forecast, but it was perfectly placid. Catching Will's eye, he said, 'Should be quite a stunt.'

'Hmm,' said Will, 'I believe I heard the same said of Loos.'

Bathurst frowned tolerantly at this. 'Oh, now, that was quite different. We'll have twice as many guns, and God knows how many more shells. I don't think you need to be concerned, Maitland.'

'Only that I'm not sure about the *wire*, sir. Shelling can't always be relied upon to destroy it. But wire-cutters are –'

'No, no, you don't follow,' Bathurst broke in, with emphasis. 'There is to be a barrage, almost continuous, for five days. By the end of it one isn't likely to see another living *thing*, let alone a living German. The wire will be – an irrelevance.'

Will, having received reports from night patrols that wire on the German line had been virtually untouched by shelling, was inclined to argue the point, but he sensed that this would be construed as wilful pessimism. Bathurst had stood up and was craning interestedly towards the cricket bat affixed to the wall over Will's desk.

'Yours?'

'It belonged to a friend of mine. Andrew Tamburlain.'

'Ah, Tamburlain . . . Never saw him bat. I gather you played yourself.'

Will nodded, and Bathurst turned to Otway. 'Ever see this fellow at the crease?'

Otway shook his head. 'More of a golfing man, sir.' He was making an effort to appear interested in the bat.

'I keep it as a sort of good-luck charm,' Will explained.

Bathurst gave a grimace at this, and said, 'Didn't he – kill himself?'

'Yes.' He sensed Otway and Bathurst exchanging a look. The former broke the silence with an uneasy chuckle. 'Doesn't sound much like a lucky charm.'

'It got me through at Loos,' he replied with a small shrug.

'Yes, well . . .' muttered Bathurst awkwardly. Repetition of the name had unsettled him; it had already become a byword for catastrophic mismanagement. At some invisible signal Otway had stood up, and the Lieutenant Colonel cleared his throat as a prelude to their leave-taking. The atmosphere had taken a sudden plunge into gloom, for which Will knew he was chiefly responsible.

'Keep up the good work, Maitland,' said Bathurst, and having saluted, bent his head to clear the dugout doorway. Otway gave Will a neutral nod and followed after.

For some moments Will stood there, as a fugitive thought hovered on the edge of his brain. At first he wondered if it was the mention of Tam that had triggered it. He had dreamt of him lately, though it was Tam wrested out of context; he was in uniform, for one thing, and he wasn't carrying a bat but a crude toy rifle. He had called to him, and Tam had walked right past, his face deep in shadow. He was moving headlong into a maelstrom of keening metal, and Will wanted to stop him, wanted to say – *You can't walk into that with a toy rifle.* But the figure ambled on, unheeding.

Then Will realised it was something else on his mind, something Bathurst had said which had caught on his consciousness, like a thistle of wire snagging on his battle-dress. A name, perhaps. But he was damned if he could remember.

Following inspection the next morning, Will was at his desk when he heard voices raised outside the dugout. Someone was enraged about the fly-tipping he had seen at the far end of the sector yesterday evening, and Meadows could be heard trying to placate the affronted party.

'It's a bloody disgrace. My company arrived exhausted from the march last night, and what do we find – the place knee-deep in rubbish!'

'I'm sorry to hear that, sir, but I have –'

'I want to see your commanding officer this minute.'

'Beg your pardon, sir, but I believe he's busy –'

'Busy?! Plainly not with keeping the line in decent order.'

As the exchanges grew more heated Will rose to his feet, reluctant to involve himself but driven to spare the estimable Meadows further blasts of the officer's indignation. He pushed open the dugout door and began composing his features into a semblance of responsibility. He hadn't thought his carelessness would come home to roost quite so soon. Over Meadows's shoulder he glanced at the furious face of the officer, a shortish fellow, his mouth twitching beneath his moustache. Meadows had heard him emerge, and began to explain.

'Sir, Captain Beaumont here has made a complaint –'

Will was barely listening as he stared at the newcomer. My God. 'Louis?'

The man's expression suddenly altered on being thus addressed. He squinted back at him, equally stunned. 'Will . . . ? *Will?* Good Lord, what on earth –' The next instant they were pressing each other's hands warmly, laughing at this outrageous coincidence. As he ushered Louis into the dugout, he turned to his batman and asked him to bring them coffee. Meadows, pleased to have had the combustible atmosphere defused, hurried off. They fell naturally to talk of the front. It turned out that Louis was a captain in the 8th Dartmoor Light Infantry, part of the Division which had been drafted in to join the attack on Mametz. Neither expressed much confidence in their present prospects. Of a sudden Louis broke off talking shop to gaze at Will.

'Of all the people! It must be – how long . . . ?'

Will smiled wryly. 'Four years, I'd say. Your cousin's wedding.'

'By Jove, I believe you're right! Now, weren't you rather fond of –'

'Constance.' He had not said the name in a long time. It felt strange on his tongue. 'How is she?'

'Oh, Mother told me she was in Paris. Working in a hospital.' His gaze became far away. 'I think the last time I saw her she'd just come out of prison. You know she was with the suffragists?'

'Yes, I remember. The last time I saw her was at Tam's funeral.'

Louis nodded sombrely. 'Dear God . . . I read somewhere

that you, um, found him –' and at this his face was seized by a helpless grimace. 'Sorry. I should have written to you . . .'

Will shook his head, brushing the thought away. He moved to his desk, took the 'Tamburlain Repeater' off the wall and handed it to Louis, who examined the bat with the reverence of a schoolboy. Will, amused by the cartoonish mobility of his friend's face, asked him to guess its provenance.

'Ah . . . I should say – Lord's, July '05 . . . ? The one that cleared the pavilion.'

'Spot on!' laughed Will. They were still reminiscing about Tam and the Priory when Meadows arrived with the coffee. As he handed over one of the tin mugs, Will noticed a distinct tremble in Louis's hand. Louis rather innocently remarked upon it himself.

'Started about six months ago,' he explained. 'We weren't even under fire. One minute it was fine, the next thing it just – gave way. Couldn't stop it shaking! I took some leave, which helped, but it still comes and goes.' He held up his hand to observe the tremor, in the interested manner of a neurologist.

'You haven't been . . .' Will mimed raising a glass to his lips.

'Good Lord, no. That is, not more than usual! I'm afraid it's just that I've been here too long.'

Will offered a sympathetic moue. Any time spent in this place was too long. 'I dare say you've heard about the push . . .'

Louis nodded. 'It seems we're to attack some trenches in front of Mametz. The whole brigade's going in.'

'Then we'll be fighting right alongside one another,' said Will, though his cheerful tone did nothing to clear Louis's knitted brow. To fill the silence he took out two cigarettes, lit one, and handed the other to his friend. Louis smoked absently for a while, then appeared to wake up to the anomaly. 'I didn't know you *smoked.*'

'Another filthy habit I've picked up over here,' he replied.

'Sullivans,' said Louis, failing to make the connection. Perhaps he had also forgotten that he had introduced Connie to him. That was June, too, Will was pretty certain – the June of that extraordinarily hot summer. Now, far in the distance, he could hear the guns start up. The crump and boom, the steady, dreary rhythm of it. Louis was staring intently at the tip of his cigarette. When he spoke his voice had altered.

'Will. D'you ever wonder if . . . your time might be up?'

Will nodded thoughtfully. 'We've come this far, though, haven't we?'

'But that's just it. When you see so many others drop around you . . . I don't know, you begin to think – why not me? There's only so much luck to go round.'

'We've all got to die, Beau.'

'Yes, but – so soon?'

There was a look of hopeless appeal in his eyes. Will had never talked to a fellow officer in this way before, and felt momentarily at a loss. He had got into the habit of throttling his own fear, as if it were a small animal, looking away and twisting the neck until it snapped. He knew that of all officers on the front the one with the shortest life expectancy was captain; he supposed Louis knew it, too. But what was to be done? He exhaled a long plume of smoke and shrugged in a fond way at Louis, who finally dropped his gaze and said, in a resigned voice, 'I'd better be getting back.' They stood.

'I'll send some men,' Will said at the door, 'to help clear up that mess at your end – with my apologies.'

Louis smiled ruefully at the mock formality. He was going to step out when Will stayed him with a hand on his shoulder. 'Listen to me. We're going to make it through this. I know we will. See that?' He pointed his thumb at the cricket bat on the wall. 'I'll let you have that on the day this is all over.'

Louis narrowed his eyes for a moment. 'Do you swear it?'

'On my honour.'

When he had gone, Will tore a strip from his notebook and wrote on it, *In the event of my death, this bat is bequeathed to the care of Capt. Louis Beaumont, 8th Dartmoors. W.M.* He taped it to the splice of the bat, and set it back on its mount.

II

On the morning of the 24th, the bombardment opened. In the preceding days Will had watched the batteries being hauled into position, and had wondered at the narrowness of the space into which so many horses and artillerymen had poured. It seemed a physical impossibility to fit them all into a sector already choked with infantry. Guns stood almost wheel to wheel. If it was like this the whole length of the line then perhaps they really would 'wipe the floor with the Boche'. A concentrated barrage bumped and thundered for an hour and twenty minutes, like the rumbling of a celestial giant's stomach, his hunger unappeased. In the afternoon Will glassed the horizon through the big periscope, intending to check the state of the wire. The enemy trenches had been strafed by the shelling, and certain parts looked a good deal knocked about. But while he could spot gaps in the wire here and there, most of it appeared intact. He would have to send out a team of wire-cutters. It would be a dangerous crawl for them, he knew; but if the job wasn't done properly now it might be calamitous for hundreds of soldiers come zero hour.

The days limped on, and a mood of dull anxiety settled

over the men. They were caught between worlds, longing for an end to the waiting yet dreading the moment that lay beyond it. Will found himself in a queerly dissociated frame of mind, performing routines so mechanically that he no longer felt aware of them. He had set out to inspect the men one morning when he realised he hadn't shaved; on returning to his dugout he discovered from the mirror that his cheeks were smooth – yet he had no memory of touching his razor.

Early on the morning of the 28th, a runner arrived at Will's dugout with a message from Louis, asking him urgently to a meeting at the dugout of a certain Captain Marsden. Will hauled on his riding boots and made his way along the zigzagging trench towards the Dartmoors' sector. The fine summer weather had turned, and rain was leaking steadily out of a grubby white sky. On arriving he was surprised to find a little party of subalterns crowded around a table in the dugout. Louis, edging through them, greeted him with a look of tense excitement, and ushered him forward towards the object of their interest. At first sight it looked like an architect's model for a golf course, with undulating hills, clumps of trees, fairways, greens and bunkers. He was staring at it quizzically when Louis nudged him.

'Will, this is Captain Marsden.'

He shook hands with a pleasantly boyish, dark-eyed fellow of about his own age, clean-shaven, with a pipe clamped to the side of his mouth.

'This is yours?' said Will, gesturing at the model.

'Indeed. Perhaps I'll send it to the gallery. I've never seen such a show of interest in my work,' Marsden replied, in a deep ironic drawl. Will was wondering why he had been summoned to inspect it when he realised, abruptly, that it wasn't a golf course at all. It was a sector of the front. Their sector. 'Papier mâché and plasticine,' the artist explained.

354

'Made it while I was on leave, in case you think I've been wasting army time.' The subalterns cleared a little space to allow Will a closer look. And now he saw how beautifully made the thing was, each part of the landscape individually painted – greens, greys, ochres, duns, blacks – while every dip and hillock duplicated its contours in miniature. Tiny copses and farm buildings had been fashioned from matchsticks. The whole trench system was outlined in meticulous grids, painted white.

'It's – remarkable,' said Will.

Marsden lifted his chin in casual acknowledgement. 'I didn't have time to make four thousand infantry,' he said with a chuckle. He took the pipe from his mouth, and pointed the stem at the right flank of the model. 'So, to begin. This is where Seventh Division are camped, and this –' he took a tiny flag and pinned it on the front line '– is where 120th Brigade, us lot, will go over.' Still using his pipe as a pointer, he outlined the next day's plan of attack. Their objective was a line of German trenches in front of the village of Mametz, about four hundred yards from a small copse. 'Now *here*, once we're beyond these trees, no-man's-land suddenly slopes, like so, and we'll be advancing over completely open ground.' He looked directly at Will. 'Do you see the problem?'

'If you mean the wire,' he replied, 'I sent out two of my best men the night before last to shear it, with decent wire-cutters. They reported to me that they'd given it a proper haircut.'

'Yes, I'd heard that,' said Marsden, with an approving nod. 'But look again.' He was pointing at a little clump of trees overlooking their approach. 'This is Anselm Copse, with that wayside shrine on the ridge. There's a German machine-gun emplacement, hidden right there. Did you know?'

Will stared at it, then shook his head. 'Are you sure?'

'Sure enough. And before you ask, the bombardment has missed it entirely. Our shells have been flying right over the position.' He allowed Will some moments to digest this intelligence, then turned back to his model. 'So the wire won't matter. If we proceed with the battle plan submitted by Divisional HQ, the brigade will be cut to pieces before we even make it to those trench lines.'

Marsden had spoken in a coolly analytical tone, but around him Will could sense a mood of unspoken dread among the assembled, like men who had just heard their death warrant read out to them.

'Have you shown this to your battalion commander?'

'Ex-cavalry. Knows horses and not much else – he says it's a lot of fuss over nothing. I was hoping you had the ear of your man – Bathurst, is it?'

'I could show it to him, but he's no more likely to budge.' Will had not forgotten the looks of disapproval when, in front of Bathurst and Otway, he had raised the warning spectre of Loos. Disapproval tinged with scepticism. It now occurred to him that they had perhaps thought he'd got the wind up.

'Know anyone at Divisional HQ?'

Will shook his head. 'According to Bathurst, our Brigadier-General believes we'll be able to stroll into the German trenches. His words. Which inclines me to think battlefield operations aren't really his strong suit.'

Marsden fell into a deep, silent nodding. Then, with all eyes back on him, he looked around the dugout and said, 'It seems, gentlemen, our fate is on the knees of the gods. I'll see you at stand-to.' One by one the subalterns trooped out of the gloomy little den, until only Will, Louis and Marsden remained. For a while they stood there, gazing at the papier-mâché battlefield. Then Marsden broke the silence with a short gasping chuckle. 'You know, I think I could take odds on the precise spot where the Boche will get us.'

He took another of the tiny flags, emblazoned with the Dartmoors crest, and leaning across his model placed it at the foot of the slope beneath Anselm Copse. 'Pity I won't be here to collect my winnings.'

Will had just parted with Louis when another barrage started up. The rain was still coming down, greasing the duckboards and turning the sodden ground to mud. On his way back he almost took a tumble, but managed to steady himself against the parapet wall. Marsden's grim prognostications seemed to have entered his bones and rendered him sluggish. He chanced to look up as two officers passed him and saluted; one of them was wearing a monocle, which reminded him of his old pal Reggie Culver. He had walked on a few paces when something stopped him in his tracks. Culver. That was the name of the Brigadier-General that Bathurst had mentioned the evening he dropped by. Of course. Now he remembered: Reggie used to talk of an uncle, 'a brass hat' in the military, years before the war began. This had to be the same man. Reggie was an officer in the Kensington Guards, stationed somewhere hereabouts. If he could be found, he might be able to secure an audience with the old goat . . .

As he quickened his pace along the line, he spotted Bailey talking to a rations party and called him over. The subaltern's guileless expression clutched at Will's heart, and in the awkward moments of silence as he gathered his thoughts he felt an absolute unfitness to command. Why should *he* have the responsibility of so many lives? He asked Bailey to make enquiries as to the whereabouts of a certain officer in the 3rd Kensington Guards, name of Reginald Culver – he needed to know double quick. Bailey hurried off, and returned a quarter of an hour later with the news that the Kensingtons were waiting in reserve just outside Albert. Six miles away. Even if he managed to locate Reggie, there was no guarantee he could arrange a meeting with the Brigadier-General today. And tomorrow would be too late.

'Sir? I could get hold of a horse for you, if it's urgent . . .'

As urgent as your life, thought Will. If only Marsden had shown him that model a few days earlier. 'Thank you, Bailey, but I'm not sure that'll be necessary.'

'Very good, sir.'

He repaired to his dugout and wrote to Ada, whose letters had been struggling to maintain their cheerfulness of old; perhaps on the M—shire coast she could detect the mood of ominous expectation wafting from across the Channel. 'We have been encouraged to think lofty thoughts about "our boys",' she wrote, 'but when I think of you enduring the hideous discomfort and danger over there, listening to those guns roar day and night (I swear I can hear them myself), it makes me catch my breath in terror at what might happen, and I feel fit only to hide my face away and cry. My dearest love, I pray that you keep safe.' Her letter had the unfortunate effect of making *him* want to hide his face away and cry, though not for the same reasons. Eleanor, now living in Camberwell and working as a VAD, had also written, in a tone less obviously imploring, though no less concerned: 'The hospital has received instructions to clear out all convalescents and to prepare for a higher number of wounded. The waiting is horrible – the sight of row upon row of beds, sinister in their starched white vacancy, already makes me queasy. I know you will be cool-headed and brave when the moment comes. But be careful, too, Captain Maitland, because you are beloved and your sister depends on you . . .'

He was writing a hasty reply to her when Meadows knocked and entered, bearing a note from headquarters. He read it, and let out an exasperated sigh. Zero hour had been pushed back forty-eight hours. The bad weather had given them a reprieve, which was no reprieve at all. They would now go over at seven thirty on the morning of 1 July. He asked Meadows to send Bailey along – 'And tell him to fetch me that horse.'

Providence appeared to be toying with him. If he hadn't run into Louis; if he hadn't been privy to Marsden's forecast of calamity; if he hadn't glimpsed the monocle that prompted his chance recall of Reggie; if Bathurst hadn't mentioned the name of Brigadier-General Culver, Reggie's august kinsman; if, if . . . The possibility of rescue had been dangled before him, then seemingly snatched away because there wasn't time. Now, a forty-eight-hour delay may have just allowed him to go through with this wild goose chase.

Having secured permission to leave, he arrived at Albert at nine fifteen that evening. His journey, along rutted, puddled roads, had been serenaded by the continuous thump of the guns. A rich mauve-coloured sky was lit by the glare of star shells. The horse had shuddered a few times in fright but Will held him steady. He found the farmyard where the Kensington cavalry were stabled and left his mount there to be fed and watered. A passing CSM directed him to the buildings in which the officers had been billeted. He could hear singing as he climbed the stone steps to the larger of two barns; within, a few officers sat around, idling over newspapers. A servant informed him that Captain Culver had been out all day but was due back later that evening. He was handed a tea dixie from which he drank some thin but fiery beverage – plum brandy, perhaps. This, combined with the six-mile ride, had an instantly soporific effect, and he plunged down into a dream of blasted woods, of fields honeycombed with shell holes and craters, of mud the colour of fudge. He was hurrying through this forlorn landscape, wondering where everyone else had gone and why his footsteps were so clogged. Then he looked to the ground on which he trod and found it entirely made up of corpses. He could feel men's ribs cracking beneath his boots, he was trampling on torsos and legs and faces, could find no room for his steps other than on the putrid slackness of dead flesh. And, what became as frightening, he seemed to be the last man moving – running, fleeing – through this infernal terrain. He woke with a start on hearing his name called.

'Ah, the sleeping beauty awakes,' cried Reggie Culver, his grinning face lit eerily from beneath by a candle in a bottle. Will struggled up from the couch where he lay, and glanced at his watch. It was nearly midnight. His mind's eye still quivered with the phantasmal horrors of his slumber.

'Reggie,' he croaked, extending his hand. In the two years since they had seen one another Reggie had lost his monocle and gained a moustache. His air of bonhomie was unchanged.

'I could scarce believe it when one of the fellows said that a Captain Maitland had poled over for the evening. You might have given a chap some notice!'

Will smiled wanly, and confessed that his visit wasn't exactly a social one. Reggie confirmed that his uncle was indeed Brigadier-General Hubert St John Culver, ex-Lancers, now in command of the Seventh Division. 'Played golf with him this afternoon, as a matter of fact. Why?'

He explained the dubious Corps Intelligence as it pertained to 120th Brigade's orders for 1 July, and how Captain Marsden's battlefield model exposed the dangers of advancing past Anselm Copse: an interview with the Brigadier-General might obviate needless bloodshed.

'Yes, I see,' said Reggie, absently stroking his moustache. 'He's a capital fellow, Uncle Bertie, but I have to say, he's an awful stickler for following orders. He won't like his authority being challenged.'

'It's not a challenge. Honestly, Reggie, I want only an introduction. I'm not going to make a nuisance of myself.'

Reggie dismissed any such possibility with a complacent

waggle of his hand. '*Of course* I'll clear your way to the old boy. We'll be up bright and early tomorrow to catch him before he goes out.' He stood up purposefully. 'In the meantime I'll fix drinks. I think we've some plum brandy knocking around.'

Reggie was as good as his word, shaking him awake just after reveille next morning with the news that their horses were ready. They drank coffee that was thick as treacle and he borrowed Reggie's razor to shave his face. He still felt bone-tired, having listened for most of the night to the leaking gutters outside his window. By seven thirty they had saddled up and were riding down sodden country lanes towards Divisional HQ, three miles west of Albert. Reggie kept up a merry prattle along the way, though as they neared their destination his high spirits seemed to evaporate along with the early-morning mist. Will, keeping his powder dry, had made very poor company, rehearsing what he might say to 'Uncle Bertie'. Chateau Beaucaillou was set in its own grounds, approached by a long gravel avenue lined with aspens. Servants were folding back dark green shutters from the high windows and sweeping the forecourt as Will and Reggie dismounted, the latter greeted with such deference by the staff that Will assumed he was a regular guest here.

Inside he felt a low-key vibration of activity – staff officers huddled in conference and engineers fiddling with telephone wires – though the atmosphere was quite orderly and unpanicked. One would never have thought that the push was less than twenty-four hours away. Will followed Reggie through the main hall, their boots ringing on the parquet, and thence into a high hushed drawing room that stank of cigar smoke. Gleaming floor-to-ceiling windows looked out onto a wide lawn, and beyond it a placid panorama of farmland, copses, a solitary spire. While Reggie consulted with one of the minions, Will stalked about the room, unable to relax. Heavy gilt mirrors kept surprising him with his reflection. Over the fireplace hung a dark-hued oil painting of a hound, and clamped between its jaws a lifeless bird with rust-coloured feathers. A pair of Louis Quinze sofas pompously faced one another, one of them occupied by a brindled cat that watched Will with unblinking eyes, as if it were the remaining trustee of all that belonged to the requisitioned house. Had it not been for the faint thunder of the guns you might have forgotten there was a war going on at all.

Reggie, bending his knees squirishly, had also noticed Will's absorption. 'Gracious living, what? I gather the family's had the place for centuries.'

Will nodded. 'I hope they get it back in one piece.'

'Oh, they needn't worry,' said Reggie complacently. 'The Hun will never get this far.'

'No. I don't suppose they will.' His voice had dropped to a murmur. A door at the corner of the room opened, a head dipped round, and at a wordless signal he and Reggie were invited to follow. The divisional operations room was also long and airy and high-corniced, but all evidence of its former occupants had been banished. Trestle tables spread with maps had usurped most of the space, and around them hunched various 'brass hats' whose unspeculative gaze betrayed not the smallest interest at their arrival. From one knot of officers in a corner there issued a resonant guffaw, and at his side Reggie, answering it with a breathy chuckle of his own, whispered, 'That's Uncle Bertie.' Through the cigar smoke Will made out a stocky, jovial figure with an aldermanic paunch and a face as brown as a crab apple.

'Ah, Reggie!' cried Brigadier-General Culver, recovering from his laughter. 'Come to crow about that lucky putt of yours yesterday?'

Reggie smiled and shook his head. 'Wouldn't dream of

it, sir! I wanted to introduce my very good friend Captain Maitland. He's with the 1st M—shires near Mametz.'

'Jolly good,' boomed Culver, saluting. 'Lieutenant Colonel Bathurst told me we should expect some early successes there tomorrow, hmm?'

Will, hearing the interrogative note, decided to grasp the nettle straight away. 'I wish I could feel so confident, sir.'

Culver frowned at this. 'Oh?'

'If I may –' He gestured at the map and began to explain, with a fluency that surprised himself, why the Anselm Copse attack was fraught with peril.

'A machine-gun nest? Very unlikely to have survived our bombardment, hmm?'

Will now sensed that the Brigadier-General's habit of ending every other sentence with a 'hmm?' was merely a tic: he was assuming agreement, not inviting debate. He would have to plough on.

'Sir, our night patrols strongly argued that the emplacement has been missed by our shells. We would be risking an awful lot of men.'

A small twitch of disappointment was discernible in Culver's cheek. 'Captain,' he began, with a slow shake of his head, 'even if your reports are correct, we must accept that, in this sort of engagement, casualties are inevitable. The corridor running beneath Anselm Copse must be secured to allow our cavalry through. We may lose some men in the event – but sacrifices have to be made. Hmm?'

It occurred to Will he might as well be arguing with him about spirit mediums, or universal suffrage. He could make life easier for himself and everyone else by admitting that the Brigadier-General wasn't going to budge. But a moment of unanticipated scorn goaded him on. 'Sir, with the greatest respect, if we "accept" that casualties are inevitable, then of course they *will be* inevitable. But if we saw a man about to kill himself we wouldn't merely stand by and watch – we'd try to stop him –'

'Be very careful what you say –'

'– so by the same reasoning, is it not one's duty to try to prevent self-destruction on a larger scale?'

Will's voice had risen, and the room around him caught its breath. The hum of background chat of a sudden had ceased, and he observed the Brigadier-General's expression pass from narrow-eyed wariness to darkly congested fury. He turned to Reggie and said, in a tight voice, 'Kindly wait outside, sir.' Reggie, looking nervously from his uncle to Will, seemed about to speak, and then thought better of it. They waited for Reggie to exit the room, then Culver addressed him in a tone of profound displeasure.

'You dare to bandy talk of "duty" with me, sir, and yet show no evidence of understanding the word. When an order is given to a subordinate, it becomes his duty to obey it – otherwise he is not worthy of serving in this army, or of calling himself a soldier.'

Will's voice, though naturally soft, did not waver. 'Sir. I have never acted in a way to dishonour either my rank or my superiors. But I take my duty to mean more than mere obedience. I owe a duty of protection to the men of my company. It obliges me to assess what danger I may expose them to – they deserve that much – and the sort of risk entailed in B Company's battle orders, I must tell you, is wildly irresponsible.'

'It is not your place, sir, to speculate on the fitness of operation orders,' Culver snarled disbelievingly, and turned to one of the staff officers. 'Good God, are you listening to this, Drew? Is this the kind of fellow we're expecting to strike terror into the Boche?'

Drew stepped forward and muttered conciliatingly into the Brigadier-General's ear. The latter emitted a sequence of gasps and tuts as he listened, his cheek now twitching fiercely. At length, having given ear to his adviser, he said coldly, 'Get him out of here.'

Will, trembling with his own suppressed indignation, felt he had nothing to lose now, and said, 'May I expect an answer –'

But the Brigadier-General had already turned away – had dismissed him – and Drew had taken over, advancing on Will's space and backing him towards the door. He could have shouted over Drew's shoulder at his recent interlocutor, like an aggrieved defendant to a judge, but the surprise of being so summarily ejected had robbed him of impetus. Drew, having shooed Will out of the room with no more ceremony than a sheepdog with a flock, called to Reggie: 'The old man wants to see you.'

Left alone in the corridor, Will thought back to another time his outspokenness had landed him in trouble, only that time he was in a hotel dining room arguing for his friend's career. And he had won, after a fashion. Now, with his men's lives at stake, he had come up against an opponent of intransigent purpose, and been swatted away. Had he really expected any other outcome? Perhaps he was of that peculiar strain of character who could only pledge himself to a cause once it looked sufficiently lost. On the other side of the door he could hear Brigadier-General Culver's querulous bark, and other, lighter voices trying to soothe it. When Reggie emerged some minutes later he shot Will the grimacing look of a schoolboy who'd just been given a ferocious dressing-down by the beak. Neither exchanged a word as they retraced their steps through the chateau and out into the courtyard. Their horses were clear of the estate before Reggie let out a sigh and turned to Will, ambling at his side.

'Next time you decide to cross swords with the brass, William, kindly *don't* ask me for an introduction.'

Diverted from his brooding, Will said, 'I'm sorry. I suppose he thought I was windy, but . . . it was just my appeal against a death sentence.' Reggie was silent for a few moments – apparently in chastened acknowledgement of the 1st M—shires' unenviable mission tomorrow morning – and when he eventually spoke there was indeed regret in his tone.

'I don't suppose Uncle Bertie will want to see me at the regimental golf dinner.'

Will, stunned for an instant, considered replying to this, but not knowing how to begin he held his tongue, and listened instead to the guns echoing around the exhausted sky.

III

He had welcomed the dawn, for it meant the waiting was almost over. They had crept along a dismal communication trench and reached the forward line an hour ago. He looked at his wristwatch. Seven ten. Ticking down to zero. As he passed down the line he felt every third or fourth man give him a sidelong look, as if they might read in his face an indication of their chances in the coming storm. And a storm was now all it was, the barrage of artillery fire so tidal, so consuming, that it vibrated thinly down their bodies. The air did not move; the noise was packed solid around it. When he gave the order to fix bayonets, how would they be able to hear him? Bailey was helping to distribute the rum ration, a tin cup full of viscous, overproofed intoxication. Oppressed by the blank-eyed look of the men, Will busied himself checking bits of equipment – Verey lights, mortars, picks and shovels – and glanced at his watch again, like a commuter waiting for a train. About fifty yards up the line he spotted Louis. As he pushed through the press of bodies, he wondered if he should have told him or

Marsden about his abortive appeal for clemency to Brigadier-General Culver. But what would have been the point? We shall destroy all we know and then live on.

Beneath his helmet Louis's face was pale and slick with sweat. He offered a ghastly smile as Will approached, and leaned forward as though to yell something into his ear. But, perhaps sensing the impossibility of being heard above the din, Louis merely planted a kiss on Will's cheek, and they stood there for a moment, looking at one another. The next instant the earth seemed to tilt sideways as one of the British mines in no-man's-land detonated, and twenty-odd tons of explosive reverberated along the trench. When they righted themselves Louis's expression was shaken, defenceless. Will spontaneously put one fist over the other and made a swinging gesture: the swish of a cricket bat. Louis nodded, understanding, and then saluted. Their dumbshow was over. They melted away from one another into the khaki crush of men waiting by ladders. Back among his company, with all eyes fixed on him, Will felt his limbs move with the slowed, dislocated sensation of a dream: his actions no longer seemed his own. Some stranger was inhabiting his body, directing him onwards. The men had fixed their bayonets, therefore he must have given the order. The minute hand on his wristwatch was about to touch six. The barrage had lifted for a moment, and all was silent. His lips tasted metal, and he found the whistle was in his mouth. Then the men were scrambling up the ladders, so they must have heard its shrill.

And he too was over, hurrying along the parapet, helping up men who struggled beneath the burden of their sixty-pound pack. Around him long lines of soldiers were climbing out, rifles at the port, and he heard a voice, imperturbable, urging them on. His voice, it seemed. They were moving forward, uphill, with the same mechanical stride he remembered at Loos; the difference was that they were not immediately being fired upon. *Keep steady*, he said, *hold that line*. Two hundred yards ahead of them the shells began to rain down – the Germans had launched their counter-barrage – and Will could see them flash and burst in an eerily straight line. Fountains of dark earth flew up, showering clods and stones hundreds of yards around. The noise closed in, thrumming on their skin. He looked to his left, in time to see a shell burst on the Dartmoors' line and men hurled backwards, limbs flying. If they could only make it to the cover of the woods . . .

Between the ground, which trembled as if a train were passing just beneath them, and the deafening thunder of guns overhead, there seemed a little cocoon of space through which they might stagger. Just as Will thought they had reached safety a screaming, hissing sound rent the air, and he froze in his tracks – it was too near. A shock wave from the blast sent him flying, he somersaulted with the force of it, and as he landed something else slammed painfully into his jaw, flush on the chin strap of his helmet. He lay there dazed for a few moments; more than anything he dreaded the mauling of a high-explosive shell, being torn to pieces by fragments of white-hot metal. A bullet between the eyes would be a mercy in comparison . . . He could feel his legs, which was good, but there was blood trickling down his face from what had caught him on his way down. Something, a man, was lying on top of him, and as he rolled the lifeless weight of him off he saw that half of the face had been lacerated by the shell. What remained of his body he didn't want to look at. The stink of burnt flesh and the fumes made Will gag. A private he didn't recognise had squatted down on his haunches to check on him, and to his enquiring look – voices were torn away by the noise – Will nodded, and allowed the man to hand him up. The dead man's blood had soaked his tunic, and he knew then how lucky he had been. Smoke had blanketed the field, but he felt himself gravitating on unsteady legs into the sheltering cluster of woods.

The bombardment had transformed parts of the wood into gaunt blackened silhouettes, yet here and there a few trees still clung to their natural colouring. Their bark was brown, and leaves shivered feebly on their branches. Men had gathered on the edge of the wood, from where the ground sloped downhill. Will took stock of their surroundings. The company had made it this far without encountering any German machine guns; now they had to pass by Anselm Copse on their right and head for the farmhouse beyond. He marvelled for a moment at the accuracy with which Marsden's model had reproduced the battlefield; only the colour of the land was different, blasted and scarred by the pounding of the six-day bombardment, where no living thing seemed to move. Just as that thought entered his head, Will saw the Dartmoors emerge from the far side of the wood and begin their descent of the slope. Seconds later a dull metallic staccato began, a single German machine gun concealed on the ridge, exactly as Marsden had warned. Men dropped down, one after the other, as the chattering fire swept along the wave; if part of the wave was missed by the machine gun's first enfilade, back came the traverse of fire to mow down the survivors. *Jesus God . . .* Will almost swooned at the horror of what he was seeing: it was like the dream he'd had of Tam walking into enemy fire with his toy gun, only now it wasn't one man, it was scores of them. *This* was a form of suicide, too, he thought. Organised suicide. The men, ordered to walk across exposed terrain, had no better hope of survival than a man who put a revolver to his own temple and fired. The Dartmoor infantry kept pouring out, twenty, thirty of them in a line, and went no more than a few yards before the curtain of fire scythed them down. It was an open-air slaughterhouse.

Will felt a hand on his shoulder and wheeled round.

Bailey, the young subaltern, stood there, with a look of wild-eyed entreaty. '. . . sir . . . ?' was the only syllable he caught above the roar. He knew his question without hearing it: what should they do? Will knew there was only one thing they could do, and he pointed the way to Bailey: forward. The machine gun could only fire in one sweep at a time. If the M—shires could move quickly enough they might escape the enfilade that was cutting down the Dartmoors. Swallowing hard, Will waved his right hand and burst from the cover of the trees, his men following. His only plan was to get past the shrine from which the gunfire was issuing. He was half running, half creeping, aware that once they were in view of Anselm Copse they would converge with the rest of the brigade and provide an even more convenient target. Keep moving, he told himself.

Up ahead he could see a shallow ditch that ran beneath the ridge, not much more than a hundred yards away, but at that moment the ragged line of Dartmoors who had eluded the fire now came into his lateral vision. Some were making a dash for a shell hole, and he recognised the lean figure of Captain Marsden among them. They were yards from safety when they fell (six, seven, eight men) beneath the remorseless strafing. Marsden himself spun round, an arm flailing up, a plume of blood fountaining from his neck. He had dropped at the exact spot he had predicted, directly below the copse. Will broke into a run: he had to make it to that ditch. Seven or eight of his men were following, but by the time he was within jumping distance of cover, the death rattle was upon them. How could one gun do for so many? From the groans and shrieks he knew that most of them had been hit.

He rolled forward into the protective runnel of earth as bullets continued to spit and chew up the ground. They were pinned there. He felt a burning sensation in his hand. Still panting, his body pressed flat, he drew back the glove on his left hand and saw that a bullet had grazed the cushiony heel of his thumb. From above he heard a man moaning, almost lowing with pain. As the machine gun's patter briefly moved away, he raised himself on his haunches and risked a look over the brim of the ditch; behind him stretched a field of corpses in khaki. But a few yards from him lay Bailey, who had plainly been at his heels ever since they rushed from the wood. He was still twitching. Will crawled out of his shelter, heaved the stricken body over his shoulder and carried him back to the trench. The colour had entirely fled Bailey's face. His breathing was quick and shallow, and Will saw that he was bleeding profusely from his stomach.

'Bailey?' he said, dipping his head low. The boy showed no sign of responding, though his eyes were upon Will. 'Mark, I'm going to give you these,' he said, scrabbling blindly in his pack for morphia tablets. He placed them under Bailey's lolling tongue; he coughed, and a thread of dark blood leaked from the side of his mouth. He felt for Will's hand, and with great effort he forced out a noise from his throat. It was a single unmistakable word: 'Mum.' Will didn't know what to say to that, so he kept hold of Bailey's hand, and watched as the life ebbed out of him. A tiny convulsion ran through the boy's face, and Will put a hand to his neck. The pulse was gone.

He began crawling along the ditch. Up on the slope he heard a massive detonation, and some moments later a couple of the M—shires hurled themselves into the space ahead of him. He caught up with one, and after an exchange of close-quarter yelling he learned that the machine-gun nest on Anselm Copse had at last been hit. 'One of our mob landed a mortar on it!' the man said proudly. As they scuttled along, crablike, Will spotted another line of infantry advancing towards the German trenches, a captain at the head. It was Louis, who must have gone over in the second wave. They were about four hundred yards from the wire when a shell loudly scattered them; squinting through the smoke he saw that Louis was still going, and instinctively he jumped out of the ditch, revolver in hand. The two M—shires followed after him. Instead of a machine gun he could now hear discrete metal reports, like farthings pitched at a bucket: a sniper's fire. *Jesus-God-keep-going.* At that moment he conceived a violent, almost panicky urge to be alongside Louis, to shield and protect him in a way he had not been able to protect his own men. He had followed orders and led them into a death trap. *Let the guilt of it be on my head, but please God let me save this one man.* He knew – the certainty of it exhilarated him – he knew he would jump in the way of bullets if it would spare Louis. And there he was, still rallying his men forward, indifferent to the barrage falling around him.

Will was closing the gap on him. If he had shouted his name at this distance on any other day he would have been heard. But this was not a day like any other. The human voice would not pass through such close-packed tumult. They would yarn about this one day, he thought, Louis charging towards the German wire, oblivious to Will thirty yards behind him. He could even imagine Louis's incredulous laugh – 'You were following me all that time?' – and the head-shaking wonder that both of them had made it through those acres of hell. Distracted for an instant – a bullet had just hissed by his ear – Will fixed his sights back on Louis, who had stumbled briefly and was now trying to right himself. He gave a little shake of his head, like a long-distance runner who had just pulled a muscle, and slowly, slowly, sank to his knees. He'd have to carry him, he thought – that would be fine, he wasn't a big man – when Louis sank face forward to the ground. Will was aware of himself crying, madly, uncontainably, as he caught up to the prostrate figure, and knelt by him. His helmet had rolled off, revealing the smoking crimson hole where Louis's left eye used to be. The body was still warm as he held it. Not even this one had he saved. You should have taken me instead, he thought, and, as though in reply, he felt some indescribable molten pain shooting through his chest and lifting him off his feet. All he remembered was a sudden glimpse of sky whirling across his eyes before he tumbled down into oblivion.

18

With gentle fingers Connie peeled back the stained dressing on the thigh and saw that the wound was purplish black and suppurating; the flesh around it looked angrily swollen. But it was the putrid odour that gave it away, filling the nostrils with its warning of morbid decay. The patient groaned and turned his head on the pillow. She watched his eyes slowly open, as if the lids were ungluing. His name was Matthew Mullen, a twenty-year-old private who had been among the first convoy from the Somme three days before. One shattered leg had already been amputated in a field hospital before he was evacuated home. She put her hand to his forehead and felt a feverish heat pulsing beneath the skin.

Within minutes she had summoned an assistant surgeon, Dr Muir, whose look of grave complicity indicated that Connie's misgivings had proven accurate. Private Mullen would have to go under the knife once more, probably that afternoon. Having half listened to the surgeon murmuringly explain the matter to him, Connie waited for some minutes before returning to the boy's bedside. At first she thought he might want time on his own to consider it; then she decided that such news was too terrifying to bear alone. His face was pale against the pillow, and his gaze, which had been fixed on the middle distance, narrowed on her as she stood before him.

'Sister?' He gestured limply at the bedside chair, which Connie took.

'Matthew. You've talked with Dr Muir, then?'

The boy nodded, and looked away. 'Can't 'ardly believe they're takin' the *other* one off too . . .' He swallowed hard, his eyes blinking rapidly. There was a baffled hurt in his West Country accent. 'Just seems –' He stopped, and shook his head. Not yet used to the idea of one leg lost, he looked dumbfounded at the prospect of losing the other.

'I gather your mother and father will be coming up,' said Connie, trying to beguile him with a note of brightness. 'They'll be pleased to see you home again, won't they?' Mullen nodded again, miserably. He was silent for some moments, then said, with a brave little laugh, 'Won't be so easy to go courtin' any more, what with . . .' His voice failed.

'Well, with your good looks, I should think the girls will come to you.' He *was* good-looking, now she thought of it, with his dark brow and pronounced cheekbones. Perhaps some nice girl would . . . but of a sudden the feigned nonchalance had gone from Mullen's expression, usurped by candid alarm. He had a more immediate worry in view.

'The lady – the doctor who was here – *she'll* be doin' it?'

'That's right – Dr Muir.'

'Not a man, then?' His voice had dropped to a despairing undertone.

'All of the surgeons in this hospital are women, Matthew. Dr Muir is one of the best – you'll be in excellent hands.'

'Oh.' It was acceptance, but there was no conviction in it. Connie's heart turned over in agonised sympathy for the boy. Trembling herself, she gave him her best smile – she had overused it as a device these last two years, but it still got appreciative responses from the men. She stood up, and laid a hand softly on his shoulder.

'I have my rounds to do –'

'You'll come again, though?'

'Of course. Before they take you in.'

Connie glanced at her watch as she exited the ward: eleven forty. There would be another convoy of wounded arriving later this afternoon, putting pressure on their already overstrained resources. The hospital, set up by Dr Louisa Garrett Anderson and Dr Flora Murray, was run entirely by women. In the August of 1914 Connie had begun working for the Women's Hospital Corps at the Hotel Claridge, on the Champs-Elysées. When those premises proved inadequate, the Corps had relocated the following spring to London, establishing a new hospital on Endell Street, near Covent Garden. They had taken over the gaunt old Georgian workhouse of St Giles, allegedly the one described by Dickens in *Oliver Twist*. She could imagine Bumble bawling at the orphan boys every time she went through the dining hall, with its stone flags and high embrasured windows, while the little pens with padlocked gates labelled Old Males and Young Males gave a plangent echo of its former incarnation.

She proceeded from the south block, reserved for severe cases, into the open central square, now cleared of the railings that belonged to its past. In the summer the square was used as a garden for convalescents and visitors, and on high days and holidays for musical entertainments, but in the present crisis of incoming wounded it functioned more or less as an open-air ward. Those not in urgent need of treatment lay on the stretchers which had borne them in. The hospital had also received another influx of Voluntary Aid Detachments – VADs – to help cope with the numbers. Connie, as one of the thirty-six trained nurses, was often required to instruct these willing but rather unworldly novices in the care of the wounded. She had seen these girls flinch and even faint at the sight of a terrible battlefield mutilation – some soldier without a limb, without a jaw – but, unlike certain of her fellow professionals, she refused to scold them afterwards, on the simple grounds that they *were* girls. They had most of them been born into genteel homes and raised to live idly until a husband might show himself. What could possibly have prepared them for this?

She could now hear the matron delivering a stern-voiced lecture to a VAD over some footling misdemeanour. She stood listening in the corridor for a moment. The offender, loftily addressed by her surname, would respond with a quiet 'Yes, Matron' and 'No, Matron' at every pause in this verbal storm, and Connie wondered, not for the first time, why a position of influence so often begat in its owner the urge to bully and humiliate others. She had for years thought this trait peculiar to the male – since it was generally men who occupied those positions – but nearly three years of working in hospitals among women had taught her that the female of the species, if not actually deadlier, was at least as well versed in the psychological strategies of 'breaking' her subordinates. She had observed something cold and unyielding in certain highly trained hospital nurses. It was as though they had to scour all pity and understanding from their personalities before they could become truly professional.

Hearing the tone shift into a new cadenza of sarcasm, Connie tapped lightly on her door, and entered. The matron's eyes flashed with the irritation of one diverted from an indignant exercise of authority. She was a tall, rigorously poised woman whose angular features seemed to have sharpened themselves on life's hard corners. With a quick glance at the subject of her displeasure – it was an earnest, round-faced VAD named Juliet Bridges – Connie asked if she might have a quiet word.

'Can it not wait, Sister?' she said brusquely.

Connie gave a little shake of her head, and the matron,

with a peevish harrumph, addressed the VAD. 'If this happens again, Bridges, I will be forced to act. I will not have our patients put at risk. That will be all.'

She might have been addressing an impertinent child, rather than a volunteer who gave of her best in difficult conditions. As the girl shuffled, eyes downcast, out of the office, the matron tilted her head enquiringly at Connie, whose low but clear voice might have been an unconscious rebuke to her interlocutor's shrillness.

'It's about Mullen in St Ursula's –' the wards were all named for female patron saints – 'I was wondering whether his family had been sent for.'

'I believe they have. Why?'

'He's going into surgery again, this afternoon. Gangrene – in his other leg.'

The matron lowered her eyes, and her mouth twitched thoughtfully at one corner. It was as close to a reflex of compassion as Connie had ever witnessed in her. 'I gather they're farming people, in Devon somewhere – arrangements have to be made.'

'Well, I could send a telegram . . . if you're too busy, I mean –'

'That won't be necessary,' the matron rejoined sharply. The tone of nettled authority was unambiguous; this queen bee would not lightly yield an inch of her dominion. It would have been unremarkable behaviour in a man, Connie thought – rather disheartening in a woman.

'Very good, Matron,' she said, betraying not a whit of true feeling in her tone. That was another useful thing she had learned in the course of her medical career.

She was on her way to St Mary's ward, refuge of the worst burns cases, when she saw a figure cowering in a shadowed alcove along the corridor. She realised in an instant who it was.

'Bridges?'

The VAD, still smarting from her dressing-down, turned to her a face blotchy with tears. 'Sister Callaway –'

Connie produced a handkerchief from her sleeve and handed it to the distressed girl. 'Perhaps you could tell me what that was about . . .'

The kindness of Connie's tone set the girl off on another flurry of sobs, through which the story brokenly emerged that Bridges, on night duty, had fallen asleep in the ward, and by a stroke of bad luck had been discovered by Matron herself. For some reason falling asleep on duty was considered an especially scandalous breach of discipline, even though the long hours and gruelling work made resistance, on occasion, all but impossible. 'I simply couldn't help myself,' Bridges sniffled. At nineteen she was still on probation as a VAD, and plainly feared the ignominy of being dismissed from the service. 'Matron said she thought I might be sent home as – "unsuitable" . . .' Her voice quavered on the word, as if there could be no more shocking an indictment of her character.

Connie hushed her consolingly, and then, in vocal mimicry of her tormentor, said, *'That won't be necessary,'* which prompted a gluey laugh from the girl. Their complicity was secured. 'I'm sure you'll prove to Matron how conscientious you normally are.' *And sooner than you imagine,* was Connie's next thought. That the great offensive had been launched in France was all over the newspapers. *The Times* had described the lines along the British front as '90 miles of uproar and desolation'. The multiplying casualties were the proof; if they became more numerous then Matron would not have the luxury of dismissing her, or anyone. Connie waited for a few moments while Bridges composed herself, then sent her on her way. The girl was by no means among the most hopeless of the recent intake of VADs, whom the soldiers would playfully nickname 'Very Attractive Damsels' and, less gallantly, 'Victim Always Dies'. A few weeks before,

Connie had explained the rudiments of sepsis to a VAD not much older than Bridges, and when an officer with an abdominal wound was being prepared for surgery she instructed the girl to shave the patient very close – 'Don't leave a single hair,' she said. Connie returned ten minutes later to find that the stomach of the etherised patient was untouched. His moustache, however, had been removed so fastidiously that his upper lip was almost raw from the razor.

For the next hour she dressed wounds, did TPR (temperature, pulse, respiration) and supervised the new recruits as they gave the men bed baths. It was a procedure prickly with humiliation on both sides: many of the VADs had never before seen a grown man naked, while some patients baulked at being treated by such fresh-faced girls. Connie adopted a brisk method of tutoring, and split the trainees into pairs, reasoning that two together would rally better than one in conquering squeamishness about the butcher's-shop appearance of wounded flesh. The septic fingers and lice they caught from the men were merely occupational hazards. Just before lunch a message came summoning her to surgery upstairs. On arrival she found Dr Muir being dressed by theatre nurses in her green apron and hygienic face mask; rubber gloves soaped, sterilising drums opened, a familiar mood of controlled urgency at large.

'Ah, Sister, I was hoping you might assist me with our amputation.'

'Of course,' said Connie, whose apprenticeship to Henry Cluett at St Thomas's before the war was known among the senior staff. 'May I talk to the patient before we proceed?'

'Yes, but do be quick about it.'

Two orderlies were wheeling Mullen on a trolley towards the electric lift when Connie caught up with him. Fear had rendered him almost grey, and his lips, parched and violet-coloured against the ghastly pallor of his skin, were twitching as if in silent prayer. On seeing Connie he reached out to take her hand, and she felt an animal terror in his grip.

'Where am I going?' he asked in a small, wretched voice. For a moment she thought he might be posing a philosophical question, but then realised there was no guile in it

'First we're taking you to the anaesthetic room. We put you to sleep for a little while – you understand?'

She stood close to the trolley as the lift swayed upwards. The boy's hand was so tight on hers it was beginning to hurt, but she kept her eyes on him and said nothing. At last the lift arrived at the surgical ward, and they rolled him into a small side room where a theatre nurse was preparing the chloroform. They could all smell it. Connie's hand was now aching inside the boy's desperate clenched fist.

She lowered her head to his ear. 'Matthew,' she said softly. 'Don't worry. I'll be coming in with you.'

Mullen made an infinitesimally small movement of his head to show he understood. Suddenly his gaze sharpened on her, and in a steadier tone than she had heard him use before, he said, 'Sister. What's your name – your actual name?'

Surprised, and moved, she told him.

'Constance,' he repeated, as though it would be important to remember it. The nurse was now hovering on the other side of the trolley, holding the monstrous-looking rubber funnel with its tin mask of drugged oblivion. Still gripping her hand, he smiled in the same brave way she had seen that morning. 'Now for the big adventure,' he said, and she managed a smile in reply. His head lifted protestingly as the mask came down to smother his mouth ('This machine is a nuisance,' said the anaesthetist crossly), then Connie felt the boy's hand go loose around hers. She laid it at his side, and his insensible body was wheeled into the hot glare of the theatre. She hurriedly put on her own cap and mask, like a latecomer to a secret cabal, and followed after.

* * *

It was a quarter to four by the time she had cleaned herself up and changed. The blood had soaked right through to her underwear; it trickled down her legs and into her stockings. Unable to bear the thought of leaving them stained, she went down to the boiler room and fed them piece by piece into the incinerator. She had been on her feet since half past six that morning, yet only now did she realise how bone-tired she was. Even the matron, not much given to displays of concern, advised her to take 'a lie-down'. Connie would dearly have loved to rest her head, but that would have meant remaining within the hospital walls – and she had to get out, if only for a while. The afternoon was oppressively sultry, and on the streets leading through Covent Garden she tried to keep within the shadows cast by the rearing brick warehouses. The neighbourhood's costers called and whistled to one another, their loaded barrows giving off the sweetish scent of day-old fruit. But it could not banish the smell of blood from her nostrils. The high-buttoned jacket of her uniform, made from grey-green serge, was too hot for such weather, but she walked on, unheeding.

She turned at the foot of Wellington Street into the Strand, and thence into Fleet Street, where she caught a passing 23 'bus up Ludgate Hill. Seeking distraction, she stepped off at St Paul's, and made her way into the warren of Georgian shopping streets that huddled around the churchyard. She wandered into Old Change, a long narrow lane of drapers and dressmakers. At this hour leisured ladies were dipping their heads to the windows, shop assistants were loafing on the pavement, a postman wheeled past, side-saddle on his bicycle. Life was going on oblivious to the agonised struggles of young men on stretchers and tables, oblivious to the bloody-handed efforts of surgeons and nurses to save them. This was as it must be, thought Connie. If such a burden of suffering became intimately known to all, how could they carry on? She was gazing at a window, deeply abstracted from the bustle around her, when she heard a voice close at her ear.

'Constance?'

She turned to stare at a woman, her face shaded by a wide-brimmed summer hat, and at her skirts two young girls appraising her with solemn eyes. Both wore embroidered white pinafore dresses, with scarlet ribbons in their hair. It took Connie a moment to emerge from her reverie and recognise the person who hailed her as Marianne Garnett.

'Hullo,' she said. 'I'm sorry, I was miles away . . .'

'So I see!' Marianne replied with a laugh that showed her strong white teeth. She was wearing a beautiful high-necked muslin dress stitched with tiny silk flowers. She candidly studied Connie in her uniform. 'The Women's Hospital Corps. I wonder – are you at the Endell Street Hospital?'

'Yes. How did you know?'

'Oh, I'm great friends with Flora and Louisa. We marched together, in the early days. Seems ages ago now . . .' The allusion to suffrage prompted Connie to wonder how much Marianne knew of the story behind her flight to Paris three years before. On the outbreak of war the King himself had issued a remission of sentences on imprisoned suffragettes. Under a general amnesty Connie was safe to return to England, though she had not resumed contact with any of her former comrades, apart from Lily.

'The cause . . .' Connie mused ruefully. 'It appears to have been rather forgotten since – since this all began.'

'Don't believe that, my dear. It is *never* forgotten. And if women keep taking on jobs in munitions and the factories I can't see how the government will deny us again. They will have to make us citizens. We have earned the right – even though it was ours all along.'

Connie nodded, thinking of the uniformed woman who had just collected her fare on the 'bus. 'Isn't it odd how it takes an actual war for them to realise that we can do most of the same things men can?' She now noticed the intense quizzical gaze of the girls at Marianne's side. 'So – these two must be the Miss Garnetts . . . ?'

'Ah, yes, I should have introduced you. This is Nancy,' she said, patting the taller girl, 'and my younger one, Bella. Girls – my good friend Constance.'

'How d'you do?' said Connie, inclining her head. She realised that it might be her uniform that had mesmerised them. In the meantime a sly smile had crept up on Marianne's face.

'So may I – congratulate you?'

Connie frowned in confusion. 'I'm sorry . . . ?' – at which Marianne gestured at the shop window she had happened to catch her looking in. Connie now saw that it was filled entirely with bridal gowns. She had been so lost in thought she hadn't even noticed. '*Oh* . . . no, not at all. I'm – far from it . . .'

She realised she was blushing, but Marianne, unfazed by her discomfort, talked on. 'I dare say your career has given you no time to think of marriage.'

It was blithely said, but Connie felt a sting in this presumption. It attributed to her a calculation of which she felt herself quite innocent. She had indeed devoted herself to work, but not because she had renounced the idea of marriage. Why should it have to be one thing or the other? With an inward weariness she gave a little shrug.

The younger girl was mumbling something to her mother, who nodded and raised her eyes in complicitous appeal to Connie. 'Ah, would you mind, dear – we've just come from ballet class, and Bella would like to show you what she's learned . . .'

'I'd be delighted,' she said, smiling. The girl, only about five or six, had a pale, intense brow beneath which her dark eyes gleamed. She took a small step back on the pavement, as if into a spotlight, and raised herself *en pointe*. Then, with arms held aloft, she executed a dainty pirouette, first one way, then the other. She came to rest with a little bow. Her movements had been so sweetly self-conscious that Connie, as she clapped, felt tears blinding her. *That poor boy*. Marianne, joining the applause, took a moment to notice, but once she did her expression turned to alarm.

'Constance? Oh, my darling, you're *distraught* . . .' Connie had turned her face away, not wishing to upset the children.

'I'm sorry – so sorry,' she gasped, her shoulders starting to heave. The pity of the thing – you could hide from it, for a while, but it had a way of catching you eventually. She felt Marianne's hand on her shoulder.

'I suppose these last few days have been dreadful,' she murmured. 'One reads the papers . . .'

'I've just been –' Connie too kept her voice low '– I've just been in surgery all afternoon, a boy, we had to amputate his leg –' She took a deep breath, and blinked up at the sky for a moment. 'He'd already lost the other one. There was so much blood everywhere . . . We got him out of the theatre, but he didn't regain consciousness. He just slipped away.' Even the surgeon had looked devastated. She felt an inward shiver of despair. What was the use of winning the war if none of the men who won it survived?

There was a pause, then Marianne said softly, 'You poor girl. I'm sure you did everything you could for him.'

Connie heard her own choked voice again. 'Before he went under – I mean under the anaesthetic – he said to me –' she took another gasping breath '– "Now for the big adventure." They were his last words.' She shook her head, stunned that the boy's adventure – his whole life – had been so brief. He might have returned to his village in Devon, might have married and had daughters, just like these two of Marianne's – who, she now saw, were staring at her in unabashed curiosity. It provoked a kind of sobbing laugh in her, and of a sudden she recovered her command. 'Matthew, that was his name. Matthew Mullen,' she said, blotting the corners of her eyes with a handkerchief.

Marianne took the hint that Connie wished to leave the subject alone. They gave one another a meaning look, before Connie turned to the diminutive ballerina. 'That was an excellent pirouette, Bella – as you can see, I was rather overwhelmed!'

'Shall we invite Constance to your school concert, then, girls?'

They nodded consent to their mother.

'I'd like that very much,' said Connie.

'In the meantime,' Marianne continued, 'perhaps you'll come over to see us in Kensington one evening. We've turned the house into a sort of home for convalescent officers. I know they'd appreciate company.' They talked for a few minutes longer, until Connie checked her watch and said that she would have to be getting back. The girls had gathered in to nestle against their mother, forming a neat family grouping in their summer dresses, and Connie, tired and tear-stained, felt a sudden piercing envy of her friend; how lovely it would be to have nothing in prospect beyond taking one's children out for an afternoon of ballet and shopping, instead of hurrying back to the crowded wards, to the stretchers on the floor, to the men racked with their vile stinking wounds.

Marianne had leaned in to kiss her on the cheek. 'It's so lovely to see you again, dear. I'm going to make sure we don't lose touch – I mean it.'

Connie caught a number 11 going back to the Strand. As she retraced her steps up to Endell Street she heard the bell in the hospital square resound with two sonorous clangs. It signified a new convoy of wounded just arriving. She entered through the staff gate and was about to go straight to the emergency room when she stopped, and hurried down the stone flags to the mortuary. Four tables were already occupied, each corpse laid out, mummified beneath a white sheet. She asked one of the attendants to show her Private Mullen. The corner of the sheet was pulled back to reveal the mask of yellowish marble stillness, the eyelids closed, the mouth slightly ajar. It was a face so much calmer than she had seen it in life. She gazed at it for some moments, then reached under the sheet to touch the hand which had gripped hers so fiercely. She felt its chill, then nodded to the attendant. A metal clipboard was affixed to the end of the trolley, and she looked briefly at Mullen's details: date of birth, record of service, type of wound, registered entry into hospital. And at the bottom, the bald phrase that Connie herself had written, time and again. *Died of Wounds*.

During the following days the hospital was in pandemonium. The dusty rumble of motor lorries and ambulances as they passed through the gate and into the square was almost unceasing, and the wards were operating dangerously beyond their capacity of 570 beds. The small team of surgeons were so overworked that Connie found herself pressed into an ancillary role, holding retractors steady, cauterising small bleeding vessels, even sewing up wounds. She did not expect praise for this unauthorised work – it was all hands to the pump – though Dr Muir had asked for her to be seconded to the receiving room during the rush, which she supposed was a kind of compliment. But these extra duties in no way relieved her of the everyday care of the wards, where the new VADS, unused to such levels of emergency, were falling prey to septic fingers and heatstroke; to make things worse, experienced orderlies were being summoned to the front to replace wounded stretcher-bearers. Most of the men endured their discomfort with quiet forbearance, and would barely raise their voices above a whimper; but there was one, a cocky subaltern named Henshall, who drove Connie to distraction, importuning helpless VADs with demands to 'talk to Sister Callaway' at all hours of the day and night. He had been at Endell Street for three weeks, but it felt more like three months. It was like being pestered by an infant – for however much of her time she devoted to him, it was never enough to satisfy his irksome appetite for attention.

A full week after the big push was under way, Connie was about to turn in for the evening when one of the new VADs on night duty called by. She had just come from St Teresa's, the ward reserved for officers, with a message from a patient urgently asking to see her. Connie felt her shoulders slump: she had a strong intuition who it might be.

'Henshall?'

The VAD widened her eyes in confusion. 'I don't know, Sister. But he did seem rather insistent. He said he knows you.'

'That sounds like him,' she said, and sighed. She could ignore him and sneak off to her digs across the road: in all likelihood he was simply angling for a chat. 'I'll go over there in a few minutes.'

It was a quarter to midnight, the time when the hospital was at its quietest. The worst of the wounded had been exhausted into silence, or else lowed softly, like cattle. The night terrors would more often visit in the small hours, blundering into a man's dreams and replaying through his unconscious the scenes of torment. At times the wards resembled a fiendish experiment in endurance as men thrashed and cursed, then sank back, utterly worn out, to wait for the dawn. As she walked across the square, Connie's gas lamp threw giant shadows against the walls, and she thought again of Dickens visiting it as a workhouse, hearing the inmates' footfall, perhaps glimpsing some gaunt-faced waif whose face would lodge in his mind's eye . . .

She entered St Teresa's, steeped in opaque black and green shadows, illuminated only from chinks in the window blinds or the tiny night lights spaced between every fourth or fifth bed. The ward was silent but for a man moaning in his sleep. Almost tiptoeing on her rubber-soled shoes, she walked along the row towards Henshall's bed, reckoning the while how long she would have to humour him this night. To her surprise – and relief – he was profoundly asleep. She raked her lamp over the remaining beds; she had not yet checked the few officers who had arrived in this evening's convoy. In the furthest corner she saw that one of them might be awake – she could usually tell from the sound of their breathing. She took a step nearer, and as the lamp created a little pool of light in the space between them, she saw that his face was turned to the wall. Some feature of it – the set of the jaw, or the shape of the head – reminded her of someone she couldn't instantly name. Someone she knew, possibly –

The man, disturbed by the light, turned his face on the pillow. Recalling it later she thought it was his spectral paleness that caused her to step back in fright. But it was his voice that did it. 'Constance.'

The tone was not interrogative: he knew her. She brought the light so close it dazzled him, and he put his hand defensively over his eyes.

'Would you mind awfully lowering that thing?' he said, nodding at the lamp. She gasped, then, because that voice was his for certain. Will. Here, in this hospital. She put the lamp on the floor, plunging them into shadow again.

'Will . . . I'm – I can hardly – When did you –'

'I knew it was you,' he said, and she could hear a weak smile in his words. 'I saw you at the door, earlier – at first I thought I was hallucinating – then I heard some chap along the row talking about "Sister Callaway".'

In a daze she sat down on his bedside chair, and gazed into his face. It seemed so improbable he should be here. In the half-light she saw how the pale skin had stretched over his cheekbones, which had the odd effect of making him look both older and somehow younger. His hair, cropped much closer than when she had known him, lent his skull a pathetic fragility. Holding her gaze, he moved his hand slowly until it rested on hers. The touch seemed to wake her up to herself.

'What happened – I mean, what have you got?' She found that she was suddenly fearful of his being terribly maimed. Will's face tilted a fraction downwards.

'Bullet pierced the lung. Surgeon at the field hospital said I was pretty lucky . . .'

'May I look?' she asked him. In answer, he undid a button of his loose pyjama jacket to reveal his bandaged chest. With accelerating heart, she peeled back the cotton and gauze to check; as the bandage tugged she felt his body stiffen, but he made no sound. The bullet hole, puckered and purplish, was about the size of a sixpence; it had pierced the right of his chest, away from the heart. That was good. The wound also looked clean, and free of any necrotic odour. She felt his eyes on her as she completed her inspection. 'It seems to be healing,' she said, catching his eye and then looking away. 'Is there anything you need?'

He shook his head very slightly. Then, after a pause, he said, 'It's very queer meeting up again like this, isn't it?'

'I was just thinking that,' she said with a smile. 'Of all the hospitals you might have gone to . . .'

He nodded. 'I was told that they'd be taking me to some officers' hospital. But when we got to Waterloo the crush was so awful there was no chance of getting a special allocation. Then some orderly just pinned a label on me saying "Endell Street". So here I am. I gather they call it the "Flappers' Hospital".'

'Yes, they do. It's run almost entirely by women. I hope that doesn't distress you?'

He heard a tiny quiver of the old mischief in her voice, and smiled. 'Far from it. I'd heard it was one of the best in London –'

'Oh?'

' – and now that I've met the staff I know it for certain.' He gave a wheezy chuckle, which became a kind of gasping cough. Connie helped raise him up against the pillow, and made a quick check of his pulse and temperature. Neither seemed wildly irregular. In low voices they continued to talk for a few minutes more. She saw him tiring.

'I think you should try to get some sleep,' she said.

'Not yet. There are things I have to tell you . . .' Did she know about Louis? he wondered. Did she already know?

'You can tell me tomorrow, after you've rested. I'll dress that wound again.' She was standing over him now, hesitating. She could have leaned in to kiss him, but instead she took his hand and gave it a little squeeze. He held on to it as she was about to withdraw.

'Connie,' he said in a changed voice, 'I'm so very glad to see you again.'

She smiled, and released her hand. He watched as her figure receded down the ward and disappeared through the doors.

When he woke the next morning, Will was befuddled with morphia and tiredness. He wondered for a moment if he really had talked to Connie the night before, or if she had been merely a very lively figment from the distorted nether-world of his dreams. No, he was sure that he had; she had come to his bedside with a lamp. A young woman, a VAD he supposed, came to his bedside and gave his wound a tentative examination. The window behind his bed had been

391

opened, and a warm breath of honeysuckle was wafting through.

'It's a lovely morning,' the girl said brightly. 'Would you care to sit outside in the square?'

Will replied that he would. Needled by doubt, he then said, 'Could you tell me – is there a Connie Callaway working in this hospital?'

The girl giggled. 'If you mean Sister Callaway, yes. I didn't know her name was Connie,' she added. He felt a surge of relief, and began to smile as the girl fussed shyly around him. She helped him out of bed and into a wheelchair, tucking a blanket round his legs, then wheeled him, via a lift and corridors bustling with uniformed women, into the large courtyard they called 'the square'. It was already thronged with patients in bath chairs and wheelchairs, swaddled in blankets like his own, some engaged in murmurous conversation with one another. The scene resembled a quiet Sunday at a rest home, except that the pale valetudinarians here were all young men, not pensioners. The VAD, having found him a shaded corner, dipped her head towards his.

'Are you quite comfortable, sir?'

'I'd be more comfortable if you called me William. And your name?'

'Bridges, sir, I mean, um –' she said, colouring slightly.

'Well, Miss Bridges, would you kindly tell Sister Callaway I'd like to see her, when she has a moment to spare?'

The girl made a kind of curtsy, and hurried off.

He was dozing off again when he sensed a presence at his side.

'Hullo again,' said Connie. In the light of day she seemed changed to him: somewhat drawn, even stern, with a wary little corrugation in her brow. Her eyes were beautiful, still, but sadder too. He wondered then at all the horrors she had probably seen – the mutilations, the gas gangrene, the burnt flesh. The same things he had seen. But he was a man – a soldier. He was supposed to cope. 'How are you feeling?' she asked him.

How *was* he feeling? Fretful, in truth, at the thought of what he had to tell her. He gave a little shrug to her question. Perhaps he communicated his secret agitation to her, because her expression had become clouded. 'Last night . . . didn't you say that you were at Mametz?'

'Yes, I was.' When he said nothing further, she had a sudden intuitive flash.

'I had a telephone call yesterday from my mother. My aunt, Mima, has been hysterical with worry. Louis has been reported missing since last Saturday – I think she said that he was at Mametz, too.'

Without looking at her, Will said quietly, 'He was. We happened to be in the same sector, quite by coincidence.'

'You mean, you were actually with him?' There was a tiny lift of hopefulness in her voice that touched him unbearably. He was going to have to tell her.

'We met up a few times. I saw him just before we went over . . . Our battle orders were a . . . We were moving over ground that had absolutely no cover – a machine gun was going full pelt above us . . .'

The hesitant way he spoke made her uneasy. 'Did you see him – after that?' Now, finally, he turned his face to her, but before he could speak, she said, 'He's dead, isn't he?'

He nodded. When he looked at her again, her eyes were swimming, but she stood quite straight. A minute or more passed as the revelation vibrated in the air between them. 'D'you know –' Connie swallowed hard, then holding her voice tight continued '– how he died?'

'Bravely,' he said, and paused. 'He was running towards the German trenches, leading his company – what was left of it. He got – sniped. I was about twenty yards away. I'd just reached him when . . . I caught one, too. I don't remember anything after that. Some Red Cross men happened to find me.'

It was the first time he had put this into words, but he had never imagined his listener would be Louis's own cousin. At the casualty clearing station he had learned that three-quarters of the battalion had been lost at Anselm Copse. Not even Bathurst and Otway had made it back. Whenever he thought of Marsden and his battlefield model – the forewarning ignored – he felt sick with shame and fury. But of what earthly use was that? The fighting there was still going on, and the casualty lists in *The Times* indicated no respite in the numbers.

She still stood there. He said her name quietly, and when she made no reply he supposed she was too preoccupied to have heard him. But at length she turned, and said, 'I'm glad it was you who told me.' And she walked away.

That evening, when Connie returned to her digs in Shorts Gardens she found, in a bitter-sweet irony of timing, her first letter from Fred in several days. Army censors forbade reference to the name of the place he was writing from, but she knew he too had been involved in the big push. It was dated 1 July, and written waveringly in pencil.

Dear Connie,
    Don't fret when you read this. I got wounded in the action this morning – shot in the arm. I AM FINE. They'll send me home for a while. Please can you tell Ma?
    Fred

The flood of relief that broke over her felt almost shameful, following so precipitately on the news Will had told her this morning. But there was no help for it. She put the letter into her tunic pocket, and hurried out to catch a tram north to Islington. On the way she kept taking out the little note to read again. By the time her house was in sight she was struggling to control herself, a messenger ready to combust from the volatile mixture of gratitude and grief roiling within her.

She had been up so late in anxious consultation with her mother that she decided to stay over at Thornhill Crescent. It had been many months since she had slept in her old bedroom, and the sudden strangeness of being back there did not make for a restful night. The next morning had begun bright and warm, but as she was stepping off the tram at the bottom of Gray's Inn Road she noticed the sky had darkened. She walked west through Lincoln's Inn Fields and thence towards Endell Street, by which time a heavy battalion of dark clouds was massing across the horizon. With a few minutes to spare before her rounds, she decided to stop at St Teresa's and ask Will the favour which she and her mother had tentatively discussed the previous night. Mrs Callaway was to visit their Beaumont cousins in East Molesey today with the news about Louis; it was Connie's idea that she might prevail on Will, once he was well enough, to accompany her on another visit there. It might comfort Mima and the girls, she thought, to hear of Louis's last moments of bravery from a friend and fellow officer.

The orderlies were serving breakfast as she arrived on the ward. Will, who was not sitting up in bed, had declined even a cup of tea.

'Not hungry this morning?' she asked. He only shook his head. She looked at him more closely, and realised that he was drawing shallow, rapid breaths. 'How are you feeling?'

'Not too good,' he admitted. She sat down by him, and checked his pulse. It was somewhat fast and small; the heartbeat was increased, too. She investigated the bullet wound, thinking it might have become infected, but behind the pad of gauze the perforated skin looked clean. She saw that he winced when she put a hand, quite gently, on his chest.

'You do seem to be feeling a bit of pain,' she said in a reasonable voice.

'Actually, this is the worst I've felt since I arrived here.'

'Well . . . I'm going to ask one of the surgeons to have a look at you.'

A shadow of alarm passed over his face, which she thought uncharacteristic. As she stood up she gave him her most reassuring smile. 'Someone will be down to see you. Don't worry.'

She went in search of Dr Muir, but was told that she was already in surgery. The senior surgeons were also occupied. She had just managed to locate Dr Tisdall, another surgeon, and was explaining Will's symptoms when two loud rings of the bell echoed up from the square. Another convoy of wounded had arrived. In a breezy, almost cheerful tone, Dr Tisdall said, 'No rest for the wicked! I'll look in on your patient once we've got this lot out of the way.'

For the next two hours, Connie was busy sorting out critical cases that required immediate treatment from those less severely wounded who could be left to the ministrations of the VADs. She had never got used to the sight of nineteen- and twenty-year-old youths who bore the haunted, haggard aspect of old men, some blank with shell shock, some with faces blistered from gas. There was only one fainter among the volunteers that morning, when the white shin bone of an amputee's leg became rawly exposed on a stretcher; Connie was more jolted by the sudden slap of the girl's face as it met the floor.

Once the rush had thinned out, she retraced her steps to the officers' ward to check again on Will. What she now saw gave her serious alarm. He was awake, but he was gasping for his breath. Asphyxia threatened. The colour of his skin had changed to a bluish grey, and his pulse had become rapid. There was also a kind of bulging of his chest, which she knew indicated either a traumatic pleurisy or else a secondary haemorrhage. Yet what baffled her, when she felt his skin, was the apparent absence of a pleural infection – pale and clammy as he looked, Will wasn't sweating or shivering. Whatever was wrong, she had to get him to a surgeon as quickly as she could. She looked into his eyes, which were dulled and yellowish, and said, 'Will – I'm going to take you to surgery.' He gave no sign of having heard. She hailed a passing nurse, Nell Thomas, a genial and conscientious Camden girl whom she had known since her days at the Hotel Claridge.

'Nurse, this man's in pain. We have to get him upstairs, at the double.'

Nell peered over at Will, and gave a little grimace. ''E doesn't look so clever, does 'e? I'll go and get a trolley.'

As they emerged from the lift into the surgical ward, Connie's heart sank at the vista of trolleys lining the long corridor, a traffic jam of wounded men all awaiting attention; the chaos in the receiving room had been subdued, but up here it was still rush hour. In such a place there was no avoiding it, that smell, acrid and urgent with fear: the smell of mortality. The men had been brought here, without ceremony, to say goodbye to something, a limb, a damaged organ – maybe to life itself. It was a lonely place to make that farewell, but then dying always was lonely.

She looked down at Will, whose breath came now in ragged heaves, and offered a silent, desperate prayer that he might be spared. Nell, taking in the frantic disorder around them, helped wheel him into the anaesthetic room, then went off in search of a surgeon. While she was gone, Connie had another look at Will's painfully distended chest, and felt his heart, now slightly displaced – could it be a haemothorax? She had once seen Cluett at St Thomas's deal with complications from a stab wound to the chest; he had somehow opened the pleural cavity and drained it. She remembered now the dark, bloodstained, uncoagulable fluid that issued from the cut. At that moment Nell returned to the room, shaking her head. 'There's not one of 'em free, Sister. Every theatre's being used. He'll just have to wait –'

'What? He *can't* wait' she cried. 'His heart's about to go into arrest –'

Nell, working her teeth nervously over her lip, glanced at the patient. ''E might hang on . . . you never know.'

But Connie did know: the bulging veins in his neck and the bluish colour around his lips told her. She percussed his chest, and felt the hyper-resonance. They had a matter of minutes in which to act. She said, in a commanding voice she barely recognised as her own, 'Prepare a tray.'

Nell flinched with surprise. 'What for –'

'Please, Nell. He's dying.' She walked over to the sink and began scrubbing her hands. Behind her she heard Nell, after a momentary hesitation, walk across the room to fetch the chloroform canister and the mask.

'Leave that,' said Connie. 'We haven't time to put him under.'

She sensed her own movements operating from an automatic agency independent of her will: she seemed almost to be watching herself pull on the apron, gloves and mask, dunk the instruments in the steriliser, paint the brown iodine square on the patient's chest. She became aware of the seconds ticking by, narrowing the possibility of rescue. She checked the non-return valve of a syringe, then connected it via a steel-nozzled rubber tube to a hollow needle. At the last moment she discarded the small scalpel and, drawing a breath as a diver might before a plunge, she thrust the needle, dagger-like, into the upper chest wall. ('*Ohmygod,*' she heard Nell mutter.) Had she gone deep enough to reach the pleura? She hoped she had. Behind her a door had opened and someone entered, but Connie didn't look round.

Nothing less than the ceiling falling in would have disturbed her concentration. Will was making a low groaning sound, though he seemed unaware of the violent penetration of his chest. She held the syringe steady and waited. This would be the moment of truth. She pressed her thumb slowly upon the piston, and listened. Moments passed, as long as hours; then there came, quite audibly, a thin whistle of air from the needle, like a football being punctured. Connie raised her eyes to Nell, standing opposite; a beat passed between them before Nell said, in a small uncertain voice, 'Is that meant to happen?'

19

By the next morning Connie perceived herself to be an object of behind-the-hand whispering. In the hospital corridors she could sense a hesitancy in the nurses and VADs as they passed her, as though they were savouring the thrill of an outlaw among them. The story of her unauthorised emergency surgery on one of the officers had gained an instant purchase on the gossip market. At first nobody could quite believe that Sister Callaway had had the temerity to perform such an operation, single-handedly, still less that her intervention had actually saved the patient's life. At the hearing, hastily convened the previous night, the WHC committee had listened calmly to the matron's deposition of the offender – 'a gross and unconscionable breach of hospital discipline' – before inviting Connie to answer personally for her unwarranted behaviour.

The hospital commandant and the chief surgeon presided over the committee, which numbered six in total. Their first aim was to establish why Connie had seen fit to take matters into her own hands. She explained that she had not done so lightly, indeed would have preferred not to; but the patient's condition was critical, all the surgeons were otherwise occupied, and she felt quite convinced that immediate action was the only way to save his life.

'What convinced you that he was in mortal danger?' someone asked.

Connie replied by enumerating the patient's symptoms. 'Taken together, it seemed very likely to me that he was suffering a tension pneumothorax. As you know, if not treated within minutes it will cause cardiac arrest, and death.'

From the bemused glances Connie saw passing between some committee members it was clear that not all of them *did* know. The euphoria she had felt on completing the operation that morning had slowly dissipated during the day, and now she felt only a weariness. The commandant, a steely-eyed, long-faced woman in her forties, cleared her throat.

'Sister Callaway, I gather that the patient on whom you operated today was a man already known to you. Did this have a bearing on your decision to act?'

'It may have done – but if it had been a patient unknown to me I think I'd have done the same. I was intending to talk to William – Captain Maitland – when I arrived this morning . . . that was the only reason I became aware of his respiratory difficulties.'

The commandant nodded at this. 'Dr Muir has told us that you regularly attend her during surgery – is that why you deemed yourself qualified to perform this operation?'

'I didn't consider myself qualified,' Connie replied. 'I don't. There was very little time for me to calculate the chances of his survival. It may sound odd to hear it, but I found myself operating on the patient before I'd really *decided* to do anything.'

'And yet Matron claims that it is not untypical for you to "put yourself forward" and interfere in hospital business beyond your remit.'

Connie glanced at the matron, purse-lipped and righteous, and determinedly not looking in her direction. 'I'm sorry that Matron thinks that way. I have only ever tried to be helpful to her.' The commandant dipped her head to listen to something her chief surgeon had to say. After a few moments she turned to Connie and asked her to wait outside.

In the gloom of the corridor she paced quietly, and thought about the frowning expressions she had just left behind. Through an open window the smell of lime blossom wafted, and she stared out into the soft night shadows. She lit a delinquent cigarette, and stood smoking with her arms crossed, left hand cradling her right elbow. It was hard to know exactly what punishment the committee would consider appropriate to her 'offence'. Would they suspend her? Dismiss her from the Corps altogether? It would be harsh in the light of what had happened. She had hoped that women in a position of influence might prove themselves fundamentally different – might acknowledge an instinctive allegiance among their sex instead of cleaving to the old forms of hierarchy. But then perhaps women, given the chance, would exercise their authority just as ruthlessly as men; indeed, men had shown them the way. No matter. She had taken a risk, and it had paid off. Will was still in the world because of her.

The door opened, and a nurse invited her back into the room. The hospital commandant asked Connie to be seated.

'I'd prefer to stand,' she replied. The commandant looked up from the notes in front of her, and inclined her head as if to say, 'As you wish.'

'Sister Callaway – I don't think I have to impress upon you the gravity of this case. In twenty-five years of working in hospitals I have never encountered so singular a breach of protocol as the one before us today. Without consulting any of your superiors, you took it upon yourself not only to make a diagnosis of a patient but to perform an instant surgical procedure for which you were wholly unqualified. The fact that the patient was personally known to you is not an excuse – indeed, a professional surgeon when faced with such a conflict would most likely have passed on the responsibility to a colleague. It should perhaps not surprise us that these considerations failed to trouble you. You are not a professional surgeon. So I comprehend the outrage of those such as the matron' – at this she glanced at Connie's glowering accuser – 'who would have you dismissed from our staff. One might be tempted to take that step on grounds of simple expediency: it would be impossible to run a hospital with a proper degree of competence and safety if a junior nurse suddenly decided she would like to play surgeon for the day. We have a duty of care to our patients, and we cannot afford to expose them to the whims of meddling amateurs.'

Connie felt herself flinch at that disobliging epithet. The commandant had paused; when she continued, her words were directed at the assembled. 'There is another side to this case, however. In the last week the hospital has been obliged to take in unprecedented numbers of wounded men from France. It has meant that at times we have been overrun, never more so than this morning. Having ascertained the dangerous condition of her patient, Sister Callaway acted with great decisiveness in taking him directly to surgery. On finding no surgeon available for consultation, she herself took the matter in hand – and, as we now know, her diagnosis and treatment were blameless. The patient's life was saved. For this, she deserves our warmest commendation. While her action may offend the spirit of medical orthodoxy, it surely behoves an institution such as ours to defend capability, and to promote initiative. At the very least we ought to admire her courage. Your reputation, Sister Callaway, is cleared – one might say it is enhanced.'

No sound could have astonished Connie more than the spontaneous burst of applause that immediately followed these words.

*   *   *

Will had been sleeping when she visited his bedside on her rounds, and knowing that he was to have a visitor later she kept clear of the officers' ward for the rest of the morning. Nell, herself now a magnet of interest once her supporting role in the emergency-room 'incident' became known, called in at the staffroom just before lunchtime with a message.

'There's a couple of lady visitors in St Teresa's who've asked to see you, Sister. The older one's proper hoity-toity,' she added with a sardonic laugh.

'I think that will be Captain Maitland's mother,' she said. Connie guessed she had brought Eleanor with her.

'They're at his bedside, if you want to go.'

She was just leaving the room when she turned back to the nurse. 'I'm glad you were there yesterday, Nell. I told them what a help you'd been.'

Nell gave her a wry look. 'I don't mind tellin' you, Sister, I was that petrified in there I 'ardly knew *what* I was doin'.'

Connie offered her own smile in return. 'Well, then – that makes two of us.'

The bracingly imperious figure of Mrs Maitland she recognised as soon as she entered the officers' ward. The younger woman she took a few moments longer to place: not Eleanor, it seemed, but Ada, Will's fiancée. A huge vase of crimson roses glowed on his bedside table. Neither visitor noticed her approach, but Will did. Propped up on pillows, he looked quite ashen-faced, and frailer, since his brush with mortality; he raised his hand effortfully in greeting, alerting the women to her entrance.

'Ah, Sister Callaway – Sylvia Maitland,' said Will's mother, rising from the chair to shake hands. She fixed Connie with a neutral look that suggested she had no memory of the girl who had provoked her displeasure at luncheon four years ago. 'This is Miss Ada Brink, William's affianced.' Connie tipped her head in greeting, bemused by Mrs Maitland's determined conspiracy that they were meeting for the first time. There was the briefest pause before she continued. 'I gather we are indebted to you, Sister. Dr Muir said that your intervention in surgery yesterday was most – opportune . . .'

'It was – a matter of luck,' said Connie, with a modest shrug. 'I'm just relieved that he's out of danger.' She had her eyes on him as she spoke, and read in his expression a mutual understanding that this was a scene they would rather have played between themselves. Ada, in a striped voile dress, put a gloved hand to Will's forehead and murmured, 'We are *all* relieved. Now we must get you home and look after you properly.'

A silence followed, and Connie, adopting a polite tone, said, 'I wonder – how is Eleanor?' The enquiry prompted a noticeable flinch in Mrs Maitland, who now seemed bound (as Connie had intended) to acknowledge their previous acquaintance. But she recovered herself quickly, and replied that Eleanor was also working as a VAD 'somewhere in south London'. There was the faintest edge in her voice to suggest that this was not an occupation she would have wished for her daughter. The news rather cheered Connie, though she said only, 'Please do pass on my regards.' Mrs Maitland responded with a brusque twitch of her mouth, as if it were rather beneath her to be passing on Connie's or anyone else's regards.

Will, feeling the strain of the conversation, said, 'I think we should let Sister Callaway get on with her work.'

Connie, relieved to be granted an escape, offered her hand to both visitors, and told Will that she would return later to put a new dressing on his wound. She had exited the ward and was halfway down the corridor when she heard pattering footsteps behind her. She turned to find Ada, her eyes as innocent as a mooncalf's beneath her hat. She blinked quickly as she spoke.

'Sister, I – I must seem such an awful booby . . . I meant

to say how very grateful I was – I am – to you for – for saving William's life.'

Up close Connie realised for the first time how young she looked. She was perhaps twenty-two or -three, though her small features and the cornflower blue of her eyes were confoundingly girlish.

'That's kind of you,' she replied. 'I'm glad to know he's so – cherished.'

'Oh yes,' Ada said earnestly. 'William's the dearest thing to me. That he might so easily have –' She bit her lip, unwilling to say the word. '. . . well, I can't bear to imagine it.'

'You've been engaged for some time, I think?'

She gave a nervous little laugh. 'Such ages! Two and a half years now. As long as this wretched war goes on I can't see how we'll be married.'

'It won't last forever. And to have that love for one another is a comfort, I'm sure.'

'Yes, I suppose,' said Ada, sounding not at all sure. 'William seems so very changed since, well . . .'

Connie felt a surge of pity. 'We've all changed. Those who have been in France more than most. William, I should say, requires rest, long rest. Then you'll see him more like his old self.' She saw that her words had exercised a consoling effect on the girl, whose brow had begun to clear.

'I'm sure you're right,' she replied, then looked at Connie in a frankly appraising way. 'I do wish I had your confidence! William sometimes chides me for being so – what's the word he always uses?' She frowned for a moment, then shook her head, as if it were no matter. 'Well, thank you again, Sister . . .'

Beaming at Connie, she turned on her heel and walked, with a little skip in her gait, back along the corridor.

The influx of wounded from France had maintained a steady momentum, and Connie hadn't a moment to herself for the rest of that day. The balmy July temperature encouraged the less grievously injured men to rest outside in the square, where lime blossom and wallflowers scented the evening air. As the shadows were lengthening over the enclosure she went out to look for him. A group of men were singing a marching song in sad, low voices.

> *Where are our uniforms?*
> *Far, far away.*
> *When will our rifles come?*
> *P'r'aps, p'r'aps, some day.*
> *And you bet we shan't be long*
> *Before we're fit and strong;*
> *You'll hear us say 'Oui, oui, tray bong'*
> *When we're far away.*

Will was parked in his usual corner, his head propped at an angle against his hand. At first she thought he was asleep, but at the sound of her footsteps he looked up, his expression lost to thought. A book lay open on his lap, and she directed her eyes at it.

'Enjoying it?' she asked lightly.

'Hmm? Oh . . .' He picked it up and turned the spine outwards. 'Housman. *A Shropshire Lad*. One of my men lent it to me.' He didn't bother to add that the man was now dead.

'That was one of my father's favourites.'

Will nodded, pensive again. 'I never much cared for poetry. But there were a few lines I came across today . . .' He riffled the pages until he found his place, and read to her: '"Now in Maytime to the wicket / Out I march with bat and pad. / See the son of grief at cricket / Trying to be glad."' He looked up at her, and before he had even asked the question, she said, 'Tam.'

It was a strange comfort to him that she instinctively understood. 'I still think about him,' he said, 'even when I was over there, where you're surrounded by death the whole time. I kept his bat in my my dugout – d'you remember it?'

'Yes. I do.'

'I was going to give it to Louis –' he began, and then wished he hadn't. The bat had been a lucky charm for him, he was convinced. He had promised it to Louis on the day the war would end, when what he ought to have done was put it in his hands straight away – passed the luck on. Too late now. No, he couldn't explain that to her, it would sound madly superstitious. When she realised he wasn't going to say more, Connie decided to broach the subject she had discussed with her mother. It would mean so much to the Beaumont family, she said, if Will were to talk to them about Louis. 'I think – it would make their loss a little easier to bear, perhaps . . .'

He paused before answering. 'I should have done so anyway. Only – would you mind if I waited a while? I'm not sure I can quite face them yet . . .'

'But of course,' she said gently. 'You must wait until you're well enough. And there's your own family to think of.'

Will shifted in his chair, and sighed irritably. 'I'm sorry about this morning – my mother, pretending never to have met you before. Though in her case that might not be such a bad thing. And Ada – what on earth was . . . what did she say to you?'

'Only that she was grateful, and happy that you were alive.' She paused, puzzled by his brooding look. 'Why should that annoy you?'

'It's not that. I'm –' He stopped, and tried a different tack. 'She's very young, isn't she?'

'Yes. And very devoted to you.'

Will nodded, and was silent for some moments. He wanted to confess what was wrong to Connie without appearing disloyal. She would understand. But how, when he could barely understand it himself? 'I think Ada and I ought to have married when we were – when everything was as it was. We lost, I don't know, the thread of it. I mean, I've hardly even *seen* her these last two years . . .'

'You weren't to know that war would get in the way.'

He shook his head gloomily. 'And still she has this dependence on me, like – like a child. I tell her not be so passive, and she just looks at me . . . I hate this constant feeling of responsibility for everything. Is it too much to hope for a woman with a mind of her own?' The irony of this privately amused Connie, who could recall times not so long ago when such an asset would have discomfited him. But she only stood there, listening, and Will finally threw up his hands in a hopeless gesture of resignation. 'What would you do?'

Connie stared at him levelly. 'Do – about what?'

'About *this*! I am engaged to be married to a woman who barely knows me. She hasn't even asked me about the front, about what happened . . .'

'Perhaps she is afraid to hear it,' she said quietly.

'So . . . what should I do?'

'Please don't ask me that. All I know is that Miss Brink loves you and expects to marry you. Beyond that it's not for me to say.'

Will heard the reproof in her tone, and looked away. 'You're quite right, I'm sorry. I didn't mean to burden you with it.' He fancied – he hoped – that slipping in the word 'burden' would incline her to sympathy for his fretting, but instead she changed the subject.

'You remember Fred, my brother? He's coming home tomorrow.'

'He got a Blighty?'

She nodded. 'Shot through the arm. My mother's been beside herself. It will do us good to see him again.'

'I'm glad to hear he's safe,' said Will. 'Does he know yet about Louis?'

She shook her head. 'I dread having to tell him. They were close as boys, when we went on holiday together.'

Will felt suddenly ashamed of his recent plaintive tone. What right had he to feel sorry for himself, safe on land while others were pulling against such a tide of grief? To be apprehensive about one's matrimonial prospects was a privilege of the living, whose membership he had so very nearly relinquished. That he had not was entirely due to the initiative of the person before him.

Connie was checking her watch. 'Time for my evening rounds,' she said by way of parting. 'Do you need anything before I go?'

Will shook his head, but as she turned to go he called her back. 'There is one thing. About yesterday. I – I still haven't thanked you for what you did.'

She looked at him. A smile, tender and sad at once, made little parentheses around her eyes. 'You'll never have to,' she said.

The toll of overwork and exposure to viral illnesses finally caught up with Connie, and no sooner had Fred settled in at Thornhill Crescent than she was laid low with a fever. For more than a week she sweated and shivered beneath the blankets, only dimly aware of her mother's ministering and the doctor's daily visits. Fred, having expected to be cosseted as an invalid, instead found himself understudying his mother in the role of brow-mopper and broth-maker. It was characteristic of him that he saw the comic side of it. One morning, when Connie was at last well enough to sit up in bed, a knock sounded on the door and Fred walked in, holding a cup of tea. He set it on Connie's bedside table with a slight rattle, his balance compromised by his other arm being in a sling.

'How's the patient?' he asked.

'Much better, thank you.'

Fred responded to her rueful smile. 'This is rich,' he

laughed. 'I come home with my arm bandaged up, expecting my sister to nurse me. And deuced if I'm not employed as her medical orderly instead! I tell you, I've been up and down those stairs like a dog at a fair.'

Connie wheezed out a laugh and took Fred's hand. 'What a dear you are. I shall write to your CO requesting he make your transfer here permanent.'

'I shouldn't bother. Ma's probably written that one already.'

They were still teasing one another when Mrs Callaway entered, with a sheaf of post in her hand. Since Fred's return her customary air of fretful preoccupation had been superseded by a mood of almost girlish delight. Her only son had escaped, somehow, from a foreign field that was becoming synonymous with a national tragedy. Connie shared her relief – there was nobody more precious to her in the world – but she was worried by her mother's apparent blindness to the fact that Fred would, eventually, have to go back. Mrs Callaway had put her hand against Connie's forehead.

'Your temperature is down, at last. This came for you a few days ago – but you were in no fit state to read it.' She placed a letter on the counterpane. Connie recognised the handwriting, though she had not seen it for some years. She opened it and read:

Silverton House

22 July '16

Dear Constance,

Allow me to hope that by the time you read this you are recovered from illness. I was sorry indeed not to be able to bid you farewell when I was discharged from Endell Street. Having asked after you, I was informed by one of the VADs that you were confined to bed with a fever. I trust you have been well looked after; also that your brother is safely returned from the front. I am now back at home, shuffling about with a stick and feeling very like an old man, although that may be the consequence of living so much around my mother. Unfair, I know – she has been in most things considerate. Ada calls here every afternoon.

I have not forgotten your request regarding the Beaumont family. Even were I not conscious of a personal obligation to Louis's memory, I would make the visit – simply because you asked me to. Eleanor will be coming down from London for the weekend, so I am at least assured of congenial company. Like everyone else she has been apprised of your heroic handiwork in the anaesthetic room, and she would very much like to thank you in person. May I take leave to effect a meeting between the three of us when I am back in London?

These last weeks have passed for me in a kind of waking nightmare, yet I am grateful for an immense double stroke of good fortune: that I survived when so many have not; and that my path, miraculously, should have crossed yours again. That the one became consequent on the other should perhaps be counted the most remarkable blessing of the lot. It shall not be forgotten.

Believe me, sincerely and indebtedly yours,
Wm

'It's from William Maitland. He's convalescing back at home.' She looked to her mother. 'He's going to pay the Beaumonts a visit –'

'Oh, he already has,' broke in Mrs Callaway. 'Mima telephoned to say that he came down to East Molesey last week and spent the afternoon with her and the girls – told them all about Louis, and how brave he'd been.'

'That's very decent of him,' said Fred, looking at Connie. 'He must have done it as a favour to you.'

'No, not just that,' said Connie thoughtfully. 'He was very fond of Louis – they were friends at Oxford, remember . . .'

Privately, however, she could not help feeling that Will's swiftness to condole with Mima and her daughters *was* a gesture of respect to her. He could justifiably have claimed his injury as a reason not to travel; or else found some other excuse to put off what was an especially painful duty, knowing how beloved a son and brother Louis had been. It perhaps marked a change in him, she thought. He had not always been so readily sympathetic to those in need.

Mrs Callaway was descanting on Will's character: '. . . such delightful manners, too. Do you remember the day he stayed here for lunch?' Connie could practically hear the cogs and wheels clicking away inside her mother's head; so her next question did not surprise her. '. . . is he *married* now, Constance?'

'No. But he's been engaged since the war began.'

'Oh . . .' she sighed. 'He did seem so very – eligible.'

Connie exchanged a glance with Fred, who, protector of her feelings, saw his cue to interrupt. Opening the blind on the bedroom window, he remarked on the loveliness of the morning, and picked up the book on Connie's bedside table. It was a library copy of *The Mill on the Floss*.

'You could sit out in the garden and read,' he suggested.

Connie pulled a face. 'I don't feel quite up to reading at the moment,' she admitted.

'Very well, then, *I'll* read to you. Why not – I seem to be doing everything else around here!'

Will, wandering alone one afternoon, had stopped on the promontory just within the shadow of the castle ruins. To his right he could see over the Priory, its rich turf dug up and divided into allotments, to support the war effort. Men pushed wheelbarrows around the grid of the new encampment. His cricketing career seemed to belong to another age, though it was only two years since he had last walked out to the middle, bat in hand. From this vantage it was hard to imagine how the ground might ever return to its original guise. He surveyed the glimmering surface of the Channel, dotted here and there with patrol boats. A breeze was blowing north, and he became gradually aware of a distant crackling pulse. At first he couldn't place it, and cocked his ear trying to ascertain which direction it was coming from. It was monotonous, the insistent pounding of it, like an early warning of thunder. And then, of a sudden, he knew it for what it was – the noise of the guns carrying from France. It seemed queer that it should have taken him nearly a minute to recognise a sound that had once lain on his skin, hummed in his teeth, for days on end. He thought he had left it behind for a while, the crump of those guns, but they would not be blotted out, not from twenty-five, thirty miles away. He stood there for a few minutes, mesmerised by its thin crepitant echo, until he forced himself to turn and walk away.

His constitutional took him into town, where war privations had rendered the streets dowdy and lugubrious. Shop windows looked embarrassed by their paltry displays, and certain small hotels wore a look of drab defeat, as if the very buildings they inhabited were about to pack up and move elsewhere. Gildersleeves was still open for business, but even this august old stager looked weary around the edges, its stonework carious and its paint flaky. There simply weren't the men around to keep the place in good repair. On a side street he happened to pass a little shop that specialised in sporting goods, one he used to visit when he was a boy. This too had closed down, and through its murky windows he could make out faded posters advertising this or that bit of paraphernalia – Wisden squash rackets and golf clubs, Gradidge's 'Imperial Crown' cricket balls, Stedman wicket-keeping gauntlets. There was no sign of the

'Tamburlain Repeater', however. On his death the company which sponsored him had quickly withdrawn its patent; nobody would want a cricket bat with the name of a suicide on its splice.

He looked at his watch, aware that he was delaying a call of duty. Last week he had received a letter from Beatrice Tamburlain, informing him that she was about to sell the family home and move away. In the course of clearing out the place she had hesitated over personal effects of Tam's, removed from his flat in Prospect Place, and asked Will if he would care to take anything as a memento; otherwise it would all go 'to a charitable institution'. He had suffered a dreadful stab of sorrow on reading that. The idea of his old friend's possessions being anonymously dispersed seemed very hard to bear. With no great enthusiasm he caught the 'bus out of town and alighted at the quiet tree-lined road where the Tamburlain house stood, a place he had not visited since that January day he had come bearing the unhappy news. It was a house that depressed him, a tall redbrick of late-Victorian stamp with fussy gables and cloudy windows. It radiated an atmosphere of morose insularity. On hearing the bell ring within, he removed his cap and instinctively smoothed a hand over his oiled hair.

Beatrice Tamburlain was one of the few people whose appearance seemed unchanged by the war, probably because she had looked grey and careworn from the first time he had met her. Inviting him inside with her demure, apologetic smile, she immediately became grave on seeing his walking stick.

'Oh, it's nothing,' he said. 'I use it only because I occasionally become short of breath.' He gave a brief and heavily edited account of the injury he had sustained, to which she listened with doleful clucks and sighs. They talked in the drawing room with its long view out to sea. Packing crates lay about on the floor in readiness for the removal men, and shrouding white sheets had turned the furniture into stage ghosts. Will enquired as to her plans.

'I have cousins up in Lancashire – I've found a cottage near to them. This house was always too big for one. My father bought it when Drewy and I were at school – as children we rather enjoyed the place . . .' She tailed off, waving her hand in dismissal of this plaintive improbability. Outside he heard a breeze buffeting the windows. He searched his brain for something to say, but her air of spinsterish modesty had stilled his tongue.

'I'll show you his room,' she said, coming to his rescue. He followed her into the hall and up the carpeted stairs, the same ones she and Tam would have taken as children, though Will's imagination gave out when he tried to picture the place thirty or more years ago. It was as if the shadow of their father, a suicide before his son, had blotted out the light by which one might have read the house's history. On the landing Beatrice opened the second door along, disclosing a sight that caused him an inward shock. It was crammed almost to the ceiling with the baggage of a life. Tam's life. Dozens of framed photographs lay stacked against the walls. On a makeshift rail hung club blazers, tailcoats, topcoats, jackets of flannel and linen, dress shirts, a rainbow blaze of silk ties. Fishing rods and nets leaned in a corner. A rack of mottled bats. A large oak bookcase played host to an array of trophies, plaques, commemorative silver. A lower shelf accommodated a sequence of shoeboxes, each stuffed with correspondence. Will, not knowing where to start, plucked a letter at random from a box. Its postmark was dated 1895.

'That's all mail from admirers, and autograph hunters,' Beatrice said. 'About twenty years' worth of it. He never threw anything away.'

He raked his gaze about the room. On the right-hand wall two portraits of Tam had been hung, he presumed by

Beatrice. One was a large oil by Lavery, dated and signed; the other was a *Punch* caricature that featured him leaning raffishly on his bat, while behind him stood several house-holders looking aghast at a facade of shattered windows. It was joked that one always knew when Tamburlain was batting from the sound of breaking glass around the Priory.

Will stood there, dazed and speechless, until Beatrice said, 'I'll leave you to look around. The portraits and a few photographs will go with me to Lancashire. The rest – please take whatever you wish.' Again came the demure, sorrowful smile.

He heard the door close softly behind him. Two enormous travelling trunks, plastered with old steamer labels, stood open on the floor: in one he rummaged through tennis rackets, batting pads, fishing tackle, single stumps prised from the middle – the booty of victorious matches long ago. In the other lay bundles of his whites, club sweaters, gloves, caps, a pair of cricket boots whose white had gone grey, all emanating the musty compound scent of grass, sweat and sun-buttered afternoons. They seemed fraught with mournfulness, these things, now that their owner had gone. He picked up the boots, their spikes brown with rust; dead man's shoes, a pair of orphans. He remembered now that Tam had lent him boots once after he had mislaid his own – perhaps these were the very ones. Nobody would wear them again.

Melancholy had begun to press on him, surrounded by so many souvenirs. He wasn't sure that he really wanted any of it. He looked again to the bookcase, the shelf of *Wisden*s, the bound volumes of *Punch*. Tam had kept very little in the way of literature. Perhaps he had been too busy reading all that mail from his admirers. Will's eye stopped on a cloth-bound volume, its navy spine at a different parallel to the others. *The Poems of Francis Thompson* did not look like a book Tam would have acquired for himself. He

took it down and turned to the flyleaf, on which a dedication had been written in pencil. The sight of the handwriting
jolted him.

16 May 1913
For Andrew, my friend and rescuer –
With love and gratitude, Constance

The word 'rescuer' awoke a remorse in Will. He absently
turned the pages, his eyes skimming over the words, when
he found a bookmark in the middle of the volume; the short
poem it marked was entitled 'At Lord's'. He read it, then
turned to the bookmark itself, a sheet of writing paper,
folded twice. Unfolding it, he saw it was a letter in Tam's
hand, an unfinished letter, for a single line had been scored
crosswise over its closely written text. Will shrank from
intruding upon his friend's private correspondence – or
would have done, if he had not seen the name of the person
it addressed. *My dear Constance*, it began.

Thank you for your last. I am glad to learn that you are
finding the work less troublesome at the hospital. You
make fun of your alleged inadequacies as a French
speaker, but I imagine the comfort and cheer you bestow
upon your patients would transcend any limitations of
language – it is your gift. (I still recall the kindness of your
condolences to me on the death of my mother.)
    You remarked upon the 'troubled' tone of my previous
letter, for which I must offer apology. Retirement does
not go well with me; formerly, the winter would have
been occupied with a club tour to Australia or South
Africa, and I feel the absence of the game hanging heavy.
It is the price one pays for choosing a young man's profession – after one's brief spell in the sun there seems to be
too much time to fill.

But I must confess truthfully that my nervous agitation springs from a quite different source. I have hesitated to express this before now lest it alarmed you, or became an awkwardness between us. I beseech you that it will not. From the first time we met, at the Maitlands' house in the spring of last year, I conceived a feeling for you which I did not allow myself to think would ever be reciprocated, having noted the very fond attachment that existed between you and Will. When I later discovered that he intended to marry you, I naturally abandoned any possibility of pursuing my own suit, and awaited the announcement of your betrothal to him. For reasons you know well, and which I shall not here rehearse, the two of you were estranged, though I did not know this until you had been some months at Holloway. Once it was clear that Will had withdrawn himself, I considered it my privilege to be able to help you, and duly hired the services of Mr Fotheringham to expedite your release. Let me assure you that I did so without thought of return. My paramount concern was your safety, and your removal from prison. Only in the weeks following, after that sympathetic conversation we had at the Criterion, did I dare to hope that I might recommend myself to you as a devoted admirer. Your accepting the invitation to my retirement dinner at the Priory encouraged me, and when, the night before, you arrived in such evident distress at my flat I persuaded myself for a moment that your heart was as fraught with longing as my own. Alas, I was soon disabused of my error; you had come to me on no romantic mission but in desperate flight from the police. Again, I was honoured to be of service to you, only now I was obliged to mask a mood of desolation. Have I been entirely mistaken in this regard? Please do not be offended if this seems presumptuous, but I can no longer conceal those ardent feelings I have for you, nor the hope that you may one day return them. Dearest Constance, I once told you that I had pledged myself to cricket at the expense of making a life. That life – I do very humbly submit – is in your power to redeem

There was no more; the letter had been abandoned, aborted by that brusque diagonal stroke. Will stood there, stunned. He had never suspected it for a moment: Tam, agonised, pouring out his heart and soul to Connie. The date was written at the top, 6 November 1913. Just over two months later he had killed himself, and now Will was forced to contemplate the abysmal possibility that love had unhinged his friend's mind. Could it be? He, of all people, should know, having been wildly in love with her himself. And now he felt a deep flush of shame as he recalled several occasions during that summer when he had burdened Tam with his spoony, self-indulgent musings upon the loveliness of Connie. How he had droned on, unaware that the confidant listening patiently at his side was also her 'devoted admirer'. He racked his memory now for a fugitive hint of that secret ardour, but he could only recall Tam's respectful friendliness towards her. Did *she* have any inkling of it? he wondered. The letter in his hand could have been a rough draft of one sent thereafter. But he doubted it. Unfinished and hidden away in a book, it felt like something that only Tam's eyes had looked upon before now.

He stared at the walls again, muted and stacked with once precious possessions, boxes of cufflinks and collar studs, county medals, engraved tankards: a burial chamber without its pharaoh. It was too much to bear, and, with heavy heart, he felt for the doorknob and backed out of the room. Beatrice, hearing his footfall on the stairs, came out to meet him. She looked surprised to find him almost empty-handed.

'I'd like to take just this, if I may,' said Will, holding up the book of Thompson's poems.

'Oh . . . I thought you'd like one of his bats, or . . . I don't know what.'

'It's very kind of you to have asked. But I have a friend at an auction house that deals with sporting memorabilia – I once bought a bat of Tam's there. Perhaps you'd allow me to send him over to make a valuation?'

Beatrice looked doubtful. 'Is it really worth much?'

Will assured her that it was, and after a little more persuading she agreed to the auctioneer's visit. Financial security was the least she deserved, and it was one last favour he could do for Tam. She kept him talking on the step for a few minutes. As he made a valedictory sigh, she looked searchingly at him, and said, in a diffident tone, 'You know, I still wonder about him – about why . . .'

He felt the unsent letter burning a hole in his breast pocket. He could have taken it out for her to read. But how would it help? Weren't we all, in the end, a mystery to each other?

'I don't think one ever stops wondering,' he said.

On the 'bus home, the convalescent officer in uniform drew respectful glances from several of his fellow passengers, but Will barely noticed them. He was turning over Tam's letter in his mind, probing its forlorn phrases and recalibrating the perspective from which he now saw Connie. In his self-absorption he had failed to discern her effect upon Tam, which was bad enough; but in his pride and egotism he had failed to appreciate her effect upon *himself*, which was unforgivable. Stirrings, intimations of his mistake had intermittently troubled him during the last four years, but he had somehow managed to tamp them down, written them off as a nostalgic indulgence. Her unassuming graciousness, her good humour – her beauty – these qualities he had seen in her and admired. But it was something else: that fierce independence which had got on his nerves during the short time they had known one another now seemed to him, in retrospect, the very brightest part of her. Why, wasn't it this that had saved his life? Tam had understood: a woman, *this* woman, might be the antidote to death! Any man with half an ounce of wisdom would have understood, would have recognised the force of destiny and immediately devoted himself to securing her happiness. How mortifying not to have been that man. Only now did he understand that in the broken puzzle of his existence Connie was the vital missing piece. She had saved his life once. He would have to ask her, as humbly and earnestly as Tam almost had, to save it again.

As the town turned to country and the tall hedgerows slid past the 'bus window, Will felt the urgency of his mission as consumingly as a fever. He had squandered the most precious opportunity of his life three and a half years ago. By a miracle it had come round again: he would not let it slip this time.

It had taken Connie nearly two weeks to get back on her feet following her illness, and her mother flatly refused to allow her an immediate return to work. This enforced absence, though it caused her some guilt, had a gratifying upshot in enabling her to spend time with Fred, whose arm was now out of its sling. During her convalescence they would take the train from Barnsbury to Chalk Farm, then walk through Primrose Hill down into Regent's Park. One afternoon as they strolled its circle Fred spoke, hesitantly at first, of what he had been through on the Somme, an account from which Connie learnt once again the terrifyingly narrow margin that determined whether a man lived or died. Within minutes of the offensive's start Fred had come close to obliteration: deputed to lead a bombing party into no-man's-land, he had paused to regroup by a shell hole when they were suddenly caught by artillery fire from behind their own lines. The range had been miscalibrated, and the barrage was falling on top of them. 'Strafed by our own guns!' he said, shaking his head. Of the six men in his team Fred was the only one left standing. A man who had been ten yards from him was literally blown to pieces – 'about the size of a pork chop', he added. Connie had a sense that she was the only woman – perhaps the only person – to whom Fred would ever impart that appalling image.

On returning home by 'bus, their mother greeted her with a postcard that had just arrived. It was from Will, and tersely expressed: he was coming up to town the next day, and would be most obliged if they could meet.

'What does he want?' asked Fred.

'I really can't imagine,' said Connie with a shrug. 'Well, I'm at Endell Street tomorrow afternoon, and in the evening I'm going to this . . .' She picked up the stiff-boarded invitation to an officers' evening at a grand address in South Kensington; Marianne, the hostess, had not forgotten her promise to keep in touch. Connie, intrigued as much as anything by the prospect of seeing inside Marianne's house, had hoped to take Fred, but he was off to Cambridge to visit friends.

'Why not invite him?' suggested Fred. 'He might enjoy the company.'

She wrinkled her nose at first, but then came to reconsider the possibility. Will had earned her gratitude by his prompt visit to East Molesey to condole with Mima and the girls, and it would not be unpleasant to renew their acquaintance outside of a hospital. Perhaps . . . She went to the study, and plucked a pencil from a quiver of them she kept in a drawer. Without thinking too deeply about it, she wrote a short reply informing him of Marianne's 'at home', and suggested he might wish to accompany her.

* * *

423

Thus was it arranged that Will would call at Endell Street at seven o'clock and squire her to the evening's event. At the appointed hour Connie came down to the entrance hall of the hospital and found an officer seated at one of the wooden benches. It took her some moments to realise that it was Will; during his time at Endell Street she had never seen him in uniform. His posture, leaning forward with his chin propped up on joined hands, was one of profound contemplation. When she called his name he looked momentarily startled, as one woken from a deep reverie. He stood up to greet her, and she took in his severely correct attire, buttons blazing off the khaki, the Sam Browne belt across his chest and his riding boots polished to a parade-ground sheen. For a moment she thought he was going to salute her, but he merely removed his cap.

'You look awfully smart,' she said. Her own WHC grey-green seemed rather dowdy in comparison.

Will blushed, and led her to a taxi waiting on the street. The fierce early-August temperature had cooled with the onset of evening. The journey took them through Trafalgar Square, along the Mall and into Knightsbridge; Will offered a somewhat mechanical account of his recuperation at Silverton House. He confessed that his routine was to get up early and go out for the day, sparing himself his mother's company.

'But Miss Brink must be pleased to have you near,' said Connie.

'Yes, she's been very patient with me,' he replied, in an absent tone. Recalling their last conversation about Ada, Connie decided not to enquire too deeply as to how things stood. She told him a little about Marianne, and how they had known one another at school, but she sensed that Will, though he gave the impression of listening, was somewhat preoccupied. He would insert a murmured 'hmm' or 'ah' on the wrong beat, which in turn disconcerted Connie and reduced her to looking out of the window. Eventually their cab turned off Fulham Road into Sumner Place and deposited them at a tall white stuccoed house, about the size of a small hotel. A maid ushered them inside, and as they passed through the porticoed entrance they heard the strains of 'Tipperary' in the distance. They followed the sound through the hall, thronged with officers, out into a long garden, where a drum and fife band were in full flow. The musicians were all women.

'Dear God,' muttered Will. Connie smiled at this throwback to suffrage days, and only hoped that 'March of the Women' would not be part of the band's repertoire. At that moment she heard her name called, and turned to find Marianne approaching. She was at her most stately this evening, sheathed in a black satin gown that heightened the drama of her pale skin. A loop of pearls glimmered at her throat.

'I'm so pleased you could come,' said Marianne, planting a kiss upon her. Connie, turning to Will, felt an unanticipated thrill of pride in being able to introduce him to their hostess. 'I gather you've been convalescing,' she said to him.

'Yes – and very well looked after,' he replied, with a glance at Connie.

'May I introduce you to some of our residents? We have quite the little club here now.' Marianne took his arm.

Will, allowing himself to be steered into a circle of officers, was privately chagrined. He really had no interest in talking to anyone but Connie: she was to be the focus of his whole evening. He had betrayed his nerves in the cab, he knew, and was exhorting himself to keep calm. Now his scheme had been unseated and he was fraternising with pipe-smoking hearties whose company he had had quite enough of in France.

Connie, meanwhile, had just accepted a light for her cigarette from a cheery young subaltern when she heard someone excitedly hailing her from the corner of the garden, and out of the shadows walked Laura Scott. They had not seen one another since Connie returned to London last year, and the exultant nature of this sudden reunion caused heads to turn.

'Marianne told me you'd crossed paths near St Paul's a few weeks ago – but I didn't dare hope you'd allow yourself an evening like this!'

'Why ever not?' asked Connie, still holding her friend's embrace.

'Well,' said Laura, widening her eyes at the sight of Connie's uniform, 'I suppose you're too busy saving lives and patching up our boys to find time for frivolities.'

Connie gaily repudiated the idea of being too busy for a party, and for the next hour or so the two friends fell into an intimate discussion of old times and present trials – Laura was doing secretarial work at the War Office – which admitted no interruption. Their glasses were continually replenished, so that by the time Marianne emerged from the house to announce that dancing would commence, Connie was aware of being rather tipsy. A pair of officers who had been hovering nearby approached them to ask if they would care to dance, and Laura needed no more encouragement. She grasped Connie's arm and cried, 'We'd be most obliged, gents!'

Following a general exodus from the garden, they found a double drawing room with a floor on which drugget had been laid down, and the drum and fife band transformed into a small orchestra. They were playing a jaunty waltz, and one of the men, the cheerful fellow (she now realised) who had lit her cigarette, gestured her forward. She put her hand on his shoulder, and said above the music, 'I have an awful tendency to lead.' Was that a slur in her voice?

'Righto!' he replied agreeably, and they were off. The floor quickly filled up with swaying couples.

Will, still trapped in the hallway, was experiencing a kind of social purgatory. Talk among his unrelaxing fellow officers had turned to the 'Somme pictures', sanitised for consumption by a British public not yet ready to confront the realities of trench warfare. He joined half-heartedly in the mocking condemnation, and wished himself elsewhere. Now he heard the music and the eager voices from the drawing room. Edging out of the khaki circle, he followed its siren call, and saw her, at last, whirling about the room in the arms of some young pup. The waltz ended, and another, slower piece started.

'D'you mind if I cut in?' Connie looked up to find Will shouldering away her partner, who, outranked, offered her a little bow. The interruption was not elegantly done, but Will didn't care: he wanted to feel her in his arms. She lifted her face to his, and he saw that her cheeks were rosily flushed. As they moved in time, he leaned towards her ear and said, 'You seem to be enjoying this little soirée.'

Connie giggled at the word, and said, *'Oui, oui – tray bong.'* She was also enjoying the touch of his hand at the small of her back. 'I met my old friend, Laura. We were at Holloway together.'

Will nodded. Such an admission would have appalled him once; the very idea of a lady being an ex-convict – grotesque. Now it barely registered. It was not her past that concerned him, but her future. Connie seemed to respond to his closeness, for as his hip bone jutted accidentally against her she felt a muted but powerful current flare within, tingling her nerve ends, and by small degrees she pressed herself to him. The music, at once haunting and gay, caught her up in a trance of delight; on and on it purled, and for a while she felt her steps almost floating across the floor, her body fused to Will's. The warmth of the evening and the whirling motion of the dance stealthily accelerated her intoxication, and it was only after their fourth or fifth dance that she sensed a warning blurriness. She had not been properly drunk in ages.

'I need to take some air,' she said, and Will, determined not to leave her side, led her out through the double doors back into the garden. A small wicker bench stood unoccupied, and without ceremony Connie flopped down on it. She could feel the back of her blouse damp with sweat. She blew away a strand of hair that had fallen across her face.

'I wish I had a cigarette at this moment,' she said.

Will, with a sly smile, unbuttoned his top pocket and produced a packet of Sullivans. 'Have one of mine.'

She gave a bleary frown. 'But you don't smoke!' He only shrugged as he nonchalantly lit them one each, and as she stared upon the extraordinary sight – Will, *smoking* – it became in her mind all of a piece with the magically charmed evening. She blew a thin column of smoke into the purplish dark, and sighed. 'I can't remember the last time I had such *fun*,' she said with wistful emphasis, turning to Will in hope of a like response.

'I certainly enjoyed the dancing,' he said.

'Yes,' cried Connie, spurred on by the thought. 'We must have some more!' But as she stood up the toll of the wine upset her balance, and she plumped back down awkwardly on the bench.

'Steady,' said Will, with a chuckle to hide his alarm. He could not say all that was in his heart if she was too squiffy to listen. Holding his breath he said quietly, 'Would you like to go for a walk?'

She looked at him, but did not read the meaning in his eyes. 'D'you know – I think I would.' Her tone had lost none of its gaiety; she allowed him to take her hand as she stood up, and he said, responsibly, 'Perhaps we should just slip out. We can always come back.'

Outside, on Sumner Place, the white stucco of the houses glowed against the grainy, crepuscular light. She took his arm as they cut across Old Brompton Road and up the orderly thoroughfare of Queen's Gate, empty but for an occasional solitary car. She sensed a companionable air between them now, soothed by the musical resonance of his voice in her ear. She had always loved his voice: it was low but demonstrative, and pleasingly at odds with the tone one might have expected from the slightly arrogant turn of his mouth. He was telling her about his recent visit to Beatrice's house and the sad spectacle of Tam's worldly possessions boxed into a room.

'There was a tremendous amount of correspondence in there, too,' he said, unwilling to probe but unable to help himself. After a moment he added, casually, 'You wrote to one another, I think?'

Connie nodded. 'Yes – we wrote quite a few times when I was first in Paris. I think he believed I was rather lonely.' She gave a little half-laugh at the memory. 'Perhaps I was . . . but I really ought to have written to him more often than I did.' Her tone was thoughtful, even regretful, but Will knew, instinctively, that she had suspected nothing. To her, Tam was a friend – a friend who had moreover helped her out of a desperately tight spot – but he was not a suitor. The aborted letter of declaration was his secret to keep.

They had walked into Kensington Gardens, where a parade of towering horse chestnuts spread plum-dark shadows across the grass. The sun had disappeared, but there came over the horizon pinkish glints of its waning, like a fire dying in the grate. They had been following one of the park's pathways when Will, glimpsing a lonely bench beneath a tree, steered his companion towards it. There was not another soul in view as they gained this sequestered spot. They sat down together in silence, feeling the night gather around them. Connie slowly turned to him, and some yielding softness in her gaze drew him forward until his face was inches from hers. He leaned in and kissed her, and she let his mouth fit snugly on hers; as his arms encircled her she felt the effects of the wine she had drunk swell within and launch her on a stream of desire. They prolonged this kiss in such a reverent hush that it took a sudden shiver of the leaves overhead to disturb their clinch. Connie pulled back, and wondered if her face was glowing quite as fiercely as she sensed it to be. He was looking at her in a way that stirred a physical ache deep within; *this*, she intuited, was the moment at which sex should probably happen, and the consciousness of her innocence both amused and saddened her. The strait-laced moral codes of her upbringing had rendered the possibility of a physical relationship with a man as remote to her as the rings of Saturn. What irony, that she who had seen naked male bodies without number during the last two years was still, at twenty-six, a virgin. An involuntary laugh escaped her lips.

'What is it?' he asked rather sharply.

'Nothing – nothing,' she said. 'I'm not laughing at you. I'm just –' Another kiss silenced her, and the next time he broke contact his expression was imploring in its seriousness.

'Connie . . .' he began, and in that moment before he continued she was convinced that he would invite her back to his flat to do whatever he would with her. And she would find such an invitation very hard to resist. '. . . I know this may seem inappropriate, but I want to ask you –' he swallowed nervously '– to do me the honour of becoming my wife.' These last words, low and quick, caught Connie utterly off guard. For a moment she thought she had misheard, and could offer only a frowning 'What?' in reply.

Will, prepared for her surprise, spoke hastily. 'I made the most terrible mistake of my life in rejecting you. I was an ass, I admit it. When I visited you at Holloway it was just an awful shock – I couldn't cope with it at all. But I ought to have done, and I'm sorry for it. So I'm asking you – no, begging you – to give me another chance.'

Connie leaned away from him, trying to order her thoughts. The kindled mood of romantic ardour had been doused, like slack poured on a promising fire. She sensed his earnest gaze upon her. 'I – I hardly know where to begin. Perhaps I should remind you that you are already engaged to be married.'

Will gave an exasperated sigh, and briefly rubbed his palms over his eyes. 'I should never have allowed it to come to this. Ada is a dear, sweet girl, but we are no more suited to one another than a dove to a jackdaw. It would be wrong, very wrong, for us even to try to make a life together.'

'You are under an obligation to her nevertheless.'

At this Will seized her hand and said, 'That means nothing, compared with what I feel for you. Connie, please understand – you're the only woman in the world I've ever wanted. I love you, sincerely and devotedly. I have never stopped loving you. And, forgive my presumption, but I believe that you love me.'

She *did* love him, it was true, but that did not help resolve the doubts which his proposal had entrained. His present engagement might mean 'nothing' to him, but she felt certain that it meant a very great deal to Miss Brink. And if he were capable of sloughing off a serious obligation once, might he not do the same again? But this in itself was begging the question.

'Whether I do or not, it doesn't follow that I should welcome an offer of marriage.'

'Why not? Do you doubt my fitness as a husband?'

'No, not quite. But I doubt my fitness as a wife.'

'I don't understand. Why would you say such a thing?'

Connie fell silent, pondering what marriage to Will would entail. Once the first bloom of excitement and romance had faded, there would be the question of work to consider. She was not prepared to give up her ambition to be a surgeon, however long it might take. But somehow she could not imagine Will, once they were married, being sympathetic to such a course; indeed, she doubted whether he would be very keen on her *working* at all. Remorseful as he was now, he took a conventional view of things, and she suspected the limit of his requirements for her would be to learn the drill on housekeeping, clean shirts, and the rest. That, and children, of course; it was reasonable to suppose he would want to be a father. Reluctant to raise such a momentous subject, she cast about for a more practical line of argument.

'How can we talk of marriage while there's a war going on? We both have as much on our plates as we can stand.'

Will shook his head. 'That's no argument. Our being married would not interfere with our duties. On the contrary, the thought of you as my wife would support me through any trial.'

It was boldly spoken, and she acknowledged the compliment with a pained smile. But still she doubted. 'Why must it be marriage? Can we not trust one another without legal bonds?'

He squinted uncertainly. 'You mean – a free union?'

'To begin with, perhaps. Instead of making an immediate decision, we could accustom ourselves to the prospect of marriage little by little.'

'Such an arrangement would only expose us to malicious gossip, and it would go rather worse for you than for me. Why should you wish to exclude yourself from society in that way?'

'A society that would snub me on those grounds is not one I would care to be part of. Besides, I have friends who would be steadfast no matter what circumstances we lived in.'

Will could not quite believe the struggle she was putting up. He had anticipated resistance from her, but he imagined that once the awkwardness over Ada was out of the way Connie would gladly, gratefully, acknowledge his persever-ance and yield to him. He thought again of his first proposal to her four years ago, when simple bad timing had undone him. Now, it seemed that her hospital experience had trans-formed wilfulness into a steely self-confidence, and he wondered if it was really in his power to win her after all. The night shadows had thickened, but she was close enough to see how intently he looked at her.

'I cannot be sure how determined you are to put objec-tions in our way. Is the thought of marrying really so repul-sive to you?'

Connie shook her head. 'I never said that it was.'

'Well, then. If you love me, you'll put aside your doubts and accept my proposal.'

'But why should you not accept *my* proposal – that we bide our time and find out whether companionship might be the wiser – better – course?'

Will looked away, shaking his head. 'Connie, please. That kind of semi-detached arrangement won't work – it's folly to imagine it. I want you to be my wife, not some . . . companion.' He tightened his hands upon hers. 'I must repeat the question, and I beg you to consider it carefully – because I will never ask it again. Will you marry me?'

Her throat felt choked with all that she wanted to say. She was moved, as much by the persistence of his love as by the honesty with which he declared it: she knew in some way they *could* make a life together. But she also knew the compromises it would entail. Once they were bound in wedlock a gradual whittling away of her independence would be inescapable, his innate decency notwithstanding. Motherhood would seal her domestic enslavement, and she would blame him for it once she realised her hard struggles

433

through the ranks of the medical profession had been for nothing. The stakes were simply too vertiginous.

'Will, I'm aware of the honour you've paid me – truly – and were my heart to rule my head I would pledge myself to you in an instant. But I cannot be the woman you want me to be. I am too afraid of surrendering what ground I have gained. You must marry someone who will give herself to you unconditionally –'

As she spoke Will's head sank, little by little, and only at this last sentence did he make an audible response: it was a groan, wrenched from deep within, and fraught with despair. He did not look up for some moments, and when he did he saw Connie gazing at him, her eyes glittering. She had never looked more beautiful to him. She started to say something, but he cut her short.

'What you've said –' he began, his mouth trembling with the effort, 'I honestly wish you'd never saved me that day in the hospital. Because I'm just as surely a dead man now.' He stood up, wishing himself away from her, and yet longing to be close to her. The last light had gone. They were now indistinct shapes in the gloaming. He knew he should accompany her out of the park, but he could not prolong the agony another moment.

'Goodbye,' he said, and paused a moment, waiting for her response. When she very quietly echoed his farewell, he turned and walked away. Her eyes followed his receding figure until it blurred and disappeared over the rise. Will felt desolation flooding his lungs. Had he really said *everything* he could have done to persuade her? He hoped, against all reason, that she might hurry after him and beg a second chance – but no footsteps came in his wake. He kept walking, almost blindly, skirting the Serpentine and thence over Park Lane into the hushed narrow streets of Mayfair. His shadow beneath the gaslight rose to meet him, then vanished over his shoulder. He paused at Down Street Tube station, but decided to keep going, preferring the solitary gloom of a night walk. By the time he had reached Devonshire Place, a trench song had lodged in his head, maddeningly.

> *And you bet we shan't be long*
> *Before we're fit and strong;*
> *You'll hear us say 'Oui, oui, tray bong'*
>   *When we're far away.*

On entering his darkened flat he found a letter on his doormat, and walked over to the front window where he examined it by the dingy illumination of the street gaslight. It was from Brigade HQ, advising him of the date he was expected to return to France.

PART THREE

The Coming of Age

20

The chestnut-shaded walk that cut through Regent's Park was busier than usual this morning. A cyclist breezed past her; a young woman pushed a wicker perambulator; a couple of truanting schoolboys lounged on a bench, smoking ostentatiously. The temperature was unseasonably mild for March, and a silvery sun was decanting its light through the high rustling latticework of leaves. This was the route Connie took to work, so to follow the same walk now, on a day off, felt oddly pleasing, as though she were truanting herself. She turned off the pathway and directed her steps across the grass, making for the grand terrace of Nash villas that rose above the hedged perimeter. On the other side of a small clump of trees a woman – a mother or nursemaid – was kneeling upon a yellow gingham blanket and handing over drinks to two fair-haired children. A picnic, this early in the year . . . She hadn't been at a picnic in a long time, and didn't miss them, but the innocent air of this little gathering touched her, and as she passed by she smiled at the woman busying herself with sandwiches. But the woman did not respond; perhaps the children had distracted her, or more likely, thought Connie, she was rather short-sighted.

She emerged from the park and crossed over to the long terrace, complacently imperial in its Ionic arches and columns. The front door gleamed like jet. She tapped the heavy brass knocker against the plate, and was admitted by a porter who directed her up a wide balustraded staircase to the first floor. The polished oak handrail and immaculate tiled floor were more suggestive of a foreign embassy than a private residence. Somebody had come up in the world. Her knock was answered after a characteristically languid delay.

'Ah, *there* you are,' cried Brigstock. 'I'd been wondering at what hour in the morning you'd show up. Come in!' She shot an amused glance at the silk paisley dressing gown that he wore over a frayed dress shirt.

'Still too early for you to have dressed properly, I see.'

He gave his mouth a twist of wry approval: they had instantly dropped into their familiar way of conversational sparring. He did not look very changed since she had last seen him, in Paris, two years ago. His slouch had become a middle-aged stoop, and the neat pointed beard was a self-conscious attempt at *homme d'affaires* gravitas. But he was still lean as a whippet, and still with a gleam in his eye. She followed him along a short corridor to a drawing room which he had converted into his studio; the three tall bays, each framing a view of the park, offered as much light as an artist could wish for. A heavy easel stood in one corner, holding a half-finished portrait. Against the walls leaned stacks of framed canvases, which he was sorting through in preparation for a retrospective of his work the following month. He had invited Connie to 'advise' him on what to select, though she suspected that it was merely a pretext to show off.

'Have a look through 'em while I make some tea,' he said over his shoulder.

She began idly to pick out one canvas and another, and found that a vague chronological arrangement had already been imposed on the assembly. One could trace a line from his earliest landscapes, mostly of Kent and Sussex, through the Mornington Crescent paintings to the larger studies of street life from his Parisian and Venetian sojourns. Some of them she admired – sprightly still lifes, nudes in dingy bedrooms, the oddly unsettling crowds at music halls and horse sales – and some she regarded with the bemused indulgence of an old friend. Brigstock's facility in painting was at once his strength and his weakness. He could do everything interestingly, and almost nothing brilliantly. The painter, who had absented himself for perhaps longer than he needed to, now returned with a pot of tea and china cups balanced on a tray. He set it down on a table already piled high with art books, monographs and catalogues, then absently began stirring the pot.

'So . . . ?' he began, with a nod to the stacks. Connie was aware that she had never rhapsodised over his work, and that Brigstock had never quite encouraged her to.

'There are some lovely paintings,' she said, looking him in the eye. 'The Mornington Crescent ones make me feel very nostalgic.'

'Ah, the hungry years. Or, at least – the *peckish* years,' he said with a laugh. 'I've moved barely a mile from the place, but what a difference.' He made a nonchalant gesture to encompass the grandeur of his new abode.

'Gracious living,' agreed Connie, craning her gaze up at the coving.

'We all move on,' he shrugged. 'I couldn't stay in a garret forever. With the prices these fetch now it would be dishonest.'

'I notice you still smoke those foul French cigarettes,' she said, taking out a packet of Sullivans and offering him one.

'Old habits. I suppose a fat cigar would better suit my elevation in the world.'

They smoked in silence for a few moments. Then she spotted something in the far corner of the room: it was the corner of a burnished gilt frame where the oatmeal-coloured dust sheet had teasingly peeled away. The dimensions were plainly enormous. She sidled over to it.

'What's this? The portrait in the attic?'

He squinted at her through curling cigarette smoke. 'I was wondering whether to show you this. You remember I was at the front for four weeks in the summer of '18? Well, in my capacity as an "official war artist" I undertook certain commissions that were . . . out of my usual line.' He pulled back the sheet, revealing a canvas about seven or eight feet long, a group portrait of six British generals standing about casually in a conference room. Their identical tight little moustaches and swagger sticks were counterpointed by their different heights and eyelines; they had the uncertain look of actors awaiting instructions from their director. None of the officers seemed to have noticed the captain's tunic and cap thrown over a chair in the corner; or else they were determinedly ignoring it.

'They look a sinister lot,' said Connie thoughtfully.

'Hmm. I didn't much care for them,' Brigstock admitted. 'And I dare say the feeling was mutual.'

'Who's that?' she asked, pointing to the foregrounded figure, a short, choleric-looking fellow who, alone of the six, stared unflinchingly out at the viewer.

'Ah, the scarlet major . . . don't recall his name. No oil painting, is he?'

She smiled, then took another measuring look at the picture. 'It's – a remarkable thing,' she said, and meant it. 'I like the "not-thereness" of that discarded uniform in the corner.'

Brigstock inclined his head in acknowledgement. 'It's actually called *The Uniform*. I'm not sure about exhibiting it, all the same. There's a danger it may overwhelm the rest.'

Connie shook her head. 'But you *must* show it. The fact that

442

it's so different from your other work – that's significant.'

He turned on her an expression in which pride mingled with doubt. 'That's a strong steer. I'll bear it in mind.' He covered it up again with the dust sheet, as if to stare at it for too long might turn them to stone. Connie, crushing out her cigarette in a pewter ashtray, settled herself against an enormous zebra-hide cushion. She watched him while he refreshed their teacups, and found herself pleased that he had at last returned to London. He was the sort of friend with whom she could pick up a conversation as if only two hours, rather than two years, had intervened. That ease in one another's company sometimes bothered her. Had they missed a vital turning that might have transformed friendship into something deeper? Perhaps not. The disparity in age would always have ruled against them.

'So – do you notice something different about me today?'

Brigstock frowned at the question, then tilted his head consideringly. 'Different . . . Have you, um, done something with your hair?' She shook her head, and he scrutinised her now, his eyes narrowing on her body. 'You don't mean to say –'

Connie realised where his speculation was tending and gave a little laugh. 'No, no. It *has* involved a period of gestation – though a good deal longer than nine months.' He looked baffled at that, so she continued. 'I am, from today, qualified to vote. It's my thirtieth birthday.' For a moment Brigstock's mouth hung open, an expression so rare on him as to seem almost alarming. Then he found his voice again. 'Well, of all the – bravo to you, my dear!' He grasped her hand, and pressed it to his lips. 'Thirty! Hard to *believe* . . .'

'You did know women could vote now, didn't you?' said Connie, only half joking.

'Well, I read about it, of course,' he said defensively. 'I recall having other things on my mind at the time.' It was a fair point. That the Representation of the People Bill had

443

received its Royal Assent and become law one night in February 1918 was somewhat lost amid the darkness of wartime despondency. After all that had gone before, their moment of historic triumph had felt like an anticlimax. The vote had been given to them – some of them – as a reward for 'war service', rather like a treat given to a child for behaving unexpectedly well in difficult circumstances. Brigstock meanwhile had dashed out of the room, returning some moments later with a bottle of champagne and a pair of tin mugs. 'Sorry, I haven't got round to unpacking the crystal yet,' he said, tearing the bottle's foil neck and firing the cork across the room. Connie remembered the mugs from Mornington Crescent; as with his cigarettes, he could not quite forsake every remnant of his old bohemian days. 'To a very happy birthday,' he said.

'To our enfranchisement,' she replied in gentle correction. She swallowed, and felt the acid bite of the champagne in her stomach. Thirty: it was not so hard, she thought, having cushioned herself against the inevitability. What did dismay her was the negligible progress she had made in the sixteen months since the end of the war. After the hospital in Endell Street had closed in 1919, she had set about renewing her association with Henry Cluett, the surgeon whose protégé she had been before the war. But he was about to leave the place, and London itself, to take an early retirement; her wartime work, which ought to have been the making of her, turned out to have little influence in the altered world of peacetime. With nobody willing to sponsor her renewed ambitions as a surgeon, she had joined the nursing staff of the Middlesex Hospital in Mortimer Street, where she was a sister. Enfranchisement was a landmark; professional mobility was still a pipe-dream. She would have to wait, and hope. A woman voter was something society would gradually accept, but a woman surgeon still floated in the realm of wayward ideas.

Brigstock was looking at his pocket watch. 'Why don't you stay for lunch? I have some people coming round.'

Connie shook her head. 'I can't, I'm afraid. My oldest friend is getting married, and I have to be at Regent Street to offer reassurance on her trousseau.'

'Good Lord. I'm surprised there are any men *left* to marry.'

'Well . . . my friend has found one. He's charming, too.' Joe, Lily's intended, was a railway clerk with a fine tenor singing voice and a flat in Stamford Hill. She smiled, thinking of his shyly deferential manner in women's company.

'My dear, you look almost wistful. Don't tell me you're longing for connubial fulfilment yourself?'

She laughed at this pompous locution. 'No, I'm not. But is the thought of my being married so extraordinary?'

'No, no . . . I simply can't envisage you under the marital thumb, that's all. You and I are of the same kidney – sufficient unto ourselves. We don't *need* anyone.'

Connie paused, and considered a reply – but kept silent. In one way she felt flattered by his estimation; but she baulked at his admiring recruitment of her into the ranks of natural solitaries. That was not the way she felt about herself, even if it seemed so to the world. She took a last mouthful of champagne and stood up.

'I must go,' she said, collecting her hat and gloves. 'Thank you for showing me the pictures. I'll look forward to seeing them, at – ?'

'Oh, the Templeman Gallery, in Albemarle Street. You must promise to come to the private view – the middle of May, I fancy.'

He followed her as she returned along the passageway to his front door. But something rankled with her. She felt, obscurely, that her eligibility had been impugned, and she turned to him as he held open the door. 'What you said before – that I didn't need anyone – what did you mean?'

'I said that *we* didn't need anyone. It was meant as a compliment, Connie –'

'It's only that . . . would it surprise you to hear that someone – a man once asked me to marry him?'

Brigstock looked at her now with a tender-eyed sadness. 'No. That doesn't surprise me at all. I only feel sorry for the fellow.'

'Because he was deluded?'

He gave a half-smile. 'Because he wanted you badly enough to ask.'

She cut back through the park and thence down Portland Place, where she passed a horse-drawn cart delivering coal at a house. She wondered if horses, so vital out in France, had been given a reprieve since the war ended. It seemed unlikely. Outside the Langham Hotel the queuing taxis were clouded in fumes of grit and petrol. At the junction of Regent Street the traffic thickened, honking, impatient to move on. There was an eagerness everywhere, it seemed, to move on. She still brooded on Brigstock's remark, and felt annoyed with herself for reacting to it: what did he care if she had once rejected a marriage proposal? Only her nettled pride had induced her to confess it. Outwardly, her life had achieved the independence she had longed for. She was renting a tiny flat above a shoe shop in Regent's Park Road. She enjoyed her work at the Middlesex. She had a little money saved from the bequest of a distant relative on her father's side. Yet such relish of her autonomy ran contrary to the prevailing assumption that a woman was not complete if she remained unmarried, and today's milestone had reminded her of lines from a comic ditty the soldiers used to sing at concert parties:

> *Hug me, kiss me, call me Gertie,*
> *Marry me quick, I'm nearly thirty!*

446

She dodged across the frantic crossways at Oxford Circus and Regent Street, and pushed through the heavy double doors of Jay's, which she had visited years before when it was a mourning-dress emporium. It had recently, and dubiously, converted to selling wedding trousseaux. She wandered along its aisles, past smugly posed mannequins veiled in silk and muslin, past counters displaying hats and gloves and fashionable fripperies, and took the stairs to the bridal department.

'Connie!' It was Lily, standing on a chair by the window and waving while an assistant edged around, pinning the hem of an ivory-coloured silk dress. As Connie stepped towards her she began to see the elaborate lace embellishments of the material and its double satin streamer ribbon. It lent its wearer the appearance of an oversized doll. Raising herself on tiptoe she kissed Lily on the cheek.

'Hullo, Constance.' The voice came from behind her, and she turned to find Lily's mother sitting on one of the courtesy sofas, her round face stiff with disapproval. Connie now sensed the air vibrating from the aftermath of a tremendous row.

'Hullo, Mrs Vaughan,' she said, injecting a note of brightness into her voice. 'I didn't know you'd be here!'

'I might as well have stayed at home, fr'all the notice she's taking of me.' The tone was primly aggrieved. Connie turned back to Lily, who raised her eyes heavenwards in an unambiguous mime of irritation. The shop assistant, her mouth full of pins, was continuing her mute circuit of the bridal hem.

'What d'you think, then?' said Lily, anxiously reading her friend's expression.

'You look beautiful, Lil, honestly,' she replied, then glanced back towards Mrs Vaughan. 'Is something the matter?'

Lily sighed. 'For some reason Mum thinks this hemline is too high on the calf –'

'Calf?!' Mrs Vaughan almost shrieked. 'It's almost up to your *knees*. Your father would have a fit if he could see what I can.'

'I knew this would happen,' said Lily, shaking her head. 'Con, will you please explain to her? She thinks it's "indecent" to bare anything above the ankle.'

Connie, already feeling a distinct urge to be elsewhere, had turned a conciliating smile on Lily's mother and was about to speak when the latter piped up again. 'And shall I tell you another thing? That hem will make you look even shorter than you are.' The argument from morality had cut no ice with her daughter, but the argument from aesthetic principle delivered a palpable hit. Lily blushed violently, and her voice trembled with anger as she spoke. 'What a horrible thing to say. Sooner I get married the better – I won't have to listen to your spitefulness any more.' She picked up the rustling skirts of her dress, ignoring the startled assistant, and hurried off to the fitting room.

Mrs Vaughan pursed her lips in righteous offence. 'Well, *really*. I'm only trying to save her from herself . . .'

Connie went and sat down next to her. 'I think Lily's just suffering nerves – about the day. The dress is important to her, Mrs Vaughan, and she so wants your approval. I suppose the hem *is* a little high, but you know, she has such shapely legs. Isn't she entitled to show them off on her wedding day?' Mrs Vaughan continued to grumble quietly about her daughter's wilfulness, but Connie's honeyed blandishments soon coaxed her into a better mood, and then managed to effect a discreet and dignified withdrawal from the battlefield of hurt feelings.

Once she was gone, Connie tapped on the door of the fitting room. 'Lil? You can come out now.' When she received no reply, she gently turned the doorknob and craned her head around the jamb. Lily was sitting on the shallow velvet-covered bench, her figure multiplied by the angled mirrors on each side of the closet. Her cheeks were blotchy with tears, in poignant contrast to the elegant tucks and folds of her pristine dress.

'Oh, Lil,' she crooned, putting a consoling arm about her. 'You mustn't let her upset you. The mother of the bride always pokes her nose in –'

'That's not why I'm crying,' she said with a sort of laughing sob. 'I was listening to the way you talked to her, so patient – it set me off. You're just a lovely person, Con – that's all. I only wish there were some man we could find for *you* to marry.'

Connie laughed and squeezed her friend's arm. 'Don't you start! I've just been told by someone – a man, in fact – that I'm not the marrying kind.'

Lily clicked her tongue in reproof. 'Well, he's wrong about that. You've just chosen not to – though why, I'm not sure.'

She sighed, and stared back at her reflection. 'I hardly know myself. I'd always thought there were more important things to do than marry – campaigning, for a start, then having a career. I wanted to live without feeling beholden to a man. For a while I suppose I did . . .'

'You mean – during the war?'

She nodded. 'Oh, I'm glad it's over – how could I not be? – but it did make us useful. It proved to men that we weren't just feeble domestic halfwits. I mean, didn't we take responsibility? We worked so hard they eventually *had* to give us the vote.'

'So we achieved something.'

'Yes, of course. But I wonder . . . They're not letting women keep those jobs. It's "thanks a lot and you can all go home now". I could work in a hospital for another twenty years and I'd be no closer to doing what I want to do. They'll make small concessions now and then, but men still have all the cards – and they know it.' She paused, and gave

Lily's knee an encouraging nudge. 'But they're not all so bad, are they?'

'Joe had better be ready to give me more than "small concessions",' she said, giggling at the unintended hint of vulgarity. She looked round at Connie, then suddenly clapped her hand over her mouth in shocked self-rebuke. 'Heavens! I've just remembered – happy birthday, Con!' And she gave the birthday girl such a fierce embrace that Connie, after some moments, had to remind her that her bridal gown was in danger of being crushed.

'I'm treating you to lunch at the Corner House – we haven't been there for such ages,' said Lily, getting up and opening the fitting-room door. 'By the way, how did you manage to get rid of my mother?'

'Oh – I told her about the new spring sale at Liberty's. I've never seen anyone move so quickly in my life.'

It was Eleanor who had first spotted it, in the Births column of *The Times*. They happened to be staying at Silverton House while their mother convalesced from a riding accident. She had broken her wrist in a fall, and both of her children had come down from London to stay for a few days. Will read the notice which his sister placed, without comment, before him.

HOLLAND. On 16 April 1920, at Brunswick Square, Hove, to Ada (née Brink), wife of Captain T. Holland, a son.

Will stared at the announcement in silence, his heart trapped in a pincer movement of remembered guilt and relief. He had done the right thing back then, though whenever he recalled the scene of separation in its particulars it burned with the sharpness of acid. He had long dreaded the moment he would have to ask Ada to release him from their engagement; yet the miracle of chancing upon the only woman he had ever truly loved would give him, he believed, the impetus to go through with it. After all, a greater crime than abandonment would be to formalise a relationship in which neither partner was suited to the other. In the event, his fond assumptions had come to nothing. His own heart broken that August night in Kensington Gardens, he had arranged to meet Ada the day before his return to duty in France, and found himself breaking her heart in turn. It had surprised him. Will had foresight, but he was severely deficient in romantic imagination. While he knew that sundering a two-and-a-half-year engagement would be awkward, he had never properly appreciated the depth of Ada's attachment to him, and as he stuttered through a confession of his doubts about their long-term compatibility, he noticed a disbelieving expression take hold of her features that genuinely shocked him. Had she not sensed that he had been withdrawing from her? No: apparently she had not. He blundered on. The long engagement had been a trial to her – it was not fair that she sacrifice herself to him – he should step aside and yield her to a more deserving fellow. By the time he had finished, Ada's frame was trembling with an almost soundless sobbing, and for some moments she seemed unable to speak. But at last she looked at him.

'You have talked as if you were doing me a favour – yet it seems I am the one in distress. Could you not have told me as soon as you knew that I had become – a burden?' And Will then felt the full piercing shame of his behaviour. He could have flannelled a little more, but he had no spirit left in him. A few more broken phrases passed between them; when he stood up to leave he offered his hand to her – which she didn't even turn her face around to refuse. He had walked away, though he had registered through his humiliation the faint euphoric pulses of what he knew to be his deliverance.

Four years ago, almost. The single morsel of comfort he

stored on his way to the front the following day was that he had avoided the howitzer recoil of his mother's wrath. He kept hearing reverberations of it, however, in the wry tone of Eleanor's letters to him. On coming home from France at the end of the war he learned that Ada had married an officer in the winter of the previous year and was living in Brighton. By then his mother's fury had abated, and their reunion passed off without any mention of Ada or of his disobliging conduct. But he could tell from an edge in her voice, from a stiffness in her smile, what a disappointment he had been to her.

He folded up the newspaper and passed it back to Eleanor, who gazed at him tolerantly over her new reading spectacles. Well, Ada was now a mother, and good luck to her. He sighed, then pointed a finger upwards to the bedroom where they could hear their mother moving about.

'It might be a good idea if you don't let her see that.'

The first week in May, Will was back in London and walking from his flat over to Lord's, where the second day's play of an MCC testimonial match had just begun. The cricket season, about to resume in earnest for the first time since 1914, had brought in the crowds, starved of the game, as of much else. Will was eking out his last days of leisure before returning to county cricket with M—shire. He did not savour the prospect. After the five-year hiatus, he was no longer confident of drawing on his old talent. When he had turned up for his first net the previous week, the bat had felt toylike and puny in his hands, and from the number of times the ball flew past his edge he suspected his eye had lost its former keenness. Three times he heard the clatter of stumps behind him – the death rattle! – and it began to seem extraordinary to him that he had ever managed to earn a living from cricket at all. He tried to encourage himself with the reflection that most of the older players would face the same predicament, returning to a profession that seemed quite alien after what they had experienced during the war. He had longed to play when he was out in France; now, nearly thirty-three and facing the expectant gaze of peacetime, he was not sure that he still knew how.

He found the ground nearly full, even at this early hour. He could have gone to sit in the members' stand, but he dreaded encountering acquaintances from pre-war days and the stilted effort to fill in the blanks – *Which brigade . . . ? So you must have fought at . . . ?* He hated talking about it, and had assiduously avoided all the reunions and regimental dinner invitations that came his way. After the enforced gregariousness of war he found that he much preferred his own company, and sitting amid a crowd of strangers watching cricket suited him best of all. He bought a scorecard from one of the sellers, and edged his way along one of the middle rows in the Tavern Stand. Conditions were good. A phalanx of silvery-white clouds were massing overhead, and a late-spring moisture in the air would help the swing bowlers. He felt the awakened thrill of the game as it settled into its rhythm, the run-up of the bowler supported by the ring of fielders stalking in, the release of the ball, the *tock* of the bat meeting it, and then the retreat to positions to await the next ball: in, and retreat, in, and retreat, there was an organic steadiness to it, like a lung expanding and contracting. The umpire's faint call of 'over', the switching of ends, a slight rearrangement of the field – and then it started again. Oh, if he could only sit here for*ever* . . .

It was by degrees that his trance of absorption was disrupted. Usually he would forget all about his fellow spectators as he focused upon the game, his eye caught fast on the smallest ripples of activity in the middle. But from somewhere behind him a voice had crept into earshot and thrown his concentration. It was an old man's voice, by the sound, not disagreeably loud or abrasive – but insistent. It seemed that the old fellow was commenting upon the cricket for the benefit of two much younger companions, a man and a woman. It was not an occasional remark, either, but almost a ball-by-ball narrative: 'Hmm . . . he's glanced that to square leg, taken a quick single . . . End of the over – fifty-four without loss.' Will, helplessly intrigued, was soon eavesdropping on the trio's chitchat. He wanted to sneak a look at them, but could not do so without obviously and vulgarly craning around. There was a jolliness about them he liked, and a mutual ease that made him think they were related. Yet something baffled him. The young woman – Molly, he heard her called – required explanation of the game, which the old fellow patiently supplied; but the young man ('feller-me-lad'), from what Will could hear, was a cricket lover and seemed to know all about the players. So why was the old man describing to *him* the evidence of their own eyes? 'Ah, he's got that one through the covers . . . fielder's fallen on his ar—backside (pardon me, Molly) . . . over the rope it goes.'

When the lunch interval came Will tried to retune his ear to something else, but found himself listening again to his neighbours. With the players off, the old gent had ceded the conversational reins to his two companions. They were now discussing family matters, and at first Will had to strain to pick up the quieter voices of the young couple. On first hearing mention of the name he thought he had imagined it, but soon it was on their lips again: they were talking, with evident familiarity, about a certain *Connie*. He leaned back slightly, pricking his ears. Unable to help himself, he stole a quick glance round, first taking in the old cove, then the young woman, neither of whom he knew. He had to twist round in his seat to look at the young man, being directly behind him, and he started back almost in fright. He recognised that face, from a long time ago.

'Um . . . Fred?'

'Who's that?'

Will looked more closely at him, and saw there was something wrong with the eyes. *He couldn't be, surely* – 'It's Will – Will Maitland.'

'Ah!' came the reply. Will looked over in appeal to the young woman. She seemed to grasp the difficulty straight away, and with the briefest smile of reassurance she passed her hand over her eyes, a little mime that told Will for certain that Fred was blind. He now perceived a milkiness in the whites. In the meantime Fred had thrust out his hand, which Will took, and held for some moments. 'I know what you were going to say,' Fred said, amusement in his voice. '"Long time, no see."'

'I'm – I'm very glad to see you again,' Will half gasped, blushing at his ungainly repetition of the word 'see'.

'Let me introduce you. This is my wife, Molly – and my grandfather, Roger Callaway. Will is an old friend . . .' he added, with tactful vagueness.

'I've been enjoying your commentary this morning, sir,' said Will quickly.

The old man – who, on close inspection, was more ancient than Will had thought – threw up his hands, and seemed to smile beneath his drooping white moustache. '*Nyuff, nyuff.* Kind of you, sir. Young feller-me-lad here has to know what's happening.' He patted his hand gently on Fred's knee.

'So what are you doing here?' asked Fred. 'I thought you'd be playing for the county by now.'

Will replied that he would be, soon enough. When the old man was told which county, he became animated again. 'M—shire, is it? Why, you must have played with Tamburlain.'

'I did indeed, sir. He was a very dear friend of mine.'

Mr Callaway shook his head, and said quietly, 'Poor man. Never saw such a batsman, before or since. Fred, didn't you say Constance knew him a little?' He turned again to Will.

'Constance is my younger granddaughter. Perhaps you've met her – great cricket lover, of course . . .'

There was a slight pause, which enabled Fred to change the subject. 'I wonder if you'd be good enough, Grandpa –?' He rose to his feet, then explained for Will's benefit. 'I need the gents, I'm afraid . . .'

Will, rising from his seat, said, 'Perhaps you'd let me help you . . .'

'No, no. You stay here with Molly. We should be back, oh, any time within the next two hours.' He laughed as he took hold of the old man's arm, and together the pair of them began, very slowly, shuffling along the row towards the exit. Will noticed other spectators looking at them curiously, and could almost read their thoughts: the blind leading the blind. He glanced over at Molly.

'Should I have – let them go?'

Molly smiled. 'Don't worry. They always manage. I think they enjoy looking after each other.'

Will appraised her more closely now. She wore a wide-collared frock and a narrow-brimmed cloche hat; her hair was cut in a shoulder-length bob and her round, clear-skinned face was elevated from comeliness to beauty by the open charm of her smile. It seemed to suggest an eagerness to please, and an expectation that others would respond in a like spirit of warmth. They talked of how she and Fred had met. Gassed at Cambrai in 1917, Fred had been at a hospital in London to which Molly was a volunteer visitor, reading to the blind.

'When I first met him he was very depressed, of course, about losing his sight. So I would do my best to cheer him up, and started visiting him every day. That makes me sound more virtuous than I am,' she added. 'The truth is, I'd rather fallen in love, and I sought him out at the expense of the other men. You see, he had such a lovely face, and he would say things like, "When I wake up in the morning sometimes

I don't know whether I'm properly awake or still asleep –"'
She stopped, and blushed at herself. 'I'm sorry, I don't know
why I'm telling you this.'

'Please, don't apologise,' said Will. 'Do you mind my
asking – um, why does he want to come here . . . ?'

'You mean to something that he can't see? It was Connie's
idea. When Fred came back from France she used to take
him out – to the park, or wherever – and describe to him
what she saw. And then she thought to take him to the
cricket, which they both love. It was just a school match,
but she made sure he knew exactly what was happening.
Fred said it was like watching it in his head. Unfortunately,
I don't know a thing about maiden overs or leg before wicket
. . . but I'm trying to learn!'

'You have the old man to help you.'

'Yes! Isn't he a dear?' Here she leaned in conspiratorially.
'Do you know, he's *eighty-five* years old.' Her round-eyed
look of wonder was so guileless that he was almost betrayed
into laughter. He hesitated before he next spoke.

'And Connie – she's well . . . ?'

'Oh, yes. She's working at the Middlesex – otherwise she
would have been here today.'

Will nodded. There was one piece of information he was
suddenly eager to secure, but he wasn't sure how he could
without seeming impertinent. 'And is she, um, still living
at home?'

Molly took the question innocently. 'No, she's got a little
flat in Regent's Park Road. So we're quite near to one
another.'

He guessed from her use of the singular that Connie was
unattached, though he took no pleasure in it. When he
thought of their brief re-acquaintance in that August of 1916
it seemed almost to have happened in a dream. Their chance
meeting at the Women's Hospital, her dramatic surgical
intervention, the night they danced at the party in South

Kensington, and afterwards . . . it felt unreal in retrospect, a phantasmal interlude between those eternities in France. He had never been in contact with her since, partly out of an offended pride, but also out of a self-protective instinct. He could not bear to go through that again, to have come so close to catching the vital object of his life only to have it slip from his grasp. To renew the pursuit would have been mortifying, and friendship was out of the question: either he must have her entirely, or not at all. He had chosen the latter. He now realised that Molly had asked him a question.

'I'm sorry – ?'

'I was just saying – Connie is coming to dinner at Thornhill Crescent this Friday, and I thought you might like to join us.' He read ingenuous expectation in her face.

'Oh . . .'

'I mean, since you haven't seen each other in a while –'

'That's extremely kind of you, but I'm – I have another engagement. On that night.'

Her look of regret seemed so sincere that, for a moment, he was tempted to change his mind and accept. She suddenly reminded him of Connie herself. How was it that he had never won the love of such a woman? Fred had managed it – and he was *blind*.

'Oh well, perhaps another time,' said Molly brightly.

But Will was distracted, having spotted the stumbling return of Fred and his grandfather through the polite commotion of spectators standing to make way. In a reflex of sympathy he too stood and moved towards them, arms outstretched, barking his shins against the seats, rather like a blind man himself.

21

They had already sat down to dinner by the time Connie let herself in at Thornhill Crescent. Friday evenings at the hospital tended to be frantic, and she had left late, and then had stopped off at the flat to change out of her uniform. As she walked past St Andrew's she could hear the echoing strains of choir practice. Lights were coming on in the houses as the evening grew dark. This neighbourhood was so much a part of her that, a year on since her move to Camden, she still sometimes found herself absently boarding the tram to Caledonian Road.

As she approached the dining room her ear picked up voices she had not expected to hear, and she paused at the hall mirror to interrogate her reflection. She looked tired, and would now have to brace herself in anticipation of others telling her so. She quickly practised a smile – it seemed rather guarded and vulnerable tonight – and pushed open the door.

'Hullo, everyone. Sorry I'm late.'

Her arrival caused little murmurs and trills of appreciation. On either side of her mother sat Olivia and Lionel, looking sleekly prosperous; she wondered what they were doing here. They rarely came to Islington unless there was a very particular occasion. Perhaps Molly had invited them. At the opposite head of the table sat her grandfather, who rose totteringly to draw back the vacant seat next to his.

'Do sit down, my dear,' he said hoarsely. 'We've only just started.'

'Where on earth have you *been*?' asked Olivia, who had grown more matronly but no less impatient with the years.

'At work – where else?' she replied with a shrug. 'And then I had to wait for a train from Chalk Farm.'

'Some of us still have to use public transport, you see,' added Fred. 'Apparently Lionel and Olivia came here in the new motor, Con.' Connie had noticed the car parked outside the house, but had not imagined for a moment she would know the owners.

'It's a Wolseley coupé, thirty hp, just been completely overhauled,' announced Lionel, in the sort of tone that suggested that his audience might be impressed, though in fact none of them knew a thing about cars. Molly was helping her to the fish, a poached turbot in a béchamel sauce: she was an enthusiastic but nervous cook, and this dish, as she explained, was a first attempt. Connie found that it tasted better than it looked.

'It's delicious,' she said reassuringly.

'Molly always does us fish on Fridays,' said Fred, who seemed tickled by this token of his wife's Catholicism. Connie noticed Olivia's mouth pursing at the fond allusion: for some reason she had conceived a brooding suspicion of Catholics which even Molly's good-naturedness could not placate. Old Mr Callaway had also picked up the reference. 'Old colleague of mine, when I was working in Mayfair . . . he was a Catholic. Every Friday, he'd always have his lunch at Wilton's.'

'Hmm. I'm not sure that's quite in the spirit of self-denial that was intended,' said Connie.

'Oh, I dare say,' replied Mr Callaway agreeably, and then embarked on a knight's-move reminiscence of old restaurants in London he used to frequent. Connie meanwhile looked around the table, trying to decide whether she was missing some vital point to the evening. She was still baffled as to why Olivia and Lionel were present: it surely couldn't have been to show off the new car?

Next to her, Mrs Rhodes said gently, 'You look rather tired, my dear. I hope they're not working you too hard.' In truth Connie's feet ached, having pounded the wards since seven o'clock that morning, but she merely deflected Mrs Rhodes with a little shake of her head. Admitting fatigue would only rouse her mother to a tutting aria of lamentation. Across the table, Molly was carefully removing the bones from the fish on Fred's plate. That homecoming . . . He had arrived at Victoria Station from France, chaperoned by two friends from his company. Connie had gone to meet him there, having instructed herself to behave in as breezy a spirit as she could muster, for both their sakes. But on seeing the bandage blindfolding his eyes and the tufty disarray it made of his hair she felt all her hard-won professional calm begin to crumble; she, who had seen men without faces, men without limbs, was still not ready to see her own brother without eyes. When through the crowd she called his name, Fred had jerked his head, like a dog hearing a whistle, and said, uncertainly, 'Con?' At that she threw herself against his shoulder, sobbing violently, to the evident discomfiture of his two guides. But she was past caring. In that intense disabling tumult of pity, she had struggled to understand how losing one's sight could be any less terrible than losing one's life. Once her heaving shoulders had slowed, Fred put a hand to her cheek and said, with a brave chuckle, 'Good job you didn't bring Ma with you, else we'd be here all day.'

Now, watching Molly's tender ministrations, she saw that even the most wretched misfortune could resemble, in another light, a strange sort of blessing. If Fred had not been blinded, he would probably never have met the reader who visited the hospital every Tuesday and Thursday afternoon, or nurtured a friendship that would become, within months, a serious love match. Connie could understand the attraction from Fred's side – no man, blind or otherwise, would fail to be charmed by Molly's sweet manner, or the confiding warmth of her voice. As Fred once said, you could always hear the smile in it. But she could not help puzzling over Molly's willingness to pledge herself to Fred. Much as she loved him, she felt that the commitment required of a wife would be different from that of a sister. It was not just the everyday responsibility it would entail, but the haunting thought of Fred never once having looked upon her face. How could she bear it?

The dinner plates had just been cleared when Mrs Callaway turned to Connie. 'I had a telephone call from Nicoll's this afternoon, darling. They said your dress is ready to collect.'

'What dress?' asked Molly. Connie explained that she was to attend Lily's wedding in a fortnight's time.

'*Lily* – you mean your friend from school?' said Olivia, her tone incredulous.

'Yes. What's so remarkable about that?' asked Connie.

Olivia gave a little shake of her head, and said, in a voice just loud enough for Connie to hear, 'If she can find a husband, there's hope for everyone.' Across the table, Lionel stifled a chuckle. Connie felt a rush of dislike towards Olivia at that moment. What she had really meant was hope *even for Connie*.

'That's rather unkind of you, Olivia,' said their mother. 'From what I hear he's a very eligible fellow.'

'And *she's* a very eligible woman,' said Connie coolly. 'Lily's had offers of marriage before. She was just waiting for a man she honestly loved.'

'Like you, my dear,' her grandfather suggested, obliging

Connie to smile at his unsubtle gallantry. 'Now, that fellow we met at Lord's –'

Fred cleared his throat loudly at this point. 'Do excuse me, Grandpa, but I think this might be the moment to let you all know – um, I – that is, *we* have a certain announcement –' He reached out for Molly, who took his hand.

'You're expecting a child?' Olivia almost shrieked. Molly blushed deeply, her smile all the answer that was required, and the company dissolved into a ragged chorus of happy exclamations. Mrs Callaway had clasped her hands together over the shocked 'O' of her open mouth, as though the news might have been of fast-approaching disaster. Olivia was exulting in the prospect of her own two boys 'at last' having a cousin. Connie wondered if at that moment her face were registering appropriate signs of gratification. She was delighted for Fred and Molly, but their news had isolated her once more as the odd woman out: having escaped being 'the daughter at home', her role would now be the family's spinster aunt. But she would not be pitied. This was the path she had chosen in life – no one had forced her to go it alone. Amid the excited gabble of congratulation Molly shot an uncertain look at her over the table; there seemed to be a kind of appeal in it. Judging it to be hopeful of sisterly solidarity, Connie raised her glass, and offered her broadest smile.

Later, once Olivia and Lionel had left (with a fruity parp of the car horn) and the rest of the family had retired for the evening, Connie had gone to smoke in the study when she heard a knock, and Molly put her head round the door.

'I'm not disturbing you, I hope . . .'

'No, of course not. Come in. May I fetch you a drink?' Molly shook her head, and sat down on the sofa opposite, one hand absently palpating her stomach. 'I'm sorry if you were a little overwhelmed by the family,' Connie said. 'My mother already thinks you're a kind of saint – so tonight was your canonisation.'

Molly laughed, and looked embarrassed. 'I don't much enjoy being the centre of attention – especially when I've done nothing to deserve it.'

'Ah, but according to Grandpa you'll be continuing the Callaway name, remember. He seems quite convinced of it.'

'Oh dear,' said Molly, frowning. 'Will he be awfully disappointed if it's a girl?'

Connie gave a sceptical half-laugh. 'He'll get what he's given – and be grateful for it.'

Molly sat back, fiddling with a button on the arm of the sofa. After a brief silence she looked over at Connie again. 'I was going to mention this to you before, but Fred told me not to while your mother was about. When we were at the cricket on Tuesday, we bumped into someone you know – knew.'

'Oh?'

'William – Will – Maitland. Fred said you were once – friendly with one other . . .'

'*Oh.*' It was not a name she had expected to hear. After their last encounter she had thought of writing to him, once it became clear that he was never going to write to her. But in the end she had resisted the impulse. What, after all, was there to say? 'How is he? Married, I suppose?'

'No, it seems not. He gave me to understand that he had been engaged –'

'Good Lord. How *long* did you talk to him for?'

'Well, our seats were close to one another – so we had most of the afternoon together.'

Connie was curious to know how much Will had told her about the two of them. It was perfectly conceivable that he loathed the memory of her. 'Did he seem at all . . . bitter?'

'You mean about the war?' asked Molly, guessing wrong. 'He didn't talk about it, really, apart from the story of his being wounded. He said that if it hadn't been for you he would have died! It sounded very dramatic, I must say.'

Connie shrugged non-committally. It seemed that Will had given Molly a judiciously edited account of their friendship, one which, moreover, cast Connie in the best possible light. She had not expected such generosity of him. Molly was now looking at her intently. 'Actually, I got the impression that he's made an awful hash of things. He said that he'd let people down very badly, and that picking up his life again after the war was much harder than he'd imagined. I did feel rather sorry for him.'

'It sounds like he feels rather sorry for himself,' said Connie.

Molly flinched slightly. 'I think he's been through a lot, Connie. If you ask me, he seemed a little . . . lost. Fred said there was once – between you – some attachment . . .'

Connie sighed and let her gaze drop. 'It was a long time ago. I dare say we're both quite different now. But I'm sorry to hear he was out of sorts.'

'I thought of asking him to dinner, if you'd –'

'You think he would come?'

Molly hesitated for a moment, enough for Connie to notice. 'I'm sure he would, given encouragement.'

How odd, she thought, that Will hadn't married. It was a surprise. When he had asked for her hand those years ago she had wondered whether his real motivation was the *idea* of marriage, as others are spurred on by the idea of wealth, or fame. Was that at the back of her mind when she refused him that night in Kensington Gardens? He had always seemed driven by a headlong determination to 'take a wife', rather than waiting to find a woman he could love. It occurred to her now that she may have misjudged him.

'Perhaps it would be best to leave alone,' she said presently, though the conversation had stirred her to candour. She studied Molly as she sat in profile. 'D'you mind my asking – were you certain that you wanted to marry Fred?'

Molly looked almost offended by the question. 'Of course. I'd never been more certain of anything in my life.'

'But – how was that? You must have considered the difficulties of marrying someone who –' She paused, and rephrased the thought. 'Did you not worry that you were limiting yourself – that you'd never be able to share things together, like – I don't know – playing tennis, or going to a gallery?'

Molly knitted her brow in puzzlement. 'Well, it's not really about seeing. It's about understanding. I can play tennis or go to a gallery with anyone. Fred isn't like anyone else. Think of all the wonderful things about him – why would I give them up just because he's blind? *You* of all people must understand that.'

'But he's my flesh and blood. You chose him, in the knowledge –'

Molly shook her head, as though amazed that she had to explain. 'We are what we love, Connie. The secret – the thing we hope for – is having that love returned.'

They talked for a while longer about the evening just gone, then Molly rose and, kissing her goodnight, left the room. But Connie remained in the study afterwards, smoking, and thinking.

One could always find such extraordinary things in *The Times*, thought Will. Ever since Eleanor had alerted him to the news of his former betrothed's happy event, he had found himself scouring the columns of announcements – for what, he didn't know. Deaths, he observed, were never in short supply; many of them were commemorative notices supplied by the parents of young men killed in the war. One could tell it was the anniversary of a major action by the length of the lists. He wondered how many they would number come July. But something quite different had caught his eye a few days ago. It was halfway down the personal columns, squeezed between advertisements for ladies' companions and holiday homes in Margate. It was short, and to the point.

MURIEL – Worrying dreadfully. Do please send us news. Promise you no recriminations – Mother.

He speculated as to what might have estranged them. Was it a recent tiff or a long-nursed resentment? One had to suppose there was a man involved. Mother was evidently beside herself, but she was prepared to let bygones be bygones if only her errant daughter would send word. Something about the desperation of her plea nagged away at him, and after a few days he realised what it was. If he, Will, ever took off quite suddenly, who would put out a newspaper advertisement imploring *him* to come back? His own mother? Perhaps; eventually; once she had swallowed her pride. Eleanor would make it her business, he supposed. Yes, he could depend on Ellie. But, in truth, he was stuck to think of anyone – *anyone* – outside of his family who might miss him enough to worry. He had put a distance between himself and the army; the few friends he had made during his time in France were either dead or had disappeared into the anonymity of civilian life. He had been close to none of his M—shire teammates, apart from Tam. Now that he thought of it, he was more like Tam than he had ever imagined. He was respected as a player, but he could not claim to be cherished as a friend by any of them. Was he really so alone in the world?

His encounter with Fred Callaway and his wife at Lord's the previous week was the first time in ages he had enjoyed the company of others. He had warmed to the familial trio during the afternoon, particularly to Molly. It had moved him, the way she was solicitous of both her husband and the old man, then the way she had shared her sandwiches with him, a virtual stranger. When she had asked him to dinner, he had made an excuse, uncertain as to whether he could face Connie with equanimity. At the close of play he had said goodbye to them outside Lord's with the melancholy inkling that they would never meet again. It didn't matter: life would go on as before. The hardest part was knowing that he would survive.

He had been walking, aimlessly, up Albemarle Street, having returned from Lewin & Co. in the City, carrying a new set of whites. His old kit, not worn since 1914, had looked so frowsy and forlorn he had thrown it out. The shop assistant had asked him which county he played for, and Will had been silently disappointed when his name on the cheque prompted no sign of recognition. Now, recalling the moment, he heard himself laugh out loud, a short mirthless *ha!* that caused a couple passing by to turn and look at him. It didn't matter, any of it. Glancing in the window of a gallery, his eye fell upon the title card of an exhibition mounted within.

Paintings and Drawings
A retrospective of works by
Denton Brigstock, RA

Brigstock. He felt sure he knew the name: wasn't it the painter he had met that night, years ago, when he had been with Connie and Tam? A night he recalled making a fool of himself, what's more . . . A bell above the door tinkled as he entered, and he wandered unobtrusively through a set of rooms, the walls uniformly painted a card-table green. The paintings were a mixed lot, some bucolic landscapes and still lifes which he admired, then a middle sequence of melancholy interiors, blotchy, blurred and dimly inhabited by people who looked close to dereliction. The fellow seemed incurably fond of seedy back rooms and squalid public houses, painted in such a way as to make them appear even more dismal than they probably were in real life. They did not encourage a lingering appraisal, and he pressed on into the next room. A small knot of people had gathered inquisitively around the room's main focus, a huge canvas whose subject only became apparent when he had cleared a space through the stragglers.

He reared back, as if before an apparition. It was a group portrait of army brass hats, foremost among them a face he had not seen up close since the summer of 1916. The truculent set of the jaw, the roasted-looking complexion, the eyes burning like danger lamps: there was no mistaking Brigadier-General Culver. The painter had caught that haughty, impatient demeanour quite chillingly, though what impressed Will more was the accusing detail of the captain's uniform draped over the chair; would that pointed comment of the artist have given the Brigadier-General a jolt? Probably not. A man who could dispatch countless soldiers to certain death would not be easily upset by a painting. Will, on the other hand, could hear the blood in his ears; he felt a wave of impotent fury surge through his body and up into his mouth. Was that bile he could taste? Around him he sensed the murmuring throng of gallery visitors absorbed in the canvas simply as a work of art. It was quite likely none of them knew or cared about the identity of the foregrounded officer: the war was over, the world had moved on. But Will hadn't. He glanced sideways at his immediate neighbours, a tweedy fellow holding a catalogue, two women in fashionably complicated hats, all training the same neutral gaze upon one of the bungling strategists of the Somme. If only they knew. Before he could stop himself he turned to face the small assembly and, in the manner of a curator, gestured at the painting.

'I'm not sure if any of you are aware,' he began, noting their interested looks, 'but *that* man – is Brigadier-General Hubert Culver, of the Fourth Army. His battle orders at the Somme resulted in thousands of needless casualties, including the loss of three-quarters of my own company at Mametz. It strikes me as odd that his reward should be to have his portrait painted, when really he ought to have been tried for criminal incompetence.' His audience, stunned into silence, looked at him as if he might be dangerous, though his voice had remained calm. With nothing more to say, Will shrugged and walked away. He felt a little better, even at the cost of being marked as a madman. The exhibition continued on a mezzanine floor and, without a backward glance, he mounted the staircase. Entering this last room, still light-headed from his impromptu public speaking, he was pottering alongside a series of small oils when another face he knew ambushed him. And a rather more agreeable one than the first. It was a squarish portrait, about twelve inches wide, of a woman seated on a sofa, her head propped against her hand, a smile on her lips. It was that smile, the warmth and humility of it, which identified her beyond any doubt. Connie. Reminders of her seemed inescapable at the moment; first at Lord's, now here. So she had sat for Brigstock . . . He would have liked to banish the next thought, but the horrific possibility that she might have done other things for the painter was leaking into his brain like poison gas. He knew that she had lived near him in Paris – she had told him so, the night of the party in South Kensington. It was quite conceivable that they had become intimate with one another: the relationship between an artist and his model didn't tend to be chaste. Why should that dismay him now?

He stood staring at her for a long time. At one moment he was aware of people approaching at his shoulder, and then abruptly changing direction when they realised it was him, the lecturing lunatic. It suddenly became clear to him that he must have this painting, at any cost. He had looked in the catalogue but found no reference to it, so he retraced his steps downstairs and consulted one of the gallery assistants, a young bespectacled fellow who knew immediately the picture Will meant.

'Yes, it's ex-catalogue, first shown at the Beaufort Gallery, in 1912,' he said. 'And I'm afraid it's not for sale.'

Will felt this like a punch to his stomach. 'Why not?'

The assistant spread his hands philosophically. 'Er . . . because the artist doesn't wish to sell it.'

'May I ask him . . . personally?'

'You could try. But he's not here at the moment.'

Will nodded his thanks, and wandered back out onto the street. He did not give serious credence to the idea that it was 'not for sale'. He recalled the painter as a shabby bohemian sort who probably struggled to pay his laundry bills: he could hardly refuse to sell once the price was adjusted to his liking. Footsore after his tramp from the City, Will stopped at Brown's Hotel a few doors along; in the bar he found a table, and ordered a large Scotch. He asked for writing paper, and began composing a letter to Brigstock, enquiring as to whether he might be persuaded to sell him the painting. Should he mention that they had once met, through Connie herself? No; he remembered again his faux pas on the occasion. He ordered another drink, and made several attempts at redrafting the letter. He couldn't quite get the tone of it right; it seemed too pleading, and then too offhand. He wrote another, but reading it back found himself excruciated by certain phrases, including his claim to be 'a man of means'. Strike *that* . . . The drinks which kept coming to his table eventually got the better of his penmanship. When a waiter came over to ask whether he should remove the discarded drafts, Will nodded blearily, and glanced at his watch. Quarter to six. He had been brooding and failing to write a letter there for almost two hours.

Having paid his bill, he rose waveringly to his feet and made his way out onto the street, closely followed by the waiter who had served him.

'Excuse me, sir, I think you left this.' He handed Will the parcel from Lewin & Co. he had left at his table.

'Thanks. Sorry,' he replied, taking the bag. He searched in his pocket to give him a tip, but the man, with a discreet look of pity, held up his hand, and then went back through the revolving doors. Will stood on the pavement, undecided for a moment, before directing his steps back to the gallery. He thought he should have another try at persuading them. Visitors had thinned out since mid-afternoon, though his arrival was noted by the assistant to whom he had spoken earlier.

'Back again, sir?' he said, leaning away slightly as he smelt Will's breath.

'Yes. May I speak to your manager?'

The man eyed him uncertainly, then said, 'He's just over there, if you'll wait a moment.' Will watched him go to consult with an older, frock-coated gent who, after some whispers and surreptitious looks in his direction, sauntered over.

'William Greaves, sir,' he said, extending his hand.

'William Maitland,' Will replied, in an echo which sounded comically like a correction. He began to explain his purpose, falling back on phrases he had lately used in those aborted letters, though he must have started rambling because Mr Greaves interrupted him with a polite stilling gesture of his hand.

'I believe my colleague has already noted your request, sir. Unfortunately that particular painting is not for sale.'

'I don't understand,' said Will. 'This is a place of business. The painting hangs on your wall. How can it not be for sale?' Before the man could reply, Will had walked past him and was heading for the mezzanine floor where Connie's portrait was displayed. Greaves and his assistant followed reluctantly in his wake. As he bounded up the stairs he felt the afternoon's drinking begin to make his head swim. Perhaps this hadn't been such a good idea after all. He had gained the upstairs room and was heading directly for the painting when his two pursuers stepped smartly in front of him, blocking his way. He tried to dodge past, but the manager pushed him firmly away.

'How dare you raise your hands to me,' said Will, suddenly furious.

'I'm sorry, sir, but I must ask you to leave –'

'Or what?'

'Or else I'll have you thrown out.'

The potential unpleasantness of this scene was suddenly interrupted by a voice off to the side. 'Now now, gentlemen, draw it mild.' Brigstock stood there, smiling from one to the other. As he approached Will, he narrowed his eyes and came to a halt. 'Don't I know you, sir?'

Will, breathing heavily, stared back at him. 'Maitland. We met one another some years ago. I was with Miss Callaway.'

The painter's frown cleared. 'Ah, yes – the cricketer!'

'The man's too drunk to see a hole in a ladder,' said Greaves, glowering, then gestured at Connie's portrait. 'Says he wants to buy this painting.'

Brigstock chuckled. 'Nothing wrong with his eyesight, if *that's* the one he's after.' He turned back to Will. 'It's a particular favourite of mine.'

Will bristled at this, and felt his determination redouble. 'How much do you want for it?'

Brigstock smiled slyly. '*Now* I remember! – the last time we met you had a very decided opinion of my work. *Unfathomable daubs!*' He seemed delighted at the memory. 'It appears you've come round to it . . .'

Will sensed that he was being humoured. 'So – how much?'

'I'm flattered by your interest, Mr Maitland,' he said, and sighed. 'Alas, Mr Greaves here wasn't spinning you a line. The picture is not for sale.'

'Is my money not good enough for you?' sneered Will, feeling the blood rush to his face.

'My dear fellow, your money has nothing to do with it. There are very few pictures of mine I've ever really loved, but that one of Connie, I should say, is among them. How can one put a price on something one loves?' It was a reasonable question, but such was Will's agitated mood that he heard only his impertinent familiarity – *Connie*, indeed – and his maddening tone of nonchalant regret. Well, he would give him an answer to remember, and taking a step forward he swung a wild fist towards his jaw. Brigstock, too quick for him, swayed out of the line, and before Will could right himself for another try Mr Greaves's own fist had connected smackingly with his nose. Pain shot through his face like lightning, and the last thing he heard before hitting the floor was Brigstock's wincing commiseration *Oh dear*.

He must have lost consciousness for a few minutes, because when he came round he was sitting outside, propped against the gallery front. The coppery taste of blood was in his mouth, and a headache thumped behind his eyes. He looked up to find Brigstock leaning against the door jamb, smoking; there was sympathy in his gaze, though he seemed to be struggling not to smile.

'Here,' said the painter, handing him a white linen handkerchief. 'You might wish to . . .' It was only then Will realised that blood was dripping from his nose. He took the proffered kerchief and tipped his head back, trying to staunch the crimson flow. Passers-by cast pitying looks at him. His wretchedness was complete. A taxi stopped and chugged at the kerb; Brigstock straightened up and stepped over to Will's semi-recumbent figure.

'This cab was called for you. Perhaps you could give me your address?'

Will told him in a mumble, and after the painter relayed the information to the cabbie he helped him up from the pavement. Will felt a lurch in his stomach, but succeeded (small mercy) in not disgorging its contents. 'I'm sorry,' he managed to slur. 'I just wanted the painting to – to look at.'

Brigstock, his hand on the car door, turned a rueful face on him. 'That's all right, old chap. I'm sorry I couldn't oblige you.'

Will stepped in, and slumped on the seat. He noticed that he was still holding the handkerchief; taking the bloodied rag from his nose he handed it weakly towards its owner, but Brigstock waved the thing away.

'Keep it,' he said, closing the cab door and slipping some coins to the driver. Then the car was moving on and the shopfronts of Albemarle Street were sliding past Will's dulled gaze. As his brain began to clear and the hot humiliation of the afternoon set in, it occurred to him that he hadn't even been able to make a decent public disgrace of himself.

Connie was occupied in her little office at the Middlesex when she heard a tap on the glass partition, and looked round to see Brigstock beaming at her on the other side. This was a first. She rose and opened the door to him. He was wearing a dove-grey suit of a carelessly expensive cut, a gold pin skewering his silk tie beneath the stiff collar. In his hand was a malacca cane – once an affectation, now a necessity – and under his arm he carried a couple of parcels.

'Well! You look smart,' she said, inviting him in. 'Let me guess. You're either off to a race meeting – or a wedding.'

'Neither, actually. I thought if I were to visit Sister Callaway –' he nodded at Connie's nameplate on the door '– I should make the effort to look presentable.' Brigstock lowered himself into an armchair, unbuttoned his jacket and raked his gaze about the office. 'Hmm. Very cosy. Mind if I smoke?' Without waiting for a reply, he pulled out a cigar, clipped the end and fired it up. She recalled how he had joked about taking up cigars the last time they had met.

'Rather suits me, d'you not think?'

'With the beard, you look like our dear late King,' she said, squinting through the smoke.

'Good heavens!' he cried, snatching the cigar from his mouth. 'Do I really look as ancient as all that?'

Connie, hearing his plaintive tone, took pity. 'I was referring to your regal bearing, not your age.'

He eyed her narrowly for a moment, then drew his mouth into a sardonic smirk. 'Cute. Very cute. I ought to know you better than to fish for compliments . . .' He had stood up to examine his reflection in the mottled mirror that hung over the washbasin. Connie glanced at her watch.

'Have you come on a particular errand?'

'Hm? Ah – the reason for my call,' he said, turning from the mirror, 'is this.' He bent down by the armchair and scooped up one of the two parcels, encased in buff-coloured paper and tied with string. 'It's rather belated, but I'd been wondering how I should mark your birthday, and this struck me as appropriate.' He handed it to her. Connie was taken aback.

'For me?'

'None other.' She stood motionless, until he added, blithely, 'You might care to open it.' He watched her as she did so, snipping the string with her desk scissors and then unfolding the layers of wrapping. It was a framed oil, squarish, about twelve inches wide. Connie found herself staring at her own portrait. She had not looked upon it since the Beaufort Gallery exhibition eight years ago.

'I'm . . .' she began, '. . . stunned. This is really too much.'

Brigstock shrugged. 'Well, I shan't take it back. Is it something that you – like?'

Connie looked from him back to the painting, and nodded. 'It is. Very much.' As she stared she felt her eyes begin to moisten. 'Thank you.'

He observed her, and said, kindly, 'I beg your pardon, this cigar seems to be affecting your eyes . . .' He crushed it in the ashtray.

'I was just thinking, the last time I saw this displayed I was with Tam. He admired it, I remember.'

Brigstock nodded. 'He wasn't the only one. As a matter of fact, there's a story attached to this painting that might interest you. Perhaps we could go for a little stroll and I'll beguile the time with it.'

He waited while she wrapped up the picture again, and they stepped out of her office together.

Out in the middle Will was rediscovering a little of his old form. It was his first knock of the season, and he'd been timing the ball with surprising ease. Perhaps it wasn't that surprising: the opposition bowling was pretty rank, and their fielding not much better. Batting was easy when the other side couldn't put you under pressure. No one had said as much, but everyone knew that the standard of county play had suffered a steep decline. The best cricketers of 1914 had been sacrificed to the war; some had returned injured, others had not returned at all. Will had even experienced a small stab of guilt for plundering runs so freely, but what was he to do with these half-volleys and full tosses? *Fill your boots*, is what Tam would have said. Tam – if only he were here now, backing up at the other end. It was strange how he still thought of him more often than he did of any man he had lost in France.

Flossy clouds drifted across the sunless, pearly-blue horizon. A little breeze ruffled the M—shire flag atop the pavilion. Their slow left-armer had returned for a bowl. With the fielders tiring and his own score on 75, Will realised that this would be the moment to start accelerating. The first delivery was dropped short, and he advanced down the wicket to club the ball back over the bowler's head for four. As he watched it thunk against the green boundary fence, his eye was distracted by something in the crowd behind long on, a dab of colour that was filament-bright against a stand of greys and browns. It seemed unaccountably familiar to him. Another delivery drifted wide down leg, and Will, stretching forward on one knee, slogged it high over square into the Queens Road Stand. Cheers came from the crowd, and a murmurous excitement at the approach of a hundred. He refocused his gaze towards long on, and now could make out the dab as a hat, a woman's hat with a flame-coloured band. He raised his eyes to the tall gaunt houses overlooking the pavilion on South Terrace, a favourite target of Tam's. How many of those windows he had holed in his time!

A moment's thought decided him. He would try to land a ball through one of them, as a personal salute to Tam. It would remind the crowd of his old friend. A few overs later he found himself again facing the slow left-armer. He skipped down the track to the first ball, swung – and missed completely. A decent wicketkeeper would have stumped him, but decent wicketkeepers were scarce and he grounded his bat. The second ball he hit so sweetly that it seemed about to clear the pavilion, but instead struck a gable and bounced down into the stand. He was finding his range. He had reached 96. A hit out of the ground and the tinkle of breaking glass – that would be the way to bring up his ton . . . The next ball was quicker, and he failed to move his feet as he launched himself at it. Impetuous, he thought, as the ball flew off his bat, steepling; he had a sense of everyone lifting

478

their gaze as it climbed skywards, a russet speck against the serene blue, and at the moment it touched its zenith he instinctively knew that it wouldn't go the distance. As it plummeted, so did something in his stomach. The fielder at long off, watching it all the way, had steadied himself, and the ball disappeared into his safely cupped hands. Out.

He kept his head down on the walk back to the pavilion, the ripples of applause in his ears. When he looked up, he saw the woman's hat again and remembered why it looked familiar: it was very like a hat Connie used to wear, the one he recovered that day at the Savoy. Years ago now. He opened the pavilion gate and mounted the steps, doffing his cap at the old boy who called to him, 'Capital knock, sir!' Will smiled. 'Capital' was pushing it, but he hadn't done so badly, first time at the crease in six years. The bowling had been terrible, and he'd flogged it. At least he could still remember how. A desultory chorus of congratulation greeted him in the dressing room. He barely knew his own teammates; most of them were young bloods straight out of school, who treated him with the distant respect owed to a veteran. A veteran – him – at thirty-three. It was no fault of theirs that he had missed the prime of his cricketing life. He knew his reflexes had dulled, and his eye had lost its sharpness. It was entirely possible that this might be his last season for the club. As he washed at one of the sinks, he recalled Tam's melancholy warning – *Don't get old, Blue, not if you're a sportsman*. Will understood that there was something more to life than cricket. He had found it once, too; but he couldn't keep it.

Around five thirty he heard a clatter of booted feet on the pavilion steps. Stumps had been drawn. Sitting in a corner with his head draped in a towel, he did not hear the youth sidling up to him.

'Ahm, Maits?' The boy's voice sounded irresolute as to whether he should be addressing a senior player in so

479

familiar a style. Will pulled back his towel and looked up. 'There's someone out there asking for you.'

Will nodded his thanks, and hauled himself upright. His legs and back had stiffened since his innings: he really was a veteran. He ambled out of the dressing room in his stockinged feet and into the Priory's gloomy hallway, and there, through a milling scrum of players and ground staff, he saw the lady in the hat – not, after all, *like* Connie, but Connie herself, in the flesh. For a few moments they stood as still as two portraits facing one another.

Shaking off her trance of immobility, Connie stepped forward. She offered her hand, and not knowing how to begin said, 'I was sorry you didn't get your hundred.'

He gave a shrug. 'Poor footwork, I'm afraid. It's always been a fault.' They exchanged a rueful smile. *What on earth was she doing here?* Both had registered changes in the other – lines in the skin, a slight tautening around the eyes – but their interest in this sudden renewal of acquaintance eclipsed any dismay they might have felt. Connie saw his eyes glance at the package she carried at her side.

'I believe this is yours.' She handed it over, and the sight of its printed trade name – GEORGE LEWIN & CO. – caused him a spasm of cold dread. They were the cricket whites he had bought last week, now irreparably tainted by association. Connie mistook his expression for simple confusion. 'My friend Brigstock said that you left them by accident in the gallery – at Albemarle Street?'

Will felt an incriminating blush rise through his face, like mercury in a thermometer. Shame had prevented him from returning to the gallery to retrieve the lost package. He wondered how much Brigstock had enjoyed telling her about his behaviour that afternoon, though what Connie said next gave him hope that she hadn't been apprised of every detail.

'Those spots on the package look a little like blood,' she said, in a tone of innocent curiosity.

'Oh, just a nosebleed I had.' She nodded, quite satisfied by the explanation, and Will felt an inward surge of gratitude to the painter. What discretion. Then he lifted his eyes from his recovered purchase. 'Did you really come all the way down here just to return this?' Now it was Connie's turn to look awkward. She felt suddenly aware of the people around them.

'I was wondering – if you might have time . . . to go for a walk?'

He paused, and gestured at his feet. 'Would you mind waiting while I put my boots on?'

They left the Priory by the players' entrance and headed towards the esplanade. The vestiges of their estrangement were sufficiently present to keep their conversation quite formal, though as they reached the Parade Will lightly, instinctively, held her arm as they crossed. Walking along the seafront, they became heedless of everything – the grind and clang of trams, the passing nursemaids and children, the caressing advance of the tide below – everything but each other. It was only when he mentioned his chance encounter with her family at Lord's that she heard a tenderness in his tone, and the distance between them seemed to shrink. He confessed to being charmed by Molly.

'Yes,' she smiled, 'isn't she the loveliest girl? I sometimes wonder how Fred managed to catch her.'

Will took a deep breath before he next spoke. 'I suppose certain people just belong together. They're sort of – meant to be.' He paused. 'I once thought I had been lucky enough to . . .' He didn't finish the sentence. A silence lingered between them, and he felt himself trying to stifle his panic as he waited. It seemed an eternity passed before she did speak again.

'Mr Brigstock also told me about your eagerness to buy a certain painting of his. I think you know the one. He said that you offered any amount of money for it. Is that true?'

He did look at her now. 'Yes. I wanted it because – it

would remind me of a time, the only time in my life, when I felt truly happy. I thought I'd never see her – you – again, so . . . I had to have that instead.'

Connie had stopped, her heart racked with pity, and something else, which felt like love. She read a profound sorrow in his face, in the very hang of his shoulders. 'I'm sorry, Will. I'm so sorry I . . .' She didn't exactly know why she was sorry, for she realised that her behaviour those years ago had sprung from her deepest convictions – there had been something to fight for. '. . . I hurt a person I loved very much.'

'Is that what you came here to tell me?'

She paused, and looked towards the Pier, its windows glinting in the late-afternoon sun. 'I suppose it is. It's been on my mind these past years. When Molly told me about meeting you, I started thinking again about what happened between us, and – much as I suffered from it – I know I couldn't have acted in any other way. If I had given myself to you instead of obeying my . . . *instincts*, I should have suffered more in the end, because I would have been tormented in my conscience. And I couldn't dismiss the suspicion –' At this she broke off, and gave him a searching look.

'A suspicion – ?'

' – that you were motivated more by a dream of marriage than by love of a woman – of me. Please understand, I didn't set myself above Miss Brink – but we seemed so very different from one another that I could only doubt the man whose expectations and affections could be satisfied so readily.'

He took this in, before saying, 'It seems that Miss Brink has had a narrow escape.'

She smiled at the self-deprecation, and took his hand in hers. 'That's not what I meant –'

'No, it's true. I should not have asked her to marry me, not when . . . That was my mistake – to think I could somehow replace you.' He found his gaze drifting to the Pier, its stilted legs lapped by the unsteady green swell. Was it really nine years since they had first met down here? He still recalled that prickly exchange he'd had with her about his batting . . . Perhaps he should have known *then* that it was never likely to be. Well, she had made her apology; they could part as friends.

Connie felt the furious squall of nerves in her stomach like birds trapped in a cage. Brigstock had said that she didn't need anyone, but he was wrong. She had only to think of Will to know that was wrong. This would be the moment, if she was going to say it. 'Will – pardon my presumption – but there's a favour I wanted to ask. A dear friend of mine – Lily – is to be married next weekend. I had intended to go to the wedding alone, but then I wondered, that is – I hoped you might – consent to accompany me.'

Will heard the tremble in her voice. 'A wedding . . . why would you ask me?'

'Because . . .' she began, and faltered. She couldn't keep running away from him. '. . . because we'd be able to see how it's done.'

He looked at her more closely, and a slow smile began to crease the edges of his mouth. They were standing by a stairwell that dropped down to the beach; with decisive calm he tugged at her hand, and they descended the stone steps together. She felt the pebbles sharply through the thin soles of her shoes, but she didn't let go of his hand as he paced across the narrow shingled ridge towards the sea. People passing along the esplanade might have wondered at what was preoccupying the couple on the shore. The fellow in his whites, hands on hips, was nodding interestedly at the woman in the hat, who seemed to be mimicking the swish of a cricket bat. An occasional peal of laughter broke from them. It seemed they might be there for some time yet.

ACKNOWLEDGEMENTS

My heartfelt thanks to Dan Franklin, Suzanne Dean and all the team at Jonathan Cape; likewise to Rachel Cugnoni and all at Vintage, Peter Straus and his colleagues at RCW. I am especially grateful to Professor Hermione Lee, who read an early draft of the book and offered many incisive pointers; also to my sister, Dr Sarah Quinn, who patiently talked me through the symptoms and treatment of tension pneumothorax.

I could not have written this book as I intended without the help of David Frith's magnificent and haunting study *Silence of The Heart: Cricket Suicides* (2001). I must also salute Martin Middlebrook's *The First Day on the Somme* (1971), and in particular the story of Captain D. L. Martin of the 9th Devons. My thanks also to Dr Simon Robbins of the Imperial War Museum.

The books I read on the history of women's suffrage are too numerous to list here, but I would like to mention the prison diary of Katie Gliddon, composed under great stress in Holloway, March–April 1912. To read this narrative, pencil-written in the margins of her copy of Shelley's *Poetical Works*, was a genuine inspiration. My thanks to the staff of The Women's Library, where this diary is kept, and to the Wellcome Collection.

I am indebted to the love and encouragement of

my wife, Rachel Cooke. Even had she not insisted upon it, this book would always have been dedicated to her.

www.vintage-books.co.uk